TO SEDUCE A WITCH'S HEART

A Novel of Love and Magic

NADINE MUTAS

Nadine Mutas

PO Box 94

New Almaden, CA 95042

nadine@nadinemutas.com

www.nadinemutas.com

Cover Design by Najla Qamber Designs

www.najlaqamberdesigns.com

ISBN-13: 978-1545126653

ISBN-10: 1545126658

❀ Created with Vellum

For Sergej,
my own personal Happily Ever After.
You're the reason I can write about love.

ACKNOWLEDGMENTS

First and foremost, my never-ending thanks go out to my husband Sergej, who has been there for me through it all, and without whom none of this would be possible. You cannot grasp how much your support means to me. Thank you for making my dream of being an author come true.

I'd like to give more heartfelt thanks to my mom, who has been my very first fan, and who always believed in me. You never let me doubt that I had talent and could follow this crazy idea of being a writer.

More thanks to Jessica Hofmann, for cheering me on so enthusiastically when I ventured back into writing after my hiatus, and for making me want to share my stories with the world. Thanks for being my #1 fan.

To my mom-in-law, who generously supported me in the last few weeks of preparing to publish with countless hours of babysitting. I couldn't have done this without your help.

To Wendy Beck, for being an awesome beta reader, a source of inspiration, and for listening to me whinesplain about all things writing and publishing. I am so glad life threw us together in the final round of that contest.

To Debbie Disch, who has been an amazing writing buddy,

critique partner, and, above all, friend. Thanks for always having a sympathetic ear.

To Kerensa Brougham and Rebekah R. Ganiere, who read and critiqued *To Seduce a Witch's Heart* and helped me whip the story into shape.

To the ladies and gents from RCRW, for the wonderfully inspiring atmosphere of encouragement and creativity, and for proving that it can be done.

To my Insomnia girls, Dawn, Christy, Janet, and Jenna. You ladies keep me sane and going steady.

To my gals from MRW and NJRW. Thank you so much for making me feel so incredibly welcome at the conference, for taking me in, rooting for me and supporting me.

To all the contest judges who helped me with their critiques and advice.

And last, but certainly not least, to all my family and friends whom I must neglect to mention by name because the list would exhaust the space available here. Thank you for being with me on this journey and for your continuous support.

CHAPTER 1

With a heavy clang, the door of Merle's family mausoleum shut behind her. The sudden silence enveloped her, the sounds of sleepy Portland cut off. It was only Merle now, standing among the lingering energy of her forebears, in the witching hour of the night, armed with nothing but her craft and a healthy dose of despair. Enough to unbind a *bluotezzer* demon from the Shadows.

Her flashlight's beam ghosted over the walls and stopped, involuntarily, on one of the shelved stone coffins. *Rowan Mary MacKenna, 1935-2007.* The letters seemed to scowl at her—full of disapproval for the transgression she was about to commit. Her power buzzed in reaction to the residual magic drenching the air, still so strong even years after the witch's passing. She gritted her teeth and averted her eyes from her grandmother's name on the marble plaque.

"I don't have a choice." Her whisper echoed in the dark of the tomb, thrown back at her along with silent reproach. "Am I supposed to just let her die?"

Of course, there was no answer. The remains of her grandmother's energy were strong enough to glower at her, but, naturally, didn't offer any help.

The thought of unleashing a blood-eater demon tightened her chest, sucked all warmth out of her. With doubt weighing on her shoulders, she paused. The power of her ancestors sizzled over her skin, pressed down on her. What if they were right, what if this was too dangerous? Maybe she should just—

Unbidden, a flash of memory tore through her. *Lips curved at the dirty joke Merle had just told, Maeve stole a Skittle out of the bag lying between them and threw it at Merle. "You're so bad," she said around a giggle, her eyes the color of fire and smoke bright in a face dotted with freckles, framed by ginger hair so like Merle's.*

Heart laughing at the unusual display of boldness from her baby sister, Merle hugged her tight. "Made you smile, though, didn't it?"

A smile she'd never see again if she gave up now. Either she took the risk of unbinding this demon—or soon she'd watch another stone coffin being added to this tomb. The memory of laying to rest here the mortal remains of her mom, her oldest sister, and later, her grandmother, were still vivid in her mind, the loss an aching wound in her heart. Losing Maeve, too, would do more than tear that wound wider—it would rip a gorge through her soul, its size immeasurable.

Throat raw at this thought, she crushed all doubt and set to work. She placed the flashlight upright in a corner, its cone of light touching the vaulted ceiling. Next she unzipped the duffel bag she'd brought and took out the sage. Lighting it, she purified the space, ensuring no trace negativity would corrupt the spell, though the lingering power in the air would have already repelled most evil spirits. Some spaces didn't require as much cleansing as others; the burial place of a line of strong witches was one of them.

With the heavy, smoky scent of the sage still saturating the air, she threw the salt in a circle around herself. Just a precaution, a ward against intrusive spirits who might attack her while she cast the spell. After taking out five candles, setting them down at the protective points on the circle and lighting them, she sat down cross-legged on the stone floor, placed her family's grimoire in her lap. The thick tome's leather binding was soft underneath her fingers as she opened it to the section that would guide her through the process. It wasn't much, only one page of information to bind or unbind a demon from the Shadows, but it would have to do.

Closing her eyes, she reached out to the source of all that was magic and life. "I humbly beseech the Powers That Be to grant me protection," she whispered into the silence. There was no guarantee they'd comply, as they were fickle, untamed, like the magic which was worked into the world. It was a witch's greatest hubris and most fatal mistake to think to ever fully control it.

A mistake she wasn't inclined to make. She'd always been cautious with the powers she tapped, her grandmother's words of warning forever etched in her mind. *For every spell you cast, there is a loophole to undo it, hidden from your knowledge.*

She released her pent-up breath, opened her eyes and began the ritual. Her words would summon the *bluotezzer* demon to the forefront of the Shadows, close enough to hear, to listen, and to speak, but still bound and powerless. She would talk to the spirit first, gauge whether it was reasonable. Would the creature be willing to cooperate?

Not for the first time, she wondered about her grandmother's reasons for binding the demon in the magical equivalent of Hell, with a spell so powerful only one of her direct bloodline could undo it. Without a doubt, it hadn't been for a speeding ticket. No, it must have been to make the demon atone for taking an innocent life, presumably even more than one.

Shaking off the queasy feeling in her stomach, she refocused. Whatever it was the creature had done, it didn't matter right now, nor would it matter in the future as long as she kept the demon under control and made sure to bind it again once Maeve was free.

"By the magic of my line," she intoned, "with the power

passed unto me, I call upon the Shadows to obey my commands."

The air grew thicker, humid and pressing as if auguring a storm. The Shadows writhed, whispers of darkness, coiling and uncoiling in tendrils of black and gray, like the smoke of the sage had done shortly before. Only this smoke, it *lived*. The active power in the air stirred the residual magic of her fore-bears, which hummed in response.

"Bring forth the *bluotezzer* demon bound by Rowan, daughter of Ethel, of the MacKenna family."

Her ancestors' energy coalesced and filled her head with their droning, until her temples throbbed. The air became thicker still. The whisper of the Shadows echoed in the dark corners of the tomb.

Then, silence.

"Speak."

Her breath caught. Her heart raced. The voice had been in her mind, masculine, deep, and reverberating in places of her body it had no business sneaking into.

Forcing herself to breathe slowly, she checked and strengthened her mental shields, and tapped into the core of her power. No way was she going to let a demon rattle her like an untrained novice witch. Her magic might not be as strong as her grandmother's, but she could handle this. Even if it was the first time she encountered a demon.

"Who are you?" That voice again, deep and resonant, danger wrapped in velvet. It stroked along her senses, testing her shields. A shiver ran down her spine as she felt his touch against her mental defenses, a hot brush of darkness.

With a surge of power, she hid the anxiety in her aura, projecting only calm confidence that she had the means to control him. She wouldn't show any weakness. Not now, not toward him. "I am Merle," she said, her voice steady. "Daughter of Emily, head of the MacKenna line. It was my grandmother Rowan who bound you."

Her senses sharpened, focused, as she felt the presence behind the voice move. He edged closer to the veil between the worlds, hovering on the brink of the Shadows.

"Merle."

The way he spoke her name—a purr rubbing against her very core.

"I remember you."

Her skin prickled.

"Your hair was braided." He paused. The air crackled. *"Blue. Your dress was blue, like your eyes."*

Her heart beat a frantic tattoo against her ribs.

"You were a pretty girl, little witch."

His words unlocked a memory, a string of images, emotions, buried for so long, she had all but forgotten. It came back now with a jolt.

The lawn outside her house. The old cherry tree still stood, its branches swaying in the warm evening breeze. Piercing, bright eyes focused on her as the demon crouched down, leveling his face with hers. Sizzling energy, brushing over her skin, making the hairs on her arms rise.

"Hello, little witch." A smile on his lips.

"Merle!" Her grandmother's voice came from somewhere behind her.

Her heart thrummed. Those eyes held her captive.

"Merle, get back inside. Now." Merle had never heard such sharpness in her grandmother's voice.

"Listen to your grandma, little witch. You're too young to play outside after dark." The wind tousled his chestnut-colored hair then rustled through the leaves as he winked at her and stood.

Her grandmother stepped up to the male just as Merle was hauled back, dragged into the house by her mother along with hushed words of reproach and an onslaught of maternal protectiveness. But Merle's gaze never left his face.

A face of cutting beauty, laced with a subtle hint of danger that even a five-year-old understood.

She sucked in a breath at the force of the memory, the maelstrom of emotions it evoked. Wrenching herself back into the present, she tried to calm her nerves. Still, the little girl inside her trembled.

"I have summoned you to make you an offer." She sounded so much stronger than she felt.

A tight silence followed.

"You need my help." His voice dripped with smugness.

She bit back a caustic response. Antagonizing him at this point would not be clever. "Yes," she said instead. "I need you to find my sister, Maeve."

"Maeve… the little chatty one?"

She was about to correct him when it hit her—he'd been bound in the Shadows when Merle was about six. He'd only known her sister Maeve before the incident that had ripped a gaping hole in the family and stifled Maeve's spirit, rendering her a mere shadow of the lively girl she used to be.

She swallowed, heart pounding as she pushed the memory away before it could truly surface. "Yes. She's been taken by one of your kind, and I need your help to locate him."

She'd tried to hunt him down herself, but his species was rare and impossible to find by means of magic. Her power was still bruised from the rituals she'd carried out, her mind exhausted from the feverish chase for a way to find Maeve. The locator spell had failed. Her Elders had turned her away. This was her last chance. Only another *bluotezzer* demon could sense the abductor's presence, track him down.

"How long has he had her?"

"Almost two days."

"Then she's most likely dead already." Spoken with calm indifference.

"No. I can still feel her." When her mom and her sister Moira had died, and later as her grandmother had passed away, her connection to them severed. The link to Maeve remained intact.

It pulsed within her, a constant reminder of what she was about to lose.

If only the link were strong enough to trace, she wouldn't need to do this…

"I will unbind you from the Shadows so you can search for the one holding her captive," she said, steel in her voice, "but you will be bound to me, and I can find you, no matter where you run. You will cooperate with me, and you will *not* step out of line. If you spill innocent blood, I will make you suffer for it."

His presence darkened, menacing, and pressed against the veil keeping him on the other side. Then—with a flicker of his energy—he softened and brushed along her mind.

"What do I get in return, little witch?"

She bristled and pushed back the sensuous caress of his words, ignoring the rush of heat centering between her thighs. *Traitorous body.* She would *not* purr back. "You can taste life again," she said, struggling to keep her voice even. "You can breathe, drink, move, see the world… You've been in the Shadows for what? Twenty years? I'm sure you'd like a break from darkness, inertia and hunger, wouldn't you?"

A touch of his presence on her mind, a gentle teasing. *"I'll help you if you vow to release me completely afterwards."*

"You know I can't grant you that without my Elders' consent," she said through gritted teeth. No matter what, she couldn't fully unbind him—if he fell into bloodlust and went on a rampage, Merle would have to answer for every innocent life he took. And the Powers That Be kept score mercilessly. "This is your chance for a taste of freedom, and it will be all I can give you. Take it or leave it."

Ponderous silence filled the tomb. The pause was long enough to make her stomach tighten, to turn her breathing into forced, shallow gasps. What if he said no? *Gods*—part of her wished for that. Then she could go home, safe, her conscience free of guilt.

And Maeve would die.

The thought sucker-punched her right in her gut, painful enough to erase any worry about unbinding a demon from the Shadows. Chest tightening, she straightened her spine. She could do this.

"Will you feed me?" His voice was vibrant with sensuality, and her heartbeat kicked up a notch.

"Yes," she ground out, unbidden and very inappropriate tingles of excitement running over her skin.

She could *feel* his amusement filling the small silence that followed.

"Then we have a deal, little witch of mine."

His endearment wrapped around her soul, stroking, enticing, taking root. She drew a deep breath and reinforced her mental shields to counter the effect his voice had on her. *Gods dammit*, it was just a voice.

"All right," she said quietly, steeling herself. "Ready?"

"I am if you are."

A twinge of doubt made her falter. The danger she was about to unleash... She clenched her jaw and buried that thought. Not like she had any other options left.

On an inhale, she bundled her power, and focused on infusing her next words with the magic that transformed ordinary language into a spell.

> *"From hunger, pain and darkness,*
> *bring unto the light,*
> *the spirit bound by Rowan,*
> *in never-ending night.*
> *Relinquished from the Shadows,*
> *as per my decree,*
> *its form released,*
> *its power leashed,*
> *it will be chained to me."*

Her magic struck, fused with the innate power of the words,

and clashed with the sentient force of the Shadows. For a moment they bristled, recalcitrant and ever-hungry as they were, but then they yielded. Coiling, they became a mass of stygian, impenetrable darkness in front of her eyes, merging into a form on the floor.

She held her breath as the writhing black stilled and molded into the motionless shape of a man, lying on his back. The last of the Shadows fell away from his body with a whisper, reluctantly letting him go, and slowly all color came back to his form.

And—*gods have mercy*—what a form.

Heat shot up to her face. He was completely, utterly naked.

She hadn't been prepared for that. The grimoire hadn't mentioned he'd be like this, so nude and—*gorgeous*. Damn, this wasn't fair. This *so* wasn't fair. There should have been a warning.

Impressive muscles bunched underneath his ivory skin, skin she ached to touch, her fingers twitching. She curled them into her palms instead. Her eyes, however, devoured him. His shoulders and chest were well-defined, wrought with iron strength, though far from bulky. He was all lean muscle, athletically toned, not an ounce of fat on his delectable body. Her gaze involuntarily followed the faint trail of dark hair from his chest over his ripped abdomen to his groin.

She drew in a harsh breath and averted her eyes. The room temperature shot up to rival a sauna.

She would not look back. She would not look back at his—

"Like what you see?"

The murmured question pulled her undisciplined gaze —*dammit*, she'd looked back—from the captivating sight of his package up to his face. His eyes were now open, focused on her, glinting with male arrogance. Dark brown hair framed the clear-cut beauty of the face she'd seen so long ago it seemed like another life. She'd been so young then, a child, and though she'd been drawn to him with equal measures of fear and fascination, it had been a child's eyes that looked upon him.

Not anymore. The flush rolling over her skin, the urge to touch, taste, feel, the whisper of want that prickled warm in low, feminine places—it was very much adult. Right here, right now, she was further removed from childlike innocence than she'd ever been.

"You grew up beautiful, little witch," he said, his voice raspy from decades of disuse. Eyes of pale, bright green met her own, searing, intense, daring in the overt appreciation they displayed.

A slight movement drew her gaze to his loins again before she could stop herself. Oh yes, he appreciated her presence, all right. Her mouth turned dry. Closing her eyes tight, she fought the waves of embarrassment rushing through her. She didn't ogle men like they were a yummy piece of cake. No, she didn't. No matter *how* yummy.

"You know," he said, a whisper of dark need behind his words, "I don't mind posing nude for females."

She opened her eyes again and glared at him. Damn if his self-satisfied smirk didn't make him even hotter.

"But as much as I'm enjoying your attention, I am kind of starving right now."

Of course he was. His demon aura, still faint because of his weakened condition, flickered with the kind of hunger born of years of deprivation. He'd been starving for the past twenty years, denied any nourishment in the Shadows. Though his body hadn't degenerated—obviously—he would have suffered from terrible hunger. Well, *that* she was prepared for.

She snapped into action and turned to the duffel bag, pulling out a unit of blood. From the little information she'd found in the grimoire, she knew his demon species fed off human blood, having given rise to the vampire myths among different cultures. Folk memory and superstitions had distorted the truth over time, creating the legend of the undead. *Bluotezzer* demons, however, were very much alive, and they had never been human to begin with.

Since she wanted to avoid giving him her blood—the less he took from her the better, whether it be blood or anything else—she'd gone to the lengths of snatching a unit from the hospital on her way here.

Breaking the circle, the salt crunching underneath her shoes, she came forward to crouch next to him and gingerly held the bag up to his mouth.

The wicked glint in his eyes barely concealed the desperate hunger lurking underneath, as he shook his head slightly. "Merle." His voice was low, rasping, humming over her skin. "You know it has to be fresh."

Ah, crap. She hadn't known that. But maybe he was toying with her—he could be making it up, for all she knew. Plus, letting him drink her blood was probably exactly what she shouldn't be doing. The way her skin prickled—as if in eager anticipation of his feeding—was a clear warning sign. She couldn't risk losing control.

Narrowing her eyes, she shoved the unit back in his face. "You can't have my blood. This will have to do."

He snorted, refusing to bite. "Your loss, then."

For a long moment they stared at each other. Her hand held the bag to his mouth. His lips remained sealed. It was a play of power, of give and take, she knew that much. And in this round, she'd have to give. She needed his help to find Maeve, and for that, he had to be fed and moving and functional.

With a muttered curse, she chucked the blood back into the duffel. "Just so you don't get any ideas," she said with a glare at the demon, "know that if you kill me, you'll automatically be kicked back into the Shadows. Failsafe measure." The lie tasted bitter on her tongue, the truth a rock in her throat.

He narrowed his eyes, and his jaw hardened. For a second, his aura darkened, like ink spilled into water. Then, the muscles in his face relaxed, the lines around his mouth smoothing out as his lips curved up. "Don't worry, little witch. I'll be on my best behavior."

"You better be, or I swear I'll kick your ass so hard you'll wish the Shadows would have never released you." This one wasn't an idle threat. The section on *bluotezzer* demons in her grimoire said his species was susceptible to blows of raw power. Her abilities might still be developing, but bursts of undiluted magic she could manage. Now, if only she could convince her jackhammering heart to calm down and believe her.

Mental shields steeled against any attack, she pushed up her left sleeve and held her wrist to his mouth. His tongue slipped out and slowly, languorously, licked across the sensitive under-side. She gasped and froze at the tingles shooting up her arm—and into other, more intimate parts of her body.

His pale blue-green eyes glowed as he spoke against her pulse. "Your neck." His fangs grazed her skin. "I want your neck."

Her heartbeat sped up even more. No, no, no, she shouldn't get all excited by that idea. But running a close second to the panic inside her was a warped sense of arousal, and he could totally tell, if the smug flicker in his aura was any indication.

"C'mere," he murmured, his voice dark velvet over her skin.

She managed to glower at him as she slowly leaned over, pushed her hair aside and exposed the curve of her neck. His lips touched her skin. A shiver ran down her spine and her heart fluttered. He inhaled deeply, drawing in her scent with a sigh, a sound so erotic it had her trembling, inching closer to him. Her pulse thrummed against his lips as he kissed her neck, nipped at her skin—and then he bit.

A flash of pain, a strangled cry, muted in her throat by the avalanche of sensations washing over her. Her skin was on fire, waves of heat rolled through her body in the rhythm of his strong pulls. Tingles of excitement spread like wildfire, unpre-dictable, uncontrollable, taking down her defenses, one by one. She heard herself moan, a distant sound that startled her. She was enjoying this way too much.

With an effort she drew back. She had to stop this before he went too far.

His hand shot up to her neck, took hold of her nape and pulled her back down. "More."

Hell, no. Reaching inside herself, she tapped into the glowing core of her powers, and pulled up a thread of raw magic. She struck out—and he blocked it as easily as if swatting away a fly. Her heart stuttered. Panic iced her spine. He shouldn't be able to do this. The grimoire had said he'd be susceptible to—

He bit her again. She gasped, not at the pain but at the... pleasure. Rolling heat, her senses moaning at the strokes of lust, silken darkness caressing her mind, her body. This shouldn't feel this good.

The demon's muscles tensed, vibrant with the energy he stole from her. Just like that, he brought her on her back, not breaking contact with her neck. His groan—an erotic sound despite the situation—sent impossible zings of excitement through her. His weight pinning her down, he clutched her with predatory possessiveness. Hot little licks of his tongue brushed over her skin while he sucked harder, igniting more sparks of liquid fire. It ran through her veins, pulsed in time with his pulls. She felt all the way down to the lowest levels of her soul. *I don't want it to end.*

It was this thought that sobered her.

She blinked, shook off the haze clouding her brain. He'd gotten to her, had sneakily infiltrated her mind. Mental shields slamming down once more, she lashed out with a flash of white-hot magic. It hit the demon square in the chest. He grunted, released her throat, and reared back. *Yes!* The trail of aggressive raw magic glowed inside her. She'd have to pay for it later, but it was better than losing her life.

Striking the demon again with a measured blast of undiluted power, she shoved at his chest at the same time. It was enough to topple him over. Not enough, however, to knock him out. Snarling, he grabbed her neck and pulled her back down on top of him. His skin was warm, silky, and oh-so-strokable underneath her hands as she sprawled across him, and—*by the gods, what is wrong with me?* She should concentrate on fighting him. Pressing her lips together, she punched him in the throat and rolled off.

The demon coughed and cursed, his aura clouding with darkness. Eyes narrowed at her, he sat up—and lunged. Her back hit the stone floor before she could so much as grab a thread of magic. All air left her lungs on a whoosh. The demon pinned her down, her wrists locked in his grip. Heat and dark power charged the air between them. Her magic flickered, waned. *Dammit*, not now. Wiggling, she made an effort to break free of his hold, but all she succeeded in doing was to rub her body against his.

He licked the curve of her neck up to her ear. "Keep doing that, little witch," he murmured, his breath hot against her skin. "Feels amazing."

She stopped moving, and with a disappointed *tsk* he resumed drinking.

Oh, gods. She tried to grasp her weakening magic, only to have it slip through her mental fingers. Her body turned to rubber, black bleeding into her vision. He was so much stronger than he should have been. She took a rattling breath. "Failsafe measure."

The reminder of how he'd be kicked back into the Shadows if he killed her made him pause. He stopped drinking, shifted far enough to pin her with his piercing gaze. "You're bluffing."

She was. Not that she would let him see that, though. "Try me," she whispered, infusing the words with as much daring bluff as possible.

His thumb gently rubbed her lower lip. "Maybe I will." He gripped her neck and bit again.

A cascade of sensations rushed through her, from her neck down to her toes, prickling heat, pulsing pleasure, an ache for more. His lips were hot on her skin, his energy stroking her senses, making her want... *No.*

Drawing in a fortifying breath, she gathered what was left of her strength. She reached deeper than ever before, focused on the brightest spark of magic she could find, and stoked it into a fire. It blazed. *More.* She nurtured the flames, fanned them higher, until the force of her magic was a glaring inferno inside her. Outward she pushed, against the influence of the demon's dark energy seeping through her shields, and she shoved, shoved, shoved.

Searing white light exploded from her. It hit the demon full-force, catapulting him off her. Groaning, he crashed into the opposite corner of the mausoleum and slumped down.

She scrambled to her feet, swayed, and steadied herself on the wall. The candles flickered, casting an eerie play of light and shadows in the tomb. Panting, she watched the demon stir. His aura darkened even further as he heaved himself up, his eyes glowing, burning a path through her soul. Yep, he was pissed. Well, so was she, for that matter.

Widening her stance, she lifted her chin, ready to meet him head-on. Carefully, she gathered the last of the bruised, exhausted magic inside her, drew it close. It would hurt like hell, but she still had enough to hit him again. And this time, she'd knock him out.

He took a step toward her. She clutched her power tighter. It churned, eager to be let loose. His energy sizzled, made the air crack. One more deep breath, and then she'd hurl—

She never got the chance. One second he stood nine feet away from her, the next he was right in her face. *Damn, he's fast,* was her last coherent thought before everything happened at once.

His hand shot out, tangled in her hair. Primed and ready, her power surged to the surface. His other arm wound around her waist, yanked her to him.

And his mouth covered hers in a kiss that had everything grinding to a halt.

Her grip on her magic slackened like a taught rope being cut. His lips were hot as they crushed against hers, his tongue demanding as he licked at her, all but ordering her to open up. On a flash of reason, she clamped her mouth shut tight. He bit her lip then, just lightly, but enough to sting.

"Ow!" She reared back. "Damn you, you bas—"

Her next words died a shameful death as he took full advantage of her open mouth. His tongue stroked inside her, branding her down to her now fizzling powers. His taste was exquisite, a drug to her senses—dark spices, sultry heat, kissed with a hint of iron from her own blood. His energy enveloped her while he pulled her closer, pressed her suddenly sensitive breasts against his hard chest. A flood of lust slammed into her. It tore down her defenses with terrifying ease, transformed her anger into something primal, voracious and aggressive.

Next thing she knew, her hands were on his shoulders, yanking him closer, her nails digging into the heat of his skin. She licked and tasted and met his tongue, driven by need and hunger. He growled into the kiss, ground his body against hers, and—*good gods*, the feel of his hardness against her hip. Everything else dissolved, until there was only heat, maddening pleasure, and the need to draw blood.

Fully lost in a spiral of lust, she didn't see it coming. Breaking the kiss, the demon swiped her legs out from under her. For the second time this night, she crashed down on her back on what had to be the hardest floor ever built. Pain shot through her, from her spine to her fingertips, in biting, razor-sharp currents. Breath knocked out of her, she couldn't even wheeze.

In between the black dots dancing in her vision, the demon rose above her. His one hand had cradled the back of her head during her fall, and now glided to her throat. He squeezed gently and gave her a taunting smile.

"Let's do that again sometime," he said, kissed her nose, and was gone.

The gaping door let in a rush of cool night air, brushing over her shivering body. Her chest heaved as she gasped for breath. The rush of adrenaline slowed, and the aftermath of the fight took its toll. Her magic—weakened, almost depleted—had simmered down to a mere glimmer. Her body ached in a million places at once. If she'd been exhausted before, now she felt like road kill come back to life and run over by a truck again.

That damn sneaky bastard demon. He'd savaged her, almost killed her, had left her nearly broken lying on the floor. Even worse, he'd had the audacity to *kiss* her—and make her like it.

She would have his ass for that.

CHAPTER 2

Pain.

Rhun took a deep breath and soaked up the aroma of hurt as it erupted from the man he'd been hitting. The guy's human aura quivered, woven with threads of agony spreading like fine mist in the air. *More.* He needed more. Twenty years bound in the Shadows, and he was so starved for the sharp taste of hurt that beating two thugs to a pulp didn't even take the edge off. He'd quenched his thirst for blood with the little witch in the tomb, but his other two nourishment requirements had yet to be met. Well, he was working on doing just that.

Rolling his shoulders, he surveyed the scene. Two of the three gang members lay lifeless behind the dumpster that concealed this corner of the back alley from the street. The third did his best to merge with the wall behind him and disappear from Rhun's view. The gang's victim—a scrawny runaway teen —sprawled on the garbage-strewn ground, still unconscious from what his abusers had mockingly called "play time."

Due to the hour of the night, it had taken Rhun a while after leaving the cemetery to find a trail of suitable prey and an isolated corner to enjoy his feeding. He'd then taken his pick of the thugs' clothes before he'd started—the white T-shirt from

Idiot One, dark blue jeans and the boots from Idiot Two, and the jacket from the third guy. Yep, clichéd bad boy leather jacket, straight out of the starter kit for thugs. It fit best of all three guys' jackets, though, so Rhun had shrugged it on with a self-ironic bow to his evil, evil demon nature.

He now knelt down next to the third thug, whose horrified expression matched the acidic flavor of fear in his aura. So different from the aggressive overconfidence he'd flaunted when Rhun had stepped from the shadows of the night, interrupting the gang's quality time with their victim. How fast things could change. He flipped the man's knife in his hand a few times, anticipation rushing through his blood. Slicing the jerk to pieces with his own blade *would* be fun.

Most human minds lacked any shields, which made it easy to manipulate them, and it only took a little mental nudge to convince Knife Guy to get rid of the rest of his clothes. He then delved deeper into the man's mind to keep him subdued and silent while he set to work on his exposed skin.

Darkness bucked within Rhun, rose to the surface and swirled around him. The knife cut, again and again, and the man jerked and writhed, pain exploding in the air. Rhun drank it in. He savored the taste, drew strength from it. Bit by bit his hunger lessened. The clawing need inside him slowly died.

Sated, he let go of the thug's mind as it faded into darkness. He licked the blood from the blade, pocketed it, and turned to the gang's victim. It was tempting to feed off him as well, and deep down, a part of him hungered for more of what he'd just tasted. *More pain, more blood, more death.* It was the dark, nefarious side of his nature urging him to finish what the gang had started, whispering that he wasn't so different from them, that he needed this, so why not take what was so clearly meant to be his?

The boy was still down for the count, half-undressed, bruises on his hips and stomach, eyes swollen shut from punches of three men double the teen's size. This, Rhun thought, was what made the difference. He enjoyed causing pain, yes, even reveled in it, same as those men he'd just killed. But there were lines he didn't cross. Harming children was one of them. He'd never given free rein to the darkest part of his nature, and he wouldn't start now.

He slipped into the teen's mind, prodded him awake and erased what little memories there were of his presence and involvement in what had happened. Walking past the wide-eyed young human, who trembled at the sight of the three dead men around him, Rhun patted his shoulder. "Run along now. Find some shelter."

After mentally reinforcing his words with a compulsion, he turned his back on the scene. He had to check back on a certain scrumptious little witch.

Now that he'd fulfilled two of his nourishment needs, his head was much clearer, his power calmed. Walking through the streets of Portland, the Oregon rain a whisper on his skin, he absent-mindedly took in the changes in his city while he pondered his strategy.

One thing was for sure—he would never go back into the Shadows. For twenty fucking years, he'd known nothing but pain, darkness, hunger, and more pain still. It had eaten him, slowly, inexorably, gnawed on his mind, his soul, chewed him up until he was not much more than a broken shadow himself.

For the longest time, he'd imagined Rowan might give him the benefit of the doubt and unleash him again. Considering the tenuous friendship they'd had, the years they'd been working together, she could have at least given him the chance to explain. In the end, though, her distrust of his kind had won out, and she'd reverted to treating him as the natural-born enemy any demon was to witchkind. When he'd felt her die a few years back—through the faint bond tying him to her after she'd bound him—the bitter knowledge that she'd really left him to rot in the Shadows had eroded whatever altruism he might have had left.

Now that he finally had a shot at his freedom, he'd do anything to gain it, to avoid returning to the Shadows. *Anything.* He'd have even killed the pretty little witch—would have been a first to take a female's life, and a real pity considering she was a beauty, but if it assured his freedom, he'd have done it in a heartbeat.

A ruthlessness born of two decades in pain and darkness.

However, her mention of the "failsafe measure" had thrown him for a loop. He couldn't be sure whether she spoke the truth, and he wouldn't risk his freedom finding out. So, as he'd fought her in the dark of the mausoleum, feral hunger shredding him from the inside, he'd decided to switch tactics. There was another way to break the bond that leashed him to her, one requiring patience and skill. He'd have to win his freedom bit by stealthy bit, had to coax her to give in to him. Which was fine, as long as the result was the same.

He followed the pull of the leash to Merle, and not surprisingly, it led him to the MacKenna residence. He'd already guessed she'd go straight back home, where all her supplies would be. She would have to mix up something—one of those witchy decoctions that resembled mire but held impossible power—to replenish her blood and energy before she could track him down as she'd threatened.

Well, no need for that. He came to her willingly.

Shaking his head at the irony of that, he approached the veranda of the old Victorian. It hadn't changed much in the past twenty years. Proud and sturdy, its lavender walls and white décor weather-worn and chipped, it rose up at the end of the long driveway like a small castle. For a fleeting moment, he half-expected Rowan to walk out and greet him as usual—with an impossible, fragile blend of trust and suspicion in those gray eyes of hers.

The wind picked up and whipped at him, rustled the leaves in the nearby trees, and he blinked, focused, pushed the past and all regrets into the darkest place inside him.

Eyes trained on the faint shimmer of the magical wards protecting the house, he took the steps to the veranda and paused, his hand almost touching the edge of the spell. The buzz of power brushed his skin. He couldn't break down the wards, but he might get in anyway. There was no guarantee this would work, though. If it didn't, he'd bounce off and probably crash down hard in the driveway, feeling like a mosquito that had tried to snuggle with a bug zapper.

Holding his breath, he pushed forward. The witch magic sparked at his touch, a slight charge electrifying the air, a precursor of the power that would strike him down if the ward decided he was unwelcome company. Heart racing, he waited. The hum in the air quieted. Slowly, the prickling on his skin subsided, and with a sigh, the magic gentled. His hand slid through the shimmer and touched the door.

He blew out his pent-up breath. *Well, what do you know?* He'd taken so much blood from Merle that the ward had indeed recognized it in his veins and allowed him in.

With a small mental command, he unlocked the door, stepped into the foyer and stopped for a moment. He'd never been inside the house, what with the wards and Rowan's cautious nature, her deep-seated mistrust of demons, even after decades of knowing him.

He inhaled the various scents that hung in the air, among them—most prominently—Merle's natural perfume, a delectable fragrance that stirred his hunger in more ways than one. Underneath it, though, hovered the combined scents of all the witches who had lived here over the decades, laced with the smell of the wood and the stone of the old Victorian, the herbs of all the potions that had been mixed and sampled here, topped with the unmistakable aroma of active magic.

Brushing his fingertips over the wallpaper, he closed his eyes for a moment and absorbed. Beneath his skin, the walls hummed with power, so strong, so vibrant, simultaneously drawing him closer and repelling him. *Witch magic*, he mused, *is a curious thing.* So different from his own, less intuitive and more of a craft, as it demanded careful study and vast knowledge to be wielded right. And yet, it could be so powerful.

It had been this fascination that had brought about his downfall. Yanking his hand back from the wall, he clenched it into a fist. He wouldn't make the same mistake twice.

He followed the pull of the leash and the freshest trace of Merle's scent to the living room, where he found her slumped on the sofa, sound asleep. There was a pitcher containing some unidentifiable sludge on the coffee table, and her fingers loosely held an empty glass tainted with the same kind of muddy residue. Yep, she'd mixed up some herbs for a potion that would recharge her batteries, energy- and blood-wise, and she'd likely passed out from exhaustion as her body regenerated. Witches might not have the accelerated healing of most otherworld creatures, but the Powers That Be favored them, and they had more magic and magical remedies at their disposal than anyone else.

Halting in the middle of the living room, he studied Merle's sleeping form. Her face was still pale, though not as ashen as it had been when he'd left her in the mausoleum. She had the usual fair complexion and ginger hair of the MacKennas, with freckles sprinkled over her nose and cheeks. The tantalizing curve of her neck was bare of any bite marks—he'd made sure to lick the wounds sealed before he'd left—and not a drop of blood stained her clothes. Well, he was nothing if not neat. At least when it came to females.

Merle's chest rose with her slow and steady breaths, drawing his attention to those feminine curves that had felt heavenly pressed against him. He wanted to explore that softness, inch by luscious inch, wanted that fair skin of hers flushed pink with arousal. Two decades of sensory starvation had left him ravenous, aching for touch, for the sizzling heat of skin-to-skin contact and the mad tumble into the depths of carnal pleasure. Merle was a package of witchy hotness, everything he hungered for in a female—not only lush curves and silken skin, but a fiery strength to her aura, a hint of danger in her power that he craved to play with.

The kiss—which had been meant to distract her—still heated his blood, made him yearn for more. Her passionate, wild response surprised him, revealing a hidden streak of temper. His own personal little witch volcano.

Right now, though, her magic was curled inwards, her energy pattern subdued and faint in sleep. She looked delicate, fragile. Sure, there was a core of strength in her, so powerful he could sense it even with her magic all but dormant, and he'd seen the spark of her fighting spirit in her eyes when they'd quarreled in the mausoleum. As he studied her now, however, the way she lay there with her guard down, peacefully asleep, she was all soft, vulnerable female.

A twinge of pain in his chest, a stir of doubt. If he went through with his plan, he would render her even more vulnerable, would smother that fire inside her, leaving her bereft and broken. He gritted his teeth until something painful popped in his jaw. Closing his eyes, he tried to breathe past the pressure on his chest. If there was another way...

But there was none. It was either this or a return ticket to the Shadows. And he'd win his freedom at all costs, so he grabbed that annoying, persistent sliver of a fucking conscience and beat it into silence.

Reaching out with his power, he prodded Merle. Her shields were airtight even in sleep, testament to her strength as a witch, but she would still feel his nudge as a mental knock. And, sure enough, she came awake with a jerk and a gasp. Eyes wide, she scanned the room, locked on to him, and froze.

Her gaze slid down his body, and to his great surprise—as well as enjoyment—he sensed an emotion in her that trumped the fear and shock in her aura. Amusement curling inside, he turned to study the contents of the shelf on the wall, giving her an unobstructed view of his fabulous backside. The flavor of appreciation in her energy pattern surged, and he barely stifled a chuckle.

He brushed his fingers over the backs of what looked like thin VHS cases, and threw a glance at her over his shoulder. "Ah. She's awake at last." Turning his attention toward the collection on the shelf again, he lightly added, "Wonders will never cease."

Fury boiled in Merle's aura, and with an adorable huff, she hurled the glass she'd still been holding straight at him. He casually caught it in midair. And there was that fiery temper of hers. *Beautiful*. Bringing the glass up to his nose, he sniffed at it, grimaced and gingerly set it on a side table.

"You should work on that recipe. Maybe a little less..." He made a show of searching for the word, snapping his fingers, then pointed triumphantly. "...mold."

She narrowed her eyes and fixed him with a stare close to lethal. "You!"

"Yes. Me." He pulled a case out of the shelf, opened it and studied the interior. *Huh*. A disc, like a CD, though it supposedly featured the movie *Ghostbusters*. Weird. He returned it to the shelf, aligning the back precisely with the other movie CDs. "I have a name, you know." He met her gaze. "It's Rhun."

"How did you get past the wards?"

He pursed his lips. "Must be all that sweet, sweet blood of yours coursing through my veins."

Merle's aura flared with anger. Her power flickered, all but throwing visible sparks around the air. It was a tangible force humming over his skin, making him want to step closer, rile her up some more so he could relish the strength of her magic.

She stood, keeping a wary eye on him. "Where did you get those clothes?"

He gave a nonchalant shrug. "Took them off some guys."

"Are those guys still alive?" Her voice was deadly quiet.

Tilting his head, he smiled at her. "What do you think?"

"I think," she said, her power drenching the air, thickening, clearly ready to clash with his own, "that I told you not to spill innocent blood."

"Ah. But they weren't innocent." He could still taste the humans' auras, dark and tainted with death and pain. That kind of flavor, it came from killing. As in plural.

"I should just bind you in the Shadows again."

"You could, and maybe you should, but then how would I be able to help you?" He strolled over to the impossibly flat TV and crouched down in front of it, examining what looked like some morphed version of a VCR underneath it.

Merle's energy flickered with conflicting emotions, most of them dark, though there was a hint of arousal—just like when they'd kissed in the cemetery. *Interesting.* He deliberately flexed his muscles. The touch of arousal deepened, much to his delight.

He stood up again and trailed his fingers along the top of the TV. Where was the back of it? "We do have a deal, don't we?"

She blinked at him, her face a study in incredulity. "You're really going to help me after all?"

"What, you thought I'd renege on our agreement?"

"You attacked me, almost drained me within an inch of my life, and then left me there to rot. What was I supposed to think?"

He pressed a hand to his heart. "You wound me, little witch. That you'd think I have no honor..." Sighing dramatically, he gave her his best look of long-suffering sainthood. "Besides," he added with a smile, "I wouldn't want to miss out on all the fun I could be having with you."

"*Fun?*"

"Why, yes." Oh, he was already enjoying this. Pushing her buttons proved to be a whole lot of fun he hadn't anticipated. And that wasn't even part of the plan. He caught her gaze and prowled toward her. "You promised you were going to feed me."

Her heart thumped loud enough for him to hear. "You drank my blood. Lots of it. You should be sated."

"My species' name," he said as he came to a halt inches in front of her, "is misleading. Blood is only one of the components a *bluotezzer* demon requires for sustenance. Besides blood, we feed off pain..." He raised his hand to touch her cheek. "...and pleasure." His finger ran down the line of her jaw, and she trembled. *So soft, so delicate.* "I have had your blood. I have caused some pain. Now I need...pleasure." With deliberate slowness his finger followed the tender curve of her throat down to the neckline of her sweater, lingering there.

Merle swallowed, obviously trying hard to appear unfazed. The beautiful blush creeping up her cheeks told a different story. "Pleasure? As in sex?"

"Hmm."

"You want to sleep with me?"

His hunger rose, snapped at him from the inside. He reined it in. "Of course. You're beautiful, intriguing, and sexy, and there's nothing I'd rather do than lock myself in a secluded room with you and make up for twenty years of involuntary celibacy. But—" He stroked her mental senses with his power, teasingly, gently. "—since I don't want to overwhelm you right now, making you come will do."

"No." Her voice was husky, and the enticing scent of her arousal spread in the air, in blatant denial of her outward refusal.

"No?" he asked softly. His finger rubbed her collarbone.

"No," she repeated, even as her nipples visibly hardened underneath her sweater. "You won't get that from me."

"I need to feed in order to help you." He studied her, those clear blue eyes, the alluring blush on her cheeks, her quickened breathing. If she really didn't consent, he wouldn't force her, and not just because it would be difficult to take pleasure from someone who wasn't into it. But she *was* interested, if ambivalent. He decided for another push. "Do you want me to take it from someone else then? I do so like debauching the innocent."

It was only partly an ultimatum—mostly it was the blunt truth. He *would* have to feed in order to be in full command of his powers, and if she refused him, he'd have to find someone else. Even with the whole of the city at his disposal, though, he'd rather take pleasure from Merle. It would bring him one step closer to winning his freedom, yes, but that aside, he simply *wanted* her.

She took a step back, putting space between them. The unmistakable fragrance of female interest followed her retreat, belying her harsh words. "Why don't you find some not-so-innocent woman to lavish your charms on? A murderous slut maybe?"

He had to smother a laugh. She really did have some spunk, and damn if he didn't like it. Giving her a sufficiently insulted look, he said, "Believe it or not, I do have certain standards." Tilting his head, he then looked up as if remembering something, a slow smile spreading on his face. "I think I'll pay a visit to that luscious blonde a few houses down. She looked very much agreeable." And with that he turned to leave.

Behind him a firestorm of emotions erupted from Merle. The air was so charged with her power—buzzing louder and louder the more her control on it seemed to slip—that the lamps in the room flickered. The hairs on his neck rose. His own magic, so much simpler and more instinctive in nature, surged in response to the power brushing up against him.

Keeping it tightly under control, he continued walking out of the living room.

He was about to open the door in the foyer when Merle blew out a breath that was laden with enough conflicting emotions to make a psychiatrist giddy with excitement.

"Wait."

CHAPTER 3

His hand on the doorknob, Rhun glanced at her, the corners of his eyes crinkling. "Yes?"

Merle ground her teeth together. Was she really going to do this?

Even as every female hormone in her body screamed, *Yes, yes, yes, jump him like you know you want to*, she couldn't ignore the nagging feeling of foreboding. She shouldn't let him get any closer to her. The fine line she was walking by having him barely leashed would get thinner with every piece of herself she ceded to him. If she wanted to keep him under control, she'd have to prevent him from gaining more power over her, and letting him take pleasure from her required a measure of trust that would hand him a great deal of power.

But just the thought of allowing him to feed from someone else sent her into a fit of worry. What if he snapped? Took more than just pleasure? He was her responsibility—she'd freed him from the Shadows, and it was on her to make sure he didn't hurt anyone innocent.

She put her hands on her hips. "I'm not letting you loose on the female population. At least I can defend myself against you." Being a witch gave her some means of keeping him under control, and if he snapped with her, she'd be able to fight him. Letting him go to take a human woman, on the other hand, would be like sending a wolf into a herd of sheep.

He narrowed his eyes. "Just what kind of beast do you think I am?"

"You're a demon."

"Ah, and that means I'm a rapist bastard, is that right?" His tone was light, but his hand tightened on the doorknob until his knuckles flashed white, and his aura flickered with such darkness, almost as if…

She blinked, baffled. Had she insulted him?

Rhun glared at her, the clear-cut beauty of his features more pronounced in his obvious anger, his lips pressed together in a tight line, and the way he held himself—rigidly dignified like someone who'd just been slapped for no good reason.

"Uh." Great, now she felt bad for assuming the worst about him. Still, how was she supposed to know he might have some decency? Clearing her throat, she said, "Sorry. It's just… No offense, but your track record doesn't exactly put you in a good light."

A flicker of something—*regret?*—showed in his eyes, but it was gone again so quickly she wasn't sure she'd seen it. Rhun's aura gentled, though, and he leaned against the doorjamb and cocked his head. "For your information, all the women I've been with were more than happy to feed me, and I left each and every one alive and well." He glanced up and paused as if in consideration. "Although some of them were passed out in bliss."

When he looked back at her, the force of his heated gaze jolted her. Slow, tantalizing waves of prickling warmth rolled over her skin, sensitized her nerves, until her clothes were too heavy, chafing. A pulse of heat and *want* centered between her thighs, deliciously wayward. Judging by how her body reacted to him, he was aphrodisiac on legs—every lithe movement a whisper of dark sensuality that promised swooningby-ecstasy. She suddenly didn't doubt his last statement anymore.

"So, little witch," Rhun said, the timbre of his voice evocative of languorous seductions between rumpled sheets, "will you feed me, then?"

The last twinge of doubt drowned in a surge of desire that almost made her knees wobble. She mentally stomped on the last bit of worry, and simply surrendered to the part of her that wanted to take what Rhun offered, and *gorge* on it.

"Yes," she said, her voice gone husky. It was just sex, nothing more, and gods knew it had been a while since someone had pleasured her but good.

A wicked smile snuck onto his lips, enhancing the raw sensuality he threw off in scores. He was sex wrapped in danger as he crossed the foyer, closing the distance to her.

"I will not sleep with you," she said hoarsely, tilting her head up to look at his face, into those eyes glowing with calm predatory attention. They had such a striking color, a mélange of bright blue and light green, a forest lake in midsummer. "You'll just...you know…"

"Make you writhe on my hand until you moan my name?"

Heaven help me.

She pressed her thighs together. "My clothes," she ground out while choice parts of her body wantonly throbbed with anticipation, "will stay on."

His eyes flashed. "Hmm, a challenge. I like that." He brought his hand up to the nape of her neck, tangling his fingers in the strands of her hair. "Where do you want to do it?"

"Where do I—" She shook her head, perplexed, rattled, and not a little distracted by the hand massaging her neck. "What?"

"You know," he said, shrugging, "where would you like it best? On the couch? The table? The carpet?" His gaze flicked to the side, and he raised his eyebrows. "Up against the wall?"

All of the above? "Uh." She cleared her throat, struggled for sanity. "I don't—it doesn't matter."

His hand slid from her nape to the front, grazing the sensitive skin over her racing pulse. "No preferences?"

"No. Let's just...get this over with."

"Then we'll do it my way?" His voice was a purr that caressed her senses, stroked her in hot, intimate places.

"Sure," she croaked. "Whatever."

"Well, then." His hand stilled. The air between them shimmered. "*Run.*"

Her heart skipped a beat. "What? Why?"

"Because," he muttered, leaning in closer, dark power rippling off him, "I like a good chase."

She only stared at him for a second.

Then she ran.

Sprinting out of the living room into the library, she threw a glance over her shoulder. Rhun stood in the foyer, watching her run. He was giving her a head start. *All right then.*

She'd just barged into the dining room, when a change in the air signaled Rhun was now fast on her heels. His heat and power brushed up against her back as she skidded round the corner into the kitchen. Demonically fast, he made a grab for her when she wanted to dart past the cooking island. She yelped, jumped to the side, and he missed her by an inch. The frantic rhythm of her heart echoed the racing speed with which she ran. Next she made a mad dash toward the game room.

She was on the secondary staircase when Rhun caught up. With a pounce reminiscent of a feline predator, he tackled her, brought her down on the steps in one fluid motion, cushioning the fall with his arms. She didn't shriek so much from the impact of crashing into the stairs, then, as from the visceral fear of being caught. Her heart thrummed in her chest, excitement rushed through her veins, every cell of her body aware of the powerful male pressed against her back.

Who knew being chased—and captured—could be so thrilling?

"On the staircase then?" Rhun's breath brushed her neck.

"Kinky."

She only wheezed in response. Her wheeze turned into a soft moan of surprise when he nibbled at her earlobe and then rubbed his cheek against hers. With a carefulness that amazed her, he turned her around to face him. Braced on his arms and knees above her, caging her in on the stairs, his hungry gaze raked her body.

"You sure about the clothes?" His voice was scraped gravel.

Every heavy breath she took brought her breasts in brief contact with his chest, brushing male heat and vibrant power. It made her breathe so much faster. "Not feeling up for the challenge after all?"

In answer, he cocked a brow and lowered his head on hers with single-minded intent, only to stop short at her hand on his lips.

"No kissing on the mouth," she whispered.

"Why not?" Spoken against her palm, eyes fixed on hers, burning through her.

"Too personal." It might sound moronic considering what she was about to let him do to her, but this was another one of those lines she'd better not let him cross. She'd allow him to touch her, yes, but it would just be sex, purely physical, part of their agreement, nothing more than her body reacting to stimulation.

If she allowed him to kiss her, though, well—that would open up a whole other set of reactions, and she damn sure didn't want to go there. That one kiss in the mausoleum had already been enough. His taste was still branded into her every cell, the feel of him indelibly etched into her consciousness, making her want more. A kind of *more* she couldn't allow, not when she needed to keep her emotional distance from him.

"Pity," Rhun muttered, still against her palm, his hot breath tingling on her skin. "I'd love to kiss you."

When she tried to pull her hand away, he grabbed it and held it in place. He licked a slow, hot circle on her palm, firing up her nerve endings all the way down to the juncture between her legs. A moan escaped her lips at the incredible sensation, and she pressed her thighs together. He still didn't let go of her hand but held it up as he let his tongue trail to her wrist, nipping gently at her pulse, and then licked his way down the sensitive underside of her forearm while pushing up her sleeve. At her elbow, he stopped for a kiss in the crook of her arm, playfully making use of his tongue.

She was already mush at that point.

He released her arm to cup one of her breasts, rubbing his thumb over her nipple, and even through two layers of fabric, it hardened instantly. Making an appreciative sound, he plucked it until her breathing grew erratic and her skin was covered with a sheen of sweat. The smile Rhun rewarded her with was pure male satisfaction.

She didn't have time to glower at him for that, though—the very next second he bit her nipple and now sucked it with utmost delight, unperturbed by the clothes still covering it. Jolts of pleasure shot through her body, sizzling down straight to her core. One of his thighs was wedged between her legs, rubbing against her in the same rhythm as his tongue now teased the nipple of her neglected breast. Breathing heavily, she dug her fingers into the carpet on the stairs.

Her body was high-strung, her pulse running in overdrive, and she ached for more touch with a need that scared her. Driven by instinct, all thought of propriety thrown out the window, she pushed her hips against his thigh.

He lifted his head from her breast, kissed a slow trail up to her neck. When he withdrew his thigh a little, she was about to moan in protest, but then his hand slid between their bodies, cupped her throbbing core over the fabric of her jeans. "Want my fingers inside you?"

She nodded, face heating with embarrassment. "*Yes.*"

"You got it, little witch."

Skimming over the front of her jeans, his fingers found the

button and made short work of it. Her zipper followed suit. With delicate care, he pushed aside her panties, grazed her curls, caressed the sensitive flesh beneath. Her breathing hitched. His thumb stroked her clit with the lightest touch while two fingers brushed her entrance, teasing her most intimately, making her writhe. She panted heavily by now, her hands holding on to the carpet with a death grip.

He slid his hand farther down and pushed those two fingers inside her. A moan caught in her throat, her body shuddering at the intense feel of the erotic invasion. Skillfully, he moved his fingers, with knowing precision and intent, and brought her close to the edge in a matter of seconds. The tension in her body built up, and she was close, so close, squirming against him, but even so, release wouldn't come.

"*Merle.*" His hand stilled.

She whimpered in frustration.

"Look at me."

Vision clouded with pent-up desire, she met his gaze.

"Just let go and enjoy." His face was so close to hers, she breathed him in. He let his energy envelop her senses, a warm, tingling embrace.

She opened her mouth to speak, found she couldn't. How was she supposed to let go, surrender, if only for a few seconds, to a being she'd been taught to mistrust, even fear? She didn't *know* him. And how could she enjoy this, how could she find her pleasure here, now, while Maeve was being held, suffering only gods knew what kind of hell? How could she allow a demon to *pleasure* her, when another one tortured her baby sister? How—

"Stop." He cupped her face with his other hand, gently forced her to look at him when she wanted to turn away. "Stop thinking, Merle." He bound her with her name on his lips, his gaze holding hers. "I don't mean you harm." A slow, soothing caress on her cheek. "All I want right now..." His voice was a low murmur. "...is to make you feel good..."

Her breath hitched, burned in her throat.

His eyes drew her in. Such a beautiful color, like dewdrops on young grass, and the way he looked at her now…as if he could see through to her soul, her heart, read her fears and hopes. As if he knew of the painful tangle of worry and guilt, knotting her chest—holding her back.

"It's okay to let go," he said, his eyes still intent, reassuring her. "And it's okay to enjoy this. It's all you can do for now. Just let go, and I'll take care of you."

She exhaled, trembling inside and out. "Okay."

His fingers lightly, carefully, teased her again. "Put your hand around my neck."

She obliged, the embers of arousal rekindling.

"Close your eyes."

Hesitating, she did. The rhythm of his fingers pushing in, sliding out again, became faster, demanding, and the tension inside her surged again. Desire sparked, hot and consuming. She clutched at his neck, held on tight, her hips moving against his hand, riding him.

"That's it." His deep voice in her ear, breath brushing her skin. "Go with it."

Little moans left her lips, her breathing turned to pants, and then, she let go. Her climax came with a vengeance. She writhed against him in a frenzy of overwhelming pleasure and sweet, sweet relief, as he brought her down with slowing strokes and murmured words of intimacy. His hot breath came in fast, shallow pants, sawing past his elongated fangs—evidence of his own arousal.

For a long moment, neither of them moved. His palm remained on her pulsing core, her fingers tangled in his hair. Eventually, he withdrew his hand with a last gentle teasing that had her shuddering against him.

She opened her eyes, coming to her senses again, and let go of his neck as if burned. Heat shot up to her face and realization sucker-punched her in the guts, closely followed by embarrassment of the finest sort.

His grin scorched the last of her pride. "A little late to be bashful, don't you think?"

"Get off."

"Is that an offer?"

By way of an answer, she shoved at his shoulders, to no visible effect whatsoever. It was like trying to move a stubborn block of concrete.

Anger, mixed with shame, had her breathing faster with flashes of heat. "You got what you wanted, now move!"

He chuckled, a low, masculine sound that was as arrogant as it was sexy—and annoyed her to no end. Even worse, he had the unbelievable nerve to kiss her on her nose before rising to his feet. Holding out a hand to help her up, he said, "Come on now, little witch, don't be too hard on yourself. It's okay to admit I gave you a mind-blowing orgasm which you most thoroughly enjoyed."

She scrambled to a stand without deigning to accept his outstretched hand, and readjusted her clothes with shaky fingers. "Oh, don't get all cocky. You didn't make me moan your name, did you?"

The smile he gave her was all sensual promise. "Next time, then."

And at that, equal parts of panic and anticipation gripped her tight. She had to get rid of him again, the faster the better. Already, she could feel a difference of power between them— he'd taken more from her than just blood and pleasure. The energy leashing him to her had shifted by a minuscule fraction, and she had a sinking feeling if she wasn't careful, she might find herself on the wrong end of that leash.

"Come on," Rhun said, watching her with all-too-perceptive eyes, "let's find your sister."

She nodded. "Yes, let's go."

Time was running out, and not just for Maeve.

CHAPTER 4

R hun watched Merle stalk away from him toward the kitchen, the scent of her anger mingling with the aroma of her arousal that still suffused the air. Such an intoxicating combination, wrapping around Rhun's senses and challenging his self-control. It was all he could do not to tackle her again and keep his promise to make her moan his name.

He closed his eyes and took a deep, calming breath—which only intensified the effect of her alluring scent. Bad idea. *Really* bad idea.

Sure, he'd fulfilled his need for nourishment, but it had done nothing to slake the bone-deep hunger for pleasure within him. His own desire remained painfully unfulfilled, his hard cock straining against the fly of his jeans being evidence of that. It had taken an amount of self-restraint he'd never known he was capable of not to rip Merle's clothes off on the staircase and drive more than just his fingers inside her.

His hands clenched to fists and he opened his eyes, his gaze inexorably drawn to the swaying movements of Merle's hips as she walked away and disappeared behind the kitchen door. He had to get a grip on himself. No matter how luscious and tempting she was, no matter how much he wanted her pinned naked underneath him, her legs wrapped around his hips while he thrust inside her until she saw stars and—wrong train of thought.

Breathe.

Jumping her like some uncivilized incubus would be counterproductive. The line he was walking was thin, and he could only push her so far toward his ultimate goal before she'd throw him back into the Shadows. Proposing to have hot monkey sex would *probably* be a bit too much—for now, anyway.

So instead of giving chase after her like his predatory instinct urged him to do, he stood and waited, arms crossed and leaning against the wall, his eyes trained on the kitchen door. How long until she'd notice?

The door swung open and Merle walked back in, her face a study in forced nonchalance.

Ah, a minute, he thought, pursing his lips.

"So," she said, clearing her throat, "how do we go about this?"

"And here I thought you had it all figured out—what with the impressively confident way you stormed out of here." Rhun shook his head. "Alas, I stand corrected."

The fire in her eyes made him smile—he liked her a bit angry. It brought out an uncontrollable, passionate part of her that he itched to tangle with. She was beautiful and attractive, yes, but her mouthwatering looks notwithstanding, it was during outbursts of anger or lust—as he'd just witnessed on the stairs—that she became a truly powerful, sensual female who stirred his own passion. Even though it went contrary to his intention of charming her pants off, he was tempted to lure that side to the surface, to annoy her just enough to stoke the fire inside and watch anger erupt. Witch volcano, indeed.

"Well?" she prompted, looking daggers at him. "What's the plan?"

"First of all," he said, "you need to change your sweater and bra. Don't get me wrong, I do appreciate the visual—a lot—but it *will* chip away at my concentration if you flaunt those goodies in front of me like that." And with a wave of his hand, he indicated the wet spots on her chest where he'd lavished his attention on her breasts. He was only half-joking—the sight of the wet fabric clinging to her hard nipples almost had him pouncing on her again.

Merle glanced down at her compromised clothing and uttered a feminine sound of dismay. *Fucking adorable.* She then peered up at him again, her face flushed beet red, much to Rhun's enjoyment. She looked yummy when she blushed—a reaction he intended to elicit a lot more. Preferably when she was splayed out before him. Naked.

"I'll be right back," she muttered and started for the staircase behind him, then apparently realized she'd have to brush past him to get there. Her face took on a panicky expression, which only intensified as he gave her a salacious smile and wiggled his brows. She whirled around and vanished into the kitchen again, presumably to take the other stairs. "And don't you dare follow me!" she yelled.

Busted, Rhun stopped midway in his ascent up the secondary staircase, chuckled and waited in the foyer instead.

Merle came back down the stairs a few minutes later, now sporting a wide sweatshirt that did a good job of hiding her scrumptious curves. He nodded approvingly. For now, that would do. He'd peel it off later.

"Okay," she said, her face all business and tense concern. "How do you track that bastard?"

He snapped into serious mode as well. "I need a starting point, somewhere he's been so I can pick up his signature."

Her brows drew together. "Signature?"

"His energy pattern. We all leave traces of it behind when we use our powers, similar to a scent trail. But since it fades over time, the fresher the track is, the better I can profile him."

"And then? Do you follow his trail?"

He narrowed his eyes at her. "I'm not a dog."

"Obviously not," she muttered. "Dogs have manners."

"For someone who needs my help," he drawled, his brows raised, "you sure are treating me a bit rudely."

She studied him for a moment, her features twitching with some restrained reaction. "Sorry," she ground out. "Didn't mean to be snappy. You just...rub me the wrong way."

"Well, that's better than not rubbing you at all."

The following nervous tick of her eye delighted him to no end.

"Anyway," Rhun said, "to get back to the problem at hand—no, the sparks of power we emit don't work like a scent trail. We don't leave a continuous energy trace behind, only parts of it when we tap our innate magic. But all *bluotezzer* demons share some form of connection on a psychic level, and once I know his signature, I can narrow my focus on him. It'll give me a rough idea of where to go to find him, a sense of direction and distance."

She nodded, grim and pensive.

Crossing his arms in front of his chest again, he asked, "So, do you have a starting point?"

Again she nodded, her face shadowed by so much pain, her voice quiet. "Maeve's apartment. He snatched her from there."

For a moment he was silent, studying her, frowning as he felt something tense inside him, an unpleasant, inexplicable sensation. Shaking it off, he refocused. "How do you know he took her from there?"

Sky-colored eyes met his, startling in their clarity. "I saw it."

Something in the way she said it, a twist in her voice, made him understand. "A vision." He regarded her with newly sparked interest. "You have the second sight. Like Rowan."

She lowered her eyes. "It's not nearly as powerful as hers was. I rarely ever *see* and I don't have much control over it." Her gaze found his again, and there was steel in it, forged in pain. "But every one of the visions I have had was correct to the smallest detail, and I saw that demon take her. I even saw his power, his aura. I felt it as if I'd been there."

He held her gaze. "How do you even know he's a *bluotezzer* demon?" But even as he finished the question, the answer came to him. The flicker in her aura gave it away. "You saw him drink from Maeve. In your vision." And there was only one demon species who fed off human blood—and looked human itself.

She blinked, slowly, and it was the only emotional reaction she showed, the rest of her face a stark mask of motionlessness, her aura tightly controlled. "Can you work from her apartment?"

Gritting his teeth, he nodded. He didn't like this look on her face, this tone of her voice—this much hurt in her eyes. It made him want to stoke that fire inside her again. Not that he cared about how she felt—after all, she was a means to an end, the key to his freedom. Still, he didn't like seeing her sad, it made him...uncomfortable. "Let's go."

Merle grabbed her keys and they went out to her car, their footsteps on the paved driveway the only sounds in the quiet of predawn. It was still dark, probably an hour before sunrise, and the air was crisp, the night at its coldest. Rhun took a deep breath, inhaled the scent of early spring, of the impending morning, of nature and *life*. It had been so long, he'd almost forgotten what it was like.

This had always been his favorite time of the night, despite his own energy and powers waning due to his demon nature. The world around him was just about to be newly born, fresh, untainted, imbued with innocence so profound nothing could touch it. It always seemed life stood still at this hour, as if taking a breath and holding it, shortly, before moving on to another day with the first light of dawn.

The sound of the car door opening brought his attention back to Merle, who slid into the driver's seat. In some way, he should probably feel grateful toward her. If she hadn't unbound him, he'd still be confined to suffocating darkness, plagued by insatiable hunger and pain.

But even as the thought crossed his mind, something inside him bristled against it. What she'd done wasn't for his benefit, and all foolish feelings of gratitude would be misplaced and wasted. After all, she was not only the one who'd freed him, but would also be the very one to kick him back into his dungeon of darkness once he'd served his purpose.

Which was exactly why he wouldn't allow himself to feel anything else for her than lust—certainly not gratitude. He was past caring for anyone or anything else. It was a weakness he couldn't afford, not with the Shadows waiting to take him back.

He got in the car next to Merle as she started the engine. While she backed out of the driveway, he studied the interior, inhaling the enticing aroma of her that had condensed in the small space, and his eyes locked onto something lying on the console between the seats. He picked up the small piece and examined it closely.

"If this is a vibrator," he said after a moment, "they surely have taken the whole notion of making electronic devices smaller a bit too far."

Merle winced and the car veered to the left. "Say what?" Her voice sounded slightly higher than usual.

"This." He held out the tiny piece of electronic...something to her. "Don't tell me this actually gets you off. I mean, with certain things, size *does* matter."

The car swerved once more on the road as she snatched the lame excuse for a sex toy from him and stuffed it back into the console. "It's not a—why would I have a vibrator in my car?"

He shrugged. "I don't know. For when you get horny on your way to work?"

"I don't—"

"Ah," he went on, interrupting her flustered exclamation, "now there's a nice mental image of you."

"Rhun!"

A glance at her told him she had a lovely red face again. A bit rosy this time. *Interesting.* He filed that information under the newly opened section of Merle's Various Shades of Blushing.

Her hands tightened on the steering wheel until her knuckles flashed white. "Before you get any other inappropriate ideas—it's an MP3 player."

"What does MP3 stand for? Merle's Private Porn Panorama?"

Now the car almost crashed into a street sign. Taking a shaky breath and steadying her hands on the steering wheel again, she said with visibly forced calm, "It's a device to store and play music."

"Oh. So no vibrating then?"

"No."

He regarded the piece again. "You know, if they made it bigger and let it vibrate in sync with the rhythm of the music it plays, they could make one hell of a fortune with it."

She shot him a sideways glance, her eyes narrowed.

"Well, just think of all the women out there who could climax to the tunes they love. *Moan along to your favorite song.*"

"*Rhun!*"

Laughing, he looked out the window. Teasing her was just so much fun. And, as a nice side effect, he'd changed her mood from sad and uncomfortably pained to…well, angry and embarrassed. Which was still better than the consuming grief she'd been drenched in before, as far as he was concerned. He knew some other ways to make her flustered out of her mind, but he'd save those for later, since they were best executed on a comfy mattress. Or maybe in a shower. He sighed. How he longed to take a shower.

About half an hour later, Merle parked the car in front of an apartment complex in a rather decrepit neighborhood in East Portland. They'd crossed the whole city to get here—this place was probably as far away as one could get from the MacKenna family house without leaving Portland proper.

They got out of the car, and Rhun frowned at the eyesore of a building in front of him, puzzled at Maeve's choice to move here. He'd seen the old MacKenna Victorian, knew there were more than enough rooms in it to accommodate the two sisters. It wasn't uncommon for witch families to have several generations living under one roof—the bonds of blood and magic were tight, and most families took care to keep it that way. All the more strange that Maeve should have chosen to move away from her sister.

He followed Merle up to the graffiti-adorned entrance. "Why did Maeve live *here*?"

"She didn't want to stay with me anymore." Suppressed emotions echoed in her calm voice.

"How come?"

Opening the door and stepping inside, she threw a cold glance at him over her shoulder. "What does it matter to you?"

He shrugged and followed her upstairs, the stench of garbage and mold assaulting his nose. "Just curious as to what would drive two witch sisters apart." Mindful not to touch the grimy handrail of the stairs or the wall covered with what looked like maybe a biological weapon, he steered around pieces of trash. *Shower.* He really wanted a shower now.

Merle was silent for such a long moment, he almost thought she'd abandoned the conversation. With measured, quiet steps she took the stairs, her movements laced with graceful grief. "Maeve is not exactly a witch," she said without looking at him.

He paused on the steps for a second. "She's a MacKenna." Born of a long line of witches, each of them endowed with an innate spark of magic.

"She never had any powers to speak of, or at least not to my knowledge. If she did, my grandmother would have nurtured them, even if they were weak."

Yes, Rhun thought, Rowan would have fostered her granddaughter's powers if there had been any. Still, a descendant of a witch line—by nature all of them were female—who did not inherit the family's magic was unheard of. But the lack of any powers on Maeve's part explained at least something else.

"She had no means of defense against him," Rhun observed.

Since Merle walked in front of him, her face turned away, her aura under cold control again, the only reaction he saw was an almost imperceptible stiffening of her spine. "No." Her voice had that pained edge again, the one that cut something inside him. "No more than any human would have."

In other words—none.

They had reached the third floor landing and Merle approached and unlocked the door to the apartment on the right. Hesitating for a moment before stepping inside after her, Rhun tilted his head and frowned.

"No wards?"

Merle let out a breath, a soft sound close to a sigh, and shut the door behind him. "Not anymore. I put some in place when Maeve insisted on staying here, but..." She rubbed her forehead and closed her eyes briefly. "I don't know what happened. They just...vanished."

He sensed her unspoken words in the tense silence that followed. "You think they failed because you didn't make them strong enough." It was a statement, not a question, and he didn't need her answer. He could read it clearly in the guilt shadowing her face.

He only noticed he'd inched closer to her when Merle flinched, her head tilted up, eyes wide and locked on his. Unperturbed, with a quiet calm belying his inner agitation, he raised his hand to capture a strand of her ginger hair, softly twirled it between his fingers. "Why would you think that?"

It took her a moment to answer, her gaze glued to the movement of his fingers. "I'm not as strong as my grandmother was."

He could hear her faint, shallow breaths, and there, underneath that creamy skin on her neck, beat her pulse, enticing, inviting. It had quickened as he'd stepped closer, just as her breathing had sped up, and he couldn't help brushing a finger over the heartbeat at her neck, feel the rush of her blood beneath the skin, the power coursing through her body.

"When Rowan was your age," he said quietly, his eyes fixed on the graceful curve of her throat that he wanted to trace with his tongue, "she wasn't half as strong as you are now."

Merle softly sucked in a breath, which drew his attention to her mouth and those lush lips of hers. "You don't need to lie to me." Her voice was low but steady.

He wrenched his gaze away from her tempting mouth and instead met her eyes. "You're right."

Something flickered in the blue that bound him.

"I don't need to lie," he went on, his finger stroking over her pulse in the rhythm of his own heartbeat, "because it's true."

It really was. Why he told her that, though, he didn't know.

His hand now curved around her nape, his fingers playing with locks of her hair, hair that seemed to have sprung from fire. "I've known Rowan since long before you were born, and though she was always a powerful witch, her strength grew over time. You're comparing yourself to a witch in the zenith of her life, when you've only just started tapping your own potential."

And it was great, he could tell, undeveloped powers coiling deep inside her core, waiting to be nurtured. If she opened her mind to him, he could even better assess the strength of her magical abilities. Well, he could do much more if she ever did open up to him like that. The mere thought of connecting that intimately with her, of tangling with that pure, potent energy, made his pulse speed up, his own power hum with anticipation and hunger. A very male, very primal hunger.

Merle studied his face for a long, silent moment, and he wasn't sure whether she was aware that she slightly leaned into his hand on her nape. "How old are you?"

His lips curved up. "Take a guess, little witch of mine."

He could almost see her mind working inside that pretty head of hers, as she apparently put together what information she had on him and his species. "A century?"

His smile widened. "Close enough."

The air between them was charged with energy, parts of hers, parts of his, colliding a thousandfold in the space separating their bodies. Jerking with sudden awareness, Merle pulled back, out of his hold, and took several flustered steps away from him.

"The demon," she said, clearing her throat, "attacked her in here." And with that she walked into the living room.

Ten measured breaths were necessary for Rhun to tamp down the overwhelming urge to grab a hold of Merle and pull her closer again, to feel the vibrancy of her power meshing with his own, her body pressed to his. Once he was convinced he could follow her without charging her like a horny incubus, he stepped into the living room as well.

The space was small but clean and well-tended, the furniture simple and scarce, though there were little feminine touches scattered about. An ornate candle here, a delicate figurine there. He picked up one of the numerous colorful picture frames decorating the room, and studied the laughing faces in the photo. Three little girls with flaming hair, hugging each other tight.

"Moira," he said, tapping the eldest of the sisters. She'd been ten when he'd been bound in the Shadows, but he remembered her too, remembered the fleeting glimpses he'd caught of the designated heir of the MacKenna line, a young witch raised to lead and inherit the full power of the family. Her absence in Merle's struggle to save Maeve was a statement in itself, but even so, he asked. "Where is she?"

The air in the room stood as still as Merle. Silently, slowly, as if afraid to break herself, she crossed her arms and looked away.

"Such pain," he muttered, setting the picture frame back on the wide top of the TV.

"The trace?" Merle prompted, her voice so soft he barely heard it. "Can you pick it up?"

"Tell me what happened to Moira."

"Pick up the trace."

"I will, after you tell me what happened."

She swallowed, still not looking at him. "She died."

"I got that much. How?"

For a moment, she was silent. "It was an accident. A spell gone awry. It killed her."

There was such hurt in her voice, such devastating grief about her, it whispered of a loss even deeper than the one she had just acknowledged. A suspicion crept up on him, and as he looked back at the picture frames, the snapshots of the people that had been loved by Maeve, he saw one face appear again and again, a face he'd known in passing before the Shadows—and it was frozen in time.

There was not a single picture showing Emily MacKenna older than her mid-thirties.

He looked back at Merle. "It killed your mother, too."

"This," she said, her lips trembling, "is not about them." Finally she faced him, and instead of the fragile vulnerability he'd expected to see, there was strength in her eyes, quiet and pained, but strength all the same. "Let's concentrate on finding the one that's still alive."

Rhun nodded. "Yes." And for the first time, he felt like he should mean it.

Expanding his senses, he mentally scanned the room, sampled the different traces of energy that lingered between the layers of the world, tasted their essence. There was Merle's power, curling in the air in the finest tendrils, some old, some new, all of them as alluring as her scent. Amidst it all was a much more delicate, faint force—so faint, in fact, that he would have almost missed it. It was intriguing, strange, but he let it go, since it wasn't the one he was looking for.

There, suspended in the air like mist permeating the

substance of the atmosphere, was the trace of a power akin to Rhun's—dark, menacing, and consuming in its hunger. He homed in on the particularities of the signature, studied the intricacies of its design, and memorized the defining elements.

When he had soaked up the essence of the other demon's spiritual trace, he closed his eyes and focused on the fine threads linking him to all of his kind, the subtle connection he shared with the collective energy he'd been forged from. He probed, felt, tested the different threads emerging from the common field, searched the mass of unseen power for a spark of the energy pattern he was looking for.

Frowning, he opened his eyes after what had felt like hours, though one look at the softly changing light outside told him it had been far less. He turned to Merle, who was watching him with tense attention, and he shook his head.

"Something's off."

Her body tensed impossibly further. "What do you mean?"

"I can't sense him. It's like...his signature doesn't exist."

She joined him in his frown. "Are you sure?" Then, something flashed in her eyes. "Is he dead?"

He considered it then shook his head again. "If he'd died, it had to have been very recently, because you've seen him take Maeve just two days ago. If he'd died since then, though, there would still be a residual energy trace of him on the psychic plane." Searching for the right comparison, he paused for a moment. "It's like the lingering body heat that only slowly fades after the onset of death." His gaze flicked to the window. The sky was now a shade of gray, streaked with the finest hues of rose. "There might be another reason I can't locate him right now." He jerked his head toward the advancing dawn on the horizon. Already, he could feel his energy waning as the night retreated. A few more minutes at best and he'd be human for all intents and purposes, except he was still almost impossible to kill.

Merle's gaze followed his to the brightening sky, and she

nodded, softly. Her chest heaved with a breath that seemed laden with an invisible weight. "We'll have to wait until sunset." And, almost inaudibly, she added, "He'll have her another day."

Something rasped along his senses, chafing him on the inside, and it had nothing to do with his fading powers. "He won't be able to feed from her during daytime."

Her eyes met his, scorching him. "That doesn't mean he can't hurt her," she whispered, and turned to go.

CHAPTER 5

They drove back in heavy silence in the quiet of dawn. Rhun stared out the window, while Merle was lost in thoughts so dark they threatened to break her. She'd been foolish enough to assume they would track down the demon without delay—through the anguished haze in her mind, strung out by the desperate need to rescue Maeve, she'd completely forgotten Rhun couldn't use his powers during the day. By the laws of nature, he was a creature of the dark, his magic inextricably linked to the reign of the night.

She mentally reached out to sense his aura, but all she encountered was the average vibrancy of a healthy male mind and body, and though it appealed to the woman inside her, it differed little from a human energy pattern. Like his demon powers, Rhun's distinctive preternatural aura lay dormant for the day.

The same would hold true for Maeve's captor, but Merle didn't fool herself. Her sister would still suffer torment at the hands of the demon. Reduced to human powers and strength he might be, but a man didn't need magical means to inflict pain on a woman. Just thinking about it made Merle sick to her stomach, made her hands tighten on the steering wheel until she couldn't feel the leather anymore.

If—no, not *if*—*when* she found that son of a bitch who'd dared lay a hand on her baby sister, she'd rip him apart limb by limb and watch it all grow back, several times, before she'd let Rhun kill him. Yes, *that*—and only *that*—might soothe the searing wrath in her blood.

Glancing to her right, Merle watched Rhun stare at the dawning sky, his eyes drinking in the display of vivid colors like a starving man might devour a sumptuous buffet. *Right, he hasn't seen the sun rise in twenty years.* Two decades of darkness and pain, a prison that would win any contest for Most Cruel Confinement, hands down. Considering the pain he must have suffered, he was surprisingly sane and…civil.

As she turned the car onto the street leading to her house, Rhun picked up her MP3 player again and browsed through the content. He stopped short after a moment and peered at her, one eyebrow arched.

"Don't tell me the Rolling Stones are still alive." His voice dripped with disbelief.

"Yeah, well, more or less."

He grunted. "Impressive. I'd have thought they'd have partied themselves to their graves by now."

"I know," she gave back, joining in his casual conversation before she knew what she was doing. "I never thought they'd outlive half of the Beatles."

Now he fully turned to her. "Which one of them died?"

"George."

"So it's down to Paul and Ringo now, huh? Pity." He clucked his tongue. "Who else of the Bold and Beautiful bit the dust?"

"Michael Jackson."

"Seriously?"

"Yep. Whitney's gone, too."

He threw up his hands. "I leave this world alone for twenty years and look what happens." He shook his head. "Next you're gonna tell me David Hasselhoff still tortures humankind with his *music*."

Merle bit her lip. "Well…"

He closed his eyes and held up a hand. "Please."

Smiling despite herself, she said, "You know, Arnold Schwarzenegger was governor of California."

Rhun glared at her. "Now you're just being cruel."

She had to chew hard on the inside of her mouth to stop her laughter from bubbling up, laughter which felt so out of place right now, inappropriate considering the sorrows weighing her down. But for a precious moment seemingly stolen from another life, before stifling responsibility, loss and pain, she felt lighthearted, free, in the mood to joke. She wanted to tease, and it startled her. Amusement and joy didn't come easily. She barely ever got playful, only laughed when Lily and Basil— friends who had grown as close as family—set their minds to it and coaxed it out of her, and it had been like this since long before Maeve's abduction.

Ever since her grandmother's death, Merle had had to carry the weight of her inheritance as the family's head, and slowly, surely, it had taken its toll. The balance of the magic abundant in the world was a frail one, easily disturbed, hard to control, and each line of witches was integral to this balance, with the head of the line being the vital part. Merle's own essence had become intricately interwoven with the powers beyond as she'd assumed her responsibility, and—just as her fellow witches— she now had to take measures to uphold the balance. Sometimes, all it took was a small offering.

Sometimes, small wasn't enough.

Merle shivered at the memory of the last time she'd had to appease the Powers That Be, had to pay them back for the magic she'd used. *Fractured parts of her soul, blood that wouldn't stop flowing…*

She shook her head, pushed the feeling of nauseous help-lessness and growing depletion far away, locked it into the place reserved for the darkest of memories. It was the same place that held the image of a burning cherry tree, the smell of scorched flesh, the sound of screams echoing in the late afternoon. Screams that were her own.

This, she thought, was why lighthearted laughter eluded her. It had died that day, sixteen years ago, long before her grandmother's passing, long before Maeve had disappeared. For Merle, careless joy was part of a childhood which had ended too early, burnt to cinders like the tree she'd used to climb.

She parked the car, got out and trudged up the steps to the veranda, with Rhun trailing behind. He was humming "Bad" by Michael Jackson, and he did it with such glee that Merle wanted to smack him.

Once inside, she made a beeline for the library, where she perused the shelves, pulled out a volume here and there. Coughing at the dust whirling around her, she dumped the books on the large desk in the middle of the room. Rhun had followed her and now sauntered around the study, frowned at the mess of books and papers cluttering the carpet and the table, and then leaned against one of the floor-to-ceiling shelves. His arms crossed in front of his chest, he focused those piercing bright eyes on Merle with an intensity that made her squirm inside.

"What are you doing?" he asked. "Trying to create a vortex of chaos?"

She barely stopped herself from throwing the volume she was holding straight at his head. The book was too valuable. "I'm doing research," she said instead, rubbing her forehead with her free hand.

"On what exactly? How to keep order? Because I can see you need some improvement in that field."

I can't kill him, I can't kill him, I can't... She dropped the volume on a pile on the desk. "Maybe there's something I've missed, some other way to find that bastard—"

"Don't bother. There isn't." He said it matter-of-factly, but still, the finality of his statement sucker-punched her in the guts. "That aside, you really should spend the idle daytime hours until sunset better than by uselessly skimming through dusty books. I think you should—"

"If you're suggesting I have sex with you..." she cut in, anger bubbling in her veins.

Smirking, he shook his head. "You know, not everything I say is aimed at getting me into your sweet little panties." He raised an eyebrow. "Unless you want me to."

"I don't." Even to her own ears, her answer had come too quickly to be credible. Images of Rhun poised above her as she'd lain on the stairs flashed before her inner eye, and the parts of her body he'd touched heated in remembrance. The mere thought of what it would feel like to have all that impressive male strength between her legs, skin on skin, pumping fast, working her up until— "I don't," she repeated, her face flushed with all-too conscious embarrassment.

"Uh-huh." Rhun gave her a knowing look that only fueled the fire spreading in decidedly feminine parts of her body. "Well, as I was saying before you so rudely interrupted me with your Freudian slip-like suggestion—now, please, would you put down that book? There's no need to start throwing things at me."

"Get to the point," Merle snarled.

He clucked his tongue. "Impatient, are we?"

The book she'd been holding slammed into the shelf— missing him by a good three feet. Merle groaned. Never, even if her life depended on it, had she been able to hit a godsdamn mark.

Rhun had not even deigned to move, he'd just watched the literary missile fly past him, and now turned to Merle again, eyes dancing.

"Maybe if you aimed for a spot a few feet to my right, you'd hit me." He caught the next book in midair and pinned her with a serious look. "Merle. Stop throwing for a sec."

"*What?*"

"When was the last time you slept?"

That startled her like nothing else, made her pause. "I was asleep when you broke in here." She lowered the book she was currently holding. "You know, after you left me bleeding on the mausoleum floor?"

"Are you still mad at me about that? I did come back to you, little witch, didn't I?" He strolled over, all sinuous moves and casual arrogance, his eyes intent on hers. When he stopped right in front of her, only inches away, his body heat brushed over her like a physical caress. "And just for the record, I did *not* leave you bleeding. I closed those holes." He raised his hand and tapped one finger on the pulsing vein on her neck.

It was such a fleeting, light touch, and yet it short-circuited Merle's entire system. How could he affect her like this? He didn't even have his damn demon powers! She checked her mental shields, reinforced them with meticulous effort, and yet...they hadn't been breached in the least.

"And back to my point," he continued, examining her with a look that seemed to strip her bare, "that bit of sleep you caught a short while ago was what? Half an hour? A quick nap at the most. Now tell me, when was the last time you *really* slept?"

Something inside her crumbled, and she closed her eyes, suddenly feeling the bone-tiring exhaustion she'd been fighting back with the force of her despair. Every muscle ached, her limbs burdened with lead. "Three days ago."

Rhun's hand curved around her nape again, a touch so intrinsically possessive that it should have made her back away. At this moment, though, it somehow felt...right. Too tired to fight his slow erosion of her defenses, Merle relaxed in his hold, leaned her forehead against his chest. *Just a little, just for a moment.* By the gods, he felt good. Warm, hard, uncompromisingly male. She wanted to wrap him around herself.

His breath brushed the top of her head. "You should rest." Slowly, languorously, his fingers stroked her neck, and it was so damn soothing despite all her common sense. "You'll be of no use to Maeve if you're weak and tired. Sleep, and we'll look for her come nightfall." His other hand had come up to her lower back, a pleasant pressure, pushing her toward him.

It was then that Merle realized she was letting him *hug* her. *Oh, hell no.*

She snapped her eyes open, pulled back with a start, and stumbled as she stepped away from him. "You're right." Her heart pounded, her thoughts were a flustered mess. Avoiding eye contact, she started for the door, stopped, half-turned. "I'll lie down for a few hours. You can watch TV, or read something, or do whatever demon stuff you usually do during daytime, as long as you stay inside and away from me. And don't even try to leave—I'll cast a spell that alerts me if you choose to skip and run, and believe me, you don't want me chasing you down." Thus spoken, she marched off out of the room and went upstairs.

Damn sneaky demon.

While walking to her bedroom, she cast the warning spell under her breath. "Within these walls, all hold and hide, allow no breach from either side." It was actually more of a reinforcement of the wards to also work inwards, but it would do. Good thing her grandmother had made sure she learned basic spells by heart so she wouldn't have to consult the grimoire except for more complicated rituals.

And right there, she stopped in her tracks. *The grimoire!* She'd left it in the mausoleum when she'd scrambled out to get home and replenish her energy. Closing her eyes, she thumped her head against the doorjamb to her room and remained like that, her arms hanging down her side.

For a moment, she pondered driving back to the cemetery to retrieve the book and her tools, then decided against it. If she didn't fall asleep behind the wheel on the way to the cemetery, she'd sure as hell collapse there in the mausoleum. Rhun was right, she needed to rest, and the last place she wanted to sleep in was a graveyard. She'd locked the mausoleum on her way out, so her belongings would be safe until she'd pick them up later, after she—

"Didn't make it to your bed?"

Merle whipped around—staggering—to find Rhun standing behind her, lips curved with unconcealed amusement.

"You know," he drawled, "I'd have carried you upstairs and made sure to tuck you into bed if I'd known you were *that* tired. I mean, you have to admit, sleeping against a doorjamb is not exactly comfortable…"

Her eye twitched. And her exhaustion had little to do with that.

He sauntered past her through the door. "So, this your bedroom?"

She followed, keeping a wary eye on him. The way he prowled around her private sanctuary was a truly disturbing sight—a dark predator stalking the lair of its prey. He brushed his fingers over her dressing table, her jewelry, sniffed at her bottles of perfume, and studied the photo collage of her family and friends she'd hung on the wall above her bed. All the while, he moved with such disconcerting poise among her personal effects—as if he owned it all. It made her skin break out in goose bumps.

"Listen, you really need to—" She stopped short and stared at him, baffled, and not a little terrified. "What are you doing?"

He'd shrugged off his leather jacket and draped it over the back of the chair in front of her dressing table, and was now in the process of taking off his shirt. He paused in pulling it up. "You've seen a man undress before, haven't you?"

She was too shocked to get mad at his quip. "Why are you doing that?"

"Well, usually, people don't go to bed in their street clothes. I certainly don't. In fact, I prefer to be naked when I join a female in bed."

She stared. Blinked. Closed her eyes and rubbed them with the fingers of one hand. "You are *not* joining me in bed. If you want to sleep, use one of the other rooms." She opened her eyes again and waved at the door.

"You know that's not going to work." His eyes crinkled at the corners, and he exuded an amount of male arrogance that was impossibly disarming. "I'd just steal into here and snuggle up to you at some point anyway."

If she hadn't been so weary, she might have smacked him for his smugness. And for sneaking the image in her mind of him snuggling up to her. *Breathe.* "I'll lock the door then."

For a moment, he was silent, eyebrows arching. Then he laughed. And laughed. And just kept on laughing. While Merle gaped at him in outrage, he pulled off his T-shirt, still chuckling, and laid it neatly on top of the leather jacket.

Merle continued gaping at him, only now it wasn't in outrage anymore. Her gaze was glued to the display of rippling muscle and lickable skin in front of her. *Why, gods, why?* Of all the demons to recruit for help, she had to pick one with a swoon-worthy body.

She mentally slapped herself back from lust-induced insanity. "I could just bind you in the Shadows again for the day."

"You could." He kicked off his boots and proceeded to unbutton his jeans.

Merle averted her eyes. Somewhere in this room must be her senses. If she didn't look back at him, she might find them again.

"But, then you'd have to unbind me again at sunset, which means you'd have to feed me your blood again. And—seeing how the Shadows tend to starve me out after only a few hours —I'd have to nearly drain you—*again*. You don't want a repeat of that, do you?" Unhurriedly, with a natural confidence that was as magnetic as it was intimidating, he strolled over to her. Naked. Temptingly so.

Merle shook herself before she did something undignified like drooling at him. "Flesh and bone, still as stone," she whispered harshly, infusing the words with magic.

Her power surged, charged the air, and then whipped at Rhun. He froze. Features strained as if he were lifting a massive weight, he stared at her.

"That's not fair," he pressed out through gritted teeth, obviously fighting against the magic holding him in place as if petrified. "I just wanted to snuggle."

"Uh-huh." Merle raised one eyebrow and crossed her arms in front of her chest so he wouldn't notice her hands shaking from the effort it took to keep the power flowing. "Maybe I'll just leave you like this until nightfall. Like a classic demon statue."

At that, his lips twitched up. "I *am* gorgeous to look at."

Everything female inside her sighed in affirmation. Not that she'd ever tell him that. Or the fact she wouldn't be able to keep up the paralysis spell for much longer. Even if she wasn't strung out from lack of sleep and the strain of recent events, she'd have trouble holding him like that for the day, since for all its simplicity, the spell was energy-draining. Still, as far as a display of power went, it was quite impressive. She *hoped*.

"You will get dressed and get out of here," she said, as she felt her magic weaken. The spark inside her flickered, her control over the spell slipping. "I can easily freeze you again if you don't comply, and I'll make sure to mute you as well so I won't have to listen to your complaints." She didn't have enough power left to pull that off, but he didn't need to know that. She took a deep breath, and deliberately let go of the spell before it broke on its own and betrayed her waning strength.

Rhun inhaled with noticeable relief—and then did a series of lazy, delicious stretches that all but eroded Merle's ability to think rationally. Or think at all, for that matter.

Mouth gone dry, skin heated and heart hammering at the erotic sight of his powerful frame in slow motion, she struggled to form words. All she managed to get out, her eyes riveted on the perfect firmness of his backside, was a rather unconvincing, "Now leave."

Ignoring her order, he moved toward her, slowly, giving her enough time to back away.

She didn't—couldn't—but she tried for some presence of mind nevertheless. "I'm not letting you in my bed. Go sleep somewhere else."

Coming to a halt right in front of her, he took a hold of her oversized sweater. "Merle." He tugged a little. She was about to snap at him, when he quietly added, "Please?"

That stumped her. Baffled, she met his eyes. They held a glint of such honest yearning that something hard inside her cracked.

"I just don't want to sleep alone. I have been by myself for the past twenty years and…" He paused, held her gaze, no sign of wickedness in his expression. "I really need some company."

Merle swallowed, past a still dry mouth, past a growing lump in her throat, and an unbidden ache of sympathy in her chest. She couldn't deal with him like this. If there had been the slightest indication he was trying to manipulate her, she'd have thrown him out without batting an eye. If he'd been as cocky and pushy as before, she'd have snarled at him and fought him. But this…this was more than she could handle. This genuine need in his eyes, this candor in his voice.

"All right," she said, closing her eyes and rubbing her forehead with one hand. "You can sleep in my bed." She didn't have the heart to send him off, and quite frankly, she was also too tired to argue about this much longer. He was still convinced killing her would kick him straight back into the Shadows, so he didn't pose a threat in that respect. As for the much more probable result of letting him into her bed… "No sex," she added with narrowed eyes.

He smiled, a subtle, seductive curving of his lips. Lips she kept telling herself she did *not* want to kiss. Did. Not. No, no, no. Wrenching her gaze away from his mouth, she looked at her closet door, her dresser, the ceiling, anywhere except at the temptation in front of her.

His hand holding the seam of her sweater moved up until his fingertips grazed the skin above her waistband. Merle felt that touch much, *much* lower, and it had her trembling.

"You can't feed during the day anyway," she managed to say.

Another slight caress of his fingertips. "Who says I want you for nourishment?"

"*Rhun.*" A warning. As much for him as for herself.

"Hmm." He stroked along the waistband of her jeans, just a little, just enough to make her breathe faster. "You're right."

Now she did look up at him, her gut knotted tight in suspicion.

"You should get some rest first. I *can* be demanding."

She opened her mouth to verbally slap him, but he shut her up by laying a finger on her lips.

"Now, my little witch," he said, "I'm going to peel this sweater off your body like I've been planning to do since you came down those stairs, and you're not going to squirm because that's all I'm going to do. Understood?"

She stared at him, into his mesmerizing eyes now holding a quiet, spellbinding assurance. Seconds ticked by, along with her heartbeat. She gave a small nod.

"Good." His finger was still on her mouth, now rubbing her lower lip. "However, I'd be delighted to help you out of those jeans, too, if you'll let me."

She shook her head, half in a trance. For a moment there, though, she'd considered it.

"Too bad," Rhun muttered.

And then he lifted her sweater.

His fingers and knuckles brushed her skin as he pushed up

the fabric, without any haste, as if he had all the time in the world and had reserved it solely for relieving Merle MacKenna of her sweatshirt.

"Arms up," he ordered, his voice calm.

He never took his eyes off hers, holding her gaze with quiet force, even when she raised her arms and let him pull the sweater off over her head and throw it to the side. Only then did he lower his eyes—and stilled.

He became absolutely, inhumanly motionless, his gaze so intent on her exposed skin, he might as well have touched her—it felt the same. Standing there, in front of him, bare-chested except for her bra and rooted to the spot by Rhun's undivided attention, Merle got an inkling of what it must be like for a deer when a panther focused before it pounced.

She sucked in a sharp breath. Immediately, Rhun's pupils dilated, his eyes taking in the movement of her breasts as she inhaled. The sight of him unhinged her. Even divested of his powers, the way he looked at her now, the way he kept himself preternaturally still, feral hunger whispering behind a thin veneer of control, she realized he was the most dangerous creature she'd ever come toe-to-toe with.

"Rhun," she whispered. Her heart racing, she didn't dare move or say anything else. It might just make him snap.

He blinked, once, twice, then raised his eyes to meet hers. Bit by bit, he regained a more sane expression, though the single-minded intent was still plainly visible on his face. "You," he said, his voice rough and low, "make it hard to be good."

Gods only knew, she so wanted him to be bad right now. Apparently, she had a suicidal streak. Before she could act on that, though, she took a hasty step back and muttered, "I'll put on my pajamas."

She didn't wait for his reaction and hurried to her closet, opened it and picked a set of shorts and a tank top. Hidden from Rhun's gaze by the open door, she pulled on the tank top and proceeded to get rid of her bra underneath. Next she discarded her jeans and quickly put on the shorts. Sliding into the bed without looking at Rhun, she turned to lie on her side and covered herself with the blanket up to her chin.

Her hands shook. Whether from the extreme exhaustion, which had gotten worse, or from the striking awareness of the naked demon who was getting in bed behind her just now, she didn't know. Probably both.

The mattress dented beside her, and the next moment Rhun had slipped underneath the blanket and up to her. Her whole body tensed and she stopped breathing.

"Shh." His breath tingled on her neck. "Relax. Just snuggling up, remember?"

"Right," she ground out. His rock-hard erection pressed into her backside, and—*gods have mercy on her soul*—made her want to push back and rub up against him, give in to the warm tingles of excitement rushing through her body, melting her core. This was so wrong on so many levels. And yet, she didn't even think of scooting away from him.

"Take it as a compliment," he said, and she could feel his lips curve against her neck.

Slinging his one arm around her waist, he replaced the pillow under her head with his other arm and entwined his legs with hers. His hand slid up her torso to her rib cage, stopped there below the swell of her breasts, and pressed her back to his chest. It felt like he had wrapped himself around her.

Merle was encased in immovable male strength, heat and raw power just short of overwhelming. She should have been terrified to be locked into his embrace like that—instead, she found herself relaxing into his touch.

Yep, she was definitely suicidal. Maybe she'd gone delirious from her lack of sleep?

"Don't you dare make a move on me while I'm asleep, or I swear, I'll make you regret it."

"Don't worry. It's much more fun when you're awake and blushing." He nuzzled the sensitive spot where her neck met her shoulder. "Now sleep, little witch of mine." Pressing her closer to him, he took a deep breath, his fingers curling into the thin fabric of her tank top, and it seemed as if he inhaled the essence of her being. He made a sound of utter relish and slowly exhaled.

As Merle drifted off to sleep, she realized she was royally screwed.

For nothing had ever felt more right than being wrapped in Rhun.

CHAPTER 6

"**W**hat the fuck is going on here?"

Merle woke with a jolt, bolting upright. Eyes popping open, she stared at the source of the voice—and cringed.

Lily Murray, fellow witch, best friend since kindergarten, partner in crime, and royal pain in the ass when pissed, stood in the open door, brandishing a baseball bat as a weapon. As a friend of the family, she'd been allowed in by the wards and now tilted her head, ebony locks falling around her shoulders, her dark blue gaze darting between Merle and Rhun.

Flinching, Merle realized what the scene must look like—she was sitting in bed, her hair ruffled, the sheets rumpled, and a very naked Rhun lay next to her, his arm slung around her waist in a casual display of possession.

He yawned, stretched, and gave her an impossibly gorgeous sleepy smile. "Morning, little witch."

"Merle?" Lily finally asked in the same voice one might use on a friend that was about to jump off a high building.

"Umm…" Merle cleared her throat, embarrassment heating her cheeks. "It's not what it looks like."

"Oh? So…you're not cuddled up to a naked demon in your

bed?" Lily asked, undoubtedly having picked up the faint trace of Rhun's demon aura, even toned down as it was during the day. She arched one black eyebrow, her body still in battle mode.

Merle grimaced. The heat in her face increased. "I can explain."

Lily didn't loosen her alert stance, holding the baseball bat ready-to-swing above her shoulder and eyeing Rhun as if he were a rabid dog. "Yeah? I'd like to hear that. Why is there a demon in your bed? And why the fuck is he naked?"

"Oh dear," Rhun said from his sprawling position. He peered up at Merle, a worried expression on his face. "Has no one told her yet?"

Merle stared at him, too stunned to react.

Propping himself up on his elbows, he turned to Lily. "All right, it pains me to be the one breaking it to you—I think that's your parents' job, but since you asked..." He sighed. "Well, grown-up men and women—yes, even witches and demons— have certain needs, and when a woman feels especially needy—"

He didn't get to finish that explanation. The pillow Merle smacked down on his face effectively shut him up.

Her best friend gaped at Rhun, dumbstruck. Rendering Lily Murray speechless was quite an achievement.

"Let's step out for a moment, shall we?" Merle scooted to the edge of the mattress and was about to get off the bed when the embarrassment factor of her situation shot up by several points.

"Lil, I checked downstairs, all clear," a familiar male voice called from the hallway, seconds before Basil Murray walked in the room. "Find anything up—" Lily's twin brother froze and fell silent as he beheld the scene.

Different from his sister as day was from night, with dark blond hair and eyes the color of molten chocolate, he was indisputably handsome. Add to that the air of protective warmth and quiet strength that he exuded, and he was a prime male specimen, appealing to women on the most visceral level. In fact, if Merle hadn't grown up with him, her feelings toward him those for a brother she'd never had, she'd have been one of his drooling female admirers.

However, the fact she considered him her brother didn't make it any less embarrassing that he'd walked in on her being in bed with a naked male.

"Uh…" Basil's gaze darted from Merle to Rhun and back to Merle. "I guess that explains why she hasn't been answering her phone all day," he said to Lily, cocking one eyebrow.

"It's not what it looks like!" Merle threw up her hands.

"That hitch in your voice," Rhun said while gazing up at her, "is that despair?"

Lily turned to her brother. "She was just about to tell me what she's doing in bed with a naked demon."

"He's a demon?" Basil's head whipped around and he pinned Rhun with a lethal stare.

"And I'm naked." Rhun waved at the nude length of his body and grinned.

Merle stared at the floor, waiting for a hole to open up and mercifully swallow her.

"Hold this and watch him," Lily said to Basil, and, handing him the baseball bat, she motioned for Merle to follow her out of the room.

Merle narrowed her eyes at Rhun as she got off the bed. "Behave. And, for the love of the gods, *get dressed.*"

"Yes, honey."

She caught Basil's appalled look and cringed. "It's not— we're not—" Sighing with resignation, she muttered, "It's complicated."

Basil said nothing as she walked past him, simply raised his eyebrows and returned to staring at Rhun as if the demon were a mold fungus in his breakfast cereal.

"All right," Lily said as soon as Merle had closed the door

behind her, "what in the world is going on here? First you tell me Maeve's been taken by a demon, then you fall off the grid for almost two days, you don't answer your phone, and then we find you having a pajama party with another demon. *What the hell is up with that?*"

Merle took a deep breath before venturing to answer. The air was suddenly as thick as fog. "I unbound him from the Shadows to help me find Maeve. He's a *bluotezzer* demon, same as the bastard who took her." She held up a hand as Lily started to reply. "He's still leashed to me and I'll send him back into the Shadows once we find Maeve."

Lily stared at her, indigo eyes wide. "You unleashed a demon that was bound in the Shadows? Have you gone insane? What if he turns on you?"

"I made him believe he'll be automatically bound again if he kills me." *Believe* being the operative word.

"What if he finds out the truth?"

"Let's pray he won't," was Merle's quiet answer. She reached out to squeeze Lily's hand. "Look, I'm sorry I was out of touch—I turned my cell on mute before I unbound Rhun, and I had no idea you've been trying to reach me. I didn't mean to spook you guys."

Lily's deep blue eyes darkened, and the lines of her face softened as she studied Merle for a moment. "Why didn't you tell me what you were going to do?"

Merle's heart weighed heavy in her chest. "Because I know you, Lily Murray. You'd have tied me to a chair to keep me from doing it."

"Damn right I would have—it's a suicide mission!"

"It's the only chance I've got to find her. I've tried every other way I could think of, believe me, but nothing worked. And I have to find her, Lil." It was not a question of choice, but of simple survival. A part of her would die along with Maeve, the part that mattered most.

"So you unleash a monster to catch a monster."

"I can't give up on Maeve. She's out there, at his mercy." Merle took a shaky breath, fought down the urge to cry. Weakness wouldn't get her anywhere. "I'd unleash a thousand monsters to find her."

Lily regarded her for a long moment with eyes that had always put Merle's motives to the test, challenged her in the best of ways. While being loyal to a fault, Lily was also the one person who never sugarcoated her opinion, and her unwavering honesty had helped Merle more than once positively question herself, and grow in the process.

Now, Lily nodded and gave her a grim smile, tempered with grief matching her own. Although she'd always been closer to Merle, Lily had never considered Maeve any less than a sister by choice, too. "Yeah, and since I can't stop you from risking your neck, I'll be right behind you, saving it."

Merle returned her best friend's smile, her heart a bit less heavy at the display of a bond that was as thick as blood.

"Okay," Lily said more lightly after a moment, "now explain to me why that demon hunk in there is nude. Have you two...?"

"No, I'm not sleeping with him. He's just...really difficult to handle."

Lily crossed her arms in front of her chest, fine lines forming on her forehead. "I've been doing some research on *bluotezzer* demons since you told me about Maeve, and they seem to have a special kind of diet."

"I know." Merle rubbed her forehead with one hand. "Blood, pain, and pleasure."

Lily's gaze bored into her. "Please tell me you're not providing him with that."

"As little as possible," Merle said after a taut silence, "as much as necessary." She parried Lily's concerned reproach. "I need him strong enough to find that other demon. For that, he needs to feed. Would you rather I let him loose on others, innocents, maybe?"

"I'd rather we feed him intravenously. You know, maybe chained to a bed."

Merle couldn't help giggling at that mental image, and Lily joined her involuntary amusement with a grin.

"Seriously, though." Lily's expression sobered. "I'm worried about you. Be careful with him, all right?"

"I'm trying."

"And let me know how I can help you with all this. You know you won't get me off your back now, don't you?"

"I wouldn't have expected anything else." Merle gave her a small smile. "And speaking of which, there *is* something you can do."

"Shoot."

"Keep collecting info on *bluotezzer* demons, as much as you can—strengths, weaknesses, habits, whatever you can find. And while you're at it, please do some research on the binding spell, too. If I'd had more time, I'd have prepared better before unleashing him. I had to rush into this with very basic info, and I have to be careful with what I look up while Rhun is around. The less he knows, the better."

Lily nodded. "Got it."

"Another thing—let's keep the lid on this, okay? Don't tell anyone about Rhun, not even your mom and least of all Isabel. The last thing I need is for the Elders to get wind of this."

"Yeah, they won't be happy to hear you unleashed a demon without their consent." Lily raised one of her sleek dark eyebrows.

"Exactly. I really don't want them breathing down my neck." Merle shuddered. "I have my hands full as it is just dealing with Rhun."

Lily's eyes danced. "He looks like more than just a handful."

"Lil!" Merle gaped at her.

"What? I may not like demons, but I'm not blind!" She leaned in closer, dropping her voice. "Now, this is totally off the record, and I'm saying this as a woman, not a witch, but—he's like Gorgeous Central! Talk about sinful temptation."

"I know," Merle groaned, thumping her forehead against the doorjamb. "Why can't he be one of those demons with scaly skin and foul breath? Do you have any idea how hard it is to remind myself why I shouldn't just jump him? I'm a mess of raging hormones!"

"Well," Lily said, patting her shoulder, "if you ever need a reminder, I'll be happy to swing by and kick some sense into your butt."

"Appreciated."

"That's what friends are for. All right, so what's the battle plan from here?"

Merle heaved herself off the doorjamb. "What time is it?"

"Half past five."

"In the afternoon?" Her voice shook with disbelief.

"Yeah."

No way. That meant she'd slept almost twelve hours straight, without waking up once. Never, in her entire life, had she slept that long, and especially not that soundly—peacefully. And she'd have probably kept on slumbering if Lily hadn't barged in. *Incredible.*

"Everything okay?" Lily's gaze was scrutinizing.

"Yeah, I'm fine." *More than fine...* Merle shook herself and refocused. "Well, we'll have to wait for sundown, then we can start searching again, when Rhun regains his powers. I don't know how fast we can track that demon down, so in any case you should keep gathering information. Call me if you find anything significant."

"You too, all right?"

Merle nodded.

"Are you sure you'll be okay on your own with Mr. Tall, Dark and Dangerously Handsome? Baz could come with you."

Merle shook her head. "I can take care of myself. Besides, I have a feeling if Basil tags along, he and Rhun will end up at each other's throats…"

"True." Lily's gaze flicked to the closed door. "Speaking of which, let's check on the guys. It's awfully quiet in there."

A sinking feeling settled in Merle's stomach. "Maybe they're only exchanging I'll-kill-you-scowls?"

For a second, they stared at each other. Then they rushed into the room.

CHAPTER 7

When Rhun came downstairs into the kitchen, Merle was sitting at the cooking island, glaring at him over her bowl of cereal. Ever since that other witch and Blondie—whom he'd successfully stared down in Merle's room—had left, Rhun was in an exceptionally good mood, and after taking his first shower in twenty years, he was humming under his breath and walking with a bounce in his step. Much to Merle's annoyance, as he could tell by the look she gave him. He met her glower with his biggest grin and enjoyed the following nervous tic of her eye. Ah, he'd never tire of teasing the hell out of her. It was just too much fun.

She'd showered as well, and had put on fresh clothes, the scent of her laundry detergent mingling with her natural aroma in a special blend that made him want to inhale deeper. Made him want to close the distance between them and *taste* her, in every possible way.

Hunger, raw and brutal, roared awake inside him. The sun was just now setting, and with every passing minute, with every glimmer of light that faded and died, his innate magic returned more to life, flowed through him like the blood through his veins.

His needs, too, came back with a vengeance.

One by one, his senses sharpened, and so did his awareness of Merle, sitting there, all clean, fresh-smelling and soft, her body underneath her clothes a lush landscape he wanted to explore—and claim. The image of her standing in front of him in her bedroom, her breasts barely concealed by her bra, was still vivid in his mind, and just thinking about it made him rock-hard.

At that moment, he'd been teetering on the brink of losing control. It had been long, so long, since he'd last laid eyes on a sumptuous female body, so long since he'd *touched*, he'd been about to go bat-shit crazy over that bit of skin exposure in front of him. Like a godsdamn teenage demon overwhelmed by his own dark instincts. *Fucking embarrassing.*

And that had been with his powers dormant and his senses dulled. Now, though, every part of him that was intrinsically male and demon was hyperaware of the appetizing woman within his reach. Merle's heartbeat drew him like a beacon, the sweet scent of her blood as it coursed through her veins an intoxicating enticement…

"Rhun."

He hadn't been conscious of walking over to where she was sitting, of stopping behind her back and bending down to her throat, until her voice, quiet and uncertain, yanked him out of his trance. He now stilled with his nose in her hair. So soft, so fragrant, so *Merle*. "What?"

"You're sniffing at me." She held her back rigid and didn't move apart from breathing.

Like prey standing still in shock.

Dark urges clawed beneath his skin, fighting to rise to the surface. With deliberate slowness, lest he snap his own leash, he brushed his lips over the curve of her neck. "I'm hungry."

Underneath his lips, her pulse picked up speed at the same time as her scent changed. The faint aroma of fear pricked his senses, but stronger yet was another note, one that nearly stripped him of the last of his civility and had his cock harden impossibly further.

"I see you're looking forward to feeding me," he whispered in her ear, and then he let his teeth—fangs extending bit by bit —graze the delicate skin over her heartbeat. He wouldn't bite, not yet. Being considerate, he'd let her finish her own food first. But it was damn hard to restrain the raging desire to break skin and take what he craved.

She swallowed, her throat moving underneath his lips, the sweetest temptation. "I am not looking forward to that."

She turned her face to the side, toward him. The subtle contact of their cheeks made his power coil inside him, ready to strike, to claim, to slake all of his needs at once, with or without her consent. Her quiet poise saved her as much as himself at that moment. If she'd cringed and backed away from him, he would have given chase with vicious intent, unable to control his predatory instincts to hunt, seize, and never let go. Something that would have broken him as much her.

"Interesting," he said, a whisper against her skin, "your scent says different." Her arousal was a delicious aroma in the air, soothing the darkness inside him.

He watched with rapt fascination as a rosy color flushed her cheek.

"Maybe your sense of smell is confused," she retorted. "I may have used too much deodorant."

He laughed in her hair, despite himself, despite the dark hunger gnawing at his self-control, his sanity. Lighthearted amusement spread inside his chest, tamed the violent instincts in a way that astonished him. "No, my little Merle." He kissed the top of her head. "If there is one fragrance I'll always pick up, it's the scent of your arousal."

She stiffened. "I am not ar—"

"Shush." Trailing his fingers along her shoulders, he walked around her back to take a seat to her left. "Finish your breakfast."

He gave her a smoldering look designed to get under her skin, to sensually sneak into well-guarded places and take root. It didn't miss its mark. When she raised the spoon to her mouth again, her hand trembled ever so lightly. *Good.*

Reining in his demanding hunger as well as he could, he casually asked, "So, who's Blondie?"

It took her a good few seconds to understand what—whom —he was talking about. "Basil." Her voice held an edge of irritation. "His name is Basil."

"Right. Whatever. Who is he?"

She cocked her head and narrowed her eyes, studying him curiously. "Why is that important to you?"

"I asked you first."

"You're being childish."

"I'm merely trying," he said, enunciating each word carefully, "to have a nice, civil conversation with you, which you— for whatever unfathomable reason—are trying to sabotage."

She pointed at him with her spoon. "That is *so* not true, you devious, tricky—"

"See? Now you're calling me names and threatening me with silverware. All because I asked you a simple, unassuming question." He threw his hands in the air. "I rest my case."

For a moment, she looked as if she wanted to skewer him with the spoon, an inclination he found delightfully charming. She had some real fire underneath that prim and proper attitude she sported most of the time, and he wondered what it would take to infuriate her enough to grab a knife and lunge at him.

Now there was a thought... For a moment he was lost in the mental visualization of a sexy sparring session involving a naked witch with knives and ending in a tangle of limbs and moans of pleasure.

Merle's voice pulled him out of his reverie. "All right." Her shrewd eyes sparked with a glint of calculation. "I'll answer your question if you answer one of mine."

He inclined his head to her, impressed by her sense of strategy. "Fair enough."

She nodded and ate another spoonful of cereal. "Basil is Lily's twin brother."

He stopped short. "Lily's a witch."

Merle kept on eating.

Confusion made him grind his teeth together. "But Blondie's a guy."

"You are," she said around chewing, "so very perceptive."

Chuckling at her sarcasm, he processed the information. A male descendant of a witch line was just as unusual as a female born without powers—it appeared Maeve was not the only anomaly in the local witch community. But learning about Surfer Boy's family affiliations was not at the top of Rhun's list of priorities right now.

Tapping his fingers on the counter, he watched Merle with an intensity that threatened to erode him from the inside out. "You and Blondie seem to be close."

She ate another spoonful, regarding him with such coolness he wanted to bite her. "That is not a question. Now it's my turn."

He clamped down on the swirling darkness within him, a darkness unlike the one he already knew. "Ask away."

"What was the nature of your relationship to my grandmother?"

Cocking his head, he gave her a slow, wicked grin. "Why, my little witch, are you afraid you're related to me?"

She spluttered her mouthful of cereal across the kitchen island. Her face pale with shock, she stared at him. "Oh gods— please tell me I'm not—we're not—are we?"

She looked so horror-stricken and lost, he almost felt bad for the joke. *Almost.* "No." He handed her a napkin. "We're not. If we were, that would make me a sick bastard, and though I am a bastard—a sneaky one, as you pointed out—I do consider myself basically sane. Besides, my kind is only fertile when mated. I never was. And just so you won't wrack your delicate mind, your grandmother and I were never intimate. Not even close. She'd have strung me up by my balls if I'd ever even *tried* to make a move on her."

After staring at him for a moment, she exhaled, relaxing bit by bit. She cleaned up the cereal mess on the island then studied him again. "That doesn't answer my initial question."

He leaned back, weighing his words. "Rowan and I used to work together."

"What kind of work?"

"Our bargain was for one question. I answered it, and then some." He pinned her with a look that visibly made her twitch. "Do you want to bargain for more?"

Silence stretched taut between them. She held his gaze. "Okay. Ask."

"No. I'll answer your questions, as many as you like, but I want something else in return."

Her heart skipped a beat. It was loud enough for him to hear. "What?" she whispered.

"When I feed from you," he said, his voice soft despite his roaring hunger, "you'll lower your shields."

The air grew thick with her panic. "No."

Lowering her mental shields would mean absolute exposure. She'd be open to him on the most visceral level, completely vulnerable. He'd taste her power, her essence, see and feel her without any barriers, the ultimate insight into her heart, her soul. Used with malicious intent, this kind of connection could inflict pain beyond comprehension and leave a trail of destruction in the layers of the mind.

On the other end of that extreme, it would intensify any pleasure felt by a thousandfold—for both parties. Rhun was itching to get her like that, for it would not only be one hell of a thrilling experience, it would also temporarily entwine his essence with hers and make her more likely to give him what he wanted.

He caught her wary gaze and brushed her mind with a sensuous caress. "I won't hurt you." *Not unless you ask me to...*

Emotions flickered across her face, through her aura, among them a shy kind of curiosity, but she shook her head. Her suspicion won. "No," she repeated, and stood to carry her bowl to the sink.

"Okay," Rhun said after a moment, watching her closely as she rinsed the bowl.

Her rejection was a minor setback, but one he'd accept. Pushing her on this now would only prove counterproductive. He'd have to move on with care, going slow while gambling for time. The fact he hadn't been able to locate the other demon the night before was an unforeseen turn now playing into his hands, a real complication he could use for his own benefit.

Truth was, Rhun was in no hurry to find Maeve's captor—doing so would only get him kicked back into the Shadows, and he'd be damned if he willingly rushed toward that result. So instead of making up an elaborate lie to gain time enough to execute his plan, he could now stall the search with the truth. Ah, the ironic beauty of it.

An unbidden, inexplicable pang of guilt followed at the heels of those thoughts, and he had to suck in air at the sudden tightness in his chest. *No. Don't go there.* He couldn't allow himself to feel sympathetic. He couldn't deal with that, not now, not ever. Not if he wanted to be free again. *I am a demon, after all. Time I started acting like one.*

He stood and walked over to Merle, who still had her back turned to him, drying the bowl. Slowly, partly so as not to spook her, partly to control himself, he placed his hands on the counter on either side of her, trapping her with her back to his front, in an intimate cage of heat and hunger. She was so deliciously small he could wrap himself around her.

Wait—he'd already done that. He smiled at the memory.

Along with it came another memory—the feel of her silken skin, her soft curves pressed against him, her scent weaving a web of allurement with a devastating effect on his mental state. Not to mention his body.

His hands tightened on the counter, knuckles flashing white.

How she could make him so fucking needy was beyond him. And he *hated* being needy. Soon, he'd have her soon, and then he could flush her out of his system—by taking her any which way until they both were spent and sweaty. Yep, he couldn't wait to get her all sticky.

And surely, she only affected him like this because he'd been in the Shadows for so long, because he was now starved for pleasure. That had to be it. There couldn't be anything more to it.

But even as he repeated that like a mantra, as his power darkened with hunger and familiar lust, underneath it, something even more demanding awoke. Indefinable, new and confusing, it hummed under his skin—a strange kind of dark, disconcerting...*tenderness*?

He gritted his teeth.

It had started when he'd held her in his arms while she slept, when he'd felt her relax and curl into him with a trust that still rattled him. Then, it had been a fleeting feeling. Now, it threatened to spread, like mist rising, unstoppable, permeating everything in its path.

Muscles locked in a silent fight with himself, he focused on Merle's oscillating aura. Attuning his own power to hers, he bent down and brushed his lips over her cheek at the same time as he caressed her mind with a stroke of his energy. A non-threatening move, unobtrusive but effective. Her aura flickered, her breath caught.

"This time," Rhun murmured against the soft skin of her neck, "I won't have to take as much blood." He watched as a tiny trail of goose bumps followed the movements of his lips on her skin.

Merle nodded, silent, but her pulse thundered.

"I also need pain and pleasure." He kept his voice low and

caressing, and brushed his power against her mental senses again, a teasing, flirtatious touch. "We could restart the search faster..." A kiss on her hammering heartbeat. "...if you allow me take all three from you." He let his words hang in the air. And while his skin prickled with anticipation, he became hunting quiet.

"Not pain," Merle said, her voice trembling.

She shifted, and he moved back far enough so she could turn around and face him.

Head tilted up, she set her mouth in a firm line. "I won't give you that."

He raised his right hand to her throat, closed it in a gentle grasp while holding her gaze. "Pain," he said very quietly, his lips curving into a smile filled with sensual knowledge, "can be pleasurable if done right."

Her breathing went erratic. Her scent exploded into a myriad of intriguing nuances. One of them, he knew well—it was the one fragrance he'd always pick up. His smile widened.

Merle cleared her throat, the movement underneath his hand spurring him to caress her silken skin. "Not going to happen." Her voice trembled more than before, had taken on a husky note doing all sorts of sinful things to his already overactive sexual imagination. "You will have to take that from someone else."

Close, so close.

His thumb stroked over the side of her throat, and her aura flared with excitement. "Anyone specific you'd like me to hurt? A cheating ex-boyfriend of yours, maybe?"

She blinked, stared at him. The corners of her mouth twitched upwards.

"Why, Merle mine," he said, an unfamiliar joy bursting inside his chest, "is that a *smile*?"

She pressed her lips together, but her eyes sparkled with amusement—and he wanted to kiss her so badly right now, it hurt. When she took a deep breath, her breasts brushed against his chest, and it nearly did him in.

"Take it from someone who deserves it," she said. "No one innocent."

He clucked his tongue in reprimand. "I don't hurt innocents."

"Oh? But you like debauching them."

He chuckled, and it was as much a teasing as the stroke of his hand down from her throat to the neckline of her sweater. "Ah, but debauchery only hurts the frigid minds of religious prudes." His index finger traced the swell of her breast, found her nipple, and circled it. "Everyone else seems to enjoy it."

Her escalating heartbeat was music to his ears. He leaned down to nip at the curve of her neck and found her pressing herself oh-so-slightly against him. *Yes. More.*

"Now," he murmured, his fangs tingling with anticipation, "may I feed?"

She made a sound close to a whimper, then managed to steady herself. "If you want to chase me again, forget it, I'm not feeling up for a run."

"Oh, don't worry. I have something different in mind." Taking her hand, he tugged at it for her to come along.

The fact she didn't hesitate, didn't question him, simply followed his lead, it did something to him. He breathed past the tight knot in his chest and led her to the living room, stopped in front of the large couch.

She glanced at the couch, then at him. "I will not—"

"...sleep with me, I know. Fine. You don't have to. But this time, your clothes come off." When she started to protest, he cut her off. "I've been wanting," he said, lowering his voice to a timbre he knew would shake her aura, "to lick you inch for luscious inch, and that's what I'm going to do. I promise you'll be rewarded with the most intense sexual pleasure you've ever felt."

Her breathing hitched, a small sound so erotic, his whole body hardened in response.

"You are incredibly arrogant," she whispered, her cheeks flushed pink.

"No, my little Merle, I am simply well aware of my skills."

Something flashed in her eyes then, and her aura pulsed with anger—no, not anger, but a related emotion. "All right." Lips pursed, she regarded him with narrowed eyes. "Show me."

Ah, defiance. Rhun grinned as he recognized the emotion in her aura. His grin slipped, however, in a wave of astonishment when Merle pulled off her sweater without much further ado and threw it to the side. Heat rolled through him, blood boiling at the sensual sight of Merle in her bra, skin creamy perfection and beckoning to be kissed. Licked. Nipped at.

"Well?" Hands on her hips, she met his gaze with a challenge in her eyes—and an unapologetic flare of lust in her energy pattern. "Let's get started. I expect to be well-pleasured."

He blinked, stumped for a moment by the change in her attitude. Seemed like his little witch had shed all pretense of shyness, reluctance or modesty, and instead jumped right into enjoying feeding him. And damn if it wasn't like a shot of aphrodisiac straight into his veins, the way she unabashedly sought her pleasure.

He moved forward and nudged her onto the couch and was on top of her a second later. She gasped, her eyes wide, dark blue with desire, her heartbeat a thrumming wild rhythm. Leisurely, he claimed every bit of skin not covered by her bra with his hands, his lips, his tongue. Licked, caressed, tasted her. Just like he'd craved.

She was soft, silken, and she smelled so fucking good, it was all he could do not to rub himself all over her like a brainless dog. Well, he did rub a little, and buried his nose in the supple swell of her belly—he liked a woman with *curves*—which earned him a delighted moan from his favorite little witch volcano.

Sliding his hand underneath her back, he lifted her torso toward him, licked a line from her throat to the sweet valley between her breasts, and unhooked her bra. He pushed the straps down one by one, following the movements with playful strokes of his tongue, a little nip here and there.

Merle watched him with rapt attention, her eyes glazed with lust, her lips parted. She looked so deliciously kissable, he had to fight—fight fucking *hard*—not to claim her mouth and do with it what it was so clearly made for.

She must have picked up on his intention, because she cringed and said—in that husky voice that was so damn sexy it would make him go nuts—"Don't kiss me again."

He suppressed a disapproving growl, instead gave her a look laden with sensual promise. "Not on the mouth, no." He tore away her bra. "But on every other damn spot I deem kissable."

She might have tried to say something in response, but she never got the chance. He'd gone for her breasts before she could voice any thought.

He sucked her nipple into his mouth, circled it with his tongue, groaning at the taste of her, and reveled in Merle's answering moan. Closing his right hand over her neglected breast, he squeezed. It had the perfect size, a good handful, and it molded into his palm as if made for it. He found he liked the feel so much, he tore his mouth away from her other breast and then cupped it too, squeezed and rubbed and stroked, a demon in the mood to play. Underneath his hands, Merle melted into his touch, undulating, her skin heating. Her rising pleasure colored the air.

It was a thing of beauty.

Fine tendrils of her power curled and writhed, and her aura pulsed with deep streaks of desire, a display of feminine sexual rapture. He soaked up the waves of her pleasure, his own power meshing with hers, electrifying the air between them.

He opened her jeans then, pulled them off, and then covered every inch of her he laid bare with licks, kisses and nips, drowning in the taste and feel of her skin, her scent, her heat. He made sure to graze her with his fangs every so often, making her gasp. When he crawled back up her legs, she trembled with the force of her excitement, panting, her fingers dug into the cushion of the couch.

He traced the lines of her panties, brushed the fabric over her core, found it was soaking wet. Suppressing the urge to pounce on her, he pulled off her panties, his patience running thin.

He had to finish this soon, or else he'd lose control and be inside her. Take her. Hard, fast, feeling her clench tight around him in ecstasy while he spent himself in her heat. And then take her again, and again, until neither of them would be able to walk for a week. As his vision hazed over with desire, he had more and more trouble reminding himself that would not be a good move. *Not yet.*

His hands tightened around her hips as he fought the force of his desire. Merle's shocked gasp and the spike of fear in her aura brought him back a little. Reining in his consuming need, he spread her thighs and had just settled her legs on his arms when she gave a startled cry.

Rhun stopped and looked at her, heart skipping a beat. "What's wrong?"

"You—you're not going to do...*that*, are you?" Her eyes were wide, her face as red as he'd never seen it before, her aura trembling with embarrassment.

His gaze flicked to the triangle of ginger curls between her legs, to the tempting pink flesh underneath, glistening with her arousal. He looked back at her face. "Do what? Eat you up like a delicious dessert?"

She squealed and squirmed, delightfully bashful again.

He bit back a grin. "I want to taste you. And not just your blood." Brushing her mind with a wave of pure sexual intent, he ran his hands down the sensitive inside of her thighs, to her entrance, grazed it with his fingers.

She panted even faster.

He traced the curve of her swollen nether lips, slick with her desire. "I am going to lick you..." He pushed one finger inside her. "...until you scream with pleasure." Cock twitching at the erotic feel of her—hot, wet, tight—he stroked her, rotated his finger inside, found the spot that made her buck and push her hips toward his hand.

A strangled moan escaped Merle's throat. Her energy rippled with waves of lust.

"Give in," he murmured against her intimate flesh.

And she did. Closing her eyes, she relaxed and let her head fall back against the couch. She was all his.

It drove a thunderbolt through his entire system.

He tamped down the fire burning in his veins and made good on his promise. With sensual cruelty he teased her, swiping his tongue along her sensitive skin, licking and sucking just short of the most pleasurable spot, until she writhed and pressed herself against him. Her desire was a palpable force in the air, swirling, strong and demanding, and damn straight delectable.

"Rhun, please."

It was a murmur, the sound of his name on her lips so intimate, a caress he felt deep inside.

He intensified his strokes, and she groaned and pushed even harder toward him. Gripping her writhing hips, he steadied her. Her moan of protest turned to a cry of pure delight when he finally licked her clit. He sucked it in and flicked it with his tongue. Once. Twice.

Her aura exploded in a dazzling burst of pleasure.

"Gods, yes!" She dug her nails in the cushion. The fabric broke.

Still she writhed, bucked underneath him, and still he licked, relentlessly.

"*Rhun!*"

Another orgasm hit her hard and lit her energy up like a supernova. Pleasure, unbridled, raw and powerful, flowed from her and suffused the air, and Rhun drank it all in. She was supreme in her abandon. The taste of her, it drove him insane, fire and spice, the heat of summer.

She came again, and when she moaned, her voice broke from the strain of it. He released her but replaced his mouth with his fingers, stroking her down with erotic care, while he kissed his way to the inside of her thigh, where her blood rushed through the femoral artery.

And that was where he bit.

Merle was apparently past cries of pleasure by now, but as he sucked, hard and hungrily, her aura shattered into a thousand sparks of ecstasy.

The rich flavor of her blood filled his mouth, intoxicating, lush and heavy with passion. He continued stroking her while he drank, and the combined stimulation of his touch and the sexual high his feeding induced had her climaxing again.

It was a feast for his senses.

He soaked up her pleasure at the same time as he took her blood, drank it all in until his hunger for both was quenched. Licking over the puncture marks on her thigh, he sealed the wounds, and looked up at Merle. Her skin was bathed in sweat, her eyes closed, her breathing still shallow and fast.

"Merle?"

She uttered a sound somewhere between a wheeze and a moan, then sighed, so deeply, deeply satisfied, it made him preen with pure, masculine pride. Then her power curled inwards, receded as it did when she fell asleep.

He stopped short. She wasn't going to…?

Sagging into the cushions, she snored softly.

"You have got to be kidding me," he muttered.

There she lay, soft, soaked, spent and sweaty, satisfied into unconscious bliss, and he was still hard as granite, to the point of pain. And not the good kind of pain.

Gritting his teeth, he was about to get up from the couch so he could go jerk off and then take a cold, cold shower, as she reached for him. He froze and stared at her. She had her eyes closed, her power dimmed inside her, and from all he could tell she was half-asleep, but her hand had curled around his arm, drowsily tried to tug him closer. With sluggish movements, she wriggled toward him, half-consciously seeking his nearness.

He remained frozen for a few seconds, indecisive how to act. Then he swore a blue streak under his breath and lay down beside her. As soon as he pulled her into his arms, she relaxed into him and uttered a sound of unadulterated contentment.

He took a deep breath, inhaling her scent. She smelled like everything good, sweet and innately feminine, and she was soft in all the right places, a perfect match for the hard planes of his body.

He was still fighting the implications of how *right* she felt there in his arms, as it happened.

"Rhun," Merle whispered in her sleep, and it fucking broke him.

CHAPTER 8

The mattress underneath Merle was kind of bumpy. A bit hard, too. *Strange, that.* She couldn't remember falling asleep on the floor. Well, for that matter, she couldn't remember falling asleep at all. Still drowsy, her mind just reconfiguring into a conscious state, she wiggled her body trying to find a more comfortable position. *Damn lumpy pillow.* Her eyes still closed, she punched the cushion—which was way too hard to deserve that name—and...it grunted.

Her eyes fluttered open. An arm blocked her sight. More specifically, an upper arm with a well-defined biceps. Her mind geared up into full consciousness and she realized the impressively muscled arm was attached to an even more impressive male body—which she currently used as a mattress.

Oh, gods.

She whipped her head up and stared into a face of cutting beauty. Recognition sank in. *Rhun.*

He watched her with calm attention, his blue-green eyes regarding her with disconcerting intensity. His one hand loosely tangled in her hair, he'd laid the other one on the bare skin of her lower back, underneath the blanket covering them both. He'd put one foot down on the floor, resting his other leg half-bent against the back of the couch, and Merle sprawled on top of him with her legs between his. The heat of his body seared her even through his clothes, and his scent surrounded her, a tantalizing embrace of her senses. It kicked her heartbeat up a notch, and stirred all sorts of warm, fuzzy feelings inside her.

One side of his mouth tipped up. "Hey there, pretty witch."

"Hey," she managed to reply. Her gaze was glued to his lips, her mind flipping through a catalog of vivid suggestions of how to use her mouth and tongue on his.

"Two things," Rhun said, and she felt his deep voice rumble in his chest from where her head rested. "First, I don't mind you wiggling on top of me. In fact, feel free to do that as often and as much as you'd like." His sly smile made her curl her fingers into his T-shirt to keep from tracing his lips. "Second, if you try to punch me into pillow shape again, I'm going to drop your delectable butt on the floor."

"Well," she said, in the mood to tease, "it's not my fault you're all hard and lumpy."

He raised one eyebrow, and in that instant, she realized what she'd said. A wave of heat rolled up to her cheeks. With his hand on her lower back, he pressed her closer, and—even though covered by his jeans—there was no ignoring that prominent hardness nudging at her hips.

"I beg to differ, little witch of mine. That right here..." He made it *twitch*. "...is very much your fault."

Lightning shot through her body, her nerve endings flaring awake, one by one, until every part of her touching him felt on fire. Gods, being splayed on top of him like this, with his arms around her, his sizzling energy brushing over her skin like a dark whisper, his gaze intent on hers, it was sinfully pleasurable. And it made it tempting, so very tempting, to enjoy him even further, to explore that rigid length pressing into her hips...

He curled a lock of her hair around his finger, tugged a little, and watched it uncurl again as he let it go, smiling with delight. "Sleep well?"

It took her a moment to realize he'd asked her a question. That insidiously kissable mouth of his had monopolized her attention again. "Um, yeah."

"You know, I've decided to take it as a compliment to my overwhelming talent in the oral arts that you fell asleep snoring after I'd lavished my amazing skills on you."

With a flash of scorching heat, she remembered what he'd done to her—and how she'd reacted to it. By the Powers That Be, she'd never come so hard in her life, and never, ever, had she been *that loud*. She flinched. Holy hell, she'd not only moaned his name, she'd screamed it. Embarrassment and newly-sparked arousal vied inside her for the position of Most Overpowering Emotion. She ignored both and went with annoyance instead.

"I do *not* snore."

"Yes, you do. And adorably so, if I may say. It's like a soft purr turning into an endearing wheeze when someone holds your nose."

She gaped at him. "You didn't!"

Rhun grinned. "To salvage your dignity, you do not drool."

She swatted his chest. "Of course I don't!"

His eyes held a warm glint as he said, "But you curl your toes when I do this." He slid his hand to the back of her head and massaged her scalp.

She couldn't stifle a groan of pure delight at the sensation. Her head flopped down face-first on his chest, her body went limp with relaxation—and her damn toes curled.

"Sneaky bastard," she muttered into his T-shirt.

"Feisty little witch."

Fingers like that should be illegal.

"Oh, I don't know." Rhun still massaged her. "I'm thinking of having them patented. Could make a fortune with that. *Rhun's Magic Fingers.*" He chuckled.

Oh gods, she'd actually voiced that thought. Where was her mind? *Well, let me see—turning to mush under a sinfully skilled demon hand?*

"Did you know," he said after a moment, "that there is a pixie colony living in your attic?"

"There is? Never noticed." Her face remained plastered to his chest, and she inhaled a good nose-full of his male scent, trying not to purr. "How d'you know?"

"I can smell them. Want me to take care of them? They can be a bunch of pesky critters."

She considered it for a moment. The tiny fairy creatures were generally benign, but known for having unpredictable bouts of mischief, and while they sometimes helped with small tasks if they felt like it, they could also wreak havoc if they were crossed. "Um, I'm not—"

A racket loud enough to wake the dead shook the house.

She jerked and lifted her head, glancing around. "What is that?"

Rhun cocked his head to the side and listened to the thumps and screeches. "That would be the sound of a pixie colony high-tailing it out of here." He glanced back at her and shrugged. "I guess they didn't like the idea of me taking care of them."

She shot him a dark look. "What did you do to them?"

He gasped, his expression the epitome of genuine indigna-tion. "I didn't do a damn thing. Those pixies have acute ears, you know. And if they decide to cheese it out of here just because I *suggested* I'd kick them out, that's their problem."

"Uh-huh," she said with a disbelieving snort, but she couldn't keep the grin off her face.

He smirked back at her, his hand on her lower back stroking her spine, and she felt the brush of his power over her mental senses, a dark, seductive force and yet—strangely reassuring. She studied his face, those clear-cut features that could turn disarmingly gorgeous when he laughed, the dark brows over eyes so piercing and bright, they seemed to take in everything with a single look. His smirk grew into a full, open smile warming his gaze as he regarded her, and her heart made a cute little somersault.

She froze.

No. This was not happening.

She could find him attractive and mouthwatering and even allow herself to enjoy feeding him. But. She. Would. Not. *Like.* Him.

He was cocky, pushy, sarcastic to the point of being rude, and a general pain in her ass. *There.* Those were some unlikable characteristics. If only his sarcasm wasn't so funny and his cockiness didn't have a strange appeal in its own right... Even though—or maybe because?—he annoyed her enough to become homicidal, he had a way of taking her mind off her sorrows, and he kept her on her toes with his charmingly disrespectful behavior—she could never guess what he might do or say next. He knew exactly how to push her buttons, and he pushed them all, the good and the bad.

No, no, no!

She brought her derailed train of thoughts back on track. He was a demon with violent instincts and a dark past, and he'd turn on her first chance he'd get. The bond leashing him to her had changed yet again, another faint shift of power between them, and it wasn't hard to conclude it was directly linked to what Rhun had done to her...with her. Whatever she was starting to feel for him would put her at risk not just emotionally.

So she had to refocus on why she'd unbound him, had to remind herself that he was an instrument to achieve her goal. She needed his assistance in finding Maeve, that was all, and she'd bind him again in the Shadows afterwards. She couldn't afford to feel any sympathy or...affection toward him. The shift in the leashing bond notwithstanding, she quite simply didn't want to *like* someone whom she needed to send back into painful darkness...

He'd studied her face after she'd tensed in his arms, and now cupped her cheek, his thumb stroking her skin. "What's wrong?"

Dammit, why did he have to be so caring now? Where was his biting sarcasm when she needed it?

"Nothing," she snapped with deliberate sharpness, bringing her unruly emotions back under control. Scrambling off him, she added, "I just think that now that you're all fed and happy, you need to get a move on and search for that bastard who took my sister."

He watched her get dressed with eyes that were too discerning. "I still need pain."

She finished pulling on her sweater, tugged it into place. "Fine. We'll go…find someone. I'm not letting you go hunting on your own. I have to pick up my tools and the grimoire from the cemetery anyway. After that, we restart the search, you locate the other…" She stopped short as she glanced at him and saw his expression.

With focused attention, he stared at a spot somewhere behind her. Holding up a finger to indicate her to wait a moment, he rose from the couch, his eyes still fixed on that something behind her shoulder. Turning, she watched him walk over to the bookshelf on the wall next to the door, where he rearranged the order of three books—the *Lord of the Rings* trilogy.

With a sigh of utter relief after he was done, he faced her. "Sorry, what were you saying?"

"What was that about?" She gestured at the books.

He glanced at the shelf and back at her, and shrugged. "They were not in the correct order. *The Fellowship of the Ring* was in the middle, *The Two Towers* to the right and *The Return of the King* to the left."

"So you just *had* to rearrange them."

He grimaced. "It was so painful to look at."

"Somehow," she muttered under her breath, "that is even

more disturbing than the fact that you're a demon." She waved at the trilogy. "If you got hung up on that, you definitely shouldn't look at my *Harry Potter* shelf."

"Harry who?"

"Ah, never mind." She shook her head and walked away in search of her cell phone.

She found it in her small purse on a side table where she'd dumped it after they'd come back from Maeve's apartment. Flipping it open, she skimmed the list of missed calls. As she'd expected, Lily and Basil had called half a dozen times, mostly before they'd shown up this afternoon, but Lily had apparently called again three times after they'd left. A text message informed her she also had a new voice mail. Frowning, she dialed and listened to the message.

"Merle, dammit, turn your fucking phone on loud!" Lily sounded not as royally pissed as her wording suggested. In fact, her voice shook with—fear? "What do you have a fucking cell phone for if you keep it on mute the whole time? Shit." A small pause. Lily softly inhaled. "Listen, you need to get out of the house and disappear ASAP. Isabel—she knows."

A tremor ran through her.

"I'm sorry," Lily went on. "I didn't mean to, I tried to avoid her and keep my mouth shut, but she knew we'd checked on you and she wanted to know if you were all right, and she fucking knew right away we were hiding something. She's got that creepy spidey sense for sniffing out secrets and…you know how she is. If she grills someone for info, she gets it."

Lily sounded so miserable Merle had the intense urge to hug her through the phone. Yes, she knew Isabel, and that's why she couldn't even blame Lily for breaking in front of her aunt. The head of the Murray family and member of the Elders was a strong, loving woman, a powerful witch—and she was intimidating at the best of times. Merle's grip tightened on the phone.

"She's informed the other Elders, Merle. They're on their way. You need to get out *now* and find some place to lie low for a while. I'll call you later to check on you. Please be careful." A pause, heavy with concern. "I'm so sorry."

The message ended and she stared at the display. The voice mail had been recorded half an hour ago. For a moment, she stood in numb paralysis, until the knowledge sank in.

The shit had just hit the fan.

Cursing, she ran, her heart pounding against her ribs. "Rhun!"

She skidded to a stop in front of him in the living room, the hardwood floor squeaking underneath her feet.

Rhun was rearranging her CDs in some OCD-compliant order and shot her a sideways glance, as relaxed as a Zen master. "What's up, little witch? You look agitated."

"We need to leave. *Now.* The Elders know about you and are on their way over here. If they catch us…"

"…we're in deep shit." His attention now fully focused on her, his eyes alert, even though he seemed a gazillion times calmer than she felt right now.

"Yep." She grabbed a hold of his T-shirt, dragging him toward the foyer. "Up shit creek without a paddle. Now, let's go!"

As Rhun picked up his leather jacket from where he'd neatly hung it on the coat rack earlier, she wiggled into her shoes and snatched her purse and coat. Her mind already raced ahead, analyzing her situation—a clear case of FUBAR—and sorting options of how to best proceed. She was about to open to the door, when Rhun's voice broke through her thoughts.

"Merle," he said quietly, but his tone held such sharpness, it made her pause. Shrugging into the leather jacket, he jerked his head at the door. "We've got company."

She stilled and listened. Sure enough, now she heard it, too. Footsteps, coming up the stairs to the veranda. A moment of utter silence as the footsteps stopped, along with her breathing, and she knew, knew without a doubt, who was on the other side of that door.

The bell rang, and everything in her jumped back to life, including her hammering heart. She grabbed Rhun's hand, indicated him to stay silent—which earned her a duh-look from him —and led him to the back of the house as fast as was quietly possible. The kitchen had a door onto the porch, and from there they could sneak into the backyard, make their way toward the rear of the property, and escape over the fence. Her neighbors surely wouldn't mind them crossing their yards in the dark.

They were a few feet from the back door when the air shook as if the pressure wave of a bomb hit. She gasped, tripped, and Rhun tightened his hold on her hand to steady her. The lights flickered.

He glanced around the room. "What the fuck was that?"

"The wards," she whispered. "The Elders are breaking them down."

If she'd had any illusions that the Elders might be lenient with her for unleashing Rhun, she was now sobered. They were here to enforce the laws of the witch community, which she'd violated by unbinding a demon from the Shadows without their approval, and they meant to punish her for it. Eminently powerful as the wards were, they not only kept out evil spirits, they were also designed to block the entry of anyone who meant harm to the residents of the MacKenna house. The fact that the Elders had to disable the wards first before being able to enter spoke of the nature of the intended punishment...

Straightening her spine, she moved forward. She didn't fear what they would do to her. Gods knew, she'd probably suffered worse in the past by keeping the balance. No, that wasn't what made her knees tremble and her hands fist, her fingers digging painfully into her palms. It was the sure knowledge they would force her to send Rhun back into the Shadows right away— force her to give up her only chance of finding Maeve.

Another tremor hit the air, and she could feel the magic oscillating, the wards shaking. *Failing.*

Her hand was on the doorknob. She neither had the time nor

the energy to keep reinforcing the wards, so they had to sneak out now before—

"Merle."

She froze at the voice coming from the other side of the door. It was Juneau, head of the Laroche family line and most powerful member of the Elders. Merle remembered how she'd used to sit on her lap as a little girl, awed into silence by the intimidating force of the older witch's energy, while Rowan and Juneau talked over coffee.

She also remembered, all too well, how the Elder's eyes had held both compassion and unshakable resolve when she turned down Merle's appeal for help in finding Maeve. Her words rang in her mind, had dug deeply into her heart.

"I'm sorry, child," Juneau said. *"We cannot risk unleashing a convicted killer, not even to find one of our own."*

"And you don't even know for sure that she was abducted by a demon," Elder witch Isabel Murray cut in, *regarding her with sympathetic sorrow.*

"But I do. I saw it."

"In a vision." Isabel pressed her lips together, heaved a breath. *"You don't have concrete proof. For all we know, Maeve could have just run away."*

"Why would she—"

"She did move out of your house," Juneau said thoughtfully. *"Left her family's home…"* She shook her head, obviously saddened by an action that was the equivalent of a slap in the face for a witch family.

Merle swallowed, her heart pierced. No matter how dead set Maeve had been on moving out and having her own place to live, she would never have run away. And Merle knew what she'd seen. It might not be enough for the Elders, but it was for her. She turned to leave.

She had a demon to unbind.

"Merle. I know you're there."

Juneau's voice called her back to the present, and she let go of the brass doorknob as if it was on fire.

"Lower the wards, girl, and let us in freely, and we will hold it in your favor when we assess your case. Do not make this worse than it already is." Juneau spoke calmly, almost friendly, but there was no discounting the force of her power suffusing the air, even through the wards and the sturdy walls of the old Victorian.

She stepped back from the door and glanced at Rhun. He watched her attentively, his harsh expression enhancing the lethal allure of his features. His aura was palpable, almost visible around him, humming, sizzling waves of energy with enough menace to shake her bone-deep. His gaze flicked to the door and back to her, his eyes holding an unspoken question. She shook her head. She wouldn't fight fellow witches, least of all her Elders. She had to face the consequences of her actions, atone for her deeds. There was no way around it.

Her chest tight as if bound with a rope, she closed her eyes and took a deep breath. The scent of herbs, spices, magic, filled her nose, so familiar, so reassuring and heartbreaking at once. Even though the memory of her grandmother and what she'd have to say to all this was a piercing pain deep inside her, it made her stand up straight with defiant pride. She was willing to take whatever punishment awaited her, with her head held high.

But now was not the time.

Turning to Rhun, she took his hand and pinned him with a warning look. "Hold on. Whatever happens, whatever you feel, do *not* let go."

He frowned. "What are you—"

"Shut up."

Something dark flashed in his eyes, even as the corners of his mouth twitched up. "Yes, ma'am."

She blew out a breath. "Let's hope this works."

At those words, Rhun shot her a look that could have been interpreted as panicked, but she ignored it and closed her eyes. There was no point in purifying the space or casting the circle with a demon by her side, so she simply sent a fervent prayer to the Powers That Be to grant her protection for what she was about to do.

"*Mahyam devadattayā mantraśaktyā...*" she murmured in Sanskrit—the ancient language sacred to the gods—speaking the words that would bend the laws of nature, tapping deep into the magic filling the layers of the world while unleashing the energy coiling inside her, fusing power with power. It curled around her, thickening, humming over her skin.

The air shook again, more violently this time. The last of the wards were crumbling.

She didn't stop casting the spell even as the magic that had protected the MacKenna house for generations slowly but surely died, taking a piece of her with it.

"*...dharmebhyaḥ ātmanaḥ vaśāya me nantum saṃdiśāmi...*"

Gripping Rhun's hand tighter, she drew on all her power. She was close, so close.

"*...atraḥ tatra, lokakālaṃ vitarāmi, anyatra vrajāmi...*"

The air pulsed with the vibrancy of the magic she wove. Just one more intricate threading...

The last ward broke.

The door opened.

CHAPTER 9

J uneau Laroche's spell hit Rhun square in the chest just as the magic Merle was weaving fused around them. The air shimmered, charged with power that seeped into his bones and changed the fabric of his being. For the span of a heartbeat lasting an eternity, every fiber in his body, down to the faintest pulse of his energy, merged with the age-old magic this world breathed. If not for the death grip Merle had on his hand, he would have dissolved into the power holding together the layers of time, space, and beyond.

But she never let him go.

When everything around him shifted and the world itself split into a thousand shards of untapped possibilities, Merle's hand pulled him through, rooted him. The air fused back together, and all around him, the dizzying kaleidoscope of colors, sounds and scents dimmed as one reality took over and solidified.

He only had a brief moment to blink at their new surroundings— a quiet street swathed in half-darkness, well-kept old houses all around, a small patch of sidewalk lined by trees— before the magic settled and the pieces of the here and now fell into place. The next second, a searing bolt of pain shot from his chest to every nerve ending in his body. He convulsed, doubled over and dropped to his knees, gasping for breath.

"Rhun!" Merle's voice, close by.

He couldn't see her, his vision darkened by the excruciating, debilitating pain spreading like wildfire. Whatever Juneau had attacked him with, it had turned the blood to acid in his veins. The magic burned him from the inside out. Every heartbeat unleashed a new wave of biting pain.

Merle's hand on his forehead, so cool against the fire underneath his skin. "Talk to me. What does it feel like? I need to know so I can recognize and break the spell."

Somewhere, somehow, through the anguish scorching him alive inside, her words registered. He tried to speak, failed. His muscles wouldn't obey. More convulsions. White-hot pain, liquid fire, searing his core.

Two hands cradled his head. "Rhun. *Speak.*"

One single word came past his parched lips. "Burns." His voice sounded as corroded as his insides felt.

A moment of silence. "Your blood? It's on fire?"

He managed to nod, barely. The motion shot more arrows of pain up and down his body.

"All right. Hold on."

Her hands left his head, and he panicked. Where was she? Straining, he tried to sense her, but his vision was still full of fire and darkness, and all he felt was heat, heat, heat. Then, her voice, drifting through flames and the roaring in his ears, and he exhaled on a shudder of relief. She was speaking in a low murmur, undoubtedly reciting a counter-spell.

The acrid smell of seared hair hit his nose, and the burning in his veins ebbed immediately. His body tingled with the aftermath of the devastating sensation, a strange feeling of peace following the pain. The night air was pleasantly cool on his still heated skin. Slowly, the darkness clouding his vision receded as well, the world shifted back into focus—and centered on a face of pale beauty, framed by ginger hair. Eyes the color of the clearest summer skies held him spellbound.

A fine tendril of smoke rose up from the ground to his right, curled in the air and caught his attention. Glancing at it, he frowned at what appeared to be a burning lock of hair—Merle's hair, judging by the color of the unburned end. *Huh.* So she'd pulled the spell out of his body and had transferred its effect to another target. Smart, that she'd cut a piece of her hair and used that for it, as it held enough residue of Merle's life energy to pass as an animate target and thus fool the spell.

He looked back at her, pride and relief mingling with something else he had no name for.

"Rhun? Can you move?"

He could. He just didn't want to. Her hands cupped his cheeks and she leaned over him, her breasts all but touching his chest, and the expression on her face... Oh, he could bask in that nurturing attention all night.

"Are you okay?" A slight crease appeared between her brows as she drew them together, regarded him with such worry, it pulled at something deep inside him.

"No," he rasped, his voice still raw from the torment of the spell. "I...need..." He sighed, briefly closed his eyes for dramatic effect.

"What?" Merle's voice had dropped to a whisper, too, as she leaned in a bit closer, probably to hear him better.

Her delectable scent filled his nose, and he barely held back an appreciative groan.

Her face tense with concern, she studied him. "What do you need?"

"This," he said, and brought his hand up to the back of her neck to pull her down for a kiss.

His move was apparently so unexpected that she didn't even resist him at first. He drew her down gently until their lips met in the slightest of touches, the soft caress he'd needed to steal. Ah, the feel of her. It soothed an ache he hadn't been aware he'd had.

After a second of astonishment, though, she obviously realized what they were doing, and tried—not very hard—to pull away. He moved his hand from her neck to the back of her head and started a gentle massage. Her aura quivered with rapture and she moaned into his mouth, her body melting against his.

He unabashedly took advantage of her parted lips, slipped his tongue inside and kissed her as she was meant to be kissed. She responded with the fiery passion he'd come to know and relish. In between hot licks and playful nibbling, she kept murmuring something that might have involved variations of "damn," "sneaky" and "demon," though it was hard to tell. The way she dug her fingers into his hair, her aura trembling with excitement, and her body rubbing over his in sensual moves, well, it did impair his attention to other details.

His blood boiled again, though now for a different reason, and far more pleasantly so. Hell, she could set him on fire any time she wanted, and he'd burn to cinders with a smile on his face.

When she broke the kiss with a strangled moan, her breath heavy and fast, her cheeks flushed rosy and her hair tousled by his hands, he had to fight the impulse to flip her over and pin her underneath him to finish what they'd started.

"We—need to—leave." Her voice had that sinfully husky note again. His fangs descended and his cock jumped in response.

Unerringly, his gaze homed in on the rapid beat of the pulse on her neck. Even though he'd recently slaked both hungers, he craved blood and pleasure—*Merle's* blood and pleasure—with a force that would have knocked him flat if he hadn't been lying down already. Judging by her state of arousal, he could probably make her come just by biting her. And *that* thought alone almost sent *him* over.

She'd obviously picked up on his idea, because her aura

shimmered with the flamboyancy of heightened desire. "No," she said in flagrant disregard of her body's response. "Not here."

He was about to suggest finding some dark corner then, when she pushed herself off him and straightened her hair.

"We need to get moving," she said, turning away from him to glance around the quiet neighborhood. Abruptly, she rounded on him, eyes narrowed, scowl in place. "And besides, you already fed from me, no need to repeat that." Her aura dimmed as if forcibly brought under control to show the least amount of emotions.

Well, well, well. His little witch turned cold on him again, just like before at the Victorian, after they'd shared a moment of relaxed intimacy. One he'd enjoyed maybe a little too much for his own liking, but that was a notion he didn't want to dwell on. Neither was he going to ponder how good it had felt when she'd snuggled in his arms. Because, just like before, her icy shutdown brought his focus back to where it was supposed to be—on executing his plan.

She was a means to an end, nothing more, and if he enjoyed her company until he achieved his goal, fine, more fun for him. But no matter what, he would *not* let her get under his skin. As soon as she didn't need his help anymore, she'd get rid of him without thinking twice, that was for sure. Returning the sentiment was the smart choice here. He'd be foolish to allow anything else. Against better judgment, he'd let her shake him up too much, and now it was high time he got his equilibrium back.

Which was easier said than done when simply looking at her made him feel like a bunch of pixies had a damn bouncing party in his chest. He gritted his teeth.

Tricky little witch.

Rising to his feet, he casually adjusted his erection, and glanced at their surroundings. "Where are we anyway, and what kind of hellacious spell did you just pull to get us out?"

She rubbed her forehead. "It's a transportation spell, delicate stuff that can easily go wrong. It only works over short distances and for destinations you know well. This—" She waved at the neighborhood. "—is just about two blocks down from my house, which is as far as I could go."

He followed her gaze to the old mansions half-shrouded in darkness. Some were Victorians like the MacKenna residence, some had been built during later periods. Here and there lights shone through the windows, and somewhere in the distance, a door shut loudly. He looked back at Merle and only now noticed the residual flicker of potent magic around her.

"Quite a powerful spell." He didn't even have to act to sound impressed. He truly was, down to his bones. He studied her with newly instilled respect, as another thing occurred to him. "You cast the spell without your grimoire—you know it by heart?" Scratch impressed, he was officially amazed.

"Well," she said with a shrug. "Lily and I used to have this competition going on about who could memorize the most complicated and risky spells, and I came across this one. I thought it'd be cool if I could jump it on her someday, but I never got around to doing it in the end." The wicked glint in her eyes was insidiously adorable. "I've wanted to try this for ages."

Warmth spread through him, centering in his chest. Before he knew it, he smiled at her with an honesty that should have alarmed all his darker instincts. "That was an incredible piece of magic you used there. Well done."

For a second, her eyes lit up with delight at his compliment. His stomach did a strange flip at the sight, but before he could dwell on that, a shadow fell over her face and the moment was gone. "Yeah, well, it comes at a price." Looking away, she pressed her lips together and then took a deep breath. "We really have to get going now."

He frowned when she pulled out a small electronic device— was that supposed to be a *phone*?—and started dialing.

"What are you doing?"

She paused and slanted a look at him. "Calling Lily. We need a ride since we had to leave my car behind, in case you didn't notice."

He snatched the miniature phone away from her.

"Hey! What the fu—"

"Stop and think, witch volcano."

"*Excuse* me?"

"You're really going to call the niece of one of the Elders? You know, the people *who are out to kick your ass*? You want to give her your location and then have her drive you around town in a car familiar to the Elders? Do you honestly think that's a good idea?"

She stared at him for a moment, her aura tightening with anger. "Fine," she grudgingly conceded, "you're right. What do you suggest then, Mr. Know-It-All? Hailing a cab?"

He tilted his head and regarded her with his smuggest smile. "Why would we do *that* when we have cars galore to choose from?" He waved in a general circle around them, and proceeded to walk up a driveway lined with conifers precisely cut into twisting rings. A posh black Mercedes was parked in front of the mansion at the end of the driveway. He pursed his lips and studied the sleek beauty. *Well, hello there.*

Merle's gasp followed him in the quiet night air. "Rhun, no!" Her voice was all hushed urgency. "You can't just steal some-one's car!"

"I'm not stealing, I'm *borrowing*."

"It's still not right. What if there's an emergency and they need their car?"

He stopped at the driver's side door. "See that impressive house there? It's dark, no one's home. Now look at this drive-way, do you see those tire tracks in the gravel next to this stun-ning example of German automobile craftsmanship? This pretty thing right here…" He patted the smooth roof. "…is just the spare car of whatever ridiculously rich family lives here.

They're probably out enjoying an avant-garde interpretation of a Shakespeare play with lots of naked actors bathed in ketchup running around an empty stage, and when they get home and find their Mercedes gone, they can still cry in their Maybach."

For all of five seconds, Merle stared at him in dumbstruck astonishment. Then, to his utter shock, she burst out laughing. Not a giggle, not a chuckle, but honest-to-the-gods heartfelt laughter. It lit up her face, let her eyes warm with amusement—and damn straight stole his heart. He could only stand and stare as the traitorous organ jumped in delight like some puppy and then fell to Merle's feet.

"You're terrible," she said, when she eventually recovered from her laughing fit. She obviously tried to sport a serious expression, with little success. Her eyes still sparkled with humor and her lips kept on twitching.

"And proud of it," he said dryly, swallowing past the tight lump in his throat.

He wouldn't stop to consider what just happened. He couldn't. With a short mental command, he unlocked the Mercedes' door and gestured for her to get in.

"Forget it, I'm not driving around in a stolen car!"

"Perfect, since you won't be driving." He opened the door and was about to slide in, when he noticed Merle's murderous glare. "What? I've seen you behind the wheel—you're a hazard to public safety. Now get in."

He slid into the driver's seat, closed the door and inhaled the rich scent of the leather interior. *Bliss.* Brushing his hands lovingly over the elegant curves of the dashboard and the console, he sighed. Car design surely had come a long way in the last twenty years.

The door on the passenger's side flew open and Merle got in, looking daggers at him. "You're a chauvinist jerk." She yanked the door closed, probably hoping for a loud bang. When the door shut with a smooth whisper, she uttered an adorable sound of frustration.

He *tsk*ed. "Now, now, I did not say that you being a bad driver has anything to do with the fact you're a woman." He started the car with another mental command, delighted at the soft purr of the engine, and swiftly backed out of the driveway. Shooting a sideways glance at her, he added with a grin, "Though I do believe it has everything to do with you being a witch."

Merle huffed. "That's still sexist."

"Oh? How so?"

"Because all witches are women, as you know full well."

"Ah," he said, nodding, "now that is sexist." She beamed in obvious triumph, when he went on, "I mean, why aren't there any male witches? Talk about gender discrimination…"

For a moment, Merle was silent, as if considering. "Well, our lore says it's part of the balance. You know, the whole endowing the 'weaker' sex with magical powers as a measure of compensation thing."

He scoffed. "So says the oh-so-impartial witch lore."

A moment's pause, then she said, "I don't think it's true."

He glanced at her, surprised.

"If it really was for compensation's sake," she said quietly, turning to the side window, "then *all* women would have magical means to defend themselves."

He didn't have to ask to know she was thinking of her sister. Her grief, spiked with bitter anger, was palpable, suffused the air, and every breath he took of it was like a sucker-punch to his guts. They drove in heavy silence for a while, Merle drenched in her sorrow, until she suddenly stirred.

"We need to go by Lone Fir Cemetery, so I can grab my supplies. Turn right at the next intersection and then—"

"I know the way." At her raised eyebrows, he said, "For your information, I used to live here, too, little witch." He focused back on the traffic. "As a matter of fact, I was born and raised and have spent most of my life in Portland."

"Really?"

He nodded. "I went abroad for a few decades when I was younger, and I've toured the rest of the country, but I came back some sixty years ago."

Merle shifted in the seat to regard him with open curiosity. "Why did you come back?"

He turned right after the red light, the shadows of the city slipping by. "I've never felt at home anywhere else."

She made a soft sound as if half-laughing, half-exhaling. It held a bitter note. "I've never even *been* anywhere else. Never had the chance to."

"Would you leave if you could?"

She was silent for a long while, so long as to have maybe left the conversation. He knew better, though, and never broke into her thoughts.

"Not for good." She tucked a strand of ginger hair behind her ear. "I guess I'd come back here, too, eventually. Too much of my heart in this city, too many living memories. Leaving that behind would be..." She paused, apparently searching for the right words.

"...like losing a friend."

She glanced at him, tilted her head, and smiled. "Yes."

"Yes," he echoed quietly, gazing at streets that were as much a part of him as his heartbeat, no matter how much might have changed in twenty years.

After he'd parked the car on SE 26th Ave, they walked the short distance to the main gate of the cemetery, which was—unsurprisingly—locked at this late hour. The night was wrapped tightly around them, and neither cars nor pedestrians were in sight, still Merle threw nervous glances around before she ventured along the chain-link fence.

"We have to climb over." Her voice was hushed despite their obvious isolation from anything remotely alive. "They used to have an open path into the cemetery over on Morrison, but they closed it a while back to keep out bums and junkies. But there's a lower section of the fence over here, where some of the barbed wire is missing…"

"Pfft." He turned to the gate. "*Climb over*," he muttered. "What am I, a squirrel?" He opened the lock with another simple mental command.

At the soft creaking sound of the gate swinging open, Merle stopped short and whirled around. "How did you do that?" She followed him through to the other side and shut the gate behind her, looking at him with narrowed eyes.

"Same way I opened and started our sweet ride." He tapped his temple with a finger. "Missed that in your anger, didn't you?"

"You're telekinetic?"

"A little. It's limited in reach and force, but it does come in handy in certain situations." He peered at her. "And it can be used so creatively…"

With a single thought, he gently pinched her nipples. Merle uttered a lovely squeal and stumbled.

"Watch your step, little witch of mine," he crooned and walked on. Or rather, *would* have walked, if his legs hadn't given out from under him as if pulled by an invisible string. With a thud, he landed on his knees, his hands barely keeping his face from making intimate acquaintance with the ground.

"Yeah." Merle strolled past him, residual magic flickering in her wake. "The asphalt seems awfully slippery tonight."

Grinning despite himself, he got up, brushed the dirt off and followed the sweet bane of his existence down the path into the heart of the cemetery.

Magic charged the air all around him. Visible fields of energy, shimmering like a desert mirage, shrouding certain spots more than others. The graves of witches. Even in death, they drew power and kept their magic close, retaining a hold on some lingering spells. Which was probably why Merle had needed to come here, to Rowan's final resting place, to unbind him from the Shadows.

They reached the MacKenna family mausoleum, a haunting neo-Gothic beauty looming above all other tombs. Stained glass windows adorned the weathered sandstone façade, pointing upward in cusped arches. The gargoyle stone figures standing watch at the corners of the roof had lost some of their menace in more than a century of Oregon rain, but still the building remained an impressive testament to the erstwhile power the MacKenna family had held.

Merle opened the gate in the cast-iron fence surrounding the mausoleum and unlocked the heavy metal door to the crypt. Gingerly, he followed her inside.

The resounding hum of the departed witches' trace energy enveloped his senses. The bite of hostility underneath the power pricked at his skin, as if the late witches knew of the demon who had set foot in their final resting place—again. *Funny, to be back here once more, with Merle.*

When he'd left the mausoleum the other night—it seemed like so much longer ago—he'd been in a hurry, driven by instinct and hunger, and in dire need to get his thoughts in order. Now, though, as he swept the dark chamber with his gaze, he took his time absorbing the details. While Merle collected her supplies that were still strewn across the stone floor, he studied the coffin slabs shelved into the walls.

The long line of MacKenna witches and their husbands, names that rang out to him here and there. He'd known some of them at some point, fleetingly, as one should be aware of potential enemies. One name, though, stood out among them all, as had its bearer when she'd been alive.

He raised his hand and traced the letters of Rowan's name and life dates with his fingers. Something tugged deep inside him, a long-buried hurt unfurling, whispering through him. She'd died six years ago, fourteen years after she'd banished him into the Shadows. Time. It was a distant concept in the darkness.

"You cared for her, didn't you?"

He blinked at Merle's soft question, and dropped his hand, turning to face her. She'd bagged her tools and now watched him, her eyes alight with quiet curiosity, as well as something else he couldn't quite name.

"You didn't just work with her, right? Who was she to you —really?"

"My best mistake."

She frowned, tilted her head, and stepped closer. The light spilling in from the door cast the lines of her face in stark relief. "Why that?"

"Did she tell you how we met?"

Merle shook her head.

He scoffed. "Figures. I imagine she'd rather have bitten off her own tongue than to admit she owed her life to a demon."

She gasped. "You saved her life?"

Shrugging, he turned away, averting his gaze from Merle's probing eyes. "She was younger than you are now, barely out of her teens, and she'd overestimated her own power. Thought she could take on two demons. I dragged her out from under them, made sure she got out safe. Like I said, my best mistake." He looked back at what remained of the vibrant witch he'd once known—stone, bones, and irredeemable silence. "Must be a special kind of irony of Fate that I saved the life of the very witch who would one day bind me in the Shadows, don't you think?"

Merle didn't answer. He glanced at her, curious despite himself to see her reaction. She regarded him quietly, her face inscrutable, her aura so controlled he wanted to strip her of her mental defenses to peer inside her, see what she was feeling.

When she spoke, it was a whisper. "Did you love her?"

He blinked, taken aback. *Love?* He'd liked Rowan, had been drawn to her exuberance, but love… "No." For whatever reason he felt the visceral need to explain this, he just did. "I cared about her, as a friend. I was never interested in pursuing her for more. We worked together, and I considered her someone to trust. As you can see, she didn't quite return the sentiment."

"What happened? Why did she bind you in the Shadows?"

Bloodstained walls, the tang of copper drenching the air, hunger eating him alive. The limbs on the floor, too many to count. He never even registered the screams, not until they died away, replaced by sounds of tearing flesh and the gush of blood. So much blood.

"Rhun?"

He yanked himself back to the present, away from a room breathing death. Giving her a sardonic smile, he said blithely, "I had one too many drinks."

The lighthearted tone in which he'd said it masked the dark truth behind his words, if only for a few seconds—then Merle apparently realized the meaning.

Her eyes widened and she took a step back, her aura quivering. "You fell into bloodlust."

He didn't dispute it. Why bother? It made no difference anyway, not like Merle would care for details. For what it was worth, Rowan hadn't been interested in finding out what really happened, and she'd known him for decades. It hadn't done him much good in the end…

"Well?" he asked, his wry smile still in place. "Did I live up to my reputation then, little witch?" Maybe she'd kick him back into the Shadows now, figuring it was too dangerous to work with him after all.

"No," she said, her voice calm and collected.

He stopped short and stared at her.

Her brows furrowed, she studied him with eyes that laid him bare. "I don't think it was bloodlust." She shook her head. "If it had been, you'd still be insane with it. It's irrevocable, right? Once seized by it, you can't shake it off?"

He nodded, too stunned to speak.

"So even after twenty years of starving in the Shadows," she went on slowly, "which should have made it worse, if anything, you were sane when I unleashed you. If you'd been seized by bloodlust before, you'd have killed me here in the mausoleum."

His mouth went dry as he stared at her.

"But you didn't. You're in control. You're sane."

He swallowed. It felt like scraping sandpaper down his throat. "Rowan didn't think so."

"What happened really?"

Shaking his head, he turned away, his chest painfully tight. "It doesn't matter now, does it? You wouldn't believe me anyway."

"Try me."

He glanced back at her. Her jaw was set in a tight line, her eyes daring, curious—and warm. Such a stubborn little witch. Stubborn and too damn caring for her own good.

"Let's go," he said, walking out of the mausoleum. "I need pain." *Badly*.

A few seconds passed before she fell into step beside him, and it wasn't until they'd reached the cemetery gate that she spoke again.

"I guess I owe you some thanks."

"For being the awesomest me I can possibly be?"

"For making that mistake." She stopped and opened the gate. "I wouldn't even exist if you hadn't saved her life when she was barely more than a teen." Her eyes glowed with warmth as she regarded him for a moment, then stepped outside.

He watched her walk toward the car, and for the first time in decades, he felt like he'd done something right in his life.

CHAPTER 10

"**G**ateway Transit Center?" Merle slanted a skeptical look at Rhun as he pulled the car to a stop in the deserted parking lot across from the MAX rail station.

His shrug made the leather jacket creak. "It's a good hunting ground."

At that, she silently raised an eyebrow to emphasize her glare.

"You want me to take pain from someone who deserves it— this is the venue for it. Lots of lowlifes milling about." Shutting off the engine, he leaned back in the seat and regarded her for a moment, shadows playing about his eyes. "You'll wait here in the car."

"Like hell I will. I'm not letting you loose to hunt on your own."

His aura whispered of darkness barely contained. "You don't want to see this."

She bristled, even though a trail of goose bumps appeared on her arms. "Last I checked, you were not a psychic, so you're in no position to tell me what I want or don't want."

"All right, let me rephrase it then. *I* don't want you to see this, Merle."

Holding his piercing gaze, she willed her breathing to slow down. It had the annoying habit of speeding up whenever he spoke her name, what with the way he turned it into a seductive murmur that entwined itself around her core. "This is not up for discussion," she said and got out of the car.

Rhun followed after a moment and locked the door with a mental command, an ability that still made her hot with envy. Walking past her, he gave her a scowl as dark as the night around them. She graciously ignored that and followed him down the shady-looking street past the station.

At this late hour, the wide space around the platforms was all but deserted, the few people hanging around clearly belonging to the less-than-fortunate part of the population. Merle gingerly side-stepped the sleeping arrangements of a bum, while casting a sinister look at the fidgety group of men in hoodies and low-slung pants a few feet away. Not that she needed to fend them off—as soon as they spotted Rhun, they quickly sidled off to the other end of the station.

"How do you know where to go?" she asked her demon guard.

"Evil has a tendency to draw our attention." His eyes were trained on the shadows unfurling between trees and dark buildings. "Same as pure innocence. It's like a scent trail luring us, much like the aroma of your favorite food would draw you closer."

Merle was about to ask another question when her phone rang. It was Lily's number. For a second, she hesitated, then answered it. Simply picking up the phone wouldn't compromise their position.

"Merle, are you okay?"

"Yes. Don't worry."

Rhun had stopped to look at her, his brows drawn together. *It's okay*, Merle mouthed, and waved him on.

"I won't ask you where you guys are," Lily continued, "and don't tell me—it's obviously better if I don't know…"

"Yeah, I think so, too."

Rhun turned and walked on, with Merle following a few paces behind.

"Listen, I'm really, really sorry about—"

"Lil," Merle interrupted gently, "don't. I'm not blaming you. It was bound to happen anyway." She skirted around trash. "I'd just hoped not quite so soon…"

"I know." Lily sounded heartbreakingly contrite. "Okay, just to give you the heads up about what's happening on this side of crazy—the Elders have virtually torn your house apart looking for clues on where you might have gone, so I suggest wherever you guys are planning to lie low, it better be a place that's not linked to you somehow. I'd pull some strings with friends of mine to get you hooked up, but same thing goes for me—they'll check all the places I know as well."

Merle listlessly kicked at a newspaper on the sidewalk. "Yeah, I kinda figured something like that." She pressed her lips together, her chest tight. "Is the house still standing?" The thought of the old Victorian reduced to rubble made her heart ache. The worn house was as much a part of her family as the people who had dwelt within its walls, and to lose it would be like the loss of yet another dear relative.

"Well," Lily said, "from the outside, yes. But you might want to hire an interior designer once all this blows over…"

Merle stopped and covered her eyes with her other hand. *Once all this blows over…* Would it ever? And then what? If the situation hadn't been FUBAR before, it certainly was now. Not only was she not one step closer to saving her sister from the clutches of a sociopathic demon, she still had another demon leashed to her who was well on the way to turning the tables on her. And in addition to the initial fuck-up of unbinding Rhun without the consent of the Elders, she had now officially gone past the point of no return when she'd defied the Elders' request to turn herself in. Even if she did manage to save Maeve and bind Rhun in the Shadows again—and no, no, no, her heart had no business cringing at that thought—there would be hell to pay with the Elders.

For a moment, for just a tiny moment, Merle allowed herself to feel like crawling into a dark hole to cry.

Listening to Lily's account of the damages done to her home, she peered after Rhun, who had disappeared into a gloomy multistory parking garage at the end of the street. Following him in, she rounded the corner behind which he'd vanished—and there she came to a stumbling halt, her eyes widening at the sight in front of her.

"Lil," she said flatly, still staring ahead, "I gotta go."

She didn't wait for Lily's response, just ended the call and watched in shock as Rhun yanked a man off a crying young woman on the ground between two cars.

"What the fuck!" the man yelled.

He didn't get to say anything more.

The next second Rhun slammed the man's back against the wall, his hand around the guy's throat, and all further protests subsided in a gagging sound.

The woman on the ground scrambled to her feet, and Merle gasped as she took in her appearance. Her face was tear-streaked, rivulets of smeared mascara running down her cheeks, and there was blood on her mouth from where a punch had obviously busted her lower lip. Merle's hands clenched to fists. *Son of a...* The woman's hands shook as she fumbled to pull down her torn skirt, and she staggered against one of the cars in her attempt to get away from Rhun and the man.

Merle started toward her. "Do you need help?"

Wide-eyed, the woman stared at her, face white as chalk. She shook her head, and stumbled away. Falling into a mad dash, she threw one more terrified glance at her attacker—and at the monster that now attacked *him*.

"Wait!" Merle made to go after her. "I can help you. If you need assis—"

A loud thump made Merle stop and turn on her heels. Rhun

had hurled the man to the ground again and now crouched on top of him, one knee pressed into the man's chest. Rhun's energy rippled, like the surface of a lake disturbed by a stone.

He grasped the right arm of the human, and with a series of seemingly effortless moves, he broke all of the man's fingers, his wrist, and the bones in his forearm and upper arm. The man convulsed and uttered strangled grunts of agony, but not one single scream came past his lips, almost as if—

Realization came over Merle with a shudder, as if a dozen spiders crawled down her back. Rhun must have mentally disabled the man's vocal cords to silence him.

The human thrashed with his remaining intact limbs, his eyes wide with horror, blood-shot and tear-filled with pain. Unperturbed, with a calm that was even more frightening than the coiling darkness of his aura, Rhun moved on to the other arm of the man, starting at his hand.

Snap, snap, snap.

He paused at the ring finger, raising an eyebrow at the golden wedding band that adorned it. Looking the human in the eye, he shook his head and *tsk*ed with unconcealed contempt. Then he overstretched the finger until it broke free of the joint, and the only part left holding it to the hand was skin. The man screamed silently, his face wrought with pain he couldn't voice.

The air around Rhun pulsed and it seemed as if he was drinking it in with every pore of his body, a dark creature of pain. Merle could only stand and stare, immobile, even though she wanted nothing more than to turn her back and run like hell. And use some brain bleach once she'd stopped trembling. After that, maybe she'd go find that dark hole to crawl into.

Rhun had gone on to break the man's legs. The guy didn't even jerk anymore, he could only pant faster in silent anguish.

For a moment, Rhun leaned back to regard his work with dark pride shadowing his face. Then he lunged forward in a lightning-fast move and bit the man's neck. The human convulsed again, uttered pained grunts that didn't lessen as Rhun continued drinking.

Merle's breath caught. So Rhun could control whether his bite was painful—or pleasurable. Automatically, she touched her neck, and a cold shiver ran over her skin like an icy draft. To think, how close she'd let him come, with the danger of his violent nature lurking beneath the surface, with all this dark power that could so easily destroy.

And yet, he had never hurt her.

The man's limbs went slack, his eyes shut. Panic surged through Merle and yanked her out of her paralysis. She couldn't let Rhun take another life, innocent or not.

"Rhun, stop! Don't kill him!"

He stilled, and even the air around him seemed to hold its breath. Slowly, he raised his head from the man's neck and looked up at Merle. She almost stumbled back at the feral glint in his eyes. His pupils were fully dilated, the black swallowing the usual pale green-blue until nothing but darkness remained. His lips were crimson with blood, his fangs extended, exposing him as the predator he was. And in his grip, clutched possessively, was the man, his prey, his kill.

"Don't, Rhun. Please," Merle whispered.

He blinked, took a deep breath, and leaned down again. She wanted to jump forward, her power humming underneath her skin, a spell on her lips, ready to be hurled at Rhun, but—he merely murmured something in the man's ear. The human's eyes flew open, widened with horror, his breathing turned erratic, and he uttered a panicked gurgle.

Rhun patted the guy's cheek and rose, stepping off him. "You may scream now," he said benignly to the man, his fangs flashing in a smile that froze Merle's bones.

Apparently he'd enabled the guy's vocal cords again, for the very next second a wail rose up from the man's throat, a scream of agony so piercing, it stopped her heart.

"Let's go," Rhun said as he walked past her without

deigning to look at the human again. "There's a hospital nearby. He'll be found by someone soon if he continues to wail like a banshee."

Merle glanced at the screaming, battered figure on the ground and then hurried to follow Rhun.

"What did you say to him?" she asked after she'd recovered enough to speak again. Her voice was shaky, though, and her insides felt like they'd been mashed.

"The truth." Rhun's eyes were almost back to normal. "That I'm a creature from Hell, that I prey on blood and pain, and that if he ever lays a hand on a female without her consent again, I will hunt him down and become his very own personal demon." He cracked his knuckles. "Don't worry about your precious witch law, though. He won't be able to tell anyone about this. Made sure to leave a block in his mind. Humans are so easily manipulated."

While she gaped at him, he simply walked on, farther away from the screams of pain that just wouldn't stop. Merle had to force herself to keep up with him, to put one foot in front of the other instead of standing still, breaking down.

Back at the car, she got in and closed the door, shutting off the man's piercing cries. Her breath stuck in her chest, her skin clammy, she stared out the front window. "You enjoyed this, didn't you?"

Rhun turned in the driver's seat to face her. "Yes."

He leaned closer, his dark energy caressing her skin like velvet. His gaze, so perceptive, focused on the trembling of her lips, flicked to her chest to note her shallow breathing, then rose to study her neck, regarding the frantic rhythm of her pulse underneath her skin.

"This," he murmured, taking her wrist and holding it up in front of her to reveal how hard her hand shook, "is why I wanted you to wait here in the car."

He leaned closer still, put his hand around the back of her neck and pulled her to him, until his forehead almost touched hers. His power prickled on her skin, raised the hairs on her arms, melted something that had iced over inside her.

"I am what I am, little witch of mine," he said, stroking her neck with the same hand that had all but shattered a human body mere minutes ago. "But I do not want you to be terrified of me. What I did to that man, I would never do to you."

Her breath mingled with his, intimate heat, shared in the space between. "But you would take pain from me," she whispered.

His gaze held hers as a sensual smile snuck onto his lips, one that ignited a slow burn deep inside her core. "Ah, yes." Gently, oh so gently, he tightened his hold on her neck. "I'd love to do that. And I am fairly sure that you would enjoy that as much as me. You see, there are different kinds of pain—pain for punishment, as you've just seen…" His lips brushed along the line of her jaw, his breath caressing her skin. "…but there is also pain for pleasure, Merle mine."

He nipped at her earlobe, and the sharp sting of his bite shot straight down to the juncture between her legs. Merle gasped. The thrill of excitement that followed the short pain sent pleasant shudders all through her body. Rhun released her, though not without intimately stroking along her neck as he withdrew his hand.

"Multiply that times ten," he said, starting the car, "and you know what it'll feel like if you ever let me take pain mixed with pleasure from you."

Gods have mercy—he'd turned her bones to liquid fire.

"Hmm." He slanted a quick look at her while driving away from the station. "That idea appeals to you, doesn't it?"

For the sake of her own soul, she wanted to deny it, but she couldn't even manage that simple lie. "Don't you have a demon to find?" she asked instead. Deflecting questions with questions seemed to be her best choice of defense here.

And he really needed to find that demon soon, not only for Maeve's sake, but for her own as well. Because, *dammit*, Merle was not nearly as wary of Rhun as she'd been in the beginning, and still should be. Hell, she should be terrified of him now that she knew how he affected her. But come to think of it, she was more afraid of that part of herself that was drawn to him like a moth to the flame, afraid of how much she wanted to let him do all sorts of things to her.

"You're right," he said, snapping her out of her dangerous musings.

"Well," she drawled and gestured, "go get started then."

"As soon as I find a quiet corner, little witch."

The quiet corner turned out to be Rocky Butte, the park on top of an extinct volcanic cinder cone rising up out of the sprawl of East Portland.

"Seriously?" Merle got out of the car and followed Rhun up the incline from the street to the stone stairs leading up to the castle-like wall hugging the top. "Don't tell me you've got better *reception* up here."

"Believe it or not, I am better at tracking energy signatures from high places." His grin was fleeting in the night, a flash of white in the dark. "The fact that this is my favorite place in the city has of course absolutely nothing to do with it." He took the remaining steps two at a time, and Merle tried hard not to notice how stunning his behind looked in motion. Nope, she didn't notice at all.

At the top, Rhun hopped onto and straddled the low balustrade. The dozen or so lanterns along the wall rimming the platform glowed with orange light, lending the place an eerie feel. Suppressing a shudder, she crossed her arms, looking back at Rhun. He closed his eyes, leaned back against the stone lamp-post behind him, and turned inward. His power flickered, curled inside, dimming as if in deep concentration. Minutes passed. Every now and then his aura quivered.

The wind was stronger this high up, whipping at Merle's hair, attacking without mercy, until she shivered at the thousand little bites of cold that slipped all the way through her clothes to her skin. She rubbed her hands together for some warmth and walked to the other side of the platform, gazing out onto the sleeping city. A sea of twinkling lights spread before her, a web of sparks in the darkness. Any other night, she'd have sighed at the view, but now it only tightened her heart, pressed it together until it cracked. Somewhere out there, Maeve suffered through an ordeal Merle couldn't, wouldn't imagine. Not if she still needed to function.

Her fingernails dug into her palms, hard enough to draw blood.

I'll find you, Maeve. I swear to the gods, I'll find you and bring you back.

"Merle."

Rhun's voice made her flinch, and she whirled around to face him. "Got him?"

He jumped down from the balustrade and shook his head, his brows furrowed. "I still can't find him."

"Why?" she bit out through gritted teeth. "Because he's Houdini?"

"Because he's being blocked."

That stunned her speechless for a few seconds. "What do you mean? How can he block himself?"

"It's not him doing it. The power that blanks out his psychic energy is not demon."

A feeling so nauseatingly cold crept up inside Merle she clenched her fists even tighter to keep from trembling. "Then what is it? Fae? Nymph?" Her voice sounded so, so desperate. She was grabbing for straws, trying, hoping for anything but...

Rhun took a heavy breath. "It's witch magic, Merle."

"No," she ground out before the blow of the heinous accusation knocked the breath out of her.

It couldn't be. Witches didn't hurt one another. It was a law carved in stone, the foundation of their community. No matter any individual differences or dislikes, harming another witch was sacrilegious, the highest form of treason imaginable. Never had there been a case of— No. It just—it couldn't be true. If it was… The ground beneath her feet opened up. She staggered, gasping for air, groped for a hold, found a lamppost to steady herself.

"You must be wrong." Her voice was but a breath away from fading.

"The pattern of witch magic is distinct," he said, his gaze intent on her. "I've felt it, even though whoever cast the blocking spell tried her best to mask it."

Her fingers clenched on the stone until her knuckles ached. "It can't be true." Underneath her skin, close, so close, her power coiled, burning with the force of her outrage. "No witch would do that to another, it's anathema to us—"

"I'm not making this up, Merle. Not even I would be that cruel." His eyes flashed as he glared at her, his jaw set in a tight line. "Whether you want to hear it or not, it's a witch backing that demon, for whatever reason."

"You're lying!" The stone underneath her fingers sizzled, and a wave of fire rolled out from her palm. She didn't even feel the burn. "You're lying to fuck with my mind! You just don't want to find him, so you're trying to turn me against my own! It can't be true, it can't be a witch, *that's impossible!*"

His aura pulsed darkly as he stared at her, his breathing as fast as hers. A muscle in his jaw ticked. The air around him shimmered with heat. Then, he held up his hands as if in defeat, toned down his energy. "Oh, I'm sorry, you're right," he said, his every word dripping with sarcasm. "I forgot witches are inherently good and biologically *incapable* of committing crimes, just as all demons are innately evil, bad to the bone, with no redeeming qualities whatsoever. Forgive me, little witch, for a moment there I slipped and saw the world in shades of gray. Won't happen again, I'm going back to black and white now."

She couldn't even take offense at his biting tone, her head swirling with the implication of his allegation. While she rejected the very thought of another witch being capable of such malice, a small part of her knew it, felt it—and broke.

She stood there, clutching the lamppost like a lifesaver, while the world around her slowly, inexorably, slipped off its hinges. "It can't be," she whispered over and over, as if the mere repetition of it could make it true. "It can't be…"

"Think about it." Rhun's voice, breaking through the darkness that crushed her. His tone had gentled, almost as though he could feel her turmoil. "You said the wards you put up around Maeve's apartment failed one day, for no apparent reason. I've seen how strong your magic is—your wards would never have vanished just like that. They were broken down." He was right in front of her now, only inches away, and his striking power steadied her as much as it made her shiver. "Tell me," he said, his voice so very, very gentle, "how many other-world creatures are able to dismantle witch wards?"

She took a shuddering breath. "None. Only another witch can do that."

Her hand slipped off the stone. Her knees gave in.

Rhun caught her as the world went black.

CHAPTER 11

Darkness curled around Merle.

This, however, was different from the cold black swallowing her whole amid her crumbling world. Instead of the icy, numbing nausea that had crawled into her every cell, the darkness enveloping her now was rich, velvety, warm. Cocooning her, humming around her, it pulsed in sync with the beat of her heart.

A part of her recognized the lethal edge in this dark energy, reminded her of the destruction this power had wrought just shortly before. She knew the danger whispering underneath it. And yet, as the darkness stroked along her senses, mingled with her own magic, nurtured it, something within Merle unfurled in the complete absence of fear.

Taking a deep breath, she inhaled Rhun's distinctive male scent, and opened her eyes—to darkness, again. She still couldn't see a thing. A slight shifting of her position told her why. Rhun had curled her up in his lap, her head pressed face-down into his chest, and he'd wrapped both his arms so tightly, completely around her that he blacked out her vision. She tried to push herself up and found the Wall of Rhun immobile, keeping her in place.

"You can let me go now." Her words came out muffled and more directed toward his pectoral muscles, since he still held her plastered facedown on his chest.

Rhun's arms tightened around her and he made a sound of languorous contentment.

She cleared her throat. "Rhun."

"Witch volcano." A lazy murmur rumbling through his chest.

"You don't need to hold on to me."

"Hmm." His hand stroked over her hair. "Yes, I do."

Another attempt at freeing herself before that warmth inside her fully bloomed into something else, something irrevocable and disarming. "Let me up."

"No." His voice lost its lazy note. "Now you listen to me. You cannot faint like that in front of me and expect me to be okay with it. You scared the living shit out of me, little witch, and you *will* let me hold you now until I feel better."

Her heart overflowed with fuzzy warmth scaring the living shit out of *her. Damn that treacherous, useless organ!*

"Of course," he added, his voice now a murmur of sensual intimacies, "there are faster ways you could make me feel better... *Umph!*"

Turned out being curled in his lap brought her in the perfect position to knee him in the ribs.

"All right, all right, I'll settle for snuggling," he muttered under his breath. "No need to witch-handle me."

Right then, she was really glad he couldn't see her grin.

Since he gently compelled her to stay in his arms, she decided to enjoy the feeling. And, oh, it was damn straight enjoyable. It had been a long time since she'd been held by someone as if she were a fragile treasure, to be protected and cherished.

Of course, Rhun wasn't holding her with that intent. He was a demon, after all, and the thought of him *caring* for anyone seemed as plausible as a lion snuggling with an antelope. But she *felt* cherished and cared for, and it was real enough for that moment. Real enough to protect her mind from the near-insanity that had clawed at her shortly before, when she'd had to realize the worst treachery imaginable had been committed by someone she likely had known and trusted her entire life.

Rhun held her like this for a long while, his heartbeat a steady rhythm against her cheek, anchoring her. When he let her go, she mourned the loss of his body heat, even though all through her limbs a new kind of warmth had spread, and it had everything to do with the demon in front of her.

"All right." She got to her feet and straightened her clothes and hair. "All right." No matter how much she'd like to keep ignoring the abounding problems, she had to face them now.

It was like a textbook case of Murphy's Law. She huffed and shook her head. Just how much more could possibly go wrong? Too much, she thought immediately, and decided not to ponder on any details, lest she give the Powers That Be some sadistic suggestions on how to fuck up her life even more.

Rhun got up, too, and dusted himself off. He'd apparently sat down to hold her on the bench of the round stone monument right next to the stairs. For a split second, Merle's unruly mind told her to go help clean him off, to get her hands on him again.

She slapped herself.

Not mentally this time, but physically, with the intended sharp pain snapping her back to reason.

At the swatting sound, Rhun jerked his head up and stared at her, frowning. "Did you just slap yourself?"

"Yes."

He looked flabbergasted. "*Why?*"

"Needed the pain."

Slowly, he arched one eyebrow. "You know, if you needed pain…"

"Not like that!"

"Just saying."

Shooting him a glare, she then took a heavy breath and returned to untangling the mess they were in. While sorting her thoughts and shoving the feeling of devastating betrayal deep into the darkest recess of her heart, she paced, one hand rubbing her forehead. "What am I going to do?"

"Break the blocking spell?"

She glanced at Rhun, who leaned against the low balustrade, his arms crossed in front of his chest. The orange glow of the lamps illuminated his face, made his light green eyes glint in the night, reminiscent of a feline predator's gaze.

"No shit," she gave back, suppressing a shiver. "And just how do you suppose I'll do that?"

"This is witch magic—that's your domain." He shrugged one shoulder, the casual movement a stark contrast to the dark vibe of his aura. "But a smart witch once told me for every spell you cast…"

"…there is a loophole to undo it, hidden from your knowledge," she finished, reciting her grandmother's favorite saying. Merle had always taken it as a warning, but now, it could just be her saving grace.

Rhun nodded, his lips curving up in a slow smile. Her heart did an annoying flip at the sight.

"Right." She blew out a breath and put a few more steps between her and that sneaky demon. "I'll have to skim through my grimoire, maybe I'll find something in there. And I'll get Lily on it, too."

"Don't."

"What?" She stopped short in the process of pulling out her phone.

Uncrossing his arms, he walked toward her. "Don't call Lily. Don't tell her what you know."

"Why not? We can use her help."

"I've told you this before and I'll tell you again, since you obviously didn't get the point." He snatched the phone from her hand.

She glared at him, not sure what irritated her more—his alpha male antics of taking her phone away, or the casual ease with which he'd pried it from her fingers before she could act on it.

"Lily is the niece of one of the Elders, the bunch of witches who are out to get you—us—" He pointed between them both, and she gritted her teeth in anger because he did so using *her phone*. "—and since Lily apparently leaked critical information to them once already, she's a weak link and a liability if you continue to confide in her. The less the Elders know about what you are up to, the better." He made a pause. A muscle ticked in his temple. "Especially since it's most likely an Elder witch who cast the blocking spell."

Merle swallowed. Her heartbeat drummed in her ears. "Why do you think that?" she whispered, even though a part of her already knew the answer.

Rhun cupped her face with his free hand, his skin a hot brand, his eyes locked onto hers. "It takes an extraordinary amount of power to dismantle witch wards, doesn't it? Same goes for casting an intricate blocking spell and keeping it up for so long. That would take the kind of power only an Elder witch wields. Am I right?"

She could barely nod to acknowledge a truth which had been gnawing at the edges of her consciousness since she'd realized a witch helped that demon. She'd desperately ignored it, hadn't even allowed herself to form it into a coherent thought, because doing so would make it real. The kind of real that could shatter the last remnants of innocent trust in the very people she'd grown up with, the ones who had vowed to save and protect their own.

"Hey." Rhun hunched down to level his eyes with hers, studying her expression. "You're not going to drop again, are you?"

She shot him her best Angry Glare.

"Good." His thumb stroked over her cheek. "I'll take that as a no."

It wasn't until his aura quivered with delight that she realized she'd been leaning into his touch, rubbing her cheek against his palm. *Uh-oh.* Even though something tugged inside her, she straightened her spine and took a step away from him.

"Okay," she said, ignoring his intense gaze. Was that disappointment in his eyes? Yeah right. Maybe she needed to have *her* eyes checked. *Focus, Merle.* "Suppose it's really an Elder witch—neither she nor the other Elders will gain any advantage by learning what we know. If anything, it might work to *our* advantage if the other Elders find out one of them has broken our most sacred law. It might actually make them persecute *that* witch instead of me, and get them off my back temporarily."

"Unless they're all in on it," Rhun said matter-of-factly.

For a good ten seconds, she could only stare at him. "Do not ever suggest that again." Her steady voice belied her inner uproar. "There's only so much treachery I can stomach before I run amok."

And he had the nerve to chuckle at that.

"I *will* call Lily and give her the update," she said, "because I don't know whether I'll find anything in the grimoire, and since I can't very well go back to my house to raid the library, I need her help in finding out how to break that spell."

"Oh, yes, right." He snapped his fingers, his voice laced with sarcasm. "Because after Lily held up so well in front of her aunt, you can completely trust whatever information she passes on to you."

"That she told her aunt about you under duress does not mean she'll let her or anyone else manipulate her into feeding me false information. She'd rather take whatever punishment they mete out to her." She looked daggers at him, daring him to contradict her.

"All right. Whatever. Go make the Call of Doom." He waved

his hands, threw her the phone and turned away. "Can't say I didn't warn you."

Ignoring his pathos, she called Lily and relayed what they found out. To Lily's credit, she neither fainted, nor did she throw a fit and accuse her of lying. In fact, she remained so calm that to anyone who didn't know her it might have suggested she wasn't the least shocked about the news.

Merle, though, who'd grown up with her and could read her friend like a book, knew the lack of emotions in Lily's reaction was the equivalent of a hysterical breakdown for her. Only during the worst of moments would the extrovert witch shut down and restrain her outgoing personality in a desperate attempt at keeping herself together.

Lily vowed to look for a way to break the blocking spell while also keeping Merle informed about any moves of the Elders. Thanking Lily from the bottom of her heart, Merle hung up and turned to Rhun—who was covered in a gazillion tiny fairies.

Their fluttering wings let the air around him hum with oscillating magic coloring the night. He stood still, his arms held at an awkward angle so as not to crush the teeny fae beings plastered to his sides. When his eyes met hers, they held a glint of resignation.

Merle pocketed her phone. "Um, need any help?"

He sighed. "They're smitten."

"Smitten?"

"With me. You know, they see me and they're addicted." Shrugging one fairy-laden shoulder, he smiled smugly. "Not that I can blame them. I *am* gorgeous."

Merle pressed her lips together lest she laugh, instead she cleared her throat. "Does that happen often?"

"Eh. Sometimes."

"And how do you get rid of them?"

"I usually wait 'til they fall off."

She stared.

"Well, they do get tired after a while, and then they can't hold on any longer."

Closing her eyes, she rubbed her forehead. "You should shake them off."

"Why? Jealous?"

She gave him a droll look. "I have no desire to plaster myself to you."

"Really? Not even if there's a little rubbing involved?" He wiggled his brows.

"No," she lied, biting the inside of her mouth to keep from saying anything else.

Checking her raging hormones back into place, she approached him and took out her old-fashioned keys to the Victorian. At the clinking sound of the metal, the fairies hissed and fluttered away. Rhun raised one eyebrow in a silent question.

"Iron." Merle pocketed her keys again. "They hate it."

"You really are a jealous witch. So heartless." He put his hand across his chest in a gesture of pain, and shook his head.

"Oh, quit it." She rolled her eyes, but the corners of her mouth felt the strangest urge to curve upwards. "Now," she said after a moment, putting her hands on her hips, "I need a quiet place where I can study the grimoire, somewhere safe and secluded. I'm kind of out of options here, because any place I can think of will be known to the Elders, too. You don't by any chance happen to know a place we can hole up in for a while?"

"Actually, I do."

She blinked. "Really?"

"Well, I have to check with someone—and technically, I don't know if he's still around, so I'll have to find him first, but I have an idea as to where he might be."

Shooting him a wary look, she considered it for a moment. "For lack of alternatives, I'll say let's try that."

They walked back to the car, and after a half-hour drive to the southeastern outskirts of Portland, Rhun parked in a back alley a little away from a dilapidated house shrouded in darkness. Neither street lamps nor lights from other buildings illuminated the gloom, and the whole area looked as inviting as a post-war zone. A sense of unease crept up Merle's spine and she felt the inexplicable urge to leave as soon as possible. Preferably *now*.

"What is this place?" she whispered, a thousand spider feet crawling over her skin, her throat closing up.

Rhun turned off the engine. "If I ask you to stay in the car again, will you do it this time?"

Instead of answering, she repeated her question, with more urgency. Anxiety pulsed underneath her skin, every muscle poised to run away, every instinct inside her screaming to turn around and leave.

"A demon bar," he said.

She stared at him, her clawing need to flee momentarily forgotten. "A bar? You guys have *bars*?"

"You know, I could take your flabbergasted disbelief as an insult, but since I am such a good-natured piece of awesomeness, I'm going to let it go."

"I never knew such a place existed."

"Yeah, well, we don't particularly advertise in the witching community. The whole natural-born enemies thing, you know."

"Funny," she sneered. Then a thought struck her. "The area is warded, isn't it?"

He nodded, locks of chestnut-colored hair sliding over his forehead, in beautiful contrast to his ivory skin. "Deterrent spells to keep humans and witches away."

And that would explain the creepy feeling she'd gotten… "So," she said, frowning, "you're fine with revealing the location of a demon bar to a witch? Doesn't that, like, break some demon loyalty code or something?"

"For that, I'd have to have some loyalty to start with."

"What do you m—"

"I'm not exactly the poster child for a good evil demon, little witch. Let's just leave it at that." His fingers tapped on the steering wheel, and his gaze turned intense. "Now—will you stay in the car while I go in and look for my contact?"

"No."

A muscle in his jaw ticked. His aura pulsed. "I really don't think this is a good idea."

"Tough luck. I'm going with you anyway." No way would she let him walk into a bar full of other demons, unsupervised.

"You're too stubborn for your own good," he muttered under his breath and got out of the car.

Merle followed him toward the dilapidated building at the end of the alley without feeling any glee about winning this argument. She was too anxious about what awaited her, and the wards now bore down with a vengeance. Every step she took got heavier, as if her feet were burdened with lead. The more she walked forward, the more that strange force pulled her away. Her sense of unease grew, spread like cancer through her body, festering, until she could hardly breathe. All she wanted was to turn around on her heels and run like hell.

At about ten feet away from the house, she abruptly stopped, against her will, and froze as if her muscles had been locked. She couldn't move forward no matter how hard she tried.

"Rhun," she ground out, her heart hammering in her chest, her throat constricted.

He paused. "Getting cold feet?"

She *so* wanted to wipe that smug smile off his face. "I can't go forward. It's the wards."

Rhun sauntered closer with dark nonchalance, stopped in front of her, his gaze holding hers. A sinister whisper of restrained power passed through his aura as he studied her with such disconcerting focus that she trembled.

"I should just leave you standing here," he murmured.

Even in the dark, his eyes were piercingly bright, and right now, they held cruel, cold calculation. He cupped her face, leaned in and kissed her nose, and then he half-turned away with a sigh. Merle was about to yell at him not to dare leave her standing there, when he brought his right hand to his mouth and bit his thumb with one fang extended.

Cringing at the unexpected and strange move, she watched him press his finger for blood. A few drops pooled at the tip, dark crimson with the distinctive trace of demon magic. Without warning, Rhun stroked his thumb along her throat, smearing a trail of blood down to the hollow between her collarbones.

She jerked back. "What the hell did you just do?" But even before she'd voiced her question, she felt it. The compulsion of the wards fell away, the restraint keeping her from moving vanished. She hauled in a free breath, the feeling of anxiety gone.

"I marked you" Rhun licked the wound on his thumb closed.

Merle turned her attention back to him. "Wait—you *marked* me? Marked as in…"

"Mine."

Her stomach made a dive for the ground. "*What?*" If looks could be lethal, she was sure hers would have killed him on the spot.

"Merle," he said, ignoring her deadly glare with astounding ease. "First, it's the only way to get you through the wards. Second, if you go in there unmarked, you're fair game to any otherworld creature that wants to lay a hand on you. Chances are high that at least one of the demons inside has lost a friend or family member to a witch at some point, which paints a fucking bull's eye on your back. You're a strong witch and I'm a good fighter, but we wouldn't last a minute against the crowd in there. With my blood on you, I've claimed you for my own. Means you're protected by our laws against any demon assault on neutral ground such as this bar."

Merle swallowed. Something funny was going on somewhere between her stomach and her chest. "This is only temporary, right? It'll wear off?"

He pursed his lips. "Sure." Before she could give in to the impulse of smacking him, he resumed walking, saying as he went, "Come on then, little witch of *mine*."

Her heart bounced at that darkly murmured endearment, much to her irritation. Gritting her teeth and balling her hands to fists, she followed him to the entrance of the building, which now looked a lot less dilapidated than before. Apparently the uninviting appearance of the house had been another effect of the wards. They had veiled the standard-issue brick stone building as a repulsive ruin.

Now, the only uninviting, repulsive aspect of the location was the man standing in front of the door. Though *man* was probably the wrong word. He could only be described as a breathing wall of muscle. Merle picked up his unique aura, and her steps faltered.

"He's a shifter of some sort, isn't he?" she whispered to Rhun.

"Yep. Tiger."

And there, Merle almost stopped and turned around. With an effort, she kept on following Rhun up the steps to the intimidating feline predator in human form. Clad in black leather from head to toe, dark hair shorn short, his ice-blue eyes night sharp and tracking Merle's every move, he was the kind of male she wouldn't want to run into alone even in broad daylight. Instinctively, she inched closer to Rhun as they stopped in front of the bar's bouncer.

The shifter's gaze lingered on Merle's throat, studying the mark of blood, and his nostrils flared as he took in the scent. "She with you?" he asked Rhun without taking his eyes off her. His voice was scraped gravel, broken through with a roughness reminiscent of his tiger's growl even in human form.

Rhun nodded. "That a problem?" His relaxed stance all but concealed the writhing agitation of his restrained aura.

Merle could feel the pulse of power in the air, sizzling between them.

After giving her another suspicious once-over, the tiger shot Rhun an intense look. "Don't let it become one." With a jerk of his head, he motioned them inside.

"I'll try my very best," Rhun muttered as they passed him and stepped into the bar.

The hum of conversation greeted them, broken by occasional laughter, over the drumming rhythm of Rock music. The room was large, though divided into a bar area, secluded booths and a couple of corners with pool tables and dart boards, everything dimly lit by scattered lamps.

"Stay close," Rhun murmured in her ear, his breath hot on her skin, sending an appreciative shiver down her back. "Don't stop anywhere without me, don't wander off alone, don't make eye contact with anyone. Oh, and try not to move in a conspicuously witchy way. In fact, try to move as little as possible."

"Like only breathe once a minute?" she asked dryly.

One side of his mouth curved up. "That's a start, little witch."

Rhun prowled the bar, glancing around for his contact, and Merle followed him on his heels. If feasible, she'd have plastered herself to his back like a fairy now. She wasn't easily scared and had means of defense as a witch, but the charged magical atmosphere in the bar had the hairs on her arms and neck standing up, and her heart rate was well on the way to breaking her very own speed record.

Everywhere she passed, the vibe coming from the otherworldly patrons changed from relaxed and cheery to wary with a sharp bite of hostility. Demons of all sorts and sizes, shifters, and nymphs, all of them focused their attention on Merle, dozens of gazes staring her down, scrutinizing her with unconcealed resentment until she felt crushed by the pressure of the barely leashed aggression.

"Witch," some of them whispered, sneering at her.

Conversations stopped, replaced by growls. A female demon hissed and bared her piranha teeth. Merle almost stumbled as she tried to ignore the hostile atmosphere strangling the breath out of her. Her steps turned sluggish, she faltered—

Then, Rhun's hand on hers, grasping her in a steadfast hold, grounding her. He threw a glance over his shoulder, gave her a cocky grin, winked—and she could breathe again. She mouthed a "thank you" and smiled.

An intriguing tremor tore through his aura and he quickly turned his head away. His hand, however, tightened its hold on hers, and she wondered whether Rhun was aware his thumb stroked the back of her hand.

They were passing by a booth when Rhun stopped so suddenly that Merle bumped into his back. While she pondered the best way to remain glued to him like that, he *tsk*ed at the person sitting in the booth, presently hidden from Merle's view by Rhun's yummy backside.

"Harassing nymphs again?" Rhun asked.

"Well, I'll be damned," a velvety male voice answered him. "If it isn't the blood-sucking pain slut."

Rhun's chuckle vibrated against Merle where she was plastered to his back.

"Says the pathetic excuse for a callboy," Rhun retorted. "Twenty years later and you still frequent the same shithole." Shaking his head, he added, "And, by the way, you *are* damned."

"Pot. Kettle. Black."

Merle inched a bit away as the other demon—still out of her line of sight—apparently got up and gave Rhun a crushing man hug.

"It's good to see you again," the demon said after a moment. "What happened? Last I heard you enjoyed a vacation in the Shadows."

There was only the smallest flicker of agony in Rhun's

energy. "Got released early because of good conduct." His voice betrayed nothing of any pain whatsoever.

Now Merle's curiosity got the better of her, and she peered around Rhun to take a look at the other demon.

"And who is this astounding beauty?" the dark-haired male asked as his gaze fell on Merle. "Your parole officer, Rhun?"

Her own personal demon chuckled at that. "Sort of."

Merle's reaction, at that moment, was limited to mindless drooling. The male in front of her was a package of sensual perfection, silken black hair, lustrous bronze-brown skin begging to be licked, strong masculine features with a touch of Persian royalty, eyes the color of crushed gold. Wearing black slacks and a dark blue dress shirt, he could have starred in an Armani ad that would undoubtedly cause a never-ending string of accidents if hoisted above a street intersection. And yet, underneath the attractive veneer, below the surface of her fierce reaction to him, there pulsed a sense of darkness that tasted *wrong*.

"Well now," he said, his voice a rich tone that might be considered foreplay in itself in the right circumstances, "that makes me want to be bad, too, just to have a parole officer like you to take care of me." He took her hand and gave it a kiss without breaking eye contact. "I'm Bahram. It's a pleasure to meet you, darling."

Every female hormone in her body was ragingly alert, homing in on the magnificent male specimen in front of her. He oozed such a vibrant, intoxicating sexuality, it was all she could do not to tear off his clothes and ride him to the ground.

"What's your name, honey?" He still held her hand, rubbing the soft skin between her thumb and forefinger in moves so erotic she almost moaned.

"You're gorgeous," Merle breathed. It was all she could say.

He gave her a swoon-worthy smile. "No comparison to how ravishing *you* are, beautiful."

"All right, that's it." Rhun slapped Bahram's hand away and

pointed a finger at him, his eyes narrowed. "Zip it, incubus, that's *my* witch. Go get your own."

Bahram sighed and raked her with a longing gaze. "They're so hard to come by these days."

Merle sobered as if thrown in an icy Norwegian fjord, and she took a wary step back. "You're an incubus?" Known for their overwhelming sexual magnetism and the nasty habit of impregnating any female that wasn't up a tree by the count of three. That explained the underlying hint of danger she'd sensed beneath the outward attraction, the sense of wrong she'd gotten despite her uncontrollable surge of lust.

Bahram bowed. "At your service, darling."

She cleared her throat and inched further away. "Thanks, but I can service myself quite well."

At Rhun's laughter, barely hidden in a cough, she realized what she'd said, her face flushing with heat.

"Although," Rhun said to her, grinning broadly, "you might have to work a bit harder for that now since we had to abandon your vibrator along with your car."

She flailed with her hands. *"It's an MP3 player!"*

"Uh-huh." Rhun pushed her into the booth, sitting down next to her.

Bahram resumed his seat, too, and when the waitress—a nymph of some sort—passed them by, Rhun stopped her to order a soda and a burger.

At Merle's frown, he explained, "It's for you, little witch. And before you ask, yes, it's safe to eat for humans."

"Thanks." She was desperately fighting the warm, tingly feeling inside her chest. "That's surprisingly thoughtful of you, demon."

"Well, I don't want you to faint from malnourishment. It's a lot harder to annoy you when you're unconscious."

"You're so sweet," she said with mock glee.

"Ain't I?"

Rhun smirked at her, his eyes glowing, and just like that, the tingly feeling in her chest took her over. She couldn't fight it any more than she'd be able to withstand the current of a wild river dragging her under. Still, she tried. For the sake of her own soul, she had to, for if she didn't, if she just gave in, she'd be headed straight for disaster.

So while Rhun and Bahram started catching up on old times, she inched as far away as possible from the demon who was stealing her heart, little by little, and she went through every mind disciplining technique she knew in order to fight a losing battle. Her food and drink arrived and she began eating, half-listening to the conversation.

"So, what did you do with my old place?" Rhun asked Bahram, putting his arm up on the seatback behind Merle, leaning toward her, his fingers playing with strands of her hair.

Focus on the food, Merle, not on how good it feels to have him close to you.

"I kept it for a while," Bahram said, "but after it was clear you wouldn't come back soon, I sold it. Not everything, though. Some of the valuable items and the more personal stuff I stored. You can look through it, see what you want to have back, now that you're free."

There was a heavy silence. Merle glanced at Rhun, whose expression was shuttered, but there, underneath the controlled veneer of his aura, pulsed a sting of pain so deep, it cut right through her.

"Yeah," Rhun said quietly, "I'll do that later. Thanks."

The knife's edge inside Merle twisted further, and she had to look away, breathing against the sudden, unbidden pain in her chest. There would be no *later* for Rhun. He wasn't here to stay, and it was no use for him to look through his old belongings, to plan for a future he didn't have.

Realizing that, it shattered something inside her.

Rhun's hand on her back, his fingers drawing small circles. "What happened to Gandalf?"

Bahram took a sip from his drink. "Morana took him in."

Rhun's hand stilled. "You left him with a werewolf? What's *wrong* with you? Please tell me she didn't eat him."

A husky chuckle from Bahram. "Don't let her hear you say that—she'll be livid. No, man, she was fond of him. I've never seen her spoil anyone like that. Rest assured, he spent the last years of his life as happy as a clam."

Rhun was silent for a moment, his hand pressing against Merle's back. "He died."

Bahram nodded. "Only two years ago, though."

Rhun whistled low. "Lucky bastard got old, huh? I always knew he'd cheat death for as long as he could."

In the meantime, Merle had finished her burger and now decided to give in to her compulsive nosiness. "Who was that Gandalf guy?" she asked Rhun. "A friend of yours?"

A slow grin spread on Bahram's face, while Rhun simply looked sheepish and cleared his throat.

"His cat," the incubus answered for Rhun.

"A *cat*?" She half-turned to gape at Rhun. "*You* had a cat? And you named him *Gandalf*?"

Rhun shrugged, still looking rather uncomfortable. "He was gray."

And right there, she couldn't keep her laughter to herself anymore. She shook with it, eyes filling with tears, and she couldn't stop even as Rhun glared at her.

"You know," Bahram said to Merle, playing with the ice in his drink, "our bad-to-the-bone demon here loved his furry little friend to death."

That set off another set of giggles in her.

"*Bahram*." A low warning from Rhun.

Ignoring him, Bahram went on, gold eyes glinting with mischief. "Picked him up from the streets, half-dead and starving. Nursed that little kitty right back to life and pampered him senseless."

Merle glanced at Rhun, pressing her lips together, her body

trembling. No use. At his expression, she burst out laughing again.

"My fist," Rhun growled, cracking his knuckles, "hasn't satisfyingly connected with an incubus's face in a long time."

Bahram cocked a brow and turned to Merle. "You should have seen him dote on that cat. He even used to cook for—"

His sentence ended in a coughed curse as Rhun's fist hit him straight in the nose.

"Ah." Rhun leaned back with the smug expression of a cat having stolen the dog's treat. "Nothing says 'welcome home' like smacking a friend in the face."

Giving him the finger, Bahram wiped the blood from his nose with a napkin.

"So," Rhun said after a moment, "I was wondering if we could crash at your place for a while."

The incubus's face was a study in incredulity. "And your preferred method of smoothing the way for my compliance is punching me in the nose?"

"Hey, you were *asking* for that one."

Bahram shrugged and grinned. "Fair enough."

"You still owe me one, you know. Remember when I saved your permanently horny ass from that shifter you were screwing? The one who tried to eat you afterwards?"

Merle choked on her ginger ale.

"How was I supposed to know she was a black widow?" the incubus grumbled. "Looked good enough in human form…"

"Let us use your place for a bit and I'll call it even," Rhun said amiably. "I'm sure you'll have no trouble finding a bunch of nymphs who are more than willing to accommodate you for a night or two."

Bahram sighed. "All right." He pointed a finger at Rhun. "But for every piece of furniture you break, I'll break one of your bones, starting with your head."

"All right."

"And no blood stains on anything!"

"When have I ever—"

"That one time," Bahram interrupted him, holding up his hand to count on his fingers, "when you came crawling back from that bar brawl, bleeding from I don't know how many wounds, and crashed at my place 'cause you didn't make it to your own." He ticked off the next finger. "That one time at one of my parties when you decided to bite that nymph and she bled all over my carpet…"

"I didn't know she was a hemophiliac!"

"…at yet another party," Bahram continued, still counting on his fingers, "when you had a little one-on-one with that leopard shifter in my spare bedroom, and I had to change the mattress afterwards…"

"She had sharp claws and was into biting," Rhun muttered. When Bahram was about to tick off another finger, Rhun threw up his hands. "Okay, okay, I get it! If there's bleeding, I'll make sure to clean it up. No need to get your panties in a twist."

Merle had been watching the exchange with a mix of shock, amusement, and a biting jealousy as unbidden as it was inappropriate. Of course Rhun had a history. And she had absolutely no reason to feel anything about that. Maybe, if she repeated that a few times in her head, the twinge in her chest would go away and her blood would stop burning.

Eyeing Merle, Bahram asked, "So how come you two need a place to hide? Gotten in trouble already, Rhun?"

He shrugged nonchalantly. "I wouldn't exactly call it *trouble*. It's more like I'm helping my favorite witch avoid certain people."

Bahram's perceptive gaze darted from Rhun to Merle and back again a few times. "Right. Just make sure those certain people won't know about my helping you." His gold eyes focused on Merle. "I have no quarrels with your kind, and I'd like to keep it that way."

"I understand," she said. "We'll keep you out of it."

The incubus nodded at her, then turned to Rhun and handed

him his key. "The address is still the same. Wards are in place, but they'll recognize you and let you through—your pretty witch as well, since you marked her."

"I'm not *his* witch," Merle said for clarification.

"Thanks, buddy." Rhun took the key.

Bahram's warm gaze fell on Merle again. "You should give me your number."

"Like hell." Rhun's growl shook the air. "She's *mine*."

At that moment, something in Merle snapped in irritation, and before she could stop herself she shouted, "I'm not *yours!*"

The bar went quiet. The crowd fell silent, even the music paused. Every single otherworld creature in the room turned to stare at Merle. The air grew thick with animosity, charged with aggression waiting to be released.

And she'd just officially denied the only reason keeping them from doing so.

Uh-oh.

CHAPTER 12

Merle's face had gone white as a sheet, her breathing shallow, and her scent spiked with fear.

Good, Rhun thought grimly. She should be fucking scared after making a blunder like that, unnecessarily putting herself in danger because of her damn pride. The thought of her being hurt set his blood on fire, made worse by the fact she'd denied his claim. A claim, of course, he hadn't intended to make, or not seriously in any case, just as a means for her protection as he'd told her. As he'd told himself.

She would never truly be *his*, not only because she was a witch, but because she was the witch who planned to kick him back into the Shadows once he'd served his purpose. And to keep that from happening he'd have to leave her—after stealing the essence of her being...

So, yeah, marking her and taking it seriously? Bad idea. Majorly bad idea. But damn if he didn't want her as his anyway. *With every furious beat of his heart.*

Trying to salvage the situation, he pinned her with a prompting glare. "Care to rephrase that, *sweetheart?*"

To her credit, she picked up on it swiftly. After swallowing what had to be an enormous lump in her throat, she loudly said, "Sorry, *honey*—I panicked. Still have some commitment issues, you know." And she gave him a dazzling smile that tugged at everything inside him he didn't want tugged.

His left hand curved around her neck in a blatant display of possession, his thumb stroking the mark of his blood on her skin. "We'll work on that, my little witch."

And he really, truly wished they could.

While the tension in the bar eased up again—the situation apparently defused—and the din of conversation and music resumed with a hint of lingering wariness, he stared at the witch who was slowly, inexorably becoming his own personal brand of poison.

He'd never cared much if the females he'd gotten involved with hadn't stuck around, they'd come and gone in his life as fun diversions, providing him with what he needed. He'd always been more than glad if they'd walked out on their own after they were done.

This one, though, he wanted to tie down and *tame*. He wanted her as *his* with an irrational drive threatening to destroy all his carefully made plans. Which he couldn't let happen.

Apparently still playing along with her role, Merle snuggled into his side, placing one hand on his chest. Her fingers dug into the fabric of his T-shirt and gently scratched circle patterns. His eyes nearly crossed at the intense pleasure of that small touch which all but short-circuited his entire system—and then shot straight to his groin.

This witch might just be his undoing.

"Uh, Rhun?"

Bahram's voice pulled him out of visions of blissful self-destruction at the feet of a ginger-haired spitfire.

"What?"

"You might want to let go of that piece of the booth you got there."

His puzzled gaze followed Bahram's to his right hand, which had been resting on the back of the seat behind Merle. He now held what was left of the wooden top of the booth—he'd apparently crushed it without noticing.

Merle had studied the damaged booth as well and now faced him again with a glint in her eyes that was on the wrong side of diabolical. When she slowly, deliberately repeated the gentle scratching caress of his chest without taking her eyes off his, Rhun knew he had met his mischievous equal.

Barely stifling a groan, his every nerve pulsing with pleasure, he couldn't help crushing the remaining wood in his hand. "You'll pay for that, tricky little witch," he ground out.

"Oooh, I'm scared."

"No, I mean that literally," he said with what he knew was his most annoying smirk. "I don't have any money on me, so you'll be reimbursing the bar for the damages done."

She quickly withdrew her hand and scowled at him. "You've got to be kidding me."

He blew her a kiss, enjoying the way she narrowed her eyes at him in anger.

"All right, you two love birds," Bahram cut in. "Get a room. Oh wait, you already have my apartment." He made lazy shooing gestures with his hands. "Go use it already to hump each other. I can't stand to watch your foreplay any longer."

That earned him a scathing look from Merle, and Rhun found it delightfully amusing not to be at the receiving end of her glare for a change.

"Well, let's finish this up, then." Bahram focused on Rhun, unperturbed by the force of Merle's resentful scowl. "Do you have a cell?"

"Sure I do." He leaned back. "Do you prefer a blood or a brain cell?"

For a moment, Bahram stared at him with what Rhun knew was the incubus's most exasperated expression. "Seriously,

Rhun, sometimes I wonder how you make it through the night without someone beating the shit out of you."

"Hey, cut him some slack," Merle piped up, looking daggers at Bahram. "In case you forgot, he missed the last twenty years, so he's not up to date on the whole technology development, all right?" Turning to Rhun, she patiently explained, "He means a cellular—mobile—phone, like the one I have. They're called cells for short." She paused, frowning at him. "What?"

He just stared at her, his lips having formed a smile without his doing, his chest seeming too tight for what he was feeling. Curling a lock of her hair around one finger, he softly said, "Nothing, little witch."

He kept his eyes on Merle even as Bahram continued speaking.

"I don't have a landline at my place, and since I figured you might not have a cell phone, I need another way of contacting you. That's why I asked for her number."

Rhun wrenched his gaze away from his witch to shoot a dark look at the incubus. "Uh-huh."

"I need to be able to call in advance if I have to swing by my place," Bahram went on, "so I won't run into you two going at it like rabbits."

From the corner of his eye, Rhun saw Merle stir—undoubtedly to give some sort of silly protest against the insinuation. So before she could voice anything that might cause trouble again, he clapped his hand over her mouth.

"Yeah, that would be inconvenient. We don't like to share." With a downward glance at Merle, her mouth still covered by his hand, he crooned, "Ain't that right, sweetie pie? *Ow!*" He jerked back and yanked his hurting hand away, glowering at the tricky witch volcano next to him. "Did you just bite me?"

She beamed at him and patted his arm. "Affectionately, *snuggle bear*. I nipped at you affectionately."

Across the table, his treacherous friend lay flat on the seat, shaking with laughter. "She's a keeper, Rhun," he said in between choked laughs, wiping a tear from his eye.

Would that I could, Rhun thought glumly. *Would that I could.*

🪷

THEY WERE WALKING BACK TO THE CAR WHEN IT HAPPENED.

Merle had just started giving him hell about how much she'd had to pay the bar for damage compensation, and he was momentarily sidetracked by how mouthwateringly hot she looked when she was infuriated, so he never saw it coming. Trust on his past to catch up with him at the precise moment when the majority of the blood in his brain had travelled southwards.

Something massive tackled him from behind, knocking the breath out of him—and his body to the ground. He hit the pavement with a thud and the unmistakable sound of bones breaking. Pain seared through him, his mental shields shook under the assault.

Gritting his teeth against the familiar attack of demon magic, Rhun sucker-punched the son of a bitch on his back with a well-aimed elbow ram. He swiftly turned around, and charged. A quick blow to the other demon's chest, supplemented by a blast of Rhun's own power, sent the attacker slamming into the wall of the building on the other side of the street. The demon—a fear-feeding one, human-looking except for the two small horns on his head—sank to the ground as if deflated.

Rhun jumped to his feet and whirled around to Merle. "You okay?"

She stood frozen, staring at him, and nodded, though her face had lost all color and her aura was subdued by her shock. He was about to take a step toward her when she flinched and screamed, "Rhun! Watch out!"

But before she'd even finished her warning, the other demon lunged at him again, catching him off-guard. And this time he attacked Rhun mentally with such a devastating blast of power that he broke through his defenses and paralyzed him. Unable to soften the fall, Rhun crashed down with the demon on top of him, his head making harsh acquaintance with the concrete.

The world erupted in white-hot explosions of pain. Rhun's vision blurred. A brutal foreign force held his mind, incapacitating him while flushing his system with waves of pain. Every vein, every cell in his body roared with agony. Still, he fought, struggled against the choking mind control, fought with every breath he had left. Only it wouldn't be enough…

Unexpected, the waves of pain stopped as if a switch had been flipped. The mind control snapped like a severed wire. Rhun was free. His vision returned, and he blinked at the thrashing, screaming demon lying next to him—and at the fire-haired witch standing at the demon's feet, power curling around her, her face ashen as she watched the attacker wail in pain.

When the demon jerked with a last rattling breath and lay still, Merle abruptly inhaled, closed her eyes briefly and then looked at Rhun. Something inside him cringed at the haunted expression on her face. Stiffly dropping to her knees beside him, she touched his head, checked his sides, her hands trembling.

"You're hurt." Her voice was so, so hollow.

"Merle."

"I've got it." She muttered a simple healing spell, keeping her eyes averted from his, her hands on his wounds. Her face had gotten even paler, every freckle standing out starkly against the white of her skin. Her breathing was as erratic as the pattern of her aura.

"*Merle.*" He grabbed one of her hands. It was ice-cold. "Look at me."

She stopped casting the spell, clenched her other hand to a fist. Pressing her lips together, she raised her eyes to meet his. There was something broken in the blue of her gaze, deep within, a painful twist striking him hard.

"Was this the first time you took a life?" he asked softly.

If he hadn't held her hand, he might have missed the infinitesimal shudder that coursed through her body. He tightened his hold on her. Silently, she nodded.

Just as silently, he sat up and pulled her into his arms. His still broken ribs screamed in protest at the movement, but he didn't so much as wince. As he held her, Merle's tense body softened bit by bit.

"He'd have killed you." The barest whisper, close to his ear.

"But he didn't. You stopped him." He rubbed his cheek against hers.

"I turned it on him." There was a hitch in her voice, echoing the broken glint in her eyes. "What he did to you. I turned it back on him."

For a moment he was silent, breathing with her in the quiet of the night, feeling her torment. He'd been young once, and there'd been a time before he had taken his first life, a time—however short—when his soul had been untainted by spilled blood. A part of him remembered, and mourned.

"It's all right, little witch." He brushed his powers along her senses, a reassuring mental embrace. "You'll be all right. You're still good."

"I don't feel good," she whispered, so low he barely heard it.

"Such innocence." He stroked her hair. "The very fact that you regret the loss of the life you took, even your enemy's, shows how good you still are, Merle mine. When you start dropping bodies without thinking twice, *then* you should fear for your soul."

He held her tighter, his witch with her soft heart, and she let him, allowing his power to soothe her. Taking a deep breath, she put her arms around him and pressed him to her. Pain shot through him as she squeezed his ribs. His aura quivered with the slightest sign of discomfort.

She picked up on it even though he'd tried to hide it. "Oh gods, you're still hurt—and I'm crushing you! Let me up."

He decided not to point out it would take a lot more than a witch of one-hundred-thirty pounds to crush him, and instead let her disentangle herself from him to resume the healing spell while he watched her expression with alert eyes. Inside him, his ribs knotted back together, tissue merged again, wounds closed. His kind healed quickly by nature, so it only took a little incentive by Merle's magic to fix him up completely.

When she was done, she nodded at him and got up. "Let's go."

She started turning away, but he was on his feet and in front of her before she could really move.

Cupping her cheek, he studied her closely. "Are you okay?"

She answered with a shaky smile. "I will be. Eventually."

And when she leaned into his palm, something inside him hurt far more than his broken ribs had done. But this pain, it was bitter-sweet.

His thumb stroked over her cheek, traced the line of her lower lip. "Thank you."

"For what?"

He gave her a duh-look. "For saving me."

A violent ripple sliced through her energy pattern, and for the tiniest moment, he thought he glimpsed an emotion so true, so shatteringly honest and warm, it made his heart stop. Then, she closed up as if she'd pulled the shutters down, her eyes turning cold, distant.

"Yeah, well," she said, an edge in her voice, "you can't really help me when you're dead, can you?"

And with that, she walked away toward the car, leaving him staring after her with a new kind of pain inside, laced with anger that had nowhere to go.

They got in the car and drove in silence for quite a while, all things unspoken between them a quiet yet deafening force. When Merle finally said something, it startled him to hear her voice.

"So what was that all about? The attack on you."

He kept his eyes on the road. "I guess that's what I get for showing my face around in a demon bar."

She turned in the seat. "What's that supposed to mean? You're one of them. Why would they attack you?"

"Well," he hedged, still focused on the street, "let's put it this way—I wouldn't exactly win a popularity contest among demonkind."

She banged her head back against the seat and uttered a cute sound of frustration. "Gods, getting some straight info out of you is like pulling teeth. What did you do to piss off your own kind?"

"Must be my stunning good looks. They just can't take the combined force of my gorgeousness."

Even without looking, he knew she glared at him. It made him want to laugh.

"Spill it already, Mr. Self-Absorbed!"

"All right, all right," he whined, "I'm telling! Just please, *please* don't witch-slap me." Putting a hand up as if to shield his head from a blow, he gave a mock sob.

The Merle-glare intensified, and he grinned, slanting a glance at her.

"What I'm doing for you now...Well, I used to do that for a living."

"Annoying the hell out of people?"

He chuckled at that. "I like your sense of humor, little witch. But no, annoying my fellow beings does not get me paid. Unfortunately so—that would be the best job ever." Sighing, he dreamily stared ahead.

Merle cleared her throat.

"Hm?" He snapped out of his reverie. "Oh. Right." Shrugging one shoulder, he said, "I used to hunt down and eliminate rogue demons."

"You were a bounty hunter?"

"Of sorts."

Silence.

Then, "Why did you do it?"

"What do you mean?"

"You're demon. Yet you chose to hunt your own kind. Why?"

He snorted. "The money, of course. What else?"

She regarded him silently for a minute, and he got the distinct feeling she was putting too much together in that clever witch head of hers.

"Who did you hunt them down for?" she finally asked.

Now *he* was silent for a moment. "Witches," was his quiet answer.

There was a small intake of breath. "That's the work you did for my grandmother, isn't it?"

He nodded. No reason to deny it.

More silence, this time charged in a way that made him edgy.

"You didn't really do it for the money."

He stared at the road, remaining quiet.

"I know for a fact," Merle went on relentlessly, "that the witch community does not have extensive funds, so whatever they paid you can't have been much. You could have gotten a better-paying job than that, easily, if you only cared about money." Her gaze bored into him. "But you didn't, did you? Why, then?" After a moment, quietly, "Was it because of her?"

He gritted his teeth, shot a dark look at her. "To make this clear, little witch, not everything I did was for Rowan."

"Oh?" She raised her brows, and he didn't like the glint in her eyes one bit. "There was another motivation? What was it?"

This damn witch was nothing if not persistent. A stubborn pain in his ass. Ignoring her would get him nowhere.

Keeping his eyes on the traffic, he said, "Whether you believe it or not, there are some things I consider morally inexcusable."

"Like what?"

His stomach knotted together into a ball of hurt. His hands

tightened on the steering wheel until his knuckles flashed white. "Eating children, for example."

That earned him a shocked silence. Merle swallowed audibly.

"There are laws," he went on. "Boundaries. Things you do and things you don't do. But in the world you and I live in, my little witch, there are few who care about where to draw the line. And there are even fewer who care enough to keep it drawn."

In the ensuing silence, he chanced a glimpse at her, and frowned at the unexpected grin on her face.

"What?" He flicked his gaze from her to the traffic and back to her. That grin of hers made him twitchy. "What's so funny?"

She slowly shook her head, still ominously amused. "I don't believe it."

"What?"

"You were a demon cop!"

He winced, and the car swerved precariously on the road before he caught himself. Grimacing, he gave her a pained look. "Do not ever say that again. That is just hurtful."

"Officer Rhun," she said musingly, the corners of her mouth twitching up, "to protect and to serve."

"Merle."

"Did you wear a uniform?"

All right, that's it. "If I say yes, will that thought make you wet?"

That effectively shut her up, and while she blushed a gorgeous shade of red, he took his turn grinning.

After a few more minutes they reached Bahram's apartment, set in a turn-of-the-century house in downtown, which had been—by the looks of it—renovated since Rhun had last been here. It now boasted the splendor of the original façade from when it had been built a hundred years ago, a fact Rhun knew because he'd been around at the time.

The apartment itself—a spacious two-bedroom suite—had

been redone, too, with new hardwood floors, state-of-the-art kitchen and modern bathroom appliances. Some of the old furniture was still in place, though, and even a few other items Rhun recognized.

Grazing his fingers over the smooth black leather of his favorite armchair, he smirked and muttered, "Stored, my ass." Seemed more like his friend had enjoyed some of Rhun's old belongings very personally. Not that he could blame Bahram, when there had been no indication of him ever coming back from the Shadows.

While he checked the armchair for scratches and stains—knowing the incubus, he'd probably enjoyed the chair together with a female at some point—Merle put her duffel bag down next to the couch. Having finished her tour of the apartment as well, she slumped down with a sigh and took out her grimoire.

"I'm going to start working through this, and it's going to take me a few hours..." She patted the thick tome with a look on her face that spoke volumes itself. "...so you might want to find something to pass the time. I saw the DVD box set of *Lord of the Rings* here on the shelf—it's the extended version, too, so if you want to watch that, you'll be thoroughly entertained for at least eleven hours."

He stopped examining a chink in the leather and stared at her. "They made it into an eleven-hour movie?"

"*Three* movies. And good ones, too. I think Peter Jackson did a fantastic job. They shot it in New Zealand." She all but bounced on the cushion with enthusiasm, her eyes gleaming. "Christopher Lee plays Saruman."

"Well," he said, rising to his feet. "Now that does sound like fun." Though he had a feeling it would be even more fun to watch it with her—he could just imagine her telling him tidbits about the production and the actors during the movies, whispered explanations that would make her eyes glow with joy, and his chest tightened with how much he *wanted* that. It tightened even more because it was something he'd never have.

Merle had gotten up to pull out a large box from the shelf apparently accommodating Bahram's movie collection, and she proceeded to put a disc looking like a CD into the player beneath the TV.

"I'll go study the grimoire in the guest room, so you'll have the living room with the TV all to yourself."

He watched her set everything up, eyeing her luscious behind when she bent over. Damn if it didn't look exquisitely strokable, the way her jeans molded to her curves...

"Enjoy," she said with a smile, and handed him a remote control.

"Hmm. I will."

After picking up her grimoire from the couch, she started for the door.

"Merle."

She faced him, her eyebrows raised.

He studied her for a moment. "Tell me why you're not a member of the Elders."

Her face fell. She peered at her feet.

"You're the head of your family," he continued, watching her expression closely, noticing how, along with her aura, she seemed to withdraw into herself, stuffing whatever she felt deep inside. He wouldn't let her get away with that. "By rights that makes you an Elder witch, too, doesn't it?"

She shook her head. "It doesn't work that way."

"Then how?"

Avoiding his eyes, she said in a quiet voice, "You have to claim your place among the other Elders."

When she started to turn away, he stepped in front of her. "Claim how?" She wasn't the only one who could be stubborn.

"You need to step up and declare you're willing to take the position, privileges and obligations and all. There's a ritual for that. A complicated one. You have to get it right or else you're rejected."

Gut churning with a mixture of inexplicable anger and

disappointment, he regarded her for a minute. "You never claimed your place."

She didn't respond, just stared at her feet again.

"Why?" It came out harsher than he'd intended.

"I didn't feel like it," she muttered.

"You didn't *feel* like it?"

"It's a lot of responsibility," she hedged.

"And it also gives you power! Gives you special rights, a say in how your own community is led. Influence among the very people who are hunting your ass right now. How could you pass on a chance like that? Why would you not claim privileges that are rightfully yours?"

He virtually *saw* when her patience snapped. Her gaze turned steely, her aura flared, and balling her hands to fists she shouted, "Because I'd have to live up to them!"

He took a breath, his lips twisting into a bitter smile. "You're scared, little witch."

"I'm not," she spit out, but from the way her spine stiffened and her energy pattern wavered with resentment and fear, he knew he'd hit home.

"You're scared you're not strong enough," he kept on. "You're hiding behind your fear instead of stepping up to your destiny and accepting who you are."

"I know damn well who I am, and I do accept it!"

"No, you don't. You're still wishing it was Moira instead of you."

She jerked back as if he'd slapped her. All color left her face.

He wouldn't give her an inch in this. Stepping even closer, he distinctly said, "You're hung up about the fact that she and your mother died and left you to take their place. You're thinking this is not your burden to bear, that you're not meant to do this. Am I right?"

She glared at him, her pulse racing loud enough to ring in his ears.

"*Am I right?*"

"Yes! Yes, okay? It was never supposed to be me, it should have been my mom and then Moira. I was never meant to lead!" She trembled all over, hands still clenched tight, her face a rigid mask.

He leaned in until their noses almost touched. "But you are now, little witch, so deal with it."

"I'm too young to be an Elder! You have to be wise and experienced and—and strong, *dammit.*" Her voice broke a little. "I'm none of that! I can't even protect my own sister." A sheen of tears glimmered on her eyes, and it tore him apart on the inside.

"You *are* strong enough," he said, his voice sharp with the force it took him to restrain the confusing anger he felt, "and it fucking beats the shit out of me why you can't see that." He made a pause and took a calming breath, studying the lines of her face, those striking eyes of the clearest blue, now wide and so full of raw emotions. "You should claim your rightful place among the Elders. You're already leading your line—I think it's time you claimed the privileges that go along with it, too."

And right there it hit him. Hit him so hard he almost staggered back. He shouldn't care about whether or not she ever claimed what was due to her. There was absolutely no use in directing a tirade at her about becoming an Elder—because when he was done with her, she wouldn't be able to claim anything with the Elders anymore. Ever.

He quickly turned away, fighting the painful twist in his heart. "Go study your grimoire, Merle." His voice sounded as weary as he suddenly felt.

From behind him came the soft pads of feet moving away on hardwood floors. She left the room without saying another word.

☙❧

Almost twelve hours and a marathon of all three *Lord of*

the Rings movies later, Rhun was indeed well-entertained and—in spite of his prejudice against movie adaptations of his favorite books—positively surprised. It had also lifted his mood, which had made a free fall for the basement after his argument with Merle.

Happily humming a tune, he was in the process of putting Bahram's DVD collection in alphabetical order—as it should be—when Merle came back in the living room. He'd heard her shuffle and move about the apartment earlier, using the bathroom and probably raiding the kitchen for food, but she hadn't come to talk to him in between, and he'd left her alone, too, figuring they both needed some space. Him probably more than her, though.

During the past hours, he'd been trying to get his head straight again, and—most importantly—his heart. It had taken up the annoying habit of beating faster for a certain witch, a witch who now leaned in the doorway, eyeing him with an unreadable expression on her beautiful face.

Dammit, he shouldn't feel such joy at seeing her. Gritting his teeth, he focused on the DVDs again.

In fact, there was a lot he shouldn't be feeling when it came to her, for it would only make it all the harder to use and discard her as he planned. If he could, he'd keep his distance from her to retain some semblance of control over his feelings, but ironically fucked up as this situation was, he had to get even closer to her in order to get what he needed.

Breathe, Rhun. You can do this. He'd never had a problem with being a cold-hearted bastard when the situation called for it. This wouldn't be any different. Right?

"Find anything in your grimoire, little witch?"

"No such luck. Would have been too easy, I guess."

He clucked his tongue and resumed rearranging the DVDs.

"Enjoyed the movies?"

"Surprisingly so, yes," he said. "Though I am begrudging the fact they omitted Tom Bombadil. Gollum, however, was a piece of art. He should win an Oscar for that split personality performance."

Silence.

Slowly, Rhun turned to Merle, his neck prickling with suspicion. She'd come closer, her eyes fixed on him in a way that made him wary. Wary as one would be of a cobra, curled up in feigned relaxation. He'd never wished for his demon powers more desperately than now—the sun had long gone up and dulled his senses, those senses that usually allowed him to read her mood quite accurately. Now, he only had the means of a mere human to guess what she was feeling. Not for the first time in his life did he pity those clueless males of her species. How did they ever survive around their females?

She still stared, all cobra-like.

"Merle?"

She blinked, slowly. "What?"

"Are you...okay?"

"Why?" Her face still had that strange expression.

"Because you look like you either want to choke me or eat me alive." *Or both?*

"Neither," she said, and her voice had that husky note, the one it got when—

All further thought abruptly dissolved into nothingness as Merle closed the distance between them, grabbed the upper hem of his T-shirt and pulled him down for a kiss. Not a peck or a chaste meeting of lips, but a full-blown, no-holds-barred, passionate kiss infused with all the fire his witch volcano possessed.

And—*fucking hell*—it inflamed him faster than a burning match thrown into dried grass.

Tangling his hand in her hair, he took control of the kiss, of her body, of *her*, and with a groan he whirled them both around and pushed her up against the wall. She moaned, panting, and jumped up to wrap her legs around his waist.

Whatever plans he'd had to play it cool, to use her without

blinking, they burnt to cinders along with his soul as she nipped at his lower lip, her fingers digging into his hair, her soft body rubbing against his hardness.

And he knew it right then.

Yep, this witch would be his undoing.

CHAPTER 13

Merle couldn't breathe. Well, not exactly. Pinned to the wall by a gorgeous bulk of uncompromising *maleness*, her mouth being ravaged in a way that turned her core to liquid fire, all she could do was gasp for air when that damn delicious demon gave her a second's reprieve.

Though what she inhaled then wasn't air—it was Rhun. It was him she drew in with every choking breath, and his essence —raw, sensual, dark—burned a path down to her soul, a scorching heat settling inside, taking possession.

She rubbed against him, aflame with a hunger she'd never felt before, not like this. Every lick of his tongue, every nip on her lips sent her farther down in a spiral of desire and need threatening to rip her apart.

His hand slid under her sweater, cupped her breast, squeezed. An erotic demand echoing her own.

Gods knew, she'd tried to stay away from him. She'd tried to tamp down her desire for him in their time apart, but he was her drug of choice. All those dull hours working through the grimoire, only to come to another dead end and find herself back in square one, had merely intensified the simmering hunger she had for him. With every passing minute, the gnawing need to feel him, the craving for his touch had deepened, until she'd been aware of nothing else but his presence in the adjoining room.

And that was when she'd decided to damn it all to hell and take what she needed more than her next breath.

She now luxuriated in the feel of him, the silken strands of hair underneath her fingers, the dark, spicy scent of him, the rasp of stubble on his chin against her throat as he kissed a trail from her mouth to her neck. And—*gods have mercy*—all that male muscle and contained strength pressing against her, between her legs, all but crushing her to the wall.

But she needed more.

Her hands travelled down his back, came around to the front of his jeans. He tightened his grip on her hair when she opened the button.

"*Merle.*" A raw, guttural warning.

She met his eyes, almost black with desire, the pupils fully dilated. Every line on his face was taut, and she knew how much he still held back. Not that she wanted him to.

She lowered the zipper, not taking her eyes off his. Her pulse raced, her blood was infused with maddening *want*, as she closed her hand around the hard length of his arousal. Hissing out a breath through clenched teeth, he grasped the back of her neck and squeezed, his other hand punching the wall.

"Fuck." His breathing turned erratic, mirroring the speed of hers.

"Yes." The corners of her mouth curved in mischievous amusement, seemingly misplaced amidst the swirl of carnal desire inside her. "Let's."

Something flashed in his eyes. His hand on her neck moved up to cup her cheek, a gentle touch, so at odds with the whisper of brutal strength in his tense muscles. "Dammit, little witch, I wanted to do this slow." His voice was hoarse, deeper than usual, rasping over her senses that were already too sharp, too sore. "But, fuck that, I can't do slow right now."

"Good. I don't want you to." Her voice was husky, too, and it seemed to erode the last of his control.

Within seconds, he'd stripped her of her jeans and panties, and before she could draw her next breath, he had her up against the wall again, her legs around his hips. He grabbed her thighs, spreading her open. His erection nudged at her entrance, which was slick with her desire.

"Wait," she breathed, her hands slamming against his chest. "Wait!"

To his utter credit, he did. Trembling with the effort it apparently took him to pause, he held himself poised, staring at her. "Changed your mind?" It was a barely intelligible growl. "If yes, I'll let you go, but Bahram will not like what I'm gonna do to his furniture then." His hand tightened on her thigh.

She shook her head, heart hammering in her chest. "Do you —you're infertile, right?" Wow, she'd actually managed to retain some common sense in the throes of her Rhun fever.

His eyes flashed as he understood her intent. "Right. As long as I'm unmated."

Her fingers curled into his T-shirt.

"And," he added before she could pose her next question, "my kind doesn't carry human diseases."

"All right," she breathed, relaxing—and then she deliberately scratched a circle pattern on his chest.

He groaned, slammed her back against the wall and thrust inside her. She cried out, her hands clutching his shoulders. He was heat and power, pleasure laced with pain, and he strained her with a demand for submission running in tremors through her body. And, oh, was she happy to oblige.

Her breath was a whispered moan as she melted against him, as he withdrew and thrust back in, setting up a rhythm of primal urgency. She clutched his shoulders, relishing the flex of his muscles underneath her hands. All of him, his lethal power, that bruising strength that could hurt and maim, now focused on her with a whole other intent. He took her with a ferocity skirting the line between rough and brutal. Her legs tightened around him, need and pleasure coiling inside her.

She was hungry for him, so, so hungry. And this raw outburst of lust, this clash of cravings too long denied, was just what she'd wanted.

With every hard, fast thrust, she held on tighter, her nails scratching over his skin underneath his T-shirt, no doubt leaving marks. A part of her wanted to draw blood. Ached to tear off his skin until they both merged as one. It was a desperate need to connect with him, the likes of which she'd never known.

He took her mouth with unbridled possessiveness, with such rough passion, she felt his claim stamped on every cell in her body.

"Mine." A murmur against her lips, in time with a shove of his hips, hard, unleashed, branding. "You're mine, Merle. *Mine.*"

Her breath hitched. Her heartbeat thudded in every inch of her heated skin. Muscles tightening with pleasure, she dug her nails in his back, feeling his skin break.

His hand closed around her throat, impossibly controlled, almost gentle. His voice was anything but. "*Say it.*"

"Yes! Yours!" She cried it out, coming apart with a climax that left her shattered in the best of ways.

He thrust even faster, harder, slamming her hips against the wall, and when he came with a groan, his face buried in the curve of her neck, he tangled his hand in her hair in a devastating mix of violence and tenderness.

It broke down the last of her defenses.

For a minute, he remained still, his breath coursing the skin of her neck, his hand in her hair. She was torn open to him on a level she didn't quite grasp, a new, deep vulnerability, as if he'd broken her down to put her back together. Fear sliced through her, kicking up her pulse.

And then, just like that, he put her back together in all the right places by massaging her skull in the way that made her toes curl.

"*Rhun.*" A whispered prayer.

He lifted his head, his eyes still dark with need, his breathing not quite back to normal. "Not enough," he said, his hand coming down to stroke her neck.

She frowned at him, uncurling her toes. "What?"

He released her and took a step back, only to hoist her up on his shoulder the next instant. "I want more." His voice was scraped gravel. Patting her bare butt, he carried her off toward the bedroom.

"Oh," was all she could say before the breath rushed out of her. Not that she'd wanted to say any more. She was very much okay with his intention.

Walking past the kitchen, he did a double take, stepped back and snatched something off the sideboard. She angled her head to see what it was, and he held up the water bottle for her to look at.

"You'll need that," he simply said and walked on, stroking his fingers up the back of her thigh, to the wet spot between her legs still pulsing with aftershocks of pleasure.

She bit back a moan at the teasing touch on her exposed, intimate skin, squirmed with the overload of sudden sensation —and received a slap on her behind for her wiggling.

Her breath caught on a gasp of incredulity. "Did you just *spank* me?"

"Affectionately, my little witch volcano," he said, dark amusement echoing in his voice. "I swatted your lovely ass affectionately."

His hand now rubbed gently over the sensitive skin of her butt cheek, turning the lingering sting of his slap to something else entirely—something insidiously pleasurable. Heat and excitement rose in her core, shot down to the thrumming beat between her legs. Face flushed, her heart pounded faster, and a totally unintentional sound of pleasure escaped her lips. *Dammit.*

"Liked that, didn't you?" Rhun murmured, and the warm appreciation in his tone almost did her in.

He reached the bedroom and set her down on the mattress, putting the water bottle on the nightstand.

"Now we can do slow." He looked at her with molten heat in his eyes, a promise of sensual depths that made her all weak and needy inside.

Sliding back to sit against the headboard, she pressed her naked thighs together as he took off his T-shirt. The sight of him, it was a feast for her eyes. Ivory skin—so *bitable*—stretched taut over toned muscles the lines of which she wanted to trace with her tongue. Every movement, however small, was a quiet testament to the strength he contained, the deadly power humming underneath the surface. And his face —that smug glint in his gaze, the smirk on his lips, spoke of an arrogance that should have infuriated her. Instead it only enhanced his allure, made him all the more damnably attractive.

Fire licked at her veins, ignited her blood. Gods, if he had the slightest idea of how he *really* affected her, of how far she was head over heels lost to him, it would be nothing short of devastating. For right here, right now, she'd let him do about anything to her.

He prowled toward the bed, his jeans half-fastened, riding low on hips that would tempt angels to fall. The bulge in the front was barely covered, revealing enough to make her drool like a dog over a treat. Swallowing, she closed her eyes, her cheeks heating. She'd never, ever, wanted to lick a man so badly. What was happening to her?

"Interesting face color, little witch."

Her eyes snapped open, focused on him. Lips curved upward, head tilted, he studied her closely with too perceptive eyes.

"What were you thinking about?" He'd prowled closer still, now putting one knee on the mattress, coming after her.

Her face, already scorched, became impossibly hotter. "I can't tell you." Even though she might have been so forward as to jump his bones, she hadn't shed all her inhibitions yet. Thinking about it was one thing, doing it another—but *saying* it? And dammit, he was cocky enough already—she almost snickered at that pun—there was no need to tell him how mouthwatering his—"I can't."

Grabbing her ankles, he pulled her down toward him, until she lay flat on her back underneath his overpowering frame. "Yes, you can." His hands, hot, branding, running over her hips, up to her waist, pulling off her sweater. "Tell me."

"No."

"Hmm." A kiss on her belly. "Later, then." It sounded like a mix between a promise and a threat.

He nuzzled the curve of her waist, one hand sliding under her back, unhooking her bra. A sigh escaped her as the material loosened and softly rubbed over nipples that were too tight, too sensitive. They ached to be touched, soothed, so much so that when Rhun removed her bra and then flicked his tongue over one hardened bud, Merle couldn't help moaning—not in relief, but in sensual agony. He licked the other one, blew a breath on it, and her body shook with the teasing sensation that wasn't enough, not nearly enough.

"Rhun," she ground out. She was *this* close to begging— which was probably exactly what he wanted.

The wicked gleam in his eyes was proof to her suspicion. "Yes, dear?"

She had the sweetest urge to strangle him for his arrogant calm. "Stop teasing me!"

He clucked his tongue. "Bossy, much?"

"You can handle it."

His smirk made her stomach flutter with a thousand fairy wings. "I can indeed, little witch of mine." And then, without warning, he grabbed her wrists and pinned them above her head.

Squirming, she wiggled against his hold, but his grasp was adamant, absolute, and she didn't gain an inch. She couldn't move. The realization of it, it sent shivers of pleasure over her skin, a tingling surge of heat down to where his thigh was wedged between her legs. He shifted by a fraction, and the sensation of the rough material of his jeans on her bare, intimate flesh zinged more pleasure up and down inside her.

"Now," he said with languorous relish, "where was I?"

"You were torturing me?"

"Torture is such a harsh word." He held her wrists in place with one hand, using the other to circle her nipples with his fingers, making her pant. "I prefer the term *playing*."

She gave him her darkest glare. "I'm not having much fun."

"Really?" He rolled one tight bud between his thumb and forefinger, pinched it.

A sharp bolt of excitement seared through her, and her back arched, pushing her breast toward him. "Well," she breathed, "maybe a little."

"Hmm." Eyes glowing with mischievous enjoyment, he bent down to suck on the neglected nipple, grazing it with his teeth.

Merle whimpered, need building inside, an avalanche of pleasure in the making, and all she wanted was for it to bury her. Rhun came up to kiss her, slowly, thoroughly, moving his thigh between her legs in the same rhythm as his tongue stroked her lips, invaded her mouth. It nearly drove her insane.

"Rhun, please." Somewhere along the way, she'd lost her pretense of being too proud to beg. She needed to feel him, all of him, a visceral craving to have him claim her once more.

"I do like to hear you say that," he muttered.

That cocky grin, it made her want to slap him—and kiss him at the same time. But—*gods be thanked*—he stopped teasing her and unfastened his jeans. She wiggled her hips in anticipation, her body tense, so tense with need, and when he pushed in, her head fell back on the mattress. How could anything feel so sinfully good?

Still holding her wrists together with one hand, he let her feel his weight as he shoved in all the way. The pressure of his body pinning her down, his fingers tight around her wrists, oh, it was enough to incite every primal female instinct in her that relished being overpowered and *taken*. He thrust in hard and then withdrew deliciously slowly, until only the tip of him was still buried inside her. He repeated the move, and the mix of roughness and slow friction made her burn oh-so-good. Just a little further, just a little more…

He stopped, almost outside her.

Her breath caught at the abrupt interruption of their slow spiral into shared pleasure, and she frowned at him, all her focus coming back to his face, his eyes—which now held a glint of wicked calculation.

"Good," he said, voice darkly sensual. "I see I have your attention. Let's talk."

"Say *what*?" He wanted to *talk*? Right *now*?

"I've been wondering," he went on casually, "about what's going on in that pretty witch head of yours."

Right at this moment? There were vivid images of how she could make a certain demon on top of her suffer a slow and painful death.

"It's day." He moved ever so lightly, pushing just a little more inside.

It was enough to make her pant. "So?"

"You don't need to feed me." He brushed a finger along the inside of her thigh, up, farther up, to where all her nerves seemed to be bundled in one spot, aching to be touched. He skirted around it. "Why did you come to me just now? You had no reason to."

She tried to focus, to keep her wits together. It was damn near impossible. "I guess I was bored."

He nipped at her lower lip. "Wrong answer."

She wiggled her hips to get closer to him, to *feel* him. A sharp swat on her butt made her freeze.

He held her hips in place with one hand. "Why, Merle?"

"Fine. All right." She trembled with how much she wanted him to move. "I had an itch that needed scratching."

His expression darkened. "By just anyone?"

She was so high-strung with desire, she couldn't lie anymore. And there was something in his eyes that made her heart cringe, made her want to tell him the truth. "No." It was a whisper. "I wanted to be with *you*."

He touched her cheek, his thumb tracing her trembling lips. "Why?"

She swallowed, mouth gone dry. "You take the weight off me. When I'm with you, it doesn't hurt as much." Her heart, it split wide open as she said those words.

For a moment, he stared at her with silent intensity, with those eyes the color of a yet-undiscovered lagoon. The kiss he gave her then was so unexpectedly tender, it broke her inside. His lips lingered on her mouth, his breath embracing her own, and his hand closed around her throat in gentle possessiveness.

"Now," he said in a timbre that was a caress in itself, "tell me what thought made you blush a blazing scarlet earlier."

"You sneaky bastard," she groaned. She still felt the pulse of her desire between her legs, around the delicious hardness that he *refused to move*. And she knew he'd remain waiting until she told him.

"Ah, I love how you talk in bed, my little witch." A smirk that could steal her sanity. "Now spit it out."

Her face glowed with heat again. "I was thinking of how much I want to lick you—everywhere." A pause, more searing fire in her cheeks. "You know. One spot, um, especially."

Raw hunger swirled in his eyes, dark shadows underneath that clear lagoon water. His hand tightened around her wrists.

"But," she went on, spurred by a sudden, wicked impulse, "I won't ever do that unless you *move now, dammit*."

"You," he ground out on a barely held-back groan, "are devious."

"That's rich coming from you."

Her amusement shattered in a scream of pure joy when he finally thrust again. Every single nerve ending in her body flared awake as he rocked against her, increasing speed, fueling the fire in her core. Just when she thought she might sob from the sheer pressure of the building yet blocked release, he put his hand between their bodies and rubbed her clit.

The world exploded into shards of pleasure. She bucked and trembled under the force of her climax, moaning the name that haunted her soul.

He let go of her wrists, only to catch her hands with his own, and at the height of his release, he intertwined their fingers. Putting his forehead to hers, he muttered something, a harsh curse turning the air blue and possibly involving the words "witch" and "undoing." Merle wasn't sure. Her mind was shaken, her thoughts scrambled, and she might not even have noticed if the building had collapsed around them.

All she knew, at this moment, was that if the building and everything else did collapse around them, he was the one thing she'd want to hold on to.

The realization of it jolted her, made her heart beat faster with fear and bittersweet agony. She was falling for Rhun, and the impact might smash her to smithereens. For he was the one thing she *couldn't* hold on to. However this all might turn out, she wasn't allowed to keep him—the Elders would make sure she'd bind him in the Shadows again.

And even if, by a miracle, she'd be able to give him his freedom back, she wasn't foolish enough to think he'd even consider staying with her. Why should he? To him, she was probably a nuisance, the witch who held him bound, who threatened to send him back into the Shadows. While he obviously enjoyed being intimate with her, that didn't mean he felt anything but a physical attraction.

So, in short, he was a heartbreak waiting to happen. If her having to bind him back in the Shadows didn't do the job, his leaving her eventually would.

Rhun stirred, reached over to the nightstand and grabbed the bottle of water, opened it and held it up to her mouth. "Drink." His voice was still hoarse, a deep tremor rumbling down to her bones.

She took the bottle and drank with greedy gulps, harboring a thirst going beyond the physical. He was still inside, his weight half-settled on her, skin on skin, his heat seeping into every cell. A caging position that should have intimidated her, but with every breath that brought her chest up to his, that increased the searing contact of their bodies, she felt a rush of purest joy in her veins.

Oh, she was so, so screwed.

Maybe she could still salvage some of her heart, her soul, her mind, maybe if she pulled back now and went cold, buried the fledgling hope for the impossible, maybe then she'd get out of this halfway sane. She'd lived through worse in her life, hadn't she? All she had to do was put some distance between them, and a major wall of ice.

While Rhun put the water bottle back on the nightstand, Merle scrambled out from under him with panic beating under her skin. She managed to crawl to the edge of the bed before Rhun's hand closed around her ankle.

"And just where do you think you're going?"

She kept her face turned away from him, lest he read the maelstrom of emotions on her face. "I'll sleep in the other room."

"Oh, no, you won't. You're staying right here." With a move of casual strength, he pulled her into his embrace, her back to his chest, one of his arms sneaking around her waist, pressing her to him. "I'm a snuggle bear, remember?" He nuzzled her neck, inhaled her scent.

Inside, she trembled. His breath coursed the skin of her

shoulder, his hand spread over her heart, and she was desperately trying to not let him take it.

"This doesn't change anything between us," she whispered. Maybe if she said it out loud, it would make it true. *One more time, with more strength.* "This doesn't change anything."

"And here I was thinking you'd wanna have my babies now." A melodramatic sigh. "This always happens to me after sex."

The giggle escaped her before she knew what was happening. Through the turmoil of emotions twisting her heart, through the fear and the anguish and the panic wrecking her on the inside, unexpected laughter rose up, streams of sunshine breaking through clouds. She giggled like mad, her shoulders shaking, her breath coming in short pants in between bouts of laughs, and the fact that Rhun chuckled behind her only made it worse.

They lay like this for so many minutes, laughing together while wrapped into one.

When they both had quieted down, Rhun kicked off his jeans and then immediately claimed her for his arms again, turning her to face him. His hand tangled in her hair, one leg put over hers, he planted a kiss on the top of her head and sighed with unconcealed contentment.

Against all odds, Merle felt strangely at peace. There was just no room in her heart for anything else at the moment. Well, except for her fear for Maeve, of course. Ever-present, it sat like a thorn embedded in her flesh, stung again each time she moved. Still, the strange, unbidden, warm and fuzzy happiness she felt in Rhun's arms, it had managed to subdue her sorrow, if only for a bit, just enough so it wouldn't crush her anymore with every breath she took.

"Rhun?" A whisper breaking the caress of silence.

"Mhm?"

Hesitating for a moment, she then said quietly, "I don't think you're evil."

The following silence was cut with a razor-edge. "I'm not exactly good either, little witch."

"You don't kill indiscriminately, do you?"

His body tensed by the slightest fraction. "No."

"How many innocent lives have you taken?"

The longest pause, woven with threads of darkness. When his answer came, it surprised her. "One."

She blinked, took a breath, and inhaled his scent, now laced with the aroma of sex. It was an intoxicating mix. "I assumed—I thought you must have taken more to be bound in the Shadows. My grandmother…"

"…saw what she wanted to believe. She didn't bother asking."

His cryptic statement made her frown. "What happened back then, Rhun? Tell me." When his silence crept into her heart, she spread her hand on his chest. "Please."

A moment of consideration. Then, trust. "Rowan found me in a room drenched in blood," he began slowly, quietly, "full of bodies, so many you couldn't see the floor. When she saw me, I was in the process of breaking the last one alive, after I'd drained him dry. I snapped his spine as she stepped in. She took one look at the room, at me, covered in blood, and bound me."

He paused, and the quiet echoed with so much pain, turned bitter with time. Her fingers curled against his chest.

"What she didn't know," Rhun continued, "what I didn't get to tell her because she never let me, was that I'd been in that room for days, weeks for all I know, immobilized and chained to the floor, starving. I'd woken up there after I'd been jumped and knocked out. The demon fuckers who'd taken me made sure to drive me insane with hunger, so much so that I halluci-nated. Then they brought the humans." A small silence, broken only by his tight intake of breath. "They killed one by one in front of me, slowly, so I could taste their blood and pain in the air without being able to feed on it. The last one, they kept for me. Before they released me, they called Rowan. They wanted me to be found by a witch who would bind me." Underneath her hand, the muscles in his chest turned to granite. "Bastards did a good job."

Merle was shocked speechless for a while. His heart beat against her palm, ten times, twenty times, thirty. She lost count. Inside her, a new sense of betrayal rose, and it had nothing to do with her own life.

"You don't believe me." His hand tightened in her hair. "Didn't expect you to. After all, I'm just a de—"

"You didn't mean to kill that man, did you?"

Only when he exhaled, heavily, did she notice he'd been holding his breath. "I wouldn't have taken his life if I hadn't been starved out of my mind."

The twist in his voice, the need in it, made her realize—this was the first time in twenty years that he spoke of what had happened, the first time he could tell his side of the story. Just the thought of what it must have been like for him to be locked away in painful darkness with a truth in his heart that he couldn't voice to anyone else, it made her ache for him.

"They set you up," she whispered, and her nails dug into his skin. Rage licked up her spine. "Why?"

"Told you. I'm not exactly demonkind's darling. My career choice was a pain in the ass for many of my brethren."

She swallowed, gut churning with silent outrage. On an impulse, she wrapped her arms around him, a gesture of comfort as much for him as for herself, for she felt a kind of hurt that could unhinge—and holding on to him, it steadied her.

"I'm sorry," she whispered.

Rhun grew still, so very, very quiet that she thought he might have been snuffed out like a candle. Then his arms tightened around her, crushed her to him, and against her cheek, his heart drummed faster than her own.

CHAPTER 14

Merle awoke to the faint sound of her cell phone ringing. With an effort, she pried her eyes open. The pull of sleep was so strong, it took her a moment to see anything at all, to get her brain working in a logical way. Her bones were molten in her body, every single muscle weighed down by blocks of concrete. She peered at the clock on the nightstand. It was half past four in the afternoon—they'd only slept about three hours. *No wonder I feel like something the cat has dragged in.*

The phone was still ringing, the sound coming through the open door to the hallway where she'd dumped her purse earlier. With a groan of exhaustion, Merle disentangled herself from Rhun, who had wrapped himself around her in his sneaky, monopolizing way. She wriggled free of one of his arms and one leg, but as soon as she pried off the other two limbs, the first two snuck around her again.

"Rhun. Phone. Need to answer."

He grunted.

"It might be something important. Let me go."

Grumbling, he did as she asked, not opening his eyes. "If it's Bahram," he said, his voice all sleep-gravelly sexy, "tell him to go fuck himself."

"Rhun!"

"What? He knows better than to call me during the day." He turned over and buried his face in the pillow.

"He's your friend!"

"That's why he knows better," came the muffled reply.

Shaking her head, Merle got up and walked into the hallway, retrieving her cell from her purse. One look at the display and the caller ID had her stomach dropping to her feet.

"Hello Sarah," she answered the call, wide awake now. "Has something happened? Is everything all right with my dad?"

"Hi," the nurse said. "Well, actually, no, that's why I'm calling." A pause, filled with a sigh. "He did it again. I'm sorry. You know we've been trying to keep a closer eye on him, but we've just gotten three new residents and things have been a little busy. He managed to sneak by me and ran."

Deep inside Merle, a part of her puffed up with pride, even as anxiety beat under her skin. "Have you informed anyone else yet?"

"No. I called you first thing, like always."

"Thank you, Sarah. I really appreciate it."

"Of course, sweetie. Just make sure to bring him back soon, before my boss gets wind of this."

If it was discovered that one of the residents of the home had the nasty habit of escaping on a regular basis, and that Sarah had not reported it, it would be her ass on the line. The nurse was a former class mate and high school friend of Merle's, and she and Merle had an unofficial agreement for situations such as these—when Merle's father fled the nursing home, it was Merle who would find and return him. She wouldn't let anyone else drag him back like an escaped inmate from a prison. It was bad enough he had to live like this.

Sarah helped her, did this as a favor for her because Merle was the reason she'd made it through high school, but it was risky and could cost Sarah her job if something went wrong.

"I know," Merle now said. "Don't worry. I'm getting him right away. Thank you so much."

She hung up and immediately dialed another number. Lily picked up after the second ring.

"Hey. You all right?"

"Lil, what's the situation at my house right now?"

A pause, the sound of footsteps as Lily apparently retreated out of someone else's earshot. "Isabel is over there," she then said, her voice hushed. "Why? Do you need something from your house?"

"No. My dad's escaped again."

"Oh shit."

"Yeah, exactly. I need to pick him up. Can you…?"

"…set my aunt's hair on fire so she runs screaming from your house? You got it."

Merle grinned despite herself. "Lil."

"I can distract her, yes. Draw her away from the house, but only for a bit, so you need to hurry, okay?"

"Thank you. You're the best."

"I know." Lily's smile shone through her voice.

"Hey, by the way," Merle said, walking into the living room, "any info on how to break the blocking spell?"

"Nope, sorry. I haven't found squat so far. But I'm on it. Raiding the whole Murray library, and you know how extensive that one is." Merle was about to express her gratitude for her help again, as Lily added, "And stop thanking me, silly."

Smiling, Merle said goodbye and hung up. She collected half her clothes from the living room and went to the bedroom for the other half. Rhun lay on his back on the bed, propped up on his elbows, frowning at her as she got dressed. And damn if he didn't look especially yummy nude amidst tangled sheets.

"What's going on?" he asked.

"We have to go."

"I got that much. What for?"

Without looking at him, she said, "My dad ran away from the nursing home he's living in, and I need to pick him up and bring him back."

Rhun moved off the bed instantly. "Your *father*? He's alive?"

"Yes." *Barely.*

"Why is he living in a nursing home?"

She walked into the hallway. "We have to hurry, come on. Lily can only get Isabel away from my house for a little bit. We have to move now."

"Wait." Rhun was in front of her a few seconds later, having dressed in record time. He grabbed her arm and forced her to face him. "Explain to me why we're going to your house if we're supposed to find your fugitive father."

She rubbed her forehead, closed her eyes for a second. "Let's discuss this on the drive over there."

After a moment, he relented, and they stepped out, got in the car and drove off.

Rhun, behind the steering wheel again, pinned her with a look brooking no argument as soon as they were on the street. "Now tell me. What's the deal with your father?"

Merle peered at her hands, watched as they clenched to fists. "My dad," she said, her voice much calmer than she felt, "was there that day when my mom and Moira died. He was closer to the spell than Maeve—she was only hit a little bit—but my dad… He survived, but he was…damaged."

It was strange, talking about it. The words held no meaning for the pain they stood for.

"My grandmother tried to fix him, but his mind was injured beyond repair. He's mostly catatonic, doesn't respond to any stimuli, doesn't really seem to recognize anyone." The more neutral she kept her voice, the better she could hide the cracks inside her, keep them from tearing open even more. "I had to put him in the nursing home after my grandmother died because I couldn't take care of him properly. Only problem is, every now and then, he has moments of half-clarity and then he...comes home."

She felt Rhun's gaze on her, hot, piercing. "*Comes home?*"

"He always runs to the same place. The only place he apparently remembers." She met his eyes, and the intensity of the heat in them had her tremble. "Our backyard. The lawn. The place where..." Her voice trailed away as the images crashed upon her.

Singed grass under her feet, green turned black, crumpled, smoldering. The old cherry tree, alight with fire, half-burned down to a stump. Next to it, there were other stumps, charred, still steaming. It wasn't wood. Burned wood, Merle thought, doesn't smell like this.

Her grandmother's voice broke through the eerie quiet. It had never been so silent.

"Merle, stop! Don't come closer! Merle!"

But Merle had already recognized what the scorched forms on the ground next to the tree had once been. Although reduced to blackened, lifeless, indefinable chunks, she knew them, would have known them both even if all that was left had been ashes on the grass. The residual energy of her mom and Moira lingered in the air, shimmered in the slant light of the afternoon.

The scream that tore out of her heart rent the sky.

"Merle."

She blinked, sucked in air. Rhun had stopped the car, had half-turned to her with one arm on the back of her seat, his hand grasping the back of her neck, the other on the dashboard. His eyes bore through her, shadows swirling in their depths. Such shadows.

"Talk to me." His voice sounded pressed, as if holding too much inside.

"I'm okay."

"You zoned out."

"Just. Memories." She inhaled deeply, her chest aching. "Keep driving."

He regarded her for a minute. "Don't do that again." His hand stroked up and down her neck, squeezed briefly, before he pulled his arm back and started the car.

The heat of his touch had revived something inside her, and she took another deep breath, the pain in her chest lessening.

"So your father was magically injured by Moira's spell, but he's not completely gone, hasn't lost all his memory." His voice was steady now, matter-of-fact, no pity, no judgment. Somehow, it made it easier for her to answer.

"Yes. So it seems." She studied her fingernails, the calm inside her barely holding up. "When he has his moments, he's clear enough to find his way back to our house, and he always sits down at the spot where it all happened, where the spell hit my mom and Moira and the cherry tree. It burned down, you know. There was so much fire..." She made a pause, flexed her hands a couple of times, took deep breaths, until the ringing in her ears stopped, until her vision didn't waver anymore. "I could have him restrained in the nursing home, but I just... I don't have the heart to bury the only part of him that's still... alive, somehow. Maybe a part of him remembers what happened there. I don't want to take that away from him."

"You think he mourns?"

She met his eyes. "You don't?"

He held her gaze for a moment before focusing back on the traffic. "Maybe he remembers something else that happened there." At her frown, he added, "Didn't he and your mother get married under that tree?"

Her heart stopped for a second, and she stared at him, open-mouthed. "Yes. Yes, they did." Why hadn't she remembered that? It was a tiny spark of warmth, that thought, a little light against the dark of the more prevalent memories of death. How less painful to assume it was this joyful event that her dad remembered, this occasion he came back to reminisce about. She regarded Rhun with curious eyes. "How do you know that?"

Shrugging one shoulder, he said, "Rowan got married at the same spot. It's the traditional venue for all the MacKenna weddings, isn't it?"

She nodded, gazing at him in ponderous silence. A beep of her phone broke the bonds of the quiet.

"It's Lily," she said after checking the text message. "She says we're good to go."

"And you trust her." The look he slanted at her spoke of what he thought of that.

"Yes." She gritted her teeth and stood her ground. "Completely."

To her great surprise, Rhun didn't argue the point further, just drove on until they reached the house. While the car rolled up toward the Victorian, both Merle and Rhun threw anxious glimpses around. Everything lay quiet, seemed deserted. No other car was parked at the end of the driveway, no sign of movement in the house.

As soon as the vehicle stopped, Merle opened her door and jogged around the veranda to the backyard. There, among grass which had once been blackened by fire, had long since regrown, sat the lonely figure of a broken man. Merle slowed to a walk, careful not to come up at him behind his back. Instead she made a wide circle, approached him from the side so he would see her coming.

"Dad."

He didn't stir. He never did. Just stared at the charred tree stump in front of him, looking into a past long gone. His face was haggard, gray whiskers growing on his cheeks, and his once light brown hair was now a shade of ash. *Like the bodies of his wife and daughter.*

Merle pushed that thought away, sat down beside him on the grass, still a bit wet from the most recent rain shower. They didn't have much time, but this moment, she had to grant him. Swallowing past the lump in her throat trying to choke her, she took his hand and squeezed it.

"Mom always said," she whispered, "that it rained cats and dogs on the day you got married here, but she didn't mind. She said you both beamed with so much joy, the sun hid in shame behind the clouds because it could never compare."

He blinked, his eyes vacant, showing nothing of the man he used to be. The man who used to tell her stories of brave princesses who saved their Prince Charmings from dragons. Merle didn't know if her words reached him, if somehow, somewhere, they touched down on the part of him that made him come out here. But still, she spoke to him as if he could hear her, because if she stopped doing that, she'd give up on him.

"When I was younger, I wanted to get married here, too," she went on softly, "and I wanted it to rain." A small smile, tinged with so much sadness, snuck onto her lips as she remembered. "I thought that would be the ultimate blessing, you know? If it rains on your wedding day, it must mean you're so happy as to make the sun and the heavens envious."

His hand twitched by the slightest fraction.

Merle held her breath. But he didn't show any other signs of having understood her words. He remained as distant as ever.

Her heart broken for the father she'd never get back, she gazed at the tree stump for a moment, then said quietly, "We have to go, Dad." She got to her feet, still holding his hand, tugging a little. "Come. Let's go back, okay?"

It was the nature of his enigmatic behavior that he always complied. He never fought her, always came along when she told him to. And yet, he remained silent, his eyes dull.

Only when they'd both stood up and turned around did Merle notice Rhun had been standing a few feet away, watching her with an unreadable expression on his face. When she led her father past him, Rhun inclined his head toward him.

"Frank."

Her father made no sign as to acknowledge anyone's presence, let alone Rhun's, but at the mention of his name, Merle stopped and stared.

Rhun's eyes met her own, pale blue-green depths that seemed to know her just as deeply. "I met him once. Before..." His voice trailed away, his gaze flicking to the burnt cherry tree.

She nodded, her heart tight, and walked on, steering her unresponsive father to the car. After she put him in the back seat and secured him, she got in the passenger seat. Rhun was already behind the wheel, scanning the surroundings with cautious glances again.

"Let's roll," he said, and they drove off.

When they arrived at the nursing home without being ambushed by the Elders, Merle breathed a sigh of utmost relief. This had been close, so close. But for once, Murphy's Law had not caught up with her. Maybe her luck was turning? *Oh, wishful thinking...*

As soon as they entered the small home, Sarah rushed toward them.

"Oh, thank goodness, you found him so fast!" She hugged Merle, squeezed Frank's hand, and beamed at Rhun, instantly mesmerized by him. "Hi."

"Hey there," he said, returning her smile.

Sarah couldn't possibly look any more dazzled.

Glaring at Rhun, her chest clenched tight with unbidden possessiveness, Merle cleared her throat. "Let's put him back in his room, shall we? I'm afraid we can't stay long this time."

"Oh, okay." Sarah wrenched her gaze away from Rhun.

Together, she and Merle led her dad down the hall with Rhun trailing in their wake. Her own personal demon looked around curiously, peering into open doors here and there, waving every now and then at someone.

"Do you know anyone here?" Merle couldn't help asking, glancing at him over her shoulder.

He shrugged. "No. Just thought I'd act friendly."

Merle missed a step. Rhun's chuckle followed her as she walked on.

They reached her dad's room and sat him down in his

armchair, facing the window. He used to watch birds in their backyard before the incident, so Merle had figured he might enjoy the view of the nursing home's small rose garden with the birdbath outside his room. Not that he ever showed it if he still did like it.

Laying one hand on his shoulder, Merle bent down and kissed his cheek. His scent was still as she remembered it from another lifetime, careless childhood days of joy.

"I have to leave now, Dad. I love you."

Gently squeezing his shoulder, she was about to straighten up again, when he lifted his head. His eyes met hers, and her heart stopped at the clarity in them. His face, it wasn't dull and emotionless anymore, it now held warmth, a silent kind of joy, almost as if… Merle's pulse sped up with fluttering hope, her chest aching with the need for her dad to *see* her, to recognize her, and she held her breath as he opened his mouth to speak.

But when he did, it broke her heart.

"Maeve?" her dad asked, his eyes searching her face.

She swallowed hard, forced herself to hold his gaze, so clear for once—though not clear enough.

"I'm sorry, Dad. It's me—Merle. Maeve is not with me right now." She didn't know how she made the words sound so steady, what with everything crumbling inside her. "She'll come along next time, okay?"

But Frank MacKenna's eyes had already turned dull again, his expression oblivious. Once more, nothing reached him.

Straightening up, Merle turned to Sarah.

"I'll take it from here," the nurse said, her face wrought with compassion. "You sure you still don't want him restrained? Sedated, maybe?"

Instantly, Merle shook her head. "Never," she whispered. If this was the only remnant of her dad's spirit, the only part not yet lost to numbness and nothing, she'd rather chew off her own hand than take that from him.

"All right, honey." Sarah squeezed her arm and gave her a small smile. "Take care."

"Thanks."

And with one last look at the man who used to be her father, she left the room, walked past Rhun, who'd watched from the doorway. She kept on walking until she stood outside the entrance to the nursing home, on the pristine lawn framed by flowerbeds, the afternoon sun streaming through the clouds overhead, glistening on the raindrops that had collected on the leaves. When the front door closed and Rhun's body heat brushed her back, she didn't turn around.

"He only ever recognizes Maeve," she said, uncertain why she told him that. The words just tore out of her. "Never me. His moments of clarity, they're so rare, and when he gets them, he *sees* her. Sometimes they can even exchange a few words. He's the reason Maeve stayed in the city when she moved out. So she could visit him." She huffed. "I've been taking care of him along with my grandmother since I was ten, but it's Maeve he recognizes. Funny, isn't it?"

Silence.

Her next words sounded light, but they were honed in fire, hardened like the shell she'd cased her pain in, the only thing standing between her and an abyss of sadness so great, it would swallow her whole. "Go ahead. Make a joke. Say something taunting. You must be itching to mock me right now, so why don't you. I can take it." And she meant it, she wanted it, craved the anger it would bring. It would harden the shell further, keep it from breaking.

Rhun didn't say anything, just silently walked around her until she faced him, and then, his eyes burning with a quiet fire, he hugged her. Her heart stuttered. She stiffened.

"Merle." His deep voice in her ear, a caress so soft she shivered. "You don't have to be strong all the time. Just let go. Be weak. Cry. Break down if you need to."

His hold was powerful yet far from crushing, an embrace of

strength that could intimidate—but right now, it felt strangely reassuring. Something inside Merle cracked, a fissure in her composure, and she tensed.

"*Cry.*" A gentle command, and it eroded part of her resistance. But it was what he said next that tore her apart on the inside, opened up the cracks she'd tried to mend. "I've got you, little witch."

The sob broke from her even as her eyes started tearing up.

"Don't keep it bottled up," he murmured, stroking her back. "Let it out."

And she did. Merle gave in, broke down on a sob, and cried like she hadn't since her family had been ripped in half. Rhun held her, unwaveringly, while she came apart in his arms. Sixteen years' worth of pain, hurt, disappointment, helplessness, anger and despair tore out of her as if a dam had burst.

She'd been afraid of falling into the abyss once she allowed it all out, afraid of disintegrating under the pressure of it all if she let it touch her. The pain, she'd thought, would take her over, shatter her if she admitted it.

It didn't.

The walls of her world didn't crumble, and while everything she'd buried inside flowed free, liberating her in a way she hadn't thought possible, she didn't fall apart—because the arms holding her wouldn't allow her to. Rhun's presence was a quiet force, a source of strength, and he never let her go, even as her knees buckled and she almost sank to the ground. He simply picked her up and carried her to the front steps of the nursing home, where he sat down with her on his lap, cradled in his arms. And he waited for the storm inside her to pass.

It did, eventually. Her sobs subsided, her sniveling eased, and she felt as if all the layers of herself had been unraveled and bared before him, vulnerable as never before.

Rhun angled his head so his face was buried in her hair, and Merle held her breath, waiting for him to speak. He could hurt her so easily now. All it would take was one wrong word, and it would cut like a razor, straight through to her heart.

"I had a sister once," he said, his voice barely above a whisper, "and I couldn't help her when she was killed in front of me."

This, it stopped her world.

CHAPTER 15

At his words, Merle had grown still in his embrace, so quiet she didn't even breathe. Once again, Rhun cursed his dull daytime senses, which left him guessing at her feelings in a vacuum. He had no idea how his revelation had affected her when she was withdrawn like this, whether he'd inadvertently broken the fragility he held in his arms.

She'd seemed so deeply vulnerable after she'd cried, so brittle as to crumble at the slightest misplaced touch, that he'd known, instinctively, he could crush her with one careless word. And that, he'd realized with surprise, would crush him as well.

So, in a visceral response to this vulnerability in her that cut right through him, he'd decided to share with her the most painful part of his past, of himself, something he'd never spoken of to anyone else. Not even Bahram, whom he considered the closest friend he had, knew how Rhun's sister had died, let alone that he'd had one to begin with. He'd locked that information away in the darkest corner of his heart, never to talk about, not even to think about, until now.

Until Merle.

Out of all the people he'd met in his life, she was the only one he'd felt the need to give this piece of himself to—maybe because she, too, knew what it meant to lose a sister.

She was still so silent in his arms, as if waiting for him to go on, and he decided to do so, anxious for a reaction from her.

"Her name was Siani," he said, and by speaking it out loud, a thousand bittersweet memories burst through the seal he'd put on them.

A small hand clasping his own. Wide eyes, the same color as his, looking up at him as if he was the center of the universe.

She'd always followed him wherever he went, had done as he did, said as he said. Clumsy child she'd been, she'd broken more than one thing while trying to impress him, a clock here, a picture frame there. And he'd always taken the blame for it in front of their parents.

"I'm sorry," Siani whispered, eyes full of tears, petting his head after he'd been punished.

"I'm not angry with you." He never could be, not with her having a face like that.

She shook her head. "I know."

"So stop crying." He couldn't stand to see her tears.

"I can't. You're hurt because of me."

She hugged him, tightly, and he sighed, knowing however small she was, she wouldn't let him go until she was sure he was all right again. Not even shaking her off would do the trick. He knew because he'd tried that before. So he said the only thing that would make her happy right now.

"I love you, Siani."

Merle stirred in his arms, her hair whispering against his lips as she moved her head. Her hand came up to rest on his chest, where his heart beat broken against his ribs.

"What happened?" Her voice was soft, as if she was afraid to scare him off.

Inwardly, he huffed. Like he'd let her go now.

For a moment, he was silent, searching for words to match the horror of his memories, finding none that did justice. So he put it as plainly as he could. "We were out playing in the woods and went too far from home. It was getting dark and we should have headed back."

Nighttime, with its allegiance to darkness beyond the visible, was not only dangerous to humans. Young demons, too, could fall prey to the predators rousing at night.

"But we were so caught up in our games that we noticed too late. Another demon found us, and he jumped at Siani." Her screams still echoed in his mind, a torture far worse than any pain in the Shadows. "I was too young to take him on, but I tried. He flung me back easily, as if I was just a fly. It wasn't me he was interested in." Lying there, broken on the ground, Rhun had had to watch—and to realize what the other demon intended, what he couldn't stop from happening right there, in front of his eyes, his vision clouded with blood. "His kind ate children alive, no matter the species. The younger the better."

Merle uttered a choked whimper, her body jerking.

"When he started..." *Sounds of tearing flesh, gushing blood, cries that shredded his soul.* He broke off, took a breath. The scent of Merle filled his nose, sweet, enticing, and he clung to it, used it as his anchor to the here and now. "I lunged at him again." With the last of his strength, he'd made his body obey, had made himself move against the pain pinning him to the forest floor. "That time, when he threw me off, I crashed down so hard I lost consciousness." A blessing, for it had spared him to watch the nightmare unfurling in front of him. "When I woke again, my parents were there. They'd found us in time to save me, but they were too late for Siani."

The remains of their attacker littered the ground, his blood seeping into the earth. The other demon had been torn to shreds, over and over again, and the liquid crimson covering Rhun's mother from head to toe like a grotesque armor bore testament to who had executed the child eater. Her eyes, wild with the mad grief only a bereaved mother could feel, were trained on the bundle of lifeless flesh and bones that Rhun's father cradled in his arms. It was all that was left of Siani.

"Oh, gods." Merle sucked in a shuddering breath.

She trembled, her hand grasping his shirt, and for a second Rhun cursed himself for heaving his pain on her when she had enough of her own to carry already. He'd overburdened her, and now she seemed close to crying again. *Way to go, dickhead.*

Then, she did the unexpected. Shifting in his hold until she straddled him, she cupped his face with both hands, blue eyes glistening with tears and a sympathy that was an unforeseen caress of his soul, and she looked at him, *saw* him the way no one ever had.

"Gods, Rhun, I'm so sorry," she whispered, and the sincerity in her voice struck something deep inside him, ripped him open, wide open.

She pulled him close then, pressed his head against her neck, against the warmth and softness of her skin. One hand in his hair, the other on his back, she stroked him, comforted him. The gash she'd torn inside him mended. She'd ripped him open, stitched him back together, and in between, she'd left a part of herself inside, inextricably linked to him.

In the sweetest reversion of roles, she now held him, soothed him, her soft embrace surprisingly strong, as strong as she was herself. He'd been wrong about her. With all the hurt in her own life weighing her down, she could still take on someone else's pain, too, and without flinching, she now carried his for those breathless moments that she held him. For what it was worth, it only seemed to make her stronger.

Rhun had never prayed to the gods, fickle as they were, but now a part of him silently begged the Powers That Be for a way to hold on to this witch. When she'd come to him in Bahram's apartment, freely come to him, and he'd claimed her with a ferocious hunger going beyond carnal cravings, he'd already been on the edge. Her quiet, caring acceptance of his past, her comfort, as freely given as her passion, had done him in. And now this.

Fuck it all, he wanted to keep her.

Though how he would tell her that, he didn't know. Even if she wanted him as well—and that was a far stretch of the imagination, since moments of intimacy didn't necessarily equal emotional attachment, as well he knew—the odds were still against them. He didn't delude himself for one second that the witching community would readily accept him at Merle's side. He *was* a demon, after all, and thus nominally their enemy. The Elders might pressure her into binding him again, whether she wanted to do it or not.

And just the thought of going back into the Shadows... His arms tightened around her, and inside him, darkness swirled, as black as the sphere he'd sworn to avoid going back to at all costs.

At all costs.

Even that of Merle's powers? Of her sister's life? Even if it might break him in the process? And it was already breaking him, for he wanted to tear himself apart for the terrible choice he had to make. He'd never meant to get attached to her like this, he'd thought he'd play her, easily, get what he wanted and then be on his way. It was never supposed to hurt so fucking much. He'd never thought he'd lose himself in her.

He wanted to give voice to the impossible, to lay himself bare before her like he'd never done with anyone else. But survival and self-preservation, those instincts he'd honed over decades of roaming on the darker side of life—they were damn hard to silence.

So, instead of telling her of the way her essence had twined around his heart, of how he wanted to keep her there, twine her a bit further, he said, "We should get moving again, little witch. Don't want to be sitting here on a silver platter for the Elders, do we?"

"Yeah. You're right."

She pulled away from him and nodded, withdrawing her hands, and damn if he didn't want to snatch them and put them back into place. *Where they belonged.* When she rose and got off him, he felt the absence of her warmth in every cell of his body. Gritting his teeth against the raw and urgent need snapping inside him, he got up and followed her to the car, *tsking* at her when she wanted to slip in the driver's seat.

"Uh-uh." He made wavy shooing gestures to the passenger's side. "Over there, you menace behind the wheel."

Even without his ability to read her aura, he could tell she was pissed at that. Eyes narrowed, hands on her hips, she glowered at him, her face flushed rose with indignation.

"You like being in control, don't you?" Belying her angry stance, her voice held a note of playfulness.

"I think," he said with a smirk, opening the driver's side door for himself, "I made that clear a few hours ago. And from what I remember of your enthusiastic reaction, you were very much okay with that."

They both got in the car, and Merle rounded on him, eyes glowing with her angry glare—as well as something else, something that, he suspected, was the reason her cheeks blazed an adorable red.

"That was then," she said. "This is now. And I don't like being ordered around."

"Except in bed."

The red flush took over her whole face, and she visibly struggled to come up with a denial, failing miserably.

"Busted." He grinned with deep self-satisfaction, and started the car.

Merle settled back in her seat and muttered something under her breath that sounded suspiciously like, "Go bust yourself."

Of course, that only made him grin all the more.

His amusement evaporated, however, when she, after some long moments of silence, said, "What I just don't understand is why that demon would keep Maeve alive this long."

He chanced a glance at her. She stared at her fingers, frowning, a curl of her fiery hair caressing her cheek. When she looked up at him, the blue of her eyes was striking in its depth.

"You said she'd likely be dead by now, but she isn't. I can still feel her through our family bond. For some reason, that demon hasn't killed her—"

Yet. He could hear that little word she'd bitten off, refused to say, and in the corner of his heart that held the memory of Siani, he understood. Oh, he understood far better than he wanted to. Hands gripping the steering wheel, he focused on the traffic.

"I'm thinking," Merle went on, her voice edged with frustration, "that it has something to do with the fact that a…witch is involved." She'd stumbled over the word, apparently still unable, unwilling, to comprehend and accept that fact. "That somehow, it is connected, in an important way, and I keep thinking and thinking about it, trying to figure out why. Why Maeve, why does a w-witch pair up with a demon to kidnap her, why keep her alive? I can sometimes feel the connection, like I already know the answer to these questions and I just can't see the forest for the trees. It drives me crazy." That hitch in her voice *did* sound a bit crazy, too, he noted.

Rhun silently debated whether he should go for it or not, knowing he should keep his mouth shut if he wanted to stick to his plan. But when he peered at her, the despair he clearly saw carved into her features tipped the scales in favor of speaking his mind. "Did you see how Moira's spell went awry that day?"

Merle blinked, obviously startled at the seemingly unrelated question. "No. I… I was at Lily and Basil's when it happened. When Isabel dropped me off at home, I saw…" She took a fortifying breath. "I only saw the aftermath."

"Rowan told you what happened?"

"Yes. Of course."

"How old was Moira when her spell went awry?"

"Why—"

"Answer the question." He knew she probably felt as if

caught in a cross-examination, but this was important in order to make sure he was on the right track with his suspicion.

"Thirteen," Merle said, her voice holding a spike of resentment at being drilled by him.

He ignored that. "A witch's powers break through when she's around six years old, right?"

"Right. How do you—"

"So," he cut her off, "she'd been handling magic for what, seven years? Eight?"

"That's about right, yes."

"Did she ever have any problems with spells before? Anything she couldn't control?"

Merle was silent, pondering that question. "No. She had excellent control. She was like my grandmother. Strong. Capable. Very careful."

Rhun had guessed as much. The glimpses he'd had of Moira had painted the picture of a formidable witch in the making, one who would wield her magic with utmost control. So the idea of one of her spells going catastrophically wrong and wiping out half her family had never sat right with him. A piece of the puzzle he'd been putting together.

His next question was aimed at another piece. "How old was Maeve when your mother and Moira died?"

The air in the car palpably tensed.

"Almost eight," Merle said, her voice laced with beginning comprehension. Even so, she shook her head. "She never showed any signs of magic, Rhun."

"Not until that day." He looked her full in the face.

"No." She shook her head again. "That's not possible. It wasn't Maeve. It couldn't have been. I mean, if it was, why didn't she have any powers afterwards?"

He was partly guessing now, but knowing Rowan, it was a likely scenario. "Maybe because her magic had been buried inside her."

Merle sucked in a breath, covered her mouth with her hand.

He understood her dismay. For a witch to lose her powers, to be unable to access her inherent magic, it was unthinkable. A cruelty like clipping the wings of a bird. And didn't that make him feel like a real bastard, considering what he intended to do to Merle.

"I think," he went on, because it was too late to hold back his opinion now, "that Maeve never lacked magic. Quite the opposite—she likely had too much. I think it was so powerful that, when it emerged with a little delay, it did so with an explosive force that killed half your family and maimed your father. Have you never wondered how it was possible Moira could have been killed by her own spell? When she was well on the way to becoming a powerful witch with a firm hold on her magic?" Now it was his turn to shake his head. "I think Rowan realized Maeve's powers might be beyond her control, might be too dangerous for her to ever learn to handle them, so she locked them inside her. It has been done before, you know, to punish those who would abuse their magic. Rowan told me she had to do it once."

Merle swallowed audibly. For the longest time, she remained silent, a myriad of emotions flickering across her face, the enormity of his suggestion sinking in. "But if this is true, why did my grandmother never tell me anything about it? Why give me a tale about how it was Moira? Why did she lie about that?"

"Think about it and be honest." He kept his voice gentle to counterbalance the cutting truth of his words. "How would you have seen Maeve if you knew she was the one responsible for the death of your mother and your sister, for debilitating your father?"

A choked sound caught at the back of Merle's throat. "She was just a child, it wasn't her fault. She wasn't able to handle her magic."

"You know that now, but back then, you were just a child yourself. Would you have understood it then? Or would you have grown up silently blaming your sister, hating her for destroying your family?"

"*Gods.*" It was a pained whisper.

The truth, Rhun thought, can hurt like a bitch.

"I think it was an act of kindness toward both of you that Rowan kept the truth to herself."

"Maeve," Merle murmured after a moment. "She never knew what she'd done. She was told the same story as me, believed it was Moira." Turning to him, she caught his gaze with eyes holding such pain. "Just imagine if she ever finds out. It will break her." And right now, it was Merle's voice that broke, as if foreshadowing her sister's fate.

What he said next was cruel in a way, he knew it, but it was meant to bring her back from a spiral of painful thoughts, make her focus on what lay ahead. "If Maeve survives this, it will take more to break her than the knowledge she killed half her family."

The pained hitch in her breathing made him ache. Even so, he went on.

"I think the key to understanding why Maeve was chosen to be abducted lies in her dormant powers. If they are as great as I suppose—and to have been able to wield such destructive magic at the age of eight, at the onset of the development of her powers, they must be enormous—then that would make her a prime target to be harvested. Her being unable to access her powers to defend herself only adds to that."

Merle pivoted in her seat to stare at him, the force of her drilling gaze hitting him almost physically. "*Harvested?*"

He hesitated for a moment, weighing his words. "*Bluotezzer* demons can absorb a witch's powers."

"What?" Her face paled. "How?" The trepidation in her voice was evident.

"I don't know the details," he lied with the ease of a lifetime of practice, against the screaming indignation of a part of himself, the part that wanted to keep the witch next to him, wanted to wrap her in fluffy cotton and protect her from any harm. *From himself.* But he went on, his voice, his expression, everything about him the epitome of sincerity, coaxing her to believe his words to be true. The skill came naturally to his species, and he'd perfected it to mastery. "I have never tried it myself—mostly for lack of knowledge..." Here he shrugged, underscoring the casual ease with which he wove the lie. "...but I know it's possible. The demon who took Maeve is very likely trying to get to her powers so he can take them."

Merle's face became impossibly whiter. "How would he even know Maeve has that kind of magic inside her?"

He held up a hand. "I'm getting to that. Now, as for the powers, I don't think he intends to keep them." He cast a meaningful look at her. "Witch magic is intricate, complex and hard to handle, for all I know. Once taken, those powers would be locked inside him, useless, since they're so different from our demon magic. He wouldn't be able to do much with them." Pausing, he then added, "Except pass them on."

Something broke in her gaze just then, a mirror of what most likely had fractured inside her. "The other witch," she whispered.

He nodded. "I'm guessing Rowan confided in someone after she bound the magic in Maeve, and that Elder witch has now decided to harvest those powers for herself."

She closed her eyes for a moment, squeezed them shut so hard, her face creased with lines from the effort, each one filled with silent pain. "You can't," she rasped. "You can't keep dropping these horrible revelations on me."

"Would you rather keep living in a world of lies?" The irony of his question, when he'd just lied to her face, was a mirrored shard of glass lodged in his heart.

"No, but I don't know whether I want to live in a world of such betrayal either."

And just like that, she twisted the shard of glass in his heart further, almost making him wince with the pain. He took a breath, his chest tight, too tight, the chaos inside him churning, and he was just about to open his mouth to tell her the truth, when Merle uttered a strangled cry beside him.

He whipped his head around. "Merle?"

She was bent forward, clutching the edges of her seat, breathing heavily. Her hair was a ginger curtain, hiding her face from his view, but from the way her knuckles flashed white against her skin where she held the seat in a death grip, he could tell she was in major pain.

He tightened his hold on the steering wheel. "What's wrong?"

She cried out again, her spine snapping straight like a rod, her head slamming back against the seat. Sweat beaded on her paling skin, her breath coming in fast pants.

"Merle, *dammit*, talk to me!"

She moaned, panted, pressed her lips together. "Balance," she ground out after what felt like an eternity in hell for him. "Have to…give…back."

"Ah, fuck…" The realization hit him like a blow to his guts. She was the head of her family, and as such, she had to bear the burden of upholding the balance. The fucking balance, he thought furiously. Nothing was for free in this world, everything came with a price, with a condition, a toll one had to pay, and for all the magic witches held and wielded—more than any otherworld creature could muster—they were not exempt from this law. The Powers That Be allowed the witches to borrow magic from the layers of this world, but they also demanded payback—from each head of a family, in the form of blood, powers, and pain.

"It'll pass," she pressed through gritted teeth, "but I need a quiet place…to get through it."

"Hold on, little witch." He grabbed her hand and squeezed it, careful not to cause her more pain, while every muscle in his body was taut and vibrated with some pain of his own that had no outlet. "I'll take care of that."

He managed the impossible task of maneuvering through the afternoon traffic while his mind splintered at Merle's obvious agony beside him. It nearly drove him insane to see her like this, and the fact he couldn't ease her suffering set his blood on fire.

He found a deserted parking lot behind a closed-up store and parked the car out of the line of sight from the street. When he turned to Merle, she was half-unconscious, drenched in sweat, trembling violently, convulsing as if caught in a seizure. He cursed a blue streak under his breath.

And then, one by one, gashes opened up all over her body. Her skin was slashed by invisible knives, cut open, her blood poured out—and evaporated. It dissolved into the air as if inhaled by the fabric of the world itself, and Rhun realized that was exactly what was happening. The Powers That Be took back the magic she had drawn from the layers of the world.

Merle's tortured screams filled the car, and Rhun's soul fractured along with hers.

He grabbed her, pulled her over the middle console and gathered her in his arms, and right at this moment, he would have given anything to carry her pain. *Anything* to stop her screams.

Take it from me, he begged, silently imploring the powers he'd shunned all his life. *Please, take it from me instead.* Over and over he prayed, as he rocked the broken body of his witch.

Merle screamed again, her voice hoarse from agony, and Rhun closed his eyes, despair lancing his heart.

"Just fucking take it from *me!*"

Pain seared through him. His eyes shot open. On the hand cradling her head, his skin split in a wide gash. Slowly, his blood poured out into the air, dissolved on a sigh of the powers beyond.

He froze, held his breath, gritted his teeth against the piercing agony wrecking him, as more parts of his body were ripped open, bled magic. In his arms, Merle grew still. Her screams stopped, subsided in labored breaths, and the wounds on her skin closed, one by one. For every gash on her that healed, another was cut into him.

And while he sat there, bleeding, burning with anguish, holding Merle's healing body in his arms, he truly knew, for the first time in his life, the meaning of mercy.

Merle had lost consciousness, and now breathed deeply, peacefully, free of pain. When his own wounds closed as well, he slumped back in the seat, every muscle in his body thoroughly wrung out, his skin chafed raw, his mind numb, as if hazed. With his blunt daytime senses now even less acute, he noticed the impending danger far too late.

So when the car door flew open, he didn't have time to dodge the spell. It hit him straight on, plunging his world into darkness.

CHAPTER 16

W ords drifted through the black velvet veiling Merle's mind. Murmurs, spoken in hushed tones, the voices familiar. Something about them should have alerted her. If only she could remember what... If only her head didn't feel as if it were about to split from the inside out, as if weighed down by a hundred tons of concrete and still pulsating painfully with every slow beat of her heart.

It was always like this after giving back to the Powers That Be.

Giving back... Yes, that was what had happened. A sliver of a memory pierced the haze inside her mind. *A car. Pain. Magic, bleeding from her body. Strong arms, holding her with such care.*

Rhun.

Merle sat up with a start as it all came crashing back, at the same moment as the identity of the voices registered. The niggling feeling she'd had formed into a certainty that chilled her blood. Her rash movement spiked another throbbing wave of pain in her head, made her gasp before she could help herself —and the hushed conversation stopped at once. Two pairs of eyes focused on her.

Juneau and Isabel stood at the large windows of the Murray's living room. The dimmed light of the chandelier glinted off Juneau's white hair, threw Isabel's face in soft relief as they both stared at Merle.

Grasping the cushion of the couch she sat on, fighting down the surge of pain from her headache as well as her rising panic, Merle stared back, unflinching. "Where's Rhun? What did you do to him?"

A slight tilt of the head from Isabel. "These are your first questions?"

Lily's aunt stepped closer, light and shadows playing on her beautiful features—benignly lined with age and experience—as she sat down in an armchair across from Merle. Her hair had the same ebony color as Lily's, her eyes were of the same dark blue, but the power they held... It spoke of magic that ran deep, so deep, it made Merle's skin prickle, let her heart beat faster. To be near a witch of Isabel's caliber, her powers among the Elders only eclipsed by Juneau's, was—as always—unsettling. Not to mention the fact that the other great witch among the Elders was also present, and now regarded Merle with eyes as cold as Isabel's.

"Considering what has happened and what you are charged with," the oldest living witch of the Murray line went on, her scrutinizing gaze holding Merle as immobile as if she'd strapped her to the couch, "your first inquiry is to the wellbeing of a demon?"

He's *my* demon, Merle thought, and the fierceness of that immediate response was an iron fist clenching around her heart. Thankfully, though, she kept that response to herself. Making any such claim right now surely wouldn't sit well with the two Elders in front of her. They were pissed enough as it was, and Merle had to tread carefully here in order not to dig herself in deeper.

Maybe, if she smoothed the waters a bit, she'd be able to talk her way out of the worst of it. Right now, Isabel and Juneau focused on her with the lethal quiet of a snake sneaking up on its prey, and Merle's every move, her every word, the smallest shift in her body language or flicker of her aura would be noted and analyzed. If she wanted to get out of here, she needed a break from that chilling scrutiny that held her, just a tiny relaxation of the thick layers of power suffusing the room—and then she'd be able to weave some magic, unnoticed, subtle threads working toward an escape.

She willed her features to calm in feigned resignation, slumped back on the sofa, her gaze dropping to the table in front of her as if in deference to her Elders. "How did you know where to find me?" A deliberate choice of words, excluding the demon that had come to be her own. The need to know where he was, though, to make sure he was unhurt, it beat against her skin from the inside, with every pounding of her heart. It was all she could do not to let it show in her aura.

"Ah," Isabel said, the slightest note of warmth in her indigo eyes, "now you are asking with more reason."

"Enough reason," Juneau cut in quietly, drawing Merle's gaze to hers, "to smooth the waters a bit."

Juneau's echo of her earlier thoughts made Merle wince before she could catch herself.

The Elder's deep green eyes studied her attentively, her power drenching the air, and Merle shrank a few inches under the force of it. The fact that the other witch had broken into Merle's thoughts and read her mind without so much as batting an eye, without Merle noticing, bore testament to just *how* powerful the head of the Laroche family truly was.

The knowledge of it stole Merle's breath, and she frantically repaired her breached mental shields. Her headache still throbbed heavily, which was probably part of why she hadn't felt the intrusion. But now that she knew what Juneau was capable of, she'd be on her guard, and she reinforced her defenses with additional care. Just how much had Juneau read? If she'd seen the convoluted mess of feelings Merle harbored for a certain demon...

Isabel now turned a questioning glance at her fellow Elder.

"Lily," Juneau said to Merle, not explaining her previous statement further, "is indeed a loyal friend of yours."

At the mention of her niece's name, Isabel's facial expression tensed. A sudden, nauseating cold crept through Merle's veins. Her gaze flicked from one Elder to the other, and she sensed the unspoken, understood her best friend had broken. Had *been* broken.

"Is she all right?" The question came out as a rasp, Merle's voice charred by her concern. There was no anger, no sense of betrayal, just bone-chilling fear for her friend's wellbeing. If Lily had been hurt because of her...

"She is now," Isabel said, ice in her voice, "that she has reconsidered where her loyalty truly lies."

And right then—as if on cue—Lily walked into the room, carrying a tray of tea. She kept her eyes averted from Merle, barely glanced at her Elders either, and set the tea down on the low table in front of the couch. Her aura subdued, her expression shuttered, she moved in a careful and measured way as she sat on the larger couch next to Merle's. Even with an experience of more than twenty years of reading each and every emotion in her friend, Merle found it impossible to gauge what Lily was feeling.

"After she so deftly lured her aunt away from your house," Juneau went on, passing only a fleeting glance at Isabel that albeit held volumes of silent reproach, "it did take some effort to glean information from Lily." A glint of sympathy shone in her eyes as she looked at Lily, and she sighed. Her gaze then settled back on Merle with a deep, regretful sadness, and suddenly, Juneau appeared as old as she really was, her wrinkled face carved with weariness. "This has gotten out of hand, child." She shook her head, closed her eyes briefly. "While I understand your motives, dear, I cannot condone your actions. You went against the law, against explicit instructions of your Elders, and you unleashed a dangerous creature you cannot control. You have risked the safety of your community to fight a losing battle. You do know we cannot let this go unpunished?"

Something snapped inside Merle. Fire flared through her veins as she glared at Juneau. "And what about the fact it's an Elder witch who kidnapped my sister? Will you let that go unpunished?"

Juneau froze and Isabel blanched. For the longest moment, the air stood still in the room.

"That," Juneau whispered, her power thrumming around her, "is a serious accusation, Merle. Unless you have proof of it, you shouldn't raise such allegations."

Merle didn't flinch, didn't back down even one inch. "The demon who took Maeve is being blocked by witch magic. Powerful witch magic."

Isabel cocked her head, her eyes narrowed. "And you know this how?"

Merle started to answer, then realized, hesitated. Setting her jaw, she said, "Rhun felt it when he searched for the other demon."

Juneau sighed and closed her eyes.

Leaning back in her chair, Isabel slowly shook her head, her expression a mix of sadness and pity. "And you take his word at face value. A demon's word."

Juneau's gaze slammed into Merle's. "A demon, no less, who is as of yet bound to you and undoubtedly seeks to free himself of that bond. Have you not considered that?"

Merle swallowed, took a shaky breath, her heart in her throat. "My wards," she said after a moment. "The ones I put up around Maeve's apartment. They were broken down so Maeve could be taken. Only an Elder witch can do that."

Isabel held her gaze for so long, it made Merle's skin crawl, turned her insides to goo. The Elder's stare seemed to strip all the years from her life, and suddenly, she was a girl again, a young, inexperienced witch, never strong enough to live up to her grandmother's expectations.

"Your magic," Isabel said, "is still developing. You know that, don't you?" Her voice was gentle, kind, as if reminding a cancer patient of her condition. "It takes time to grow into your full power. Your wards might not have been strong enough to hold by themselves."

Merle pressed her lips together, lowered her head. This time, her deference wasn't an act. The intimidating presence of two witches as strong as Isabel and Juneau truly humbled her, utterly put her in her place. Tears prickled at the edges of her eyes, and she closed them, shutting out the image of the two Elders in front of her, the sharp contrast of their power to hers. Maybe they were right. Maybe her wards really had failed. After all, she *was* still so young, her power not established yet and…

I've seen how strong your magic is—your wards would never have vanished just like that.

She held her breath as Rhun's words echoed inside her mind. Unbidden, the memory of his voice stroked along her senses, nurtured something within that had started to wither at the older witch's patronizing tone.

"After all," Isabel continued, still so gentle, "there is a reason why you are not yet an Elder."

The words cut her, harshly, reinforcing her deepest fears and—

You're hiding behind your fear instead of stepping up to your destiny and accepting who you are.

Merle's eyes snapped open. Focused on her hands, clenched to fists in her lap. On the ring circling her right middle finger, the heirloom of the MacKenna family denoting the current head of the line. Merle was so used to wearing it, she'd all but forgotten it was there—it had become part of her, a given. She'd accepted the ring after her grandmother's passing. Deep down, however, she'd never accepted the role that came with it. How could she, when her grandmother's legacy loomed over her, an example of strength to which she could never compare? When the power she held just wasn't enough to fill the gap her grandmother's death had torn?

You are *strong enough, and it fucking beats the shit out of me why you can't see that.*

The ring caught the light of the chandelier, the amber jewel flaring as if lit by a fire from within. Magic, raw, strong and unbridled, unfurled inside Merle, thrummed through her veins.

You are *strong enough.*

Merle raised her head. Straightened her spine. Met Isabel's gaze, and smiled grimly.

"My wards didn't fail," she said with a newfound strength pulsing in every cell of her body.

The power drenching the air this time held the heat of fire and the combined force of one of the oldest magical family lines this side of the Atlantic. And it answered to the call of a witch of twenty-six.

Isabel blinked, opened her mouth to speak.

The phone rang, interrupting whatever she had been about to say. Juneau and Isabel turned to the door to the kitchen, and a moment later Hazel appeared holding the phone. Hair the typical ebony of the Murrays, her features almost identical to her sister's, Lily's mother could have been Isabel's doppelganger—if it wasn't for those warm brown eyes, same as Basil's. Where Isabel radiated power and authority, making Merle's spine snap straight in attendance every time the Elder witch looked her way, Hazel's aura glowed like a hearth fire in the darkness, drawing those around her in with promises of warmth, care and love. A gentle presence in the shadow of Isabel's strength, Hazel had raised Merle and Maeve as much as Rowan.

She now handed the receiver to Juneau. "It's for you, ma'am."

Juneau took the phone, listened, her forehead wrinkling impossibly further. "Have Estelle take care of it," she said after a minute, mentioning her oldest daughter, a capable middle-aged witch with a quick laugh. "I am not finished here." Whatever was being said on the other end of the line now put a spark of anger in her eyes. "How did that happen?" The chandelier flickered with the rise of the Elder's power in the air. "Call Sophie, she will handle it."

One of the chandelier's light bulbs went out with a crack. Merle surreptitiously pursed her lips. Apparently Juneau's younger daughter was unable to handle it either. Whatever *it* was.

"Fine." A heavy sigh from Juneau. "I will be there shortly." She ended the call and turned to Isabel. "Are you able to take care of this on your own for a few minutes?"

Merle could virtually *see* Isabel's pride bristle. It had obviously taken quite a beating when Lily had outsmarted her before.

"Of course," the head of the Murray line said tersely, clearly not appreciating her competence being questioned by a fellow Elder.

Juneau nodded, glancing at each of the witches in the room, her gaze lingering on Merle, and she studied her with newly-sparked interest. "I will be back soon." And with that she left.

Isabel slanted a hard look at Lily, glanced at her sister, then stared at Merle. "I will not be made a fool of again," she said quietly, her powerful words charging the air with a lethal edge.

Lily flinched at the warning from her aunt, and sank more deeply into the cushion of the couch. Her hands trembled as she picked up her cup of tea and took a sip, holding it front of her as if hiding behind it. Hazel took a seat next to Lily, putting her arm around her daughter's shoulders. Merle, however, was beyond caring about consequences at that point.

The power she just tapped still coursed through her veins, and it gave her a sense of strength and confidence to withstand the kind of intimidation she'd have cowered away from before.

So when Isabel began to tell Merle what awaited her for her disobedience, Merle cut her off grimly.

"You should be ashamed of your hypocrisy," she said, holding her Elder's gaze steady.

Lily stifled her gasp by clapping her hand over her mouth.

Isabel leaned forward, her eyes on Merle. Power swirled in the indigo depths. "That is a strong word to use."

"Fitting, though," Merle shot back, "when you'd rather persecute me for trying to save my sister from a demon than investigate the involvement of one of your own in the abduction."

There was the slightest flicker of grief in Isabel's eyes, and Merle picked it up relentlessly.

"How can you sit here condemning me, when you lost your daughters same as I am about to lose Maeve?"

Her words hit home. Something broke in Isabel's eyes, and for a moment, just a tiny moment, Merle felt miserable about mentioning the violent deaths of Isabel's three daughters—each of them brutally slain by demons. The most recent loss—Vicky, the youngest one, full of laughter and energy at the age of twenty-two, until she'd been stripped of her skin by a vindictive demon—was still a raw, open wound to the Murray family. It had only been six months since her remains had been laid to rest next to her sisters, a macabre final reunion of siblings who had shared as much in life as in death.

Merle had grieved for each of them just as much as Lily and Basil—they had been her cousins in all but blood.

Now she swallowed past the lump in her throat, breathed through the weight crushing her chest, and pushed on, determined to make her point. Still staring at Isabel with heat in her veins, she said, "You'd have done the same as I did if it was one of your daughters in Maeve's place. Don't tell me you wouldn't go against the gods themselves to save her!"

For a long moment, Isabel was silent, her eyes looking inward. When she met Merle's gaze again, she gave her a smile that broke her heart. "What I want," the Elder said, her voice so quiet and full of regret, "and what our law allows me to do are not always in accordance."

Merle's temper boiled over. "Fuck the law!"

Isabel's gaze sharpened, would have shriveled a lesser witch. "Watch your mouth, Merle."

The chandelier's lights flickered, dimmed, and the air grew thick with menacing magic. A few seconds ticked by. The Elder witch took a breath, obviously trying to get a hold on her own temper, and picked up her cup of tea. She took a long sip from it and set it down again. Each of her movements was careful and measured now—being able to put a lid on a flaring temper and a power such as hers was another one of the characteristics making Isabel an Elder witch. She now took another deep breath, and looked at Merle. "You will bind that demon in the Shadows as soon as you've recovered your full strength." Her voice brooked no argument.

At the mention of Rhun, Merle's heart skipped a few beats and then took up a frantic rhythm.

"Isabel," Hazel said, her voice gentle. "Perhaps we should consider using the demon to find—"

The look Isabel shot at her made Hazel's words wither. "Are you questioning your Elders' decision?"

Hazel held her older sister's gaze for the span of two heartbeats, before she lowered her head in deference to the head of her family. "Of course not."

Isabel nodded, took another sip from her tea, and turned back to Merle. "We'd have bound the demon again already, but since he's still partly leashed to you, only you can send him back." She was about to say something else as she gagged, grabbed her throat, coughed, and then slumped down face-first on the coffee table as if someone had turned the lights off in her head.

Merle shot to her feet. "What the..?"

Lily gingerly rose from the couch and threw a sheepish glance at her motionless aunt, who now snored softly. "I am so screwed."

Merle gaped at Lily. "You did that? You jinxed *Isabel*?"

At that, Lily winced and grimaced. "Boy, she's going to be *pissed* when she wakes up."

"Language, sweetie." Hazel stood and gave Lily a stern glance.

"Sorry, Mom." Lily Murray's trademark evil grin snuck onto her lips the next moment, though, and she shrugged. "It was her mistake to let me prepare the tea, though. And you have to admit, she really had it coming."

Merle gaped some more, this time at Hazel, who had checked on Isabel, to make sure she was out like a light. "You're in on it, too?"

Lily's mom came over to Merle, took her hand and squeezed. Fine white lines of strain bracketed her mouth, and her eyes shimmered. "Just bring Maeve back."

"I will," Merle said, her voice cracking, her throat closing up.

Lily stepped between them, made shooing gestures toward the hallway. "Now hurry, it won't hold up for long, and you gotta get out of here before Juneau comes back or sends someone else over to check on my 'won't-be-made-a-fool-of-again' unreliable aunt."

Merle sucked in a breath. "You did that, too, didn't you? You lured Juneau away?"

"Not me—Baz." Lily's eyes danced. "He might not have any magic, but he sure can conjure up some trouble of his own when he puts his mind to it."

"What did he do?"

Lily closed her eyes and waved the question away. "You don't wanna know. *Really.*"

Merle stared at her for a second before she gave her a crushing hug. "Thank you."

"All right, all right," Lily choked out even as she squeezed Merle back. "Enough with the physical abuse. Get out and kick some demon butt already."

At that, Merle's gut clenched tight. "Where's Rhun?"

"They put him in the basement," Hazel said. "The holding room."

When Merle wanted to bolt straight down, Lily held her back with a hand on her shoulder and a solemn, searching look. "You're only using him to find Maeve, right?" There was a deeper understanding in the grave tone of her voice, as well as a warning. "After that you'll bind him again." Those dark blue eyes bore into her. "Right?"

"Right," Merle said, assuring her friend—and herself. "I'll bind him again." She nodded, her throat gone dry, her heart twisted. "Why wouldn't I?" It was meant to sound light, underscored by a casual smile—only it was her best friend she was trying to fool, and of course she saw straight through it.

But it was also *because* Lily was her best friend that she didn't comment on it, didn't give Merle a lecture on her situation and what she could and couldn't do, should or shouldn't be feeling. She simply hugged her, a tacit reassurance, an unspoken promise. *If what you shouldn't be feeling tears you apart, I'll be there for you.*

Merle hugged her tightly in return, fighting back her tears. Taking the keys Hazel handed her, she then rushed down to the basement. Fear and worry wove a knot in her stomach, and her heart beat triple time as she fumbled with the lock on the massive door to the dark cell at the end of the basement hallway.

It had been built to hold evil spirits until they could be dealt with, and the MacKenna residence featured one just like it.

Merle had seen—and even put—some otherworld creatures in it over the years, but never, in her wildest thoughts, had she imagined she'd be helping a demon escape from it.

The door swung inward with a creak, and the scant light from the hallway fell upon a slumped shape on the floor. Merle's heart stopped beating, pierced, crushed.

He was manacled to the wall, the shackles infused with magic subduing his powers, draining his energy, leaving him defenseless. A low moan of agony rose from his throat, and it tore at Merle as if someone had started to pull out her guts. Within a second, she was at his side.

"Rhun."

His head snapped up from his chest, his gaze homed in on her face, and in the blink of an eye, his whole attitude changed. All apparent agony left him, shrugged off like a coat, and a dazzling smile lit up his features. "Little witch." He inched closer to her, as much as he could. "Missed me?"

Merle stopped short. "You're not hurt?"

He snorted. " 'Course not. Takes more than a bit of pathetic spell-casting to break me."

The relief washing over her scared her with its intensity. "I thought you… You looked injured when I came in." She undid the manacles, using the keys and the proper spells to release him.

"Ah, well," he said, "I didn't know it was you at first, and I wanted to be a good sport and play along with your witch friends. They'd be so terribly disappointed if they knew they didn't hurt me." He winked at her, playful, completely at ease, as if he hadn't just escaped torture and incarceration.

As Merle undid the last shackle, she started thinking the whole situation was nothing but a joke to him—when he cupped her face with both freed hands and gave her a kiss that left her breathless. His thumbs stroking over her cheeks, he then studied her so intently, it made her quiver inside.

"Are you all right, Merle?" His tone was low with a kind of

need that scraped over her skin, a protective urgency that touched her even deeper.

All she could do was nod. There was no voice left in her.

Rhun still stared at her as if he wanted to drink her in. His aura was a contained explosion of dark violence, streaked with a tenderness that could unhinge. "Did they do anything to you?"

She shook her head, acutely aware of the heat of his palms on her skin.

"Good." He claimed her mouth again, and her world tilted sideways. "Then let's get out of here, little witch of mine," he murmured against her lips.

They hurried up the stairs and down the hallway toward the front door, where Lily and Hazel waited for them. On their way past the living room, Rhun stopped short in his tracks, staring through the open doorway. Merle followed his gaze to the figure of Isabel, still sprawled face-down on the coffee table, snoring. Rhun cocked an eyebrow at the sight.

"Don't ask," Merle muttered and pulled him forward.

He dug in his heels, looked at her and pointed with a thumb over his shoulder at Isabel. "May I take pain from her?"

"Rhun!"

"What? I'm hungry!"

"We don't have time for that!"

At that, he smiled and let her drag him on. "Ah, so you'd let me feed from her if we had more time? Let me break a few bones?"

Merle shook her head. "Don't even go there."

"Why not?" He draped one arm around her shoulders as he walked, leaned down to whisper in her ear, his breath sensually hot. "You could break some of her bones, too. I know you want to."

Merle was glad they arrived at the front door and faced a suspicious-looking Lily and a curious Hazel at that moment, saving her from commenting on Rhun's suggestion. Because

—*gods knew*—she did want to break some Elder bones, which was, however, a notion that made her extremely uncomfortable.

Hazel hugged Merle goodbye, eyed Rhun warily, and then ushered them out toward the car idling in the driveway. "Go, I'll hold up here. I'll make sure to send the Elders in the wrong direction when they go searching for you."

Merle thanked her from the bottom of her heart, and followed Lily and Rhun to the car. As they approached, Basil rose from his leaning position on the hood and enfolded Merle in a warm hug.

"You okay, sweetie?" he asked into her hair.

"Yeah. Thanks. What about you?"

"I'm fine." His sunny nature gleamed in his eyes.

She returned his smile and gave him a peck on his cheek. Merle had never had a problem being close to Basil without anything sexual getting in the way—he was too much of a brother to her, and she knew he saw her as a sister by choice, too. To the outside world, however, their interactions could sometimes seem like intimacies, a fact Merle all too often forgot until she saw other people's reactions to them.

Like now, for example, when the blunt force of a seething demon's aura brushed up against her back like a wall of heat. She turned to see Rhun staring at Basil over her head with an expression just short of murderous.

"Jerkface," Basil said politely, as if greeting an acquaintance by his name.

"Dickwad," Rhun returned just as politely, inclining his head in mock-respect. His eyes, however, shot daggers at the other male.

Merle rubbed her forehead, choosing not to comment on the display of testosterone in front of her.

"Let's go, chop-chop," Lily said, already opening the door on the passenger side. "You can compare the size of your manly parts later."

"I'm really sorry, man," Rhun said to Basil just as he and Merle were turning to the car.

They both stopped and stared at Rhun in surprised confusion.

Basil frowned. "About what?"

Rhun waved a hand in the general direction of Basil's head. "About...you know." He stopped short and grimaced. "Oh, wait. That is your face."

Merle had to jump in between them to keep Basil from lunging at Rhun. Holding them apart with one hand on Basil's chest, the other on Rhun's, she turned to her personal demon and hissed, "Get in the car. *Now.*"

"Yes, honey-bun," Rhun chirped, his eyes fixed on Basil. Leaning forward, he then grasped the back of Merle's neck and placed an openly possessive kiss on her lips before she got the chance to slap the hell out of him. And once his viciously talented tongue slipped in and claimed her mouth with maddening strokes and licks, Merle couldn't do much more than soften against him. Her brain had effectively been turned to spaghetti.

When Rhun let her go with that arrogant smirk of his and sauntered over to the car, she stumbled. *Damn sneaky demon.*

"Hell no." Basil's hand slammed down on the sedan's roof when Rhun was about to slide into the driver's seat. "You're not driving my car, demon. Get in the back."

Rhun didn't budge an inch, his hand on the open door, and he stared at Basil with calm menace. "I don't take orders from you, Blondie. Only my witch gets to order me around, and only when we're not in bed. Or up against a wall. Or wrestling on a staircase. Or naked on the couch..." He waved a hand. "You get the picture."

Basil looked as if something had gotten stuck in his throat, Lily sucked in a breath, and Merle desperately wanted to merge with the concrete underneath her feet. The heat in her face could have rivaled a furnace.

"Rhun, get in the backseat," she ground out, staring at a point past him, mortified.

"Why, of course, my dearest love."

The endearment hit her straight in the chest and burrowed deep into the place where she harbored a silent, desperate hope, one she knew would be crushed sooner or later. She didn't want his words touching her so deeply, especially when they were so clearly spoken with the intent to taunt, when she burned with anger at the way he'd embarrassed her in front of her friends just now.

Gritting her teeth, she slid into the backseat next to Rhun while Basil and Lily got in the front. As they drove off, Rhun slung his arm around her shoulders and pulled her into his side with a casual, proprietary move. It set her teeth on edge and melted something inside her at the same time.

Any attempt to draw away from him or even get him to remove his arm resulted in a kiss from him, first one on the top of her head, then one on her temple, the next one on the spot between her brows. When he'd reached the tip of her nose, she decided she'd rather give up fighting before he got to her mouth. Because if he kissed her now, her anger would evaporate in a surge of mushy feelings, and—*dammit*—she needed to hold on to that anger. It was the only thing standing between her and an avalanche of emotions that would tear her apart.

Rhun made an appreciative sound when he realized she'd stopped trying to get away from him, and now he nuzzled her hair. "May I take pain from *him*?" he asked for her ears only, indicating Basil.

"No!" Merle hissed.

"But he's *asking* for it."

"Basil's a friend and he's helping us," she whispered. "What is *wrong* with you?"

"I'm hungry! I get cranky when I'm hungry!"

Lily cleared her throat. "Sorry to interrupt the demon's

whining, but I thought I'd let you know I found out how to break the blocking spell."

Merle's whole body went taut and she leaned forward, her pulse picking up speed. "How?"

The small silence from Lily didn't bode well. "There is a ritual you can do."

"But?" Merle knew there was a *but*. There was always a godsdamn *but*.

"To do that, you need to know the identity of the one who cast the blocking spell."

The ensuing silence was so heavy it pressed on Merle's every cell. She closed her eyes and leaned back, into the heat of Rhun, and when he wound his arm around her again, his hand coming to rest above her heartbeat, she didn't fight it at all. A part of her welcomed it, sighed in relish, and wanted to snuggle closer, even as another part of her still wanted to break off Rhun's arm and then some.

"So," she said at last, speaking into the tense quiet while trying to ignore Rhun's hand stroking her skin, comforting her, "we're back to square one, then." Finding out which Elder witch had cast the blocking spell would take even longer than finding out how to break the spell in the first place. In fact, it might just prove impossible to gather that kind of information, since they didn't even have a starting point. They knew nothing about the origin of the spell, so they couldn't trace it. Merle hadn't even seen it with her own eyes, wasn't able to recognize the individual brand of magic used.

They had run into a dead end.

Lily half turned around in her seat. "I'll keep searching, maybe there's another way. I'll also keep my eyes open for how to track the origin of spells, all right?"

Lily's words barely registered through the despair engulfing Merle. She swallowed hard, past a throat gone dry, scraped with sandpaper. Shaking her head, she whispered, "It was all for nothing." The world around her lost color, just as everything seemed to lose sense. "We'll never find her." She felt the bond to Maeve, still barely there, and she saw how it would snap, all too soon, irrevocably tearing out a piece of Merle's soul.

Suddenly, there was no air left in the car. Her breathing hitched, her chest becoming as if bound by tight ropes. Sweat beaded on her skin.

Rhun's hand pressed down on her chest, rubbed in slow, measured strokes, forcing her to inhale when she wanted to choke.

"Breathe," he muttered into her ear.

Lily's gaze flicked from Rhun to Merle and back again, and she gave the slightest of nods to the demon. Her eyes then narrowed on her best friend with affectionate relentlessness. "We *will* get Maeve back," she said, holding Merle's eyes captive, not allowing her to break down. "Don't you give up now, Merle MacKenna."

Lily's faith, her stubborn loyalty, combined with Rhun's calm presence beside her, his heat seeping into her skin, his power enfolding her, it brought Merle back from the brink of despair.

"We will find her," Lily repeated.

Merle sucked in a breath, nodded, and bent forward when Rhun's hand slid to her back, pushed against her with a gentle command. He stroked along her spine as she rested her head on her knees and calmed her breathing.

"That's it, little witch." The murmur was low, intimate, meant for her alone.

When her pulse wasn't on the verge of going through the roof anymore, Merle straightened up again with a deep breath, and Rhun's hand followed her movements up until it curved around the back of her neck.

"I'm all right," Merle said in response to Lily's concerned look. "I'm fine." She leaned back and relaxed into Rhun's fingers caressing her neck. "It's just…"

Maeve's image flashed before her eyes, quiet, shy Maeve—

who had fought with Merle for her right to move out of the house with surprising persistence. Her little sister had never demanded anything for herself, but in this, she'd been adamant, arguing with Merle to the point of yelling—which had been so unlike Maeve, it had shocked Merle for days. In the end, Merle had relented. If only she'd kept Maeve by her side, though, she might still be unharmed…

"I should have never let her move out," Merle muttered. "I still don't know why she wanted it so badly—it's like she couldn't wait to get away from me." And how much that had hurt her, still hurt, she'd never told her sister. Just like she'd never told her how much Maeve meant to her, how much she'd wanted her to move back in. The old Victorian had been so empty without her quiet presence.

"It's not easy," Basil said, his voice low and bearing a note of painful understanding, "being the child without magic in a witch family."

Merle stopped short and stared at him. "She never said anything—"

"Not to you." The lights of the oncoming cars gleamed in the dark blond of his hair until it shone like spun gold. "We used to talk about it, sometimes. She felt out of place, not really belonging. See, she knew about this world beyond that of ordinary people, knew all this stuff about magic and what it can do, but she was never part of it. When you'd meet with Lily and your witch friends, she stayed on the outside, couldn't share it with you, even though she was born of a line of witches same as you. I'm guessing she was trying to build her own identity, start her own life on her own terms, and for that she needed space from you."

Merle was dumbstruck. She'd never looked at it that way, had never understood where Maeve was coming from. "Damn, I've been blind." She shook her head, seeing the pieces falling into place. All the little signs in Maeve's behavior, all the hints she'd given over the years, and Merle had been too focused on herself to notice. As she thought, for the first time, about what it must have been like—*really* been like—for Maeve growing up without magic in a witch household, she realized something else. Her gaze snapped back to Basil. "What about you? How are y—"

"Don't worry about me, sweetie." He met her eyes through the rearview mirror. "I made my peace with it a long time ago. And besides, being a male without magic in a witch family is the rule rather than the exception, so it wasn't as much of a problem to begin with."

She gave him a small smile. "Right. Plus, you've been spoiled silly by all the women in your household."

Basil laughed, even as Lily piped up.

"Not by me," she said, giving her brother a good-natured smack on the shoulder.

Merle shook her head, squeezing Basil's arm. "Thanks for the insight, though. I never knew Maeve felt like that." Rubbing her forehead, she closed her eyes for a second—and then groaned.

Rhun had slid his hand up to the back of her head and now massaged her skull the way he knew would make her toes curl. And they did, *dammit*.

"Rhun!" It was supposed to be a rebuke, but it came out as a moan since she'd melted inside.

He gave her wicked grin. "You looked like you needed a massage. Just trying to help out here."

She swatted at his hand until he withdrew it to play with her hair instead.

Throwing a sheepish glance at Lily and Basil, Merle mumbled, "He didn't... He just... He does this thing with his fingers..."

Basil winced, and Lily swiveled around to stare at the road, her hands over her ears. "TMI! TMI!"

"No, not like that!" Merle could have sworn someone had

turned up the heat in the car. "That's not what I—Oh, some-body just kill me now…"

"No can do, witch volcano," Rhun muttered, his chuckle resounding within her. "I've got plans for you."

"So," Basil said loudly, clearing his throat, "where do you want me to drop you off, Merle? I think it's best if we don't know where you've set up camp, so I figured I'll let you out some place public and you go from there. All right?"

"Yeah," Merle said, infinitely grateful for Basil's tactful igno-rance, "that's fine. Thanks."

Glancing out the window, she realized they'd reached downtown. From what she remembered, Bahram's apartment was just a few blocks away from their current position. Rhun gave her a nod.

"You can let us out here," she said to Basil.

"Sure."

He drove into the parking lot of a fast food restaurant and turned off the engine. They all got out of the car, and then Lily hurried around to retrieve something from the trunk. Reap-pearing with a small duffel bag, she handed it to Merle.

"I thought you might appreciate a change of clothes," she said with a smile.

Merle moaned at the thought of fresh laundry. "You're an angel in disguise."

Lily waved a dismissive hand. "Yeah, yeah, tell me some-thing I don't know. So," she said, her gaze flicking back and forth between Merle and Rhun, "I'll keep raiding our library and whatever other sources I can find for more information, and I'll get in touch with you as soon as I stumble upon something. And you…" Here she poked a finger in Merle's chest and lowered her voice so only Merle would hear her. "…you call me if that luscious hunk of demon gives you any kind of trouble you need help with, all right?"

"I can hear you just fine, you know," Rhun said casually.

"And by the way, thank you—I do so appreciate female admiration."

Lily froze, then slowly straightened up and—without turning around—gave Rhun the finger over her shoulder.

"Thanks, but no, thanks," he said. "I've already got a lovely witch to do that with, and I'm a one-witch kind of demon."

And that was the moment Merle decided she would eviscerate Rhun after beating him to a pulp.

CHAPTER 17

R hun's first clue to Merle being more than royally pissed at him was the fact she made him magically walk into a door. *Twice.*

Except for their first meeting, and that one time in the cemetery, when she'd made him trip—which had been playful teasing—she'd never harmfully used her powers on him, not even when he'd pushed her out of her comfort zone and tried to irritate the hell out of her.

Now, however, for some unfathomable reason, she'd lashed out at him with her magic two times in a row. And—*fucking hell* —his nose hurt like a bitch after clashing twice with the front door of the bar they'd entered in search for someone he could take pain from. The irony of that particular thought wasn't lost on him as he rubbed the bridge of his nose and set it straight again with a crack, grimacing just a little at the sharp jolt of pain. Wiping the blood off with the back of his hand, he turned around to stare at Merle.

"The fuck did you do that for?"

"I don't know what you're talking about." Her face was all innocence, good enough to fool a poker champion.

If he hadn't *felt* her magic, couldn't still taste it in the air, he might have actually believed her. *Tricky little witch.*

"That was totally uncalled for," he whined. "I've been on my best behavior, and this is how you reward me? What did I do to deserve this?"

"Don't you have a drug dealer or pimp to torture?"

He paused for a moment, trying to read her aura. She had it tightly under control, not even showing the slightest hint of any emotion. No anger, no exasperation, no humor either. Something was wrong, and he couldn't put his finger on it. She'd been much more open with him before, to the point of revealing a vulnerability that had pulled at his heartstrings, so why was she now shuttered like a storefront in preparation for a hurricane?

"Are you gonna be all right alone here for a few minutes?" He didn't much like leaving her standing in the corner while he went hunting through the crowd, but the thought of her coming along and witnessing him taking pain from another scumbag was even less appealing.

"I can handle myself." Her tone turned the air icy.

The stare she directed toward him then wasn't the usual Merle glare—it was the kind of dark scowl one might see on the face of a female who was silently plotting to kill her ex. That's how Merle was looking at him right now, as if thinking up fun ways to hurt him. Like, maybe, eviscerating him after beating him to a pulp.

With that uncomfortable thought at the forefront of his mind, he went about his hunt through the bar, a dark, grimy shithole he knew from his time before the Shadows. It had stubbornly withstood the withering of decades and the gentrification of the neighborhood, and still served as the watering hole for all sorts of lowlifes.

It didn't take him long to pick up on the twisted aura of one particularly vile character, a drug dealer who had just covertly sold a bag of pills to a twitchy kid. Rhun waited in a corner until the kid, who could be no older than sixteen, left, and the drug dealing scum made for the restroom. With one last glance in the direction of Merle, to see if she was doing okay—she was, still standing alone and unbothered—Rhun followed the man.

He made short work of him in the empty restroom. After silencing the guy's vocal cords with one mental crush, Rhun dragged the struggling figure into one of the dingy stalls, and then used some more of his demon powers to sever the sinews in the scum-sucker's body, one by one.

Pain erupted in the man's aura, oozed from his pores. Rhun absorbed it, devoured it, sighing with delight as it nurtured him. Nothing better than causing some raw hurt to make his night, to take his mind off a witch he couldn't have.

Against better judgment, driven by his hunger, Rhun sank his throbbing fangs into the man's neck. The blood tasted revolting, pumped full of narcotics, and Rhun stopped drinking after two pulls, spitting the foul stuff on the floor.

"Fucking junkies," he muttered under his breath, and concentrated on causing some more pain instead.

When he was done, the man's limbs were only held together by flesh and bone, all the sinews being torn apart, so when Rhun let him go, the drug dealer slumped to the dank floor like a puppet whose strings had been cut. He'd be unable to even crook his little finger, much less stand up and run away until someone found him here.

Rhun regarded him for a moment with a dispassionate eye. He'd have liked to make the internal organs of the scumbag pop like overheated corn in the microwave, but that would have effectively killed him in no time. Wouldn't be a loss, in Rhun's opinion, and he'd have done it without a second's hesitation not too long ago—but that was before he'd met his witch. Now, he contented himself with making the human chew up his own tongue as a parting gift, and then he strolled out of the restroom, whistling a tune.

He stopped when he saw Merle.

She leaned against the wall in the corner next to the entrance, her arms folded in front of her chest, every single sign of her body language clearly projecting a "Fuck off" vibe. Of course, though, that didn't keep the bastards who frequented this joint from trying to come on to her.

What made Rhun stop in his tracks and admire the view, however, was what happened to those said bastards. One tripped and fell on his face before he reached Merle, another was seized by a nasty bout of coughing that made him run to the bar for a drink after he'd tried to chat her up. Another one who'd been approaching her with a leer walked straight past Merle and collided face-first with the opposite wall, and even another—who'd called her something that made Rhun want to smash the guy's face in—had the sudden and irrational urge to douse himself not only with his own beer, but with that of his pals as well. Which led to a heated brawl between drinking buddies.

And all the while, Merle hadn't even moved a finger, leaning against the wall with a casual don't-mess-with-me attitude.

Standing there, staring at her, Rhun decided he'd never met a sexier female in his life.

He grinned with unconcealed endorsement and approached his witch, reaching out to stroke her cheek—and instead ended up involuntarily poking that finger in his nose. Of course, it still hurt like hell from when he'd force-smashed it into the door before.

"Done here?" Merle asked him, her voice flat, her eyes cold.

"Yes." He glared at her, magic swirling between them. "Would you let me remove my finger?"

"I don't have anything to do with where you decide to stick your fingers." She pushed off the wall, picked up her duffel bag, and walked outside.

"What the fuck did I do?" he called after her, still not able to pull his finger out of his nose.

She didn't answer him, and she didn't loosen her magical hold on him until they'd reached the apartment, which meant he was forced to walk three blocks through downtown with one finger up his nose. The looks this earned him from passers-by spoke volumes.

"So what's this all about?" he asked, closing the door to the apartment behind him. He gingerly pinched his nose, winced at the pain.

"You're a jerk." Merle dumped the duffel bag in the hallway and bent to rummage through it.

"I know, that's nothing new." Leaning against the wall with one shoulder, he watched her take out a set of fresh clothes. "Why don't you just tell me which department I fucked up in this time, I apologize, you forgive me, and we move on to have hot make-up sex?"

"So you can flaunt that in front of my friends, too?" She stood and rounded on him with fire in her eyes.

Ah, so that's what this is about. "I wasn't flaunting," he said, slightly piqued.

"Really? What were you doing, then? Trying to find out how to best embarrass me?" Her voice shook slightly, and there, in her aura, was the tiniest flicker of hurt. It felt like razors scraping over his skin.

He was about to reply something when Merle cut him off.

"You know what? Don't bother. I don't care." The tremor in her voice belied her statement. "I'm going to leaf through the grimoire again so we can get on with the search *to find my sister*, but first I'm taking a shower. *Alone*," she added with a scathing look, and then stomped toward the bathroom.

Rhun was left staring at the wake of her aura, which flickered with the turmoil of emotions she hadn't been able to shield from him anymore.

Anger, he could take—in fact, he liked her getting a bit riled so she would banter with him. It was a teasing game, irritating her just enough so she would shed her proper attitude and verbally tangle with him. But *hurt*—that was something else. He didn't want to see that in her eyes, sense it in her aura.

For a reason he hadn't reckoned with but had come to accept, he couldn't stand the thought of her being disappointed in him. With not a little astonishment, he realized it threw his world out of kilter, made him want to hold her and soothe her until it was righted again.

Such an unsettling feeling, knowing one single person held the key to his own happiness.

He thought about the irrational urge which had driven him to crudely stake his claim on her in front of her friends. No, not her friends—just Basil. The way the other male had looked at her, touched her, held her, had made Rhun's reason dissolve in a wash of visceral jealousy and possessiveness. He'd never been territorial about females, until Merle had snuck up on him and transformed him into a primitive beast staking claim on its mate.

Mate.

The word stung, just as it stung him that he'd never get to make her *his* with the most intimate, most serious bond his species was capable of. The thought of letting her go was a raw, gaping wound inside, though it didn't ache as much as the mere idea of taking her powers and leaving her stripped of her identity.

Which was why, in the long hours he'd lain shackled in the dark basement, fearing for his witch, wanting to know she was unharmed, he'd changed his mind. Oh, he would let her go, all right. But not as he'd originally planned.

Going back to the Shadows, he thought, wouldn't break him. He'd been there already, he'd survived. Betraying Merle, however, would kill something inside him.

So he'd decided not to absorb her magic, not to break the bond leashing him to her. Instead, he'd stay true to his word, would help her find Maeve, knowing Merle would have to bind him right away afterwards. It was the single most unselfish decision he'd ever made, and he marveled at the strange feeling. He'd figured it would hurt, yes, but he'd never guessed it would bring him such a bittersweet sense of peace. Of doing something *right*.

As he strolled toward the bathroom, listening to the sound of the shower running, Merle's presence on the other side of the closed door a beacon drawing him like nothing else, he knew it would be the noble thing to do to let her stay angry at him, considering she'd have to let him go, too. It would be easier on her if she became less attached to him, and being a ruthless jerk would certainly help that along. He could hurt her, make her hate him even, to the point that she'd be happy to banish him in the Shadows again once he'd served his purpose.

Yes, it would be the noble thing to do.

However, Rhun was only demon, after all, and there was only so much selflessness he was capable of. In this, he'd be selfish. He wanted to enjoy the remaining time he had with her, to savor her, what they had, this ephemeral bond they shared. He wanted to make her smile so he could take the image with him, wanted to relish how she made him feel, how she branded him in a way no one else ever had.

He took off his clothes, folded them neatly, set them on the dresser, and then went into the bathroom, disabling the lock with a mental command. Steam rolled up against him. When he slid open the glass door of the huge shower cubicle and stepped inside, Merle jumped and dropped the soap.

"Rhun! I locked the door, dammit!"

"Aren't we past that?" he asked quietly.

He picked up the soap, lathered his hands and then set the bar aside. Calmly, he took her hand and started washing her. When she wanted to withdraw, he grabbed her wrist, holding her in place.

"Stay still."

"You," she said through gritted teeth, "are such an ass. If you think you can just waltz in here and cop a feel like you have a right to…"

"Merle."

"…then you've got another thing coming. You are—"

"Sorry."

She stopped short, blinked, a rivulet of water running down her forehead. "What?"

"I'm sorry. That's what I am." He continued lathering her, stroking soap in soft caresses up her arm, her shoulder, her collarbone. "I'm sorry I embarrassed you in front of your friends." He washed her other arm, rubbing each and every finger with utmost care. "I'm not sorry, however, that I made it clear to Blondie that you're mine." Taking up more soap, he then spread it in languorous strokes over her breasts, around her puckered nipples, until her breath hitched and his own skin was on fire. "Because that's what you are. Mine."

Merle stood still now, not fighting him, her eyes fixed on his face. Her aura wavered, tinged with budding desire.

"You might not be mine for long," he said, his voice gone rough with hunger, "but you are right now, and I want us to enjoy this for the time we have left."

At that, her pulse stuttered, and her power spiked with a new kind of hurt.

Rhun stopped lathering her stomach and glanced at her face. There was a sheen of tears on her eyes, and she jerkily shook her head, taking a step away from him. The iridescent flutter of her aura stilled, brought under careful control as she shut herself off bit by bit.

"No," he said, panic surging through him, and he followed her, crowding her until her back met the tiled wall. Cupping her face, he pinned her with his gaze. "Do not go cold on me again." He couldn't let her do that. It would shatter him.

Merle's breathing went erratic, her throat worked fast as she swallowed several times, and her gaze skittered back and forth between his eyes.

His thumbs stroked over her cheeks, and his chest was tight, so tight, as he looked upon her. "When I go back to the Shadows," he whispered, "I want to take a good memory with me. I want to remember you, us, this." He pressed his forehead to hers. "Will you at least grant me that, little witch?"

At his endearment, a part of her walls came down. He could taste regret, fear—*affection*. Warmth spread through him as he latched on to the feeling, grasped it like the pathetic idiot he was. He kissed her then, brushed his lips over hers in a tender caress, a silent request for permission. Because for what it was worth, for all the raging need in him to claim her more aggressively, if she told him to let her go now, he would, even if it wrecked him.

She whispered something against his lips, her body pressing into him.

"Yes," she said more distinctly when he drew away far enough to look into her eyes. They were wide, a clear blue with depths that haunted him, and right now, they held such bittersweet longing, a desperate hunger echoing his own.

"Merle mine," he muttered, and she shivered, parting her lips.

It was all the invitation he needed.

With the water of the shower pelting down on his back, he lowered his head and kissed her again, harder this time, infused with the force of his craving. He licked along her lower lip, and she opened for him, greeting him with her tongue as he plunged into her mouth, pressed his body closer to hers. A low moan escaped her, and her aura flickered with pleasure. It only ratcheted up his hunger.

He broke the kiss, panting, his fangs punching through his gums. He was strung tight with need, for blood and pleasure and *Merle*, his cock grown hard where it pressed into her belly, but he wouldn't rush it. Not now. Not when this might be their last time together.

Licking and nibbling along her jaw, he moved down to her throat, nicking the artery there just the tiniest bit with the tip of his fangs. Merle gasped and grasped his shoulders, trembling with anticipation. He didn't sink his teeth into her neck, though, only lapped up the few drops of blood, sealing the small nicks he'd caused. The aroma of Merle spread on his tongue, and he closed his eyes, savored it while pressing a kiss to the curve where her neck met her shoulder.

"*Rhun.*" Her voice shook.

Taking a deep breath, he inhaled her scent—mixed with that of water and soap—and then withdrew a bit.

"Turn around," he said, need and raw emotion roughening his voice.

Merle obeyed without hesitation, and it almost did him in. He had to pause for a few seconds, tamping down his desire far enough that he wouldn't just bend her over and take her. It was clear she thought he'd do something like that, though, by the way she stood still, half-glancing at him over her shoulder, trembling with thrilled expectation.

Smiling, Rhun ran his hand down her spine, delighting in how it made her shiver and how she slightly bent forward in response, angling her hips toward him.

"Not yet, witch volcano," he murmured.

He picked up the soap bar instead, lathered his hands again, and proceeded to finish what he'd started. Stepping up close to her, he rubbed her back, spread the soap, kneading her muscles, and Merle sighed and leaned into his touch. He worked his way down, took care of her hips, her ass, stroked down her legs and even lathered each foot down to her toes. Straightening up again, he playfully nipped at her earlobe as he moved his hands to her front and lavished his care on her breasts again.

"You already did that area," she said, even as she leaned

more into him. Her husky voice was a stroke of pure sex over his senses.

"Not well enough."

He relished the feeling of the swell of her breasts under his hands, her supple skin, the hard buds of her nipples, the way she arched her back and pushed into his caresses. He relished and savored and memorized, and still knew it would never be enough to last him through the Shadows.

By the time he moved his hands lower to stroke her abdomen, circling her bellybutton, Merle had raised her arms and tangled her fingers in his hair, her head tilted to the side so she could half-face him. Her breath came in pants, hot on his cheek, and he held still for a moment, just reveling in her nearness, in the feel of her. His arms tightened around her, and he wished he could keep her like this. His heart splintered with the knowledge he couldn't.

She obviously felt the hard ridge of his erection pressing into her hips, because she wiggled them impatiently, ground her rear against him in sensual invitation. Grinning, he loosened his embrace enough to give her a warning slap on her ass. She sucked in air and froze while a bolt of pain shot through her aura, followed by a violent wave of pleasure.

"I said not yet, my impatient little spitfire."

She half-turned around and opened her mouth to protest, saw his expression, and clamped her lips together again. A quiver rippled through her body, her cheeks flushed a lovely red, and the tantalizing scent of her increased arousal suffused the humid air. When he curved his hand around the back of her neck and stole a kiss, she softened against him, melting something inside him, too.

With a patience belying his roaring need, he then shampooed her hair. His fingers massaged her scalp, gently worked the ginger strands—now a darker shade of red under the water—while he placed kisses on her cheeks, her temples, her forehead. She was his to take care of, at least for now, and he enjoyed every minute of it.

He maneuvered her underneath the shower's spray to rinse it all off. With her eyes closed, she let him do as he pleased, and the warm appreciation in her aura was like a balm for his hurting soul.

As the soap and shampoo flowed down her body, over skin flushed rosy by the heat of the shower, he came around to stand behind her again, his front to her back. His hands slid down over her abdomen, to her hips, and followed the curve of her thighs inward to the triangle of her ginger curls.

"There's a place I haven't washed yet," he said into her ear, and he smiled as she trembled in response.

Using only water this time, he started attending to the one spot he'd hungered to touch, had left for the finish as his own special treat. He slid his fingers through her folds, parted them, stroked her in what could hardly pass as washing. Not that Merle seemed to mind. She writhed against him, moaning with her head rolled back against his chest. Her mounting excitement tinged her aura and deepened his hunger.

Growling low in his throat, he felt his control slip. He dipped one finger inside her to check how wet she was.

Dripping.

"Hands up on the wall." His voice was barely recognizable, even to himself.

She did as told, breathing fast, and he nudged up her right leg, setting her foot on the low marble bench below the wall. Without further ado, he grasped her hips, pulled her backwards toward him and then buried his cock inside her.

Merle's choked cry made him freeze.

Gut clenched tight at the troubled flicker in her aura, he held still. "Am I hurting you?"

"No. Yes. A little." She panted, her body tense. "It's okay. I'm just a bit sore from yesterday."

"You know I take that as a compliment," Rhun said, stroking her back—and then he pulled out and knelt behind her.

When he grabbed her hips and delved his tongue inside her slick center, Merle gave an adorable squeal of surprise. "Wh-what are you doing?"

"Making it better," he muttered against her intimate flesh, and continued to lick her. Sealing the puncture marks of his bites wasn't the only possible application of his skin-surface healing ability.

In addition to soothing her soreness, he brought her to a swift climax and soaked up her pleasure as it spread in the air. This time, when he entered her, she pushed against him and let out a long moan of pure delight, echoed by his own sounds of pleasure as he moved inside her, withdrawing and plunging back into her tight heat.

While he stroked her breast with one hand, he held her hips in place for his thrusts with the other and used a fragment of his powers to tease her clit. She bucked against him in a frenzy, her hands slipping from their position on the wall.

"Stay in place," he ordered her roughly.

His command was enough to send her over the edge—and wasn't that the fucking hottest thing he'd ever seen? Waves of pleasure rippled through her aura, she cried out, cursing him, moaning his name as if it was a prayer, and he drank it in, all of it, not just her pleasure, not just as nourishment. He feasted on the layers of warmth in her feelings for him in a way that had nothing to do with carnal hunger, and everything to do with a need running much deeper, to the core of his soul.

Leaning down until his chest brushed her back, his cock still buried inside her, he embraced her, one hand gently closing over her throat.

"Drop your shields," he whispered in her ear.

Merle stilled, breath wild and heavy, her pulse fast in the wake of her orgasm.

"I want to taste you," he said, caressing the sensitive skin of her throat, a subtle gesture of possession, a promise. "All of you. I want to feel you, Merle. Without barriers." He brushed her mental senses with a reassuring wave of his powers. "Open to me. I won't hurt you."

Her breath caught in her throat, a choked sob. Rhun stroked her, physically, mentally, their bodies still linked in the most intimate of ways, and he waited patiently while her aura quivered with a storm of emotions, too many and too quick for him follow.

"I won't ever harm you, little witch." He pressed a kiss to the back of her neck.

She trembled hard in his arms now, so hard, and she seemed so small and vulnerable that he thought better and wanted to tell her it was okay, she didn't have to do this, he didn't need to feel—

Merle lowered her shields.

It knocked the breath out of him, almost brought him to his knees. Her power wrapped around him, and his heart stuttered at the unadulterated richness of her emotions, her thoughts, laid bare before him. He saw, felt, tasted, touching her mind with gentle care, humbled by her trust. The depth of her feelings was staggering, such true goodness, such pure hope and faith, and her magic—it was as strong as he'd suspected, stronger even, a power beyond any he'd ever encountered. There was a promise of greatness in her, the potential of her—given more time— growing into a witch of unparalleled force.

He voiced his thoughts directly inside her mind. *"Gods, but you're beautiful."*

Her response was visceral, swift, a wave of affection, shatteringly open and honest, and he soaked it up, bathed in it. If he spent the rest of eternity in the Shadows, this feeling would last him through it.

She held nothing back, and he saw the intricate tangle of her emotions for him, tasted it, reveled in it, wrapped it around himself. There was fear, of him being hurt by the Elders, of losing him, of her feelings for him. Laced into it was a desperate hope for the impossible, echoing his own futile wish to keep her. There was anger, too, affectionate exasperation that made him want to smile and tease her. But, above and beyond all else, there was the one emotion that ripped through his heart and stitched it back together, the one feeling he'd never tasted before, not this deeply, truly, consuming.

Merle quivered as he touched upon it, marveled at it, savored it. He was torn inside with the need to open to her as well, to let her see her feelings reflected in his own, to let her taste him as he tasted her now.

Shame kept him from lowering his shields and letting her in.

Rhun couldn't allow her to know how he'd planned on stripping her of her magic, of her beautiful, strong magic humbling him so profoundly now that he'd seen how deep it ran. He couldn't stand her disappointment, was afraid it might taint the wonder that was this feeling which she wrapped around him. So, he simply voiced what defied all definition, reduced it to words that were too small.

"I love you, too."

An explosion of emotions inside her, bittersweet, powerful, delight tempered with heartache. Her mind splintered, broke into shards of pleasure and pain, threatening to break him as well. But he held on to his witch, didn't let her drown. He latched on to the threads of purest affection, to the sparks that would ignite fire, and he nurtured and intensified them, until there was only desire and passion, heat and hunger.

Linked to her in devastating emotional intimacy, Rhun deepened their physical union as well, moved inside her, enhancing their shared pleasure in her mind. Merle met him thrust for thrust, climbing with him toward a shattering release. When he bit her neck in the throes of their passion, drank from her as if starved, it was enough to hurtle them both into bliss.

Much later, after he'd carried her out of the shower and onto the bed, after he'd taken her again, slowly and thoroughly, pleasured her until she'd fallen asleep, happy and sated, only then, when she came to again locked in his embrace, did he tell her. He could have done so earlier, but he knew it would destroy this moment he had with her, would force her back to reality and rush them both toward the inexorable end. So he only told her now, being the selfish demon he was.

"I know someone," he said, stroking her fiery hair, "who could break the blocking spell."

CHAPTER 18

Merle sat up with a jolt, fully awake within one second. Heart beating a million times a minute, she stared at Rhun. "You know someone who can break the spell? How long have you known that? And you're only telling me this *now*?"

Rhun gingerly disengaged her hands from his throat, placed them on the pillow and patted them. "I said *could*, not can. I know someone who *could* break the spell. Big difference, little witch. And even if he can, chances are he just *won't*. He's…a bit difficult."

Merle had a feeling the frown on Rhun's face was not for her benefit. "Who are you talking about?"

He cleared his throat. "Arawn."

Merle's jaw dropped. "*The* Arawn? The Demon Lord?"

"Yes and no," Rhun said. "He's not really our lord." He frowned again. "He's not even demon." The frown deepened and he grimaced. "In fact, no one's really sure *what* he is…" His voice trailed away and he stared off with unease in his eyes.

"But—he really exists? I've only heard of him in stories—you know, we witches tell our children to behave, or else Arawn will come to get them…"

"Yeah," Rhun said quietly, "we demons have the same stories."

At that, Merle only gaped at him in silent worry.

"Anyway," he went on after a minute, "Arawn does have his own set of indefinable magic, and he might be able to break the spell—if you can offer him something of value for his help. I can't guarantee anything, especially since he's reclusive and unpredictable. Now, if I could avoid it, I wouldn't draw Arawn's attention by any means, let alone ask him for a favor, but seeing that time is running out for Maeve…" His gaze was intent on Merle's, steady, supportive, unwavering. Without words, his eyes told her he would take on whatever risk lay ahead in order to help her, to right her world, and that he didn't care what it might cost him.

Merle's chest was too tight for her to take in air, so she kissed him, breathing him in instead. Her hand resting on his cheek, she then drew back a little, and the glint in his eyes made her sigh. The way he looked at her, as if she were the only thing of value in his world, it shook her to her bones.

"You've met Arawn before?" she asked before she melted into a puddle of goo on the bed.

Rhun's gaze stroked over her features in a visual caress, drinking her in with such open delight. "Our paths have crossed." His finger traced the curve of her throat, made her shiver. "I'm not one of his, though."

"His?"

"He deals in favors and binds otherworld creatures to him in servitude. His network and resources are vast." Rhun now played with a lock of her hair, expressing a fascination with it that was almost childlike in its honesty.

"So," Merle said, frowning, "it might be dangerous to ask him for a favor? What with him being so unpredictable and powerful?"

Rhun shrugged, a casual display of lithe muscle underneath his lickable skin. "The way I see it, we're damned if we do, and damned if we don't. Even if he turns on us, things can hardly get any worse, can they? If we don't ask him, we're screwed anyway."

Merle considered it for a moment, unease churning in her stomach. This was risky, and she wasn't so sure about Rhun's statement that things couldn't get any worse. She'd thought she'd hit rock bottom quite a couple of times already, only to find out she could always fall deeper, crash harder. Involving someone like Arawn—a mythical creature of unknown powers and questionable affiliation—might send everything spiraling out of control.

Then again, Rhun was right. With every passing night, the chances of finding Maeve alive and in a state of being able to recover—Merle didn't even hope for her being unharmed anymore—grew slimmer. If they tried to find another way of breaking the blocking spell or locating the witch who cast it, it might take too much time.

Merle's eyes met Rhun's. "Okay. Let's do this."

෧෯෯

STANDING IN THE LIGHT, DRIZZLING RAIN, HER ARMS WRAPPED tightly around her against the crisp night air, Merle stared at the lake's black surface in front of her. "Remind me, my darling demon—why are we here again?"

Rhun smiled at her endearment, and the beauty of it cut through her in bittersweet pleasure. "One does not simply *walk* into the lair of Arawn," he said, his voice low and ominous as he played on a quote from the first *Lord of the Rings* movie. Merle bit her lip at his humor, resisted the urge to kiss him breathless. "The exact location of his hidey hole is only known to his lackeys, and you have to get one of his gatekeepers to take you there."

"And by gatekeepers you mean sleeping fish?"

He chuckled, swatted her butt, and walked over to where

the shore's rocks fell steeply into the dark of the lake. Squatting, he dipped his fingers into the water and started making small waves. Merle half-expected him to say something like "Here, fishy, fishy," and she barely smothered her snort of laughter. The dark look Rhun shot her over his shoulder made her fall utterly silent, though. An enticing whisper rose in the gloom of the night. Merle rubbed her arms as the hairs on her neck rose in warning.

"Rhun, what—"

"Shhh."

A hand shot out of the water and grabbed Rhun's wrist. Merle jumped and shrieked. The surface of the lake shook as the creature tried to pull Rhun into the depths, but he calmly dug in his heels, his thumb stroking circles on the skin of whatever held on to him. After a minute of a silent and eerie tug-o'-war, the force on the other side stopped trying to draw Rhun under, and instead the shape of a head broke the surface of the black water.

Merle held her breath as a young woman emerged, ethereally beautiful—and stark naked. The wet curls of her dark hair clung to skin the color of moonlight, framing the face of a maiden which would undoubtedly have inspired a whole collection of courtly love songs in the Middle Ages. She'd half-risen out of the lake, her upper body—naked breasts and all— glistening in the scant light, and she still held on to Rhun's hand, her eyes fixed on his face. When she smiled, Merle felt the sudden and irrational urge to strangle her with her own hair.

"Rhun," the water nymph said, all but purring his name.

"Kalista." He returned her smile.

"It's been a while." The nymph tilted her head and regarded him with blatant appreciation.

Merle's urge to strangle the damn beauty morphed into the violent desire to scratch her eyes out first. And then maybe hack off the hand that *still held Rhun's wrist*. She mentally shook herself. What was happening to her? She'd never been that jealous of anyone.

"You look good these days," Kalista said, her voice a melodious hum in the dark of the night.

"Hm. Must be because I'm in love."

Merle froze, along with her heart.

Kalista's gaze followed Rhun's to Merle, disbelief written on her face. "With her?"

Rhun's low hum of affirmation rolled through Merle, melted the ice that had crept up, filled spaces inside her she hadn't realized had been empty and aching.

"And," Rhun went on, "I'm afraid my witchy sweetheart here will hack off your hand, scratch out your eyes and then strangle you with your own hair if you keep on holding on to me like that. She *is* rather possessive." All said with a beatific expression and such gentleness, one might think he was talking about how he'd found salvation.

At his words, Merle's pulse had stuttered into high gear, and her face blazed with heat. That damn, sneaky demon. She'd apparently maintained a mental connection to him after she'd lowered her shields, and he'd picked her thoughts from her mind like ripe fruit.

Kalista gave Merle an assessing once-over, and then released Rhun. "My apologies, witch. I didn't realize you had a claim on him. You should mark him as yours to avoid misunderstandings."

Merle blinked. "Uh, yeah, sure." She glanced at Rhun, and her heart twisted with longing. If only things were different, she would mark him any which way she could, and flaunt him as hers like a precious jewel. Hell, if she were a cat, she'd possessively rub herself all over him until he wore her scent embedded in his skin.

"I'd like that, little witch of mine."

Merle jumped at Rhun's mental voice. *"You just love taking advantage of that open connection, don't you?"* she thought right at him.

His chuckle resounded in her mind, stroking her in hot, low places. *"You betcha. And, by the way, you may rub yourself all over me at any given time, even if you're not a cat."*

"We wish to speak to Arawn," Rhun said out loud while Merle blushed with scorching heat. "Are you still in his service, Kalista?"

A shadow fell over the water nymph's face. "Yes."

"Can you take us to him?"

Her expression turned wary, and her gaze darted from Rhun to Merle and back again. "I will have to ask him for permission." And that thought clearly didn't appeal to her. There was even a glint of fear in her eyes.

"Please do," Rhun said, his voice low and reassuring.

"Wait here," Kalista told him after a long moment of consideration, and then she disappeared underneath the water without making a sound.

The night was eerily quiet all of a sudden, as if holding its breath. Merle stared at the lake, vast and black and looming in front of her, and she shivered involuntarily. A warm hand closed around the back of her neck, and then Rhun pulled her against him, enfolding her in his arms. He bent his head and rubbed his cheek over hers, a gesture of such sweetness, it tore at her. One of his hands came to rest above her erratic heartbeat, and he cocooned her with his power.

Closing her eyes, Merle smiled, relaxing. As mild rain feathered over her skin, the night lost its menace, and she marveled at how one darkness could expel another. Rhun's aura was still demon, laced with a lethal vibe that had once unsettled her. Now, however, she took the strangest comfort in it. She'd let him closer than anyone ever before, and as he held her with a strength whispering of danger and darkness, all she felt was a peace she'd never known. And wasn't that madness?

"No." Rhun's deep voice hummed in her head. *"It's the most beautiful gift I've ever received."*

"Rhun…" She brought her hand up to stroke his face. *"You've got to stop saying stuff like that."*

"Why?" An unrepentant brush of his powers against her mental senses.

"You'll turn me to mush," she whispered.

"So?"

"I don't look good as mush."

His lips curved against her cheek.

The surface of the water broke and Kalista reappeared. Another nymph followed, this one with hair of luminous gold.

"He'll see you," Kalista said. "Come."

Rhun loosened his embrace but took Merle's hand, leading her toward the rocky lake shore.

Merle frowned, suspicion unfurling inside. "Um, Rhun?"

"Yes, mushy witch?"

That earned him a swat on the arm. "Where are we going?"

"To see Arawn, of course," he said, pulling her unerringly closer to the water. "Seriously," he went on with a dramatic sigh, "I feel like half of the time you're not even listening to me. I mean, I know my good looks are distracting, but it's just hurtful if you don't pay attention to what I say." He threw her look of heartbroken sadness. "I think it's time we admitted we have a communication problem, honey."

She chose to ignore his quipping and instead glared at him as he stopped at the edge of the shore. "I mean why are you pulling me toward the lake?"

"Because that's the way we're taking to Arawn," he said, and before she could so much as flinch, he'd grasped her by the waist and hauled her into the water.

She hit the lake's surface with a splash, followed by the muted sounds of water closing in around her. The biting cold stopped her heart. Her shocked shriek turned into a gurgle as a thousand icy pinpricks pierced her skin, numbing her muscles.

She struggled, flailed, swam upward with panicky strokes, and broke the surface with a gasp, hauling in air.

"You jerk! Bastard! I'm gonna kill you!" Pedaling in the water, she searched for Rhun, so she could flay the skin off his back.

But he wasn't standing on the shore anymore. Merle paused for a second, swimming in place, and then she whirled around and punched the demon who'd swum up behind her right in the face. Her fist connected with his nose with a satisfying crack.

Rhun glared at her, wiping the blood away while swimming. "That's twice in one night you broke my nose."

She shook her hand against the pain the punch had caused. Hitting someone definitely looked easier in the movies. "You deserved that, you sneaky, two-faced—"

"Would you have jumped in if I'd asked you to?"

"Yes," she said petulantly.

He cocked an eyebrow.

"Okay, no!"

His grin flashed bright in the night. Winking at her, he threw her a kiss.

"I hate your guts," she muttered under her breath.

"No, you don't, my little witch." Rhun's voice was smooth, alluring, and with just enough smugness to make her narrow her eyes at him, even as a smile bloomed inside her.

"All right," he called out to Kalista, who had been watching their interaction with a mix of fascination and confusion. "Let's go."

As Merle was about to ask how this would work, the blond nymph swam toward her, inclined her head—and pulled Merle under. The water rushed in around her before she could voice any protest.

Darkness, cold, an unyielding grip, drawing her down, down, down with preternatural strength. Instinctively, Merle had started holding her breath, fought the urge to inhale. Her pulse hammered in her ears. The water got colder by the second, biting into her skin, icing her limbs, and she couldn't breathe, mustn't breathe, had to hold on. The blond nymph's grasp around her waist never loosened, even as Merle struggled in beginning panic.

Just as her head was about to explode, the direction of the pull changed. The nymph dragged her upward now, so fast Merle's ears rang at the sudden difference in the water pressure. They broke the surface, and Merle sucked in a breath with an undignified wheeze. *Air.* Gods, she'd never been so glad to use her lungs.

The blond nymph had let her go when they had surfaced, and now swam idly in a slow circle around Merle, studying her with open interest.

"You could have given me a warning," Merle rasped in between shuddering breaths.

The naiad simply smiled, her face all smooth with the beauty of never-ending youth. Nymphs didn't grow old—they just dropped dead one day when their time came. Merle had never made up her mind whether that was a boon or a bane.

At that moment the water splashed wildly a few feet away as Rhun emerged from the depths. Kalista surfaced at a safe distance from him, shooting Merle a cautious glance.

That's right. Merle narrowed her eyes at the water nymph. *You keep your fins off him, missy.*

Rhun laughed and dragged Merle toward the shore.

"Stop reading my thoughts," she hissed at him.

"And lose such a great source of amusement? I don't think so."

They trudged out of the lake, and Merle stopped short at the difference in their surroundings. Where before rocks and pebbles had framed the lake, set in a wide clearing in the forest, now huge trees loomed almost directly over the water. The shore had a much shallower incline, with sand instead of pebbles, and it morphed into grass the closer it got to the tree line.

"This is not the same lake," Merle murmured.

"Nope," Rhun said as he stepped onto the small beach, wringing his T-shirt and shaking his hair.

"Follow the trail until it swallows you," Kalista called from out on the water.

Merle frowned. What an odd wording. Shaking her head, she trudged on, cursing at the soaked state of her clothing. "Great, now I'm all wet," she muttered under her breath, and froze in place when she saw Rhun wiggling his brows. "Not like that!" The wave of heat rolling through her was enough to dispel the cold of her clammy clothes and the chilly night air.

"I can change that in a minute, you know."

"Rhun! This is neither the time nor the place."

"Pity," he murmured, heat in his eyes. "Let me know if you get too cold. I'll be happy to warm you up again."

"Let's just go before we catch pneumonia."

Rhun led the way, his acute demon night vision recognizing a winding path into the forest where Merle only saw shadows and more shadows still. She grabbed his hand so as not to trip, and he squeezed it in reassurance.

"I've got you," he said in her mind.

"I know." Merle's answer came without thinking, from a place that felt rather than understood.

"Before we go in," Rhun said after a moment, "a word of warning. Keep your wits together around Arawn. He can be somewhat...unnerving." It was too dark to see his face, but the nervous flicker in Rhun's energy was palpable.

Merle almost stopped in her tracks. "The very fact that *you* find him unnerving makes me a teeny tiny bit *more* apprehensive about this meeting than I already was."

Rhun didn't reply anything, and they walked in silence for a while, the cold seeping into Merle's bones. She was about to risk muttering a spell that would singe her clothes in order to warm her clammy limbs, when it happened. The earth gave way underneath their feet, and with a cry of shock, Merle tumbled down along with Rhun, through dirt and roots and darkness.

Just as Kalista had said, the trail swallowed them.

Rhun had wrapped himself around Merle, taking the brunt of the fall, so after they'd hit the ground and rolled over a couple of times before coming to a halt, it was him that looked like something a giant mole had chewed up and spit out again.

"Are you okay?" Merle disentangled herself from him, worry a tight knot in her stomach.

"Yeah," Rhun groaned. "Just peachy."

Getting to her feet and extending a hand to help Rhun up—which he proudly ignored in favor of struggling upright by himself—Merle threw glances around the hole they'd tumbled into. It was in fact a tunnel, dimly lit by—were those fireflies? She squinted at the tiny, moving sources of light floating in the air, and shook her head in disbelief. *Incredible.*

"Don't linger," Rhun said low in her ear, pushing her gently forward in the direction the fireflies were taking.

After a few minutes and several turns at intersections—the lights leading their way—the tunnel opened up into a room. Roots, as massive as tree trunks, steadied the rounded walls of earth. Here and there, the roots curled into smaller swirls of almost artful delicacy, a natural adornment. In the middle of the room lay a heap of furs and cushions—and on top of it, lounging in languorous predatory ease, loomed a giant black wolf, almost twice the size of a normal canine.

Merle stopped dead, her muscles locked in place, her heart pounding with the rush of fear. *"Rhun,"* she called out mentally, *"please tell me Arawn has ordered that wolf not to eat us."*

He squeezed her hand. *"That wolf is Arawn."*

Merle blinked, swallowed, dumbstruck for a moment. *"But...he's not a werewolf."* His aura didn't have the unique traces of shifters, the kind of otherworldly creatures who were two-natured, being able to switch between a human form and that of a particular animal.

"No," Rhun said, "*that he is most definitely not. He can change into several different shapes, though, and this is one of them.*"

Unable to respond, Merle just stared.

Rhun cleared his throat. "Thank you for seeing us," he addressed the beast.

"*Shouldn't you add* my lord *or something?*" Merle asked anxiously, eyeing the otherworldly canine predator in front of her.

"*He's not my lord.*"

If the circumstances were different, Merle might have laughed at the growl of indignation in Rhun's mental voice. As it was, she could only swallow the lump in her throat and try to keep her hands from shaking. Arawn's power was an overwhelming force tightening the air and pressing against her shields, a foreign, strange kind of magic swirling around him. Merle had never felt anything like it, and if it were up to her, she'd be happy if she'd never encounter it again. There was only so much intimidation she could take.

"We're here to ask for your help, if you can give it," Rhun continued, coming straight to the point, much to Merle's liking. The sooner they got out of here again, the better. "This is Merle of the MacKenna line of witches," Rhun went on, gesturing to her. "We're looking for her sister, who has been taken by one of my kind, but he's being blocked by witch magic. We were hoping you might be able to break that blocking spell so we can find the demon who holds her captive."

Silence.

Seconds ticked by. The wolf didn't stir, didn't acknowledge the request made to him in the least. The fact that Arawn didn't even deign to change his form to human to talk them was a blatant sign of his condescension. His yellow eyes held a glint of boredom, and he stretched one massive paw in lazy comfort as he gazed upon the two supplicants in front of him.

Rhun cleared his throat again. "We'd greatly appreciate your help, if you would be so kind," he said quietly, and Merle could only guess what it must have taken him to use this deferential tone of voice. Proud and arrogant by nature, Rhun had never struck her as the type who would easily bow to anyone, and now he was as close to begging as she'd ever seen him. It tightened her throat, knowing he did it for her.

The wolf flicked one of his ears and yawned, displaying a daunting set of sharp teeth, with fangs the size of Merle's forearm. They gleamed brightly in the flickering light of the fireflies, the white a striking contrast against the black fur.

"Now I see what you meant by unnerving," Merle said, taking a cautious step back. Her skin prickled with warning, all her senses on high alert because of the imponderable creature before her. The effect his power had on her own was that of stroking a cat's fur the wrong way.

A muscle in Rhun's jaw flexed, he took a deep breath and said, "Please consider our request...my lord."

Merle's gaze snapped to Rhun, and her heart sank.

"It's okay, little witch." The rigid way in which he held himself told a different story.

Just when she wanted to reply something, the wolf moved. With a fluid grace seemingly at odds with his giant size, he rose to his feet. The room shrank in on itself. Arawn's power compressed the air, and for the longest moment, he simply stood there, looming over Merle and Rhun, his eerie yellow eyes studying them intently. The fireflies surreptitiously floated farther away from him.

Then, he shifted.

The air around him blurred as if melted by heat, and in swirls of light and shadows, his form changed from wolf to man —a naked man.

But Merle didn't even have one second to take in the details of the nude body in front of her, because Rhun's hands immediately came up to cover her eyes.

"Rhun!" she hissed. "Quit that!"

He ignored her swatting at his hands and kept her eyes covered. *"Just preserving your modesty, little witch."*

Before Merle could mentally yell at him that he hadn't cared about her modesty when he'd paraded in front of her naked at every chance after she'd unbound him, Arawn spoke.

"I do not involve myself in the affairs of witches." His voice was a deep, deep bass, edged with a roughness that could abrade skin.

Rhun removed his hands from Merle's eyes, and she blinked at the sight in front of her. Arawn had gotten dressed in flowing black pants in the meantime, leaving his upper body bare, and he patted the head of the fox that had apparently brought him the piece of clothing. The small canine touched his muzzle to Arawn's hand and then trotted away, disappearing in another tunnel leading from the room.

Arawn turned to Rhun and Merle. His hair was of the same shiny black as the fur of his wolf form, and his build was just as massive, with muscles speaking of frequent use and a physical strength rivaling the force of his aura.

"This is not only a witch affair," Rhun pointed out politely, not showing any signs of intimidation in the face of a power like Arawn. Probably a smart move. "It's a demon who took Merle's sister, and he collaborates with a witch to absorb the girl's powers."

Arawn waved his hand. "Particulars." His eyes in human form were dark, not brown for all Merle could discern, but of some color courting shadows and depths. Right now, they still held a glint of boredom and indifference. "It is still witch magic you ask me to break." His gaze fell on Merle, and she flinched under the force. "This is a matter for your Elders, not for me. Besides," he said, turning away, "your sister is a witch. If she cannot defend herself against a demon, then maybe she deserves her fate."

The callous remark struck Merle like a blow to her guts, and she spoke up before thinking. "She can't defend herself because her powers are locked inside her!"

Arawn paused and slowly turned to her.

"*Merle.*" Rhun's voice inside her mind, warning.

"Explain," Arawn said. It was a low, quiet command, but a command nevertheless.

Merle shifted her weight, anxiety crawling up her spine on icy feet. But she wouldn't back down now, not when she'd just caught the first flicker of interest from Arawn. "My grandmother bound Maeve's magic inside her when she was a child."

"Did she now?" Arawn's voice was soft, deceivingly benign, but there was no mistaking the underlying danger in it. "Whom did your sister kill?"

At that, Merle sucked in air. Arawn was astute, and she realized too late she should have maybe kept this information to herself. Next to her, Rhun was tense enough to snap some sinews.

"*Don't,*" he said in her head.

"Answer my question." Arawn's gaze drilled into her, eroding her resistance.

"Half my family," Merle whispered.

Arawn tilted his head, the movement nothing human. "Interesting."

Underneath the focus of his scrutinizing eyes, she almost squirmed.

"How old is your sister now?"

"Twenty-four," she said, unable to stop the words from spilling out of her mouth. It was too late now anyway.

Arawn studied her for what felt like hours, with an intensity that made Merle's pulse pound in her head like drum beats.

"You are the head of your family?" he asked, the rugged lines of his face unreadable.

"Yes."

"Your witch line's affiliation is fire?"

Merle's pulse spiked. Most families kept their elemental

affiliations secret, as the knowledge could be used against them —each element had its weakness, an Achilles' heel, and exploited cleverly, it could neutralize the witch's powers. How did Arawn—?

"Answer me." His deep voice rumbled through her, made her gasp.

She fought the compulsion, and yet—"Yes." Spoken through gritted teeth, the words forced out of her by the power swirling in the air, seeping through her defenses.

Arawn regarded her for a moment with shadowed eyes. His gaze flicked to Rhun. "I assume you have a mental imprint of the blocking spell."

Rhun nodded with a grim expression. "It's too faint to trace it, though."

Arawn waved that away and looked back at Merle. "I can break the spell for you. Be aware, however, that I will ask for something in return for my assistance."

Merle swallowed past a throat gone dry. "I don't have much money, but my family has some antique jewelry pieces. They're worth a lot."

He gave her a smile that scared her lifeless. "I am not interested in money or baubles."

"What do you want?" Her voice shook.

"That, fire witch," he said, "I will tell you when I come to collect it."

"This was a bad idea," Rhun said in her mind. His mental voice was strained with urgency. *"Let's leave. We'll find some other way to break the spell. One that doesn't involve giving* carte blanche *to the bogeyman of all otherworld creatures."*

With an inconspicuous tug on her hand, he indicated her to back away. Merle didn't move, squeezed his hand instead while still looking at Arawn.

Her heart beating violently against her ribs, she asked, "One favor?"

"No," Rhun said.

"Yes," Arawn replied.

"Only one, and after that we're quit?"

"You have my word."

"Merle, don't do this. Do you have any idea what owing an open favor to Arawn might entail? He could ask you for anything.*"*

"Whatever he'll demand from me," Merle gave back bitterly, *"it can't be worse than losing one more member of my family."*

Rhun's aura spiked with irritation and fear. *"What if he asks you to swear fealty to him forever? He could make you crawl at his knees."*

Merle glanced at Arawn. "One condition."

The shadows in his eyes deepened.

"The favor will not entail me swearing fealty to you, nor will it end my life," Merle said, succeeding barely in keeping her voice from trembling. "And the same goes for my sister."

Arawn held her gaze for a long moment, unblinking, and then smiled in the way that chilled Merle's blood. "Agreed."

"Then we have a deal," she said.

He inclined his head in acknowledgment and turned to Rhun. "You will have to give me the imprint of the spell."

At the bristling in Rhun's aura, Merle realized the implication of that statement.

"Rhun," she said, her chest tightening. "I'm sorry, I didn't know that was necessary… You don't have to open your mind to him if you don't want to. I…" Owing a favor to Arawn was her decision, the price she would pay, but it wasn't her place to demand a mental strip of Rhun in front of a creature like Arawn. Even if Rhun managed to get the imprint of the spell to the forefront of his thoughts so that it would be easy to pick up without the need for further digging, Arawn would still be able to sift through Rhun's mind unchecked. "We can just leave," she said quietly, even though her stomach turned at the thought of how much longer Maeve would remain captive then.

Rhun's gaze lingered on her for a long moment, his eyes warm, glowing, before he faced Arawn. "I'll do it."

"Rhun..."

"Shush, little witch of mine."

Merle had never known her heart could break because she was loved too much.

"Very well," Arawn said, and held out his hand to the side.

Even as Merle still wondered at that odd gesture and what the hell it was supposed to mean, a tree nymph appeared from another opening in the earthen wall. Clad in sheer, flowing silks, she approached Arawn and laid a dagger in his open hand, hilt first of course. Bowing her head, she backed away again. Arawn hadn't even spared her a glance, unquestioned in his authority, and now he handed the blade to Merle.

"I require a blood oath for our agreement."

Merle winced but took the dagger. Drawing in a fortifying breath, she placed the sharp edge of the blade on her palm and slid it open. Pain shot through her, and she bit down hard on her lower lip to keep from cursing. Clenching her hand into a fist, she pressed until a drop of blood fell on the floor. "By the Powers That Be," she said, "I will uphold my promise of a favor to you, Arawn, for your assistance in finding my sister."

Another drop fell to the floor. The magic bound her.

CHAPTER 19

It was dawn by the time they stepped back into Bahram's apartment, where they would wait until they received word from Arawn. He'd told them it might take him a few hours to break the spell, so they'd decided they would spend the day resting, hoping by nightfall they could hunt down Maeve's captor. The morning's faint light had dispelled night and darkness, and Rhun's powers had almost faded completely when he and Merle stepped into the apartment—and ran into the incubus who owned it.

The demon stood in the hallway, in the process of zipping up a duffel bag. "Good," he said to Rhun, his eyes gleaming with amusement, "you're fully clothed. Was afraid I might see more of you than I prefer when I came in here. I tried to call your witch to let you know I was going to pick up some stuff, but I only got her voice mail."

"Oh. Right. My cell." Merle rummaged through her purse, which Rhun had made her leave in the car before they took the lake route to Arawn. Of course, he hadn't told her it was to keep the cell from being drowned. She'd have probably magically beaten him into finding another way to get to Arawn than by going for a swim.

"Sorry," Rhun said to Bahram while Merle checked her messages. "We were...indisposed."

"Uh-huh." The incubus surveyed their wet clothes from head to toe, and raised an eyebrow at the water dripping on his pristine hardwood floors.

"Sorry about that," Merle muttered, following his gaze and shifting her weight uncomfortably. "We'll clean that up."

"Oh," Bahram said smoothly, "no worries, honey. *You* can drip on my floors any time." He gave her a smile of sensual invitation, took a step toward her and tucked a lock of her hair behind her ear.

And that was when Rhun charged him. With a roar, he slammed the incubus into the wall, decades of friendship erased within seconds, drowned in a fit of rage and possessiveness.

"Rhun! Gods dammit, stop!"

Merle's voice filtered through the red haze clouding Rhun's vision, but it wasn't enough to make him loosen the grip he had around the other demon's throat. All he knew, right at this moment, was that he needed to eliminate the threat to his female. And then haul said female away into a cave somewhere and—

"Rhun!"

Something kicked him in the back of his knees. He doubled over, growling with pain, and let go of the male. Turning around, he faced his witch, who fisted his T-shirt—and kissed him.

His rage dissolved in a whirl of pleasure and contentment.

With a low sound of appreciation, Rhun pulled his female close and kissed her back, delighting in her scent, her softness, the way her hands stroked his neck and face. He sighed against her lips, tangled his fingers in her hair, caressed her silky skin. *Mine.* His heart filled with a tenderness threatening to melt him. As if she'd known just what he needed, Merle had reacted in the only way that could have reeled him back from his rage.

Sanity trickled into his mind, and when she broke the kiss, he noticed the glint of anger in her eyes.

Uh-oh.

"That. Is. Your. Friend." Her voice was clipped, and she emphasized each word with a swat at his chest. "What is wrong with you?"

"It's okay," Bahram said, cracking his neck and rubbing his abused skin. His golden eyes were far too perceptive when they focused on Rhun. "I was out of line. I didn't know she's your m—"

Rhun cut him off with a sharp look. "It's all right. I'm sorry I snapped. No hard feelings?"

The incubus glanced from him to Merle and back again, then shook his head. "No, man. I understand."

No, you don't. Rhun gritted his teeth. His best friend might have realized where Rhun's territorial rage stemmed from, might understand that, as a demon, he was an irrational pile of base instincts around his chosen mate, lashing out at any potential male threat to his claim. But he'd never understand the pain Rhun felt at being unable to finalize the bond with Merle.

Well, of course he wouldn't. Bahram didn't know Rhun was living on stolen time, that he was scheduled to return to the Shadows soon. Rhun hadn't had the chance to tell him. And maybe it was better he didn't. If his friend started looking at him with pity, it might just break what was left of Rhun.

"Thanks, buddy," he said instead, grabbing Bahram's neck and shoulders in an open hug.

"What's going on?" Merle asked, glancing back and forth between the two of them. "What's there to understand?"

Rhun let go of Bahram and shook his head. "Nothing. Don't worry."

It was no use telling her. It wouldn't change anything for the better, explaining to her he'd picked her to be the one he'd mate with, in an intuitive, subconscious choice defying all reason. He wasn't mated to her yet, but his heart, body and mind had already shifted into the mode for it, which was why he'd lashed out at Bahram. Up until he'd finalize the mating bond, he'd morph into a cave-demon version of himself around other males who so much as looked wrong at Merle. Even his best friend.

Telling her that would only hurt Rhun. As long as he didn't acknowledge it with words, he could pretend it didn't tear him apart that much.

He couldn't—*wouldn't*—mate with her. Doing so would render her unable to emotionally bond with anyone else, and, with Rhun bound in the Shadows, that would mean she'd wither away her life in loneliness. And as much as the thought of her with another male brought Rhun to the verge of losing his sanity, he would rather rip out his own heart than subject Merle to a life without love.

So, there it was. He'd officially turned into a pathetic excuse for a demon, brought to his knees by a female. Arawn had seen the extent of his weakness when he'd stripped Rhun's mind, had seen the emotional chaos he was in because of one fine witch—and he'd laughed. The fucking bogeyman of demons had mentally laughed at Rhun. *Arrogant son of a bitch.*

"So," Bahram said, hefting his duffel bag up on one shoulder, "how's your mission going? Any chance you could give me an estimate of how much longer you guys need my place?"

"Why?" Rhun peeled himself out of his soaked leather jacket, trying his best to shrug off his disastrous emotional state as well. "Running out of nymphs to take you in?"

Bahram's eyes danced. "Nope. Just wanna know whether I need to grab some other supplies—if you stay a few more nights, I'll take the chains with me." His gaze flicked to Merle, then back to Rhun, a wicked glint in his eyes. "Unless you plan to use them yourself…"

Merle took a step back. "Chains?" She shot Rhun a wary look. "He's joking, right?"

Rhun didn't answer right away, indulging himself with

images of a tied-up witch on silken sheets, her pale skin flushed with arousal. "Hmm."

"Rhun?" Her voice trembled with the right mix of excitement and anxiety.

He pursed his lips. "Maybe you could leave a set," he said to Bahram, not taking his eyes off Merle, who blushed an amazing red. "Just in case."

Merle uttered a sound close to a whimper, but her lack of protest against the idea of being restrained was telling. She obviously had no problem verbally tearing his head off whenever she really didn't like his behavior, so...

Bahram cleared his throat. "Uh, I'll leave you two alone, then." Always so perceptive to moods, that incubus.

"Right," Rhun said, his gaze on Merle, who backed away into the apartment, her cheeks now a beautiful pink. She had to know inching away from him only made him want to chase her.

A mischievous little smile tugged on her lips, and he grinned. Oh, she did know, all right. So when Bahram pulled the door closed behind him and Rhun charged, she squealed with delight and ran.

ॐ

THEY SLEPT FOR MOST OF THE DAY, SNUGGLED INTO EACH OTHER, and Rhun relished how she cuddled up to him, nestling against him as if he were her haven, her place of comfort. Since it was day, he couldn't sense Merle's aura anymore or read her thoughts, but he didn't need either to know how she felt. The little kisses she showered him with every time she woke, the way her face glowed when she looked at him, the smiles she gifted him with, it all mirrored the deep waves of emotion he'd tasted in her mind, and it filled him with more heartbreaking pleasure than he could bear.

Every once in a while, her eyes would shadow over, lines of tension appearing around her mouth. Rhun also didn't need his demon abilities to know her sister's fate haunted her at these moments. The ache and worry surrounding her was palpable even to his dulled senses, and chafed at him like sandpaper over sensitive skin. He'd say something silly then to make her smile, or at least swat at him in annoyance. Anything to take her mind off what Maeve might be going through right now, and how Merle couldn't help her until nightfall.

He'd already sworn to himself he'd rip the fucking son of a bitch to shreds, for what he'd done to Maeve, for the bruises he'd put into Merle's eyes.

By late afternoon, after they'd finally left the bed, showered and gotten dressed, and Rhun had repaired the dripping faucet in Bahram's bathroom, the crooked shelf in the hallway, the slanted curtain rail in the bedroom, and cleaned the whole apartment—twice—Merle had somehow managed to persuade him to watch something called *Harry Potter* with her. She'd discovered Bahram owned the whole set—*eight damn movies*—and since Rhun had trouble refusing Merle anything that made her eyes sparkle like that, he'd relented and had resigned himself to watching a bunch of kids chase each other around on brooms.

He soon found a way to make the whole experience a bit more interesting, though, and set up a nice little game he liked to call *Tease-a-Witch*. Every time someone cast a spell in the movie, Rhun would steal a kiss from Merle, he'd tickle her whenever Harry's scar hurt, pinched one of her nipples at any mention of Voldemort by name or his titles, and fondled any other available part of her body when anyone flew on a broom.

By the middle of the second movie, Merle jumped up from the couch as if seared by a firecracker, and turned off the TV, her hands shaking.

Rhun blinked at her in perfect innocence. "Something wrong, little witch?"

She rounded on him, her face flushed all shades of

intriguing red. "Yes! This! I'm aroused! Gods, I can't do this! *You shouldn't be aroused when you watch* Harry Potter*!*"

She was so adorable. Rhun laughed, ignoring her sound of irritation, and then proceeded to engage her in some activities for which being aroused was very much encouraged.

It was almost nightfall when the message from Arawn arrived—in the form of a fairy. Rhun let her in after she'd knocked on the living room window—he didn't want to know how Arawn had found out where to send his messenger—and the little winged fae creature flew into the room in graceful swirls, landing on the coffee table.

"His Grace the Lord of Demons wishes me to tell you that he succeeded in his task," the fairy said, her violet-colored hair glinting in the light of the sunset. Her wings were of a lighter lavender-shade, their shape reminiscent of a butterfly's.

"Thank you." Merle smiled, but the lines on her face were tense, undoubtedly speaking of her inner agitation.

The fairy inclined her tiny head. "My master also bid me to explain that the spell is not fully undone until you cut this thread." She held out a piece of string about two inches long.

Rhun took the thread from the fairy, grudgingly grateful for Arawn's prudence. *Smart son of a bitch.* By letting them choose the moment the spell would break, he gave them a fighting chance to find the demon before the Elder witch would rush to the site where Maeve was held. She would likely notice the second the spell was broken, and then know that Rhun and Merle were onto her.

Merle's eyes met Rhun's, and he saw the determination in them, the grim will to take the next—and final—step in her quest to find Maeve.

Her gaze then dropped to Rhun's arm and he followed the direction—to see the fairy now plastered to his biceps, looking up at him dreamily.

"You're beautiful," she said, a sigh in her voice.

He smirked. "I know. I'm a gift to the females of the world."

"Hmm. Yes." The fairy rubbed her tiny cheek against him, her wings moving in slow, dazed strokes. "Yes, you are. Beautiful demon."

Rhun watched with amusement—until Merle plucked the fairy off him, strutted over to the window, and threw her out, growling like a threatened tiger. She shut the window with a bang and then dusted her hands off.

"Now, I knew you were jealous," Rhun said, barely biting back his laugh, "but I didn't know the extent of it. In case you didn't notice, that female was the size of your forearm. Serious competition that, no doubt."

She swiveled around to glare at him, her face starting with another nice blush, the color hinting at embarrassment.

"And, by the way, you do know you just witch-handled a messenger of *Arawn*?"

Merle sucked in air and covered her mouth with her hands. "Oh gods!" She sprinted back to the window, yanked it open and shouted, "I'm sorry!"

A hiss, a smack, and then Merle stood frozen, staring out after the blur of wings that zigzagged away.

"She punched me." Her face was a study in disbelief. There was a tiny red blotch on her forehead where the fairy's fist had apparently made contact with her skin.

"Well," Rhun said, strolling over to pull her into a hug, doing his very, very best not to laugh, "I guess that means you're even."

Merle leaned into him, and he wrapped his arms tightly around her, his eyes on the setting sun on the horizon. He drank in the colors of the dusky sky, knowing this would be the last sunset he'd ever get to see.

Because before this coming night was over, he'd be bound in the Shadows again.

CHAPTER 20

Merle watched the vibrant colors of the sunset fade into the darkness of the advancing night, her whole body humming with grim excitement. *Soon.* Soon she'd get to kill the fucking bastard who'd kidnapped and tortured her baby sister, and then this whole nightmare would finally be over. The familial link to Maeve pulsed inside her, weaker than before but not broken. *Yet.* Her sister was still alive, and Merle would make damn sure they found her in time.

Time. Thinking of which…

She turned around, laid her hand on Rhun's cheek and met his eyes. "I don't know how fast the Elders are going to find us once we've rescued Maeve, but I want you to know that I'll try to convince them that you're—"

"Rhuntastic?" he asked with a grin that could be sold as an aphrodisiac.

She almost choked on the giggle bubbling up. "No. I mean, yes, you are, but—what I meant was I'll find a way to make them see that—"

"I Rhuned you for all other men? I think that's rather obvious, little witch."

"Stop it." A command that would have had a lot more impact if it wasn't undermined by her laughing.

When she was about to start once more with the promise of how she would fight to keep him, he backed her against the wall, circled her throat with his hand and kissed her. Dumbfounded, she melted into his touch, left gasping for breath by the intensity of his kiss when he broke away and nipped her lower lip with his fangs.

She sucked in air at the current of arousal that drove straight down to her core. Her whole body came to life, ignited with raw desire, as if she hadn't had sex in ages—as if she hadn't been enjoying Rhun's sensual skills for the better part of the day. By rights she shouldn't even be able to stand. But her body somehow still managed to cry out for more, every inch of her skin hungry for his touch, her heart and mind drawn to him with undeniable force.

"You need to feed," she whispered against his mouth. With the erotic pulse underneath her skin trumped by the drive to find Maeve as soon as possible, she resisted the urge to tear off his clothes and continue the games they'd been playing all day. "I think it'll be faster if you just... You know."

Rhun laughed, a throaty sound that reverberated in places of her body already primed for his touch. "Still so bashful, Merle mine? After everything I've done with you?" He rolled one of her nipples between his fingers through the fabric of her blouse. "To you..."

A moan escaped her lips. "Rhun."

"I want you to say it. Tell me what you want me to do to you, and I'll make sure to be very time-efficient." The glint in his eyes was positively wicked. "And don't be coy about the vocabulary."

She glared at him while heat flooded her face with the force of a tidal wave. One deep inhale, and then she charged forward, the words tumbling out in a rush. Speed made it easier. "I want you to make me come. Like you did the first time, with your hand, stroking me underneath my panties…inside me. And I want you to—" She broke off, licked her lips, arousal beating between her thighs.

He raised one brow, infinite amusement in his eyes. "Do go on."

"I want you to use your telekinetic power to…enhance the manual action."

Slowly, oh-so-slowly, one side of his mouth quirked up. "Like this?"

The invisible tug on her clit made her jump and utter an undignified sound of excitement. "Yes."

His smile sinfully sensual, tempered with predatory hunger, he gently squeezed her throat, gave her a languid kiss—and then whirled her around. Her back now to his front, he pressed her to him with one arm banded around her waist. Sliding his hand up to her breast, he flicked the puckered nipple with his thumb while he unfastened the button on her jeans with his free hand. A few seconds later, and her viciously talented demon had his fingers right where her desire pulsed with maddening force, his hand and his telekinetic power setting up a rhythm that had her writhing close to the edge in record time.

"Good gods, you're amazing," she moaned, head thrown back against his shoulder, hands raised and buried in his hair.

A kiss on her neck. "You didn't doubt me, did you now?"

Her answer came out as a strangled groan. With her impending climax moments from shattering her into bliss, and Rhun grazing the skin on her neck with his fangs, preparing to bite, she grasped the last bit of sense she had left and suggested the one thing that had been lurking at the back of her mind ever since he'd hinted at it. Mild curiosity had morphed into secret craving until temptation pulsed underneath her skin with every beat of her heart.

"Rhun," she whispered as he played with her nipple in a way that made her knees turn to rubber, "I want you to take pain from me, too."

He grew absolutely still behind her, his breath coursing her skin, hot and fast. His power vibrated darkly.

"It'll save us time." She swallowed, half-turning her face toward him. "If you take all three from me, we can start the search for the demon faster. Find Maeve faster."

"Merle..." It was a feral snarl, a warning. For whatever reason, he hesitated.

It made her grit her teeth. "Do it. I'm not made of spun glass and need to be coddled. I know you've been longing to take all three from me, and I want you to, so do it. You told me pain could be pleasurable—was that all talk and no show?" She was taunting him, but she didn't care. She wanted all of him, nothing held back.

Rhun growled, the low rumble vibrating against her back, and still, he hesitated. His aura blazed with all sorts of conflicting emotions. "Merle," he rasped, his voice barely human, "I don't—"

"Do. It."

He tightened his arm around her waist. His body shook, making hers tremble, too.

"*Rhun.*" She lowered her shields completely again, flooded him with the force of her desire. "Please."

Uttering a groan full of pent-up lust and hunger, he raised one hand to her throat, stretched her neck—and bit.

She cried out. It wasn't gentle this time. He let her feel the full impact of his teeth breaking her skin, sinking into her flesh. Pain speared her, rushing through her veins with the blood he drew. Then, the sensation changed, shifted, morphed into something else as he kept up the rhythm of his fingers inside her, of his power on her clit. Her inner muscles clenched around him, and within seconds she was strung tight with a kind of arousal she'd never experienced before. It felt like a full-body immersion in pleasure, her skin humming with heightened sensitivity.

He sucked harder, and another wave of pain surged, making her ball her hands to fists. Sudden pressure on her clit, exquisite, delicate movements that zinged pleasure outward from her core. Merle moaned, trembling with the force of her excitement, and just like that, the pain from his bite merged with the sensation of his strokes inside her, with the stimulation on her clit—and her pleasure skyrocketed.

Short-circuited with arousal, her body couldn't distinguish between pleasure and pain anymore, and each sting from his bite, each pull on her vein, each stroke of his fingers inside her brought her higher, higher, higher, until the shattering fusion of sensations became too much.

Merle's world shattered in a blast of pleasure, raw, powerful, consuming. Her senses exploded with overload, her mind splintered under the force of a climax that dissolved all thoughts.

Everything went black as she drowned in a vortex of blood, pain, and pleasure.

☙❦❧

THE INCESSANT RING OF HER CELL PHONE YANKED MERLE OUT OF the clutches of overwhelming oblivion. *Dammit*, she hadn't meant to fall asleep. They had to get moving and find Maeve. With a moan, she rolled over and fought to lift her eyelids against the lead weighing them down. Her whole body felt packed in cotton candy, her muscles limp, her movements lethargic, and there was more numbness inside her, a strange kind of...void.

Shaking her head against that odd feeling—and damn, that movement made the world spin around her—she got off the bed and trudged into the hallway. She picked up the still ringing phone from the chest of drawers, answering Lily's call.

"Yeah?" she asked with enough tiredness in her voice to shock herself.

"Merle, are you all right? You sound like crap."

"Gee, thanks, Lil." She continued dragging herself to the kitchen.

When Lily didn't shoot back with a quip, Merle got her first inkling that something was majorly wrong.

"I found more information on Rhun's species." The somber note in Lily's voice made Merle pause.

"Spill."

A moment of hesitation. "You're feeding him, right?"

Merle's skin prickled with suspicion. "Yes."

"Blood, pleasure...and pain?"

Now it was on Merle to hesitate. A heavy, heavy weight settled in her stomach, dragging her down. "Yes," she whispered.

"At the same time?" Lily's voice sounded pressed.

"Lily." Cold fear crept up her spine. "I swear I'm gonna kick your ass through this phone if you don't get to the point *right now.*"

The swallow on the other end of the line was audible. "Just please, *please* tell me you didn't let him take all three at once."

Invisible bands tightened around Merle's chest, choking her as her throat turned dry as desert sand. "Why? What happens if I do?"

Silence.

"*Lil.*"

"He'll be able to steal your powers."

The floor fell out from beneath Merle's feet. Spinning, spinning, the world went whirling around her, and she grabbed the marble kitchen counter to keep from toppling over.

No. It couldn't be. Rhun wouldn't have...

The void inside her ached. She sucked in air. This numbly throbbing emptiness—for the first time since she'd come into her powers, she couldn't feel her magic.

It was gone, ripped out of her like the marrow out of a plant, leaving a hollow husk. No. No, no, no. Frantic, her mind scrambled, she tried a simple levitation spell on a spoon. The utensil didn't move, not even an inch. Her hand shook. All air left her lungs.

"Oh fuck," Lily whispered on the other end of the line, "you did, didn't you? You let him take it? Merle?"

She didn't answer. Couldn't. She was unable to form even one coherent thought. Her pulse thundered in her ears.

Lily cursed violently, then caught herself. "Merle, listen, you gotta run. Once your powers are absorbed, any spell you've cast which relied on your magic to remain active will be rescinded. That means the binding spell that partly leashed Rhun to you is lifted, and he'll think he can now kill you without being kicked back into the Shadows."

"No." Merle's breathing went erratic, rising panic vying with stupefied disbelief. "He wouldn't... He could have killed me already. He didn't."

"Yeah, well," Lily said, voice dripping with cynicism, "maybe he wanted to play with you a little first."

Merle covered her mouth with her hand, choked back her sound of dismay.

"You need to get out of there," Lily urged. "Get away from him *now*. Just because he didn't kill you yet, doesn't mean he won't do it any time soon. He's a demon, he's taken your powers and you are now at his complete mercy without any means of defending yourself. So just run. Like. Hell. Forget about everything else for the time being, it's *your* life on the line now. *Get the fuck away from him!*"

Merle swallowed, her heart thumping at record speed. "I will. I'll call you as soon as I can."

The silence after she disconnected the call was deafening. Not a single sound in the whole apartment. Merle held her breath, listened, her mind struggling to work, and then she figured out what had been niggling at her since she'd peeled herself out of the bed.

Rhun was nowhere around.

Her pulse kicked up. She could just run. If she was lucky, he'd taken off, had left her, and wouldn't come back to—she couldn't even finish that thought. Wanting, needing to believe he wouldn't harm her, she tried her powers again, searched for some proof Rhun hadn't done the unthinkable, hadn't ripped her essence from her when he knew, *knew* her magic was as vital to her as the air she breathed.

The emptiness she encountered inside hurt like a torn-off limb.

Shaking her head against the onslaught of emotions barreling her cracked heart, she started toward the hallway when a faint creak made her stop dead in her tracks.

The front door clicked shut. A moment later, the heavy sound of boots on hardwood floors came from the hallway. Merle's heart skipped a couple of beats. The footsteps halted for a few seconds at the level of the bedroom door, then moved on toward the kitchen.

Fear trickled into her veins. Breathing gone shallow, she glanced around, searching for whatever she could use as a weapon, and her gaze fell on the boning knife at the sink. She made a grab for it, swiveling around just as Rhun appeared in the doorway. Hiding the knife behind her back, she forced her heart to slow down enough to speak. Maybe she didn't need to use the knife. *Yet.*

"Where have you been?" Okay, so she'd brought her pulse down to speaking level, but it was still fast enough to make her voice tremble.

Rhun's face was shadowed, his features strained. "Taking a walk." He stepped into the kitchen with measured calm, even though an underlying tension vibrated in his movements. "Had to clear my head."

She couldn't read him like that, without his aura, couldn't guess at his state of emotions, his intent. Just a few short hours ago, she'd have never believed he'd harm her—well, she'd also been convinced he'd never betray her like that. But he had.

He'd taken her powers.

The realization speared her heart, pierced through a part of her that had been untainted by the mounting betrayal surrounding her. Not anymore. That part of her heart was shriveling by the second, crumbling to dust. If he was guilty of stealing her magic, what else was he capable of?

"Sounds good," Merle said with forced calm, her eyes on Rhun as she inched toward the door, putting the kitchen island between them. "I think I'll go for a walk, too."

"Merle." He followed her, his gaze level on hers. "It's not what it seems."

"Oh?" Eyes stinging with tears, she glared at him, breathing past the panic tightening her chest. "So you didn't take my powers?" A part of her hoped against hope he'd say no, that somehow, *somehow* he wasn't responsible for the hollow ache tearing her apart on the inside.

A muscle ticked in his jaw. "I did."

What was left of her heart shattered into shards, each one stinging with enough force to puncture her lungs, make her choke.

"Listen," Rhun began, but Merle couldn't, wouldn't anymore.

"Stay the fuck away from me!" Every beat of her heart sent more fear through her veins. Her thoughts were scattered, her mind hazed, her instincts screaming *Run, run, run!*

Rhun made a move, and she snapped. With her breath caught in her throat, she threw the knife at him. It rammed into his chest, and he jerked back. Merle knew she'd hit his heart when his eyes widened and he choked, tumbling, grasping the kitchen island for support. He wheezed, his hand slipped, and he collapsed onto the floor.

Unbidden, a sob tore out of her. Even with panic riding her hard, it tore her apart to have struck Rhun down. It wouldn't kill him, would only stun him for a few minutes until he healed, and still it felt like she'd slammed that knife right into her own heart as well.

She had to leave before she joined him on the floor.

Stopping only to twist into her shoes, she fled out of the

apartment and onto the street, and then she kept on running. It was raining hard, water pouring down, flowing in torrents over the dark, deserted sidewalks and streets, and she was soaked through within seconds. But she didn't pause, didn't slow down, not until her lungs burned and her legs wouldn't hold her up anymore.

Breath coming in hard, fast pants, she turned into the roofed entryway of an apartment house, hid in the corner out of sight from the street, and then slumped down with her back to the wall. While the rain drummed down through the black of the night, Merle's scrambled mind put the pieces together.

She'd been such an idiot. Such a fucking idiot. She'd trusted Rhun, with her feelings, with herself, and he'd taken that trust and crushed it, along with her heart, not even batting an eyelash.

He'd stolen her magic.

The betrayal cut soul-deep, tearing into her, right into the dark ache where her powers should have been. She'd never, ever, felt so fucking naked and vulnerable. Rhun had wrenched away the most integral part of her identity, had left her feeling as if her very soul had been amputated.

And it hurt. So. *Much.*

She'd felt safe with him, hadn't even thought for one second he might harm her. Now, she couldn't be sure of anything anymore. The world had slipped from its axis, and on top of all the gut-wrenching treachery she'd had to encounter from her own kind, she'd just been stabbed in the back by the one person she'd come to rely on above all others during the second darkest time in her life.

How could she have been so stupid?

Fighting down the tears threatening to spill, she fumbled for her phone. Maybe she could get Lily to pick her up, but in any case, she had to start moving again soon. If she lingered, Rhun would find her, she was sure about that. She only wished she could still be so sure he wouldn't harm her once he did.

Her body had cooled down from her frantic run, and now the aggressive rain and the chill of the night took their toll. Cold clung to her dripping clothes, crept through her clammy skin and into her muscles. With numb hands, she tried to pry her cell open. It slipped through her wet fingers, tumbled down the steps of the entryway and skidded onto the waterlogged pavement of the sidewalk.

"Fuck!"

Merle staggered down to retrieve it, the incessant rain pummeling onto her back as she bent to pick it up—and caught a movement in the periphery of her vision. She froze. Her heart stopped, then leapt up into her throat.

Rhun had run around the corner a few feet away. Drenched in rain just like her, his white T-shirt bearing a dark stain over his heart, he paused as he spotted her.

Inch by inch, Merle straightened up, the phone clutched in her hand. Her eyes were locked on Rhun, and for the longest moment, they stared at each other in silence, the only sound that of the rain pelting down on them.

Then, she swiveled around and ran.

Rhun uttered a foul curse behind her, and only seconds later he slammed into her back, taking her down to the ground. For a frozen moment in time, Merle thought she'd crash head-first into the concrete and that would be it.

She never made contact with the sidewalk, though. In a preternaturally swift move, Rhun flipped them both over, cushioning her fall with his body. They came down hard, and he grunted from the impact, holding her locked in a tight grasp. For all of five seconds, the crash knocked the breath out of her, and she wheezed on top of him, her back to his front.

As soon as she could suck in air again, she struggled against him, panic pumping through her blood. She elbowed, kicked and hit any part of him she could reach, fighting with every last ounce of strength she had left.

More grunts from Rhun, followed by a snarled, "Stop!"

She didn't. She couldn't. Her brain had switched to desperate survival mode.

With a growl, he rolled them both over, turned her around and hauled her with her back up against the wall of a building.

"Stop and fucking listen," he ground out.

Pinned to the wall by his body, unable to hit him anymore, Merle went limp, all fight gone out of her.

"Save your breath," she whispered, "and just kill me."

Rhun jerked back as if she'd struck him. For a moment, he only stared at her with something akin to shock, then his expression hardened, his eyes flashing hotly. "Kill you? You think I want to *kill* you?" He gritted his teeth, drew a deep breath through his nose. "I tell you that I love you," he said, his voice rising, *"and you think I want to kill you?"*

"What else am I supposed to think? You fucking took my powers!"

"I didn't mean to!"

"Yeah, right." Bitterness turned her heart to acid. "You planned this all along, didn't you? Everything you said, everything you did, even that you loved me, it was all an act to get me to trust you so you could take my powers and break free. That's why you didn't lower your shields when I did. You didn't let me in because you didn't want me to know. Am I right?"

Breath heavy, eyes hard, he looked at her. "Yes."

And just like that, Merle's heart shattered a second time, smashed to smithereens. "You fucking bastard," she ground out, hurt beyond her capacity to understand, her breath catching on a sob. "You're such a cold-hearted son of a—"

"No," he cut her off, his eyes haunted. "Just listen. Yes, when you unbound me from the Shadows, I planned to gain your trust and take your powers so I could kill you and leave. I spent twenty years in pain and darkness after being bound for a crime I did not commit, not to the extent of warranting this punishment, at least. I didn't know you when you unleashed me. The only thing I knew was that I wanted, that I *needed* to be free, that I couldn't go back to the Shadows no matter what. I didn't care —I didn't *want* to care—about anything or anyone but me."

She shivered, from the cold, the rain, from the impossible hurt pounding inside her.

Rhun's gaze drilled into her. "But I *do*. I fucking do, Merle. Suddenly I care about saving a witch I don't know, a witch who shouldn't mean anything to me. Only she does. Maeve means something to me, because she means *everything* to *you*. When I told you I loved you, it was the fucking truth. Somewhere along the line, you snuck up on me, little witch. You snuck under my defenses and changed everything. I made the decision to give up on my plan, to stick to our deal and let you bind me in the Shadows again, because for the first time in my life, I care more about someone else than I care about myself." He made a pause, his voice going quiet. "I didn't want to take away your magic, Merle. And I didn't lower my shields because I was ashamed to let you know I ever even considered doing something like that to you. I swear I didn't mean to take your powers."

Tears, hot and scorching, spilled from her eyes, mingled with the cold rain. "But you did." She clenched her hands to fists, and in the small space Rhun had given her, she punched him in the chest. "You did take them." She punched harder, a sob tearing out of her. "You did!" More punches. "I trusted you!"

Rhun didn't stop her from hitting him, let her pound his chest with the force of the despair wrecking her inside. There was heartbreak in his eyes, echoing her own. When she finally collapsed against him, crying into his chest, he put his arms around her and laid his forehead on top of her hair, exhaling a shuddering breath.

"Why?" Merle asked after an eternity of silent tears. "You took my magic." Her voice was hoarse from crying. "Why, when you didn't mean to?"

Rhun's curse turned the air blue. "Because I didn't know it

would happen automatically. I didn't *know*." There was pain in his words, such pain. "When you asked me to take all three from you, I hesitated, because I knew taking blood, pain, and pleasure was the key to absorbing the powers. I thought I'd have to make a conscious decision to steal them, though. I didn't know—" He cursed again, drew in a strangled breath. "I shouldn't have taken all three at once, no matter what." His fingers dug into her back. "I fucked up." Pressing her closer, he buried his face in her hair. "I'm sorry, Merle. I'm so sorry."

Her tears wouldn't stop, even after she thought she had no more emotion inside her to cry out. Rhun stroked her back, held her, while she fought for breath.

"I feel so empty without my powers," she whispered, her voice as broken as her heart.

"I know." Rhun's own voice was hoarse, too, sounding as raw as if he'd scratched out his throat with a cheese grater. He swore a long streak of obscenity that would have made Merle blush if she hadn't been so empty of anything. "I want to give them back to you."

"Then do it."

Silenced stretched taut between them.

"I don't know how," he finally said, quietly, pained. Helpless.

Merle hiccupped, a sound between a laugh and a sob. "How can you not know?" She grabbed his T-shirt in a fist.

"Because even with demon magic, there is always a part that eludes you."

And didn't that just fucking figure?

He took a trembling breath. "I've been racking my brain for some info that I might have missed, trying to remember whether I knew it once. I'll find out how to do it, Merle, I swear I will. We'll find Maeve and then I'll give you your powers back, and if I have to appeal to Arawn to find out how, I don't fucking care. You'll have your magic back, little witch, and then you can bind me in the Shadows again." The last part he said softly, with a note of gut-wrenching resignation.

It tore into Merle. The pain she felt at the thought of binding him again, it tore deep, much deeper than—she drew in a sharp breath. Losing Rhun… it would hurt her more than losing her powers. With everything that had happened, she still wanted to hold on to him, against all reason and hope.

"I don't want to bind you again," she whispered, voicing the impossible. How could she feel this way, even though his betrayal was still an open cut inside her? "I want to keep you, Rhun. I want to *keep* you." Despair pulled at her heartstrings, those strings which she'd thought had snapped and withered. She almost stumbled with the confusion churning in her mind.

Rhun pressed her closer, kissed her hair. "It's okay, little witch. I know you can't." Against her cheek, his chest vibrated with his voice. "Just…tell me you forgive me. That's all I ask of you." A shuddering breath, hot in her hair. "Don't let me go into the Shadows without that."

"Rhun…"

Releasing her, he sank to his knees, grasped her hands—and bowed his head. "Please."

Merle uttered a choked sob. She stared at the demon in front of her, this dark, powerful otherworldly predator—kneeling at her feet, begging her forgiveness. The sight of it let something click into place, loosened the knot of pain and betrayal deep inside her chest.

Taking a breath, she cupped his face, turned it up so he would look at her. "I forgive you. How could I not? Gods help me, but I love you, Rhun. And I don't want to see you like this." It wasn't so much him being on his knees before her—it was the devastating pain, the genuine regret, the tormented guilt shadowing his eyes. He'd meant it when he'd told her he hadn't intended to take her powers. It still hurt like hell, but the thought of him suffering, aching because he'd done her wrong, it was unbearable, eclipsing her sense of betrayal.

Love, she thought, is feeling someone else's pain more than your own.

Leaning down, she kissed him, whispering words of forgiveness against his lips, and he breathed her in, trembling, and pulled her down into his arms. He held her like this for the longest time, his heart beating against her chest, in sync with hers.

"Don't ever run away from me again." His breath was hot on her ear. "And don't you *ever* think I'd harm a hair on your head, little witch. I'd rather slit my own throat."

She swallowed hard. "I can't promise you that."

He tensed.

"I *will* run away from you," she went on, making a small, deliberate pause, "so you can catch me on a flight of stairs again."

Rhun pulled back, stared at her—and then he kissed her so hard it stole her breath. Dragging her into another crushing hug, he only let her go when she shivered again from the cold and the rain.

After he'd brought them both to their feet, he rubbed her arms and back, studying her face. Slow warmth spread over her skin, enfolded her like an invisible blanket. He'd wrapped her in his powers. It didn't dry her clothes, but it was enough to stop her trembling.

"Better?" he asked.

"Yes."

He cupped her cheek with one hand, a smile tugging at his lips. "You threw a knife at me."

Her gaze dropped to the dark blotch on his T-shirt with the small slit in the fabric where the knife had sliced the cotton and sank into his skin. Her guts twisted, but she looked up at him again and calmly said, "I'm not going to apologize for that."

"No need." His eyes danced with amusement. "I'm rather impressed by your aim. You hit me straight in the heart."

"Yeah, well, I aimed for a spot a few feet to your right."

At her play on the throwing advice he'd once given her—it seemed like ages ago—he stared at her for the span of a heart-beat. Then he burst out laughing, his face lighting up, his eyes warm with affection.

In the aftermath of heartbreak and despair, of panic and anger and fear, such a simple thing as seeing Rhun laugh brought a smile to her face—as well as her heart.

And Merle knew she truly loved him, down to the depths of her soul.

CHAPTER 21

R hun pressed his lips together, steeled himself, and then ushered in the inevitable end. "I found him."

Merle froze in the process of pulling on a new sweater. They'd come back to Bahram's apartment once more, where he'd peeled her out of her soaked clothes, and, ignoring her protests of I-can-do-that-myself-you-domineering-male, had towel-dried every inch of her until her skin glowed rosy with warmth. Of course, he'd also insisted on kissing any spot looking like it might still be cold—just to be sure—with the result of leaving bright red hickeys in strategic places—and a nice blush of arousal on Merle's face.

Now she swallowed several times before speaking, sky-blue eyes wide. "You know where he is?" She'd immediately understood whom he was talking about, and all lingering sense of playful exasperation had left her face as if wiped away.

He nodded. "While I was taking a walk earlier, I cut the thread to break the spell and see if I could trace him. I could."

Her hands trembled oh-so-lightly when she pulled on the sweater. She straightened her spine, her eyes glinting with hard resolve. "I'm ready. We can go."

"No." He shook his head. "You're staying here."

Even without her powers, her human aura spiked with enough outrage to make the air sizzle. "Forget it, I'm coming with you. You don't honestly think I'll sit here with my hands in my lap while you take down that fucker and rescue Maeve?"

"That fucker," he replied with more calm than he felt, "is a demon like me who could snap your neck in the blink of an eye —especially now that you can't magically defend yourself. I'm not going to risk you getting in harm's way, Merle, so you'll stay here and let me do this on my own."

"The fuck I will." She narrowed her eyes and stepped up to him, and he had to quell a wave of pride at her will to fight. "I have not come this far and gotten into this much trouble just to bury my head in the sand and wait for you to return with my sister. I'll stay out of it when you kill that demon, but I want to be there when you free Maeve."

"No." His blood heated with the mere thought of Merle coming anywhere close to danger. "What part of *you can't magically defend yourself* did you not understand? You're vulnerable like this, and your presence will undermine my concentration because I'll try to protect you. I can't go in there with half my mind being on your safety, Merle. Without your powers, you're a fucking demon snack waiting to happen."

Fisting his T-shirt, she pulled him down—or rather, pulled herself up, since he refused to move—and hissed, "And whose fault is that?"

The verbal blow struck him like a sucker-punch to the guts, and he flinched.

Merle glared at him, her eyes without a trace of mercy. "Do *not* deny me this, Rhun. I need to get Maeve out of there myself. I swear I will stay back as much as I can and not get in your way, but I have to be there for her when she's freed. I *have* to." Something sparked in the clear blue depths of her eyes, a visceral need—and he understood. If it were Siani... yes, he would fight snapping and biting to be the one to release her, to make sure she saw his face first thing and knew she was safe again.

But—"Know this," he said, leaning in until her face was only a breath away, his voice gone dangerously low, "when push comes to shove, I will let him have Maeve to save your life. If I need to decide whom to help, I *will* abandon her in order to protect you."

She opened her mouth to say something when he cut her off.

"This is my condition, Merle. Take it or leave it."

She held his gaze for a long moment, then nodded, flattening her hand over his heart. "I understand."

He gave her a curt nod, tamping down the raging urge to tie her up with Bahram's set of chains so he could track down the other demon without her after all. If anything happened to Merle… He drew in a sharp breath. A thousand lifetimes of suffering in the Shadows wouldn't be enough to outweigh that kind of pain.

Laying his hand on hers, above his heartbeat, he closed the distance between them and kissed her, softly, savoring the feel of her lips.

"Let's go kick some demon ass," he then said with a grim smile.

⚝

THE HEAVY TORRENTS OF RAIN HAD FADED INTO A FAINT DRIZZLE AS they got out of the car—Rhun's old vintage Porsche 911, which Bahram had kept and integrated into his own collection of nice rides—and looked upon the isolated warehouse looming ahead. It was supposed to be abandoned, pending demolition according to the sign on the perimeter fence—also warning away trespassers—but any sensitive otherworld creature would feel the vibration of active magic in the area.

Rhun stopped in front of the gate, studying the heavy chain

and lock, and undid both with a minuscule telekinetic blow. The clink of metal echoed in the night as the chain fell down.

"That was easy," Merle muttered behind him.

Rhun shook his head. "That was just the start." His gaze resting on the warehouse shrouded in darkness a few yards away, he clenched his jaw. "The building is warded." He turned to her, his stomach knotting with frustration. "By witch magic."

"What?" Merle's face blanched, and then she cursed. "Of course. The Elder witch wouldn't leave her precious project unprotected against intruders, would she." Kicking the fence a few times, she cursed some more, not looking at him. Her faint human aura vibrated with profound anger.

Rhun was torn with some violent anger of his own—directed at himself—mixed with gut-wrenching guilt. If he hadn't taken Merle's powers, she'd have been able to dismantle the wards. She was definitely strong enough to tackle and neutralize even an Elder witch's magic. Now, all they could do was stand there and stare at the warehouse, forced to remain a few feet away.

So close, and yet so far.

Her eyes trained on the place where her sister was being held hostage, Merle took several deep breaths. "I refuse to accept this." Her aura spiked with that damn, beautiful stubbornness of hers, and she faced him. "Try to take them down."

The power of Merle's magic—so different from his own—flowed through his veins, churning, pushing at him from the inside, almost too much to contain. Rhun shook his head. "You know I can't wield your magic." The words came out pressed, his voice strained. He wanted to tear something into tiny little pieces. Wanted to rip and punch until he didn't feel so fucking helpless anymore. Here they were, having come this far, having gone through a shitstorm of emotions and turns of events, only to stare at a dead end—because he'd fucked it all up.

She took his hand, squeezed until her nails dug into his skin. "*Try.*"

"Merle," he said through clenched teeth, "I can't control your powers. Witch magic is different from demon magic. It's intricate and needs to be directed carefully, or else it might do more damage than good. You know that."

"Then I'll direct you. I might not have my magic, but I still know how to wield it. Go into my mind, and I'll show you. We'll do it together."

"Merle…" He swallowed past a growing lump in his throat. It could still go so horribly wrong. All it would take was one slip of his concentration, and they would find themselves in a major magical cluster-fuck.

Merle took his other hand as well, her eyes holding his captive. "We can do this." She squeezed his hand. "I will *not* let us turn back now. Not when we're this close. Do it, Rhun." She shut her eyes and rested her head against his chest.

"You might want to send a prayer to the Powers That Be," he said quietly.

She huffed. "Right." Sarcasm put an edge in her voice. "They have been helping us so well."

He bent his head until his breath whispered through her hair. "They did answer my prayer when I asked them to take your place in upholding the balance."

"What?" Merle's head snapped up so fast, he was sure she'd gotten whiplash. Eyes the color of endless skies searched his face. "You what?"

"I asked them to spare you and take blood and magic from me instead. They did." A wonder he still couldn't grasp, something that had sent his world-view spinning into a new kind of uncertainty.

Her aura wavered with astonishment. "You bled for me."

He shrugged. "Ah, well, it's becoming something of a habit around you, little witch. I mean, I also bled for you when you broke my nose—twice—and again when you put a knife through my heart, and I do believe I also scratched the delicate skin on my hands when you made me trip in the cemetery…"

Merle shut him up by giving him a scorching kiss. "I love you," she whispered against his lips.

It took him a moment to realize he was smiling like an idiot. On idiot crack. And the worst part was, he didn't even mind it one bit.

"Let's do this," she said and closed her eyes again.

She muttered a quiet prayer, and when she repeated it, he found himself finishing it in his mind. They *did* need all the help they could get.

With her powers gone, she didn't have any mental shields she needed to lower, and he slipped into her mind unhindered. As before, the beauty of her emotions and depth of her soul amazed him, put him into a state of blissful awe. He had to force himself not to linger and mentally roll around the magnificence of her mind like a happy wolf in a field of wildflowers.

He found the thread of memory she'd brought up from the depths, and studied the intricate workings that would break a ward spell.

"Fuck, Merle, this is too complex."

"Don't be a wuss."

Rhun blinked, taken aback. "Did you just call me a *wuss*?"

Her mind hummed with her soft laugh, glowed with her teasing. *"Oh, did I think that out loud?"* Layers upon layers of affection wrapped around him, infused him with warm, strong faith. *"You can do this, Rhun."*

Swallowing hard, he took a deep breath, and then tapped into the magic so unlike his own. He muttered the words she showed him, wove the threads of power according to the blueprint in her mind, concentrating hard on keeping a lid on the writhing force that throbbed in his blood. His own powers, dark against the blaze of Merle's magic, collided with the foreign essence. He winced under the onslaught. His body and mind weren't made to wield such magic, and they both let him feel it.

"Keep going." A mental nudge from Merle. *"I'll help you."*

He realized he'd been squeezing her hands to the point of

almost breaking her bones under the mental and physical strain. With a low curse he eased his grasp. Her mind filled with encouragement, with images of how to keep control while casting a spell, showing him how to channel, how to tame. He soaked it all up with a thankful mental sigh, and worked harder, weaving more threads of magic.

Tendrils of power twirled in the air, latched onto the vibrating force of the wards like vines onto a wall. Tendril after tiny tendril, Merle's magic dug into the protective spells, creating cracks within the wall.

The cracks connected. The air shook.

Rhun's blood burned from the force of the magic he wielded, his muscles ached, his skin raw as if scraped with razor blades. He ground his teeth together and kept up the flow of power. More cracks appeared, sending tremors through the night. The last few seconds had Rhun reeling under the dizzying potency of the magic streaming out of him, and then, with a quake that made Merle stumble into him, the wards broke.

He clutched her hard to keep himself from toppling over, and they held on to each other for a moment, one steadying the other.

Rhun was the first to catch his breath. "So," he said with a lightness belying the pain wrecking his body and mind, "how was I, babe?"

Merle swatted his shoulder, her lips curving upward. Then, her eyes widened as her gaze dropped to his nose. Her smile died, and she sucked in air. "You're bleeding."

He raised his hand, dabbed at the trickle of warm liquid running down toward his lips, then wiped it away. "See?" he said, smirking at her. "Habit."

"Rhun..."

"Don't worry about me, little witch. I'm fine." He glanced at the warehouse. It still loomed in the darkness, waiting, taunting. "Let's finish this."

She gave him a brief nod, and together they approached the building's front.

"Stay behind me," he said. "Do what I tell you. When I say run, you run, understood?"

She nodded again, not taking her eyes off the warehouse. "Do you smell that?" she whispered as they came to a halt in front of the door.

"Yes." He ground his molars together against the surge of his dark instincts. "Blood." And lots of it, by the strength of the scent. It wafted out through the closed door, tantalizing, enticing, calling on everything demon inside him. His fangs tingled, pushed out of his gums. "Stay back," he told Merle, his voice gone hoarse.

The door gave way as he opened it, he stepped inside—and right into his own personal hell.

The faint light from the street lamp outside the perimeter fence fell onto a floor coated in fresh blood, spilled in gallons upon gallons until it covered every last inch of the room. Rhun's vision narrowed, going predator sharp, taking in the carnage. Splashes of sickly sweet red painted the walls, the ceiling—the bodies littering the floor. The room breathed blood, pain, and death. Such a heady, intoxicating—*disastrous*—cocktail of scents and sensations, it catapulted him back, all the way into the last moments before he'd been bound in the Shadows twenty years ago.

Rhun stood frozen in place, his heart thumping madly in his chest, his fangs aching. Hunger churned in his veins, gnawed at his sanity, even though he'd just fed a short while back. The lingering threads of pain, the metallic tang of *so much blood* it short-circuited his mind. His senses overwhelmed, he noticed the presence of the other demon too late. Merle's scream cut through him, and he spun around.

The blond demon had dragged her inside, held her with her back to his front, facing Rhun. With his hand grabbing her hair, he'd pulled her head to the side, exposing her neck, where her carotid throbbed with the frantic beat of her heart. The smile the demon gave Rhun flashed his fangs, only an inch away from piercing her skin. His teeth were stained red—he'd been feeding recently. Ice-blue eyes met Rhun's, and the realization—the recognition—jolted him, made him stagger.

"You," Rhun rasped. He should have known right from the start, when he'd picked up the trace of his energy, should have recognized it, *him*. It had been so long, and the endless pain and darkness of the Shadows had dulled his memory, but it came crashing back now in the midst of this abattoir of a room, this eerie reenactment of the place that had broken him.

Rhun was looking at one of the demons who had held him captive, had set him up to have him bound.

The blond's smile widened. "It's been a while, hasn't it?" His eyes grew dark with the dilation of his pupils as he breathed in Merle's scent. "Your witch is damn pretty, so much like her sister. The two really do look alike. Or should I say *looked*?" His features twisted into a sneer. "Little Maeve's face isn't as pretty anymore as it used to be, I'm afraid."

A choked, anguished sound tore out of Merle. Jerking, she struggled against the demon's hold. He tightened his grasp and yanked on her hair. The sight of it pierced the red haze clouding Rhun's mind. It shattered the trance he was in, broke through the maddening grasp of hunger and hunting instincts. He growled. His muscles tensed, protectiveness swamped him, pushed back the urge to feed. Rhun's sole intent was now to rip out the other demon's heart after tearing off every patch of skin that had touched his mate. But first, he had to get him to release Merle.

"Tell me," the demon bastard said, his tone benign, "how do you like our venue? I tried to make it as original as possible for you. When the Elder told me you'd been unleashed and might show up here, I convinced her you'd appreciate a little overload of your senses." His eyes flashed with glee, and his voice dropped to a maddened whisper. "Is it working?"

Rhun's nostrils flared as he tried to block out the beguiling scent of blood. The air was thick with the aroma of pain, a delicious taste tugging at his powers, making him itch to grab whatever human he could find and cause more pain so he could drink it in. It was a powerful trap indeed, and it might have worked—if Merle hadn't wiggled her way into Rhun's heart. As it was, she was his chosen mate, and he'd rather rend himself limb from limb than touch her with the intent to harm. Nothing equaled the urge to keep her safe.

The other demon studied Rhun, tilted his head, and sneered in triumph. Rhun knew what he must look like—pupils dilated, fangs flashing in a feral snarl, aura vibrating with the intense craving to feed and kill. It must seem he was indeed overwhelmed by the onslaught of sensations, and Rhun would be damned if he let the demon know otherwise.

The son of a bitch pierced the skin on Merle's throat with his canines, cut a line of bright red over her carotid and let her blood trickle down her collarbone. The air filled with the sweet aroma of her essence, with the sharp sting of Merle's pain, the scent of her fear. Rhun's muscles strained, his instincts screamed at him, but he held himself back from going bat-shit crazy on the asshole. He couldn't risk hurting Merle in the process. Instead, he inhaled the fragrant cocktail that saturated the air, making sure to tremble with hunger.

"I'm willing to share if you are, too," the demon said, an unholy glow in his eyes. "We can even tap the sister as well. What do you say?"

Rhun licked his lips. "Yes."

Merle's eyes widened, and panic emanated from her pores. Rhun briefly debated sending her a telepathic message, explaining the act, but he needed her fear to be real to make it more credible, at least for now. He took a slow step toward them, his eyes riveted on the tantalizing trickle of Merle's blood.

The blond demon flashed his fangs in a feral grin. "That's what I thought. I'm not allowed to kill sweet little Maeve—at least not until I take her powers—but this one here..." He lapped up the trail of blood on Merle's throat, and it took all of Rhun's control to remain where he was. If he jumped on the demon now, he might inadvertently kill Merle.

"We can also have fun with the others," the demon said after he'd licked his lips, clearly enjoying the taste of Merle he'd gotten. Rhun would make sure to rip out his tongue as well.

"Others?" he asked, his voice rough as gravel from the violent emotions he was keeping at bay—barely. He moved another step closer to the soon-to-die bastard holding Merle.

"The ones I get to kill." The demon waved at the body parts littering the room.

"Hmm." Rhun was only about three feet away from him now. "Sounds good."

"Merle," he said inside her mind, not looking in her eyes, *"when I say now, jump to your right."*

Her answer was immediate. *"Rip out his fucking heart."*

If he hadn't been so pumped full of adrenaline, he'd have laughed at that. *"Will do, little witch."* He tilted his head, glanced from Merle's throbbing carotid to the demon, and gave him a grim smile. "I call dibs on fucking her first, but feel free to use her mouth while I'm at it."

Merle flinched, and the demon cackled.

"I knew you'd come around." His eyes gleamed with mad joy.

Rhun curved his hand around Merle's neck, raising one eyebrow at the other demon in a silent request for permission—and the bastard let go of Merle.

"Now."

Rhun released her, and Merle jumped to the side at the same moment Rhun lunged at the demon. He slammed him into the wall. A blast of dark power struck Rhun, making him stagger back. He still had his hand clawed into the demon's chest, though, and the son of a bitch snarled as he tumbled down along with him. They both hit the floor, blood splashing around them, and rolled over several times while pounding into each other with physical and mental force.

Knuckles bloodied, fangs flashing, Rhun struck out. He hit the demon square in the face, blocked a mental blow, caught an uppercut to his chin that made his teeth rattle. Another punch to the demon's solar plexus made the fucker wheeze and gasp for air, which Rhun took advantage of to lay him flat by swiping his legs out. Just as Rhun was about to punch his face in, the demon rolled away, sprung to his feet and rammed his elbow into Rhun's back.

Fuck. Pain exploded in his spine. Rhun ground his teeth against the waves of hurt zapping his body, forced his spasming muscles to obey. Stumbling a few paces away from the other demon, he straightened up, spat blood on the floor, and breathed past the agony in his back. The blond bastard charged again and slammed into him.

Dammit. The other demon was strong, well-fed and would have made a worthy opponent on the best of nights. Now, though... Rhun cursed as his back hit the floor, shooting more whit-hot pain up and down his spine. He'd lost a significant amount of strength when he'd wielded Merle's magic, enough to tip the scales in this fight.

His breath sawing in and out through clenched teeth, his body a wreck, muscles exhausted and sluggish as if he'd run a marathon, he blocked the other demon's strike, hardened his mental shields—and focused on the one thing that kept him going beyond what he thought he was capable of.

Merle.

Rhun unleashed the full power of his wrath unto the bastard, and—fuelled by the raw need to annihilate the male who'd laid a hand on his mate—he beat, struck, broke and tore into his adversary with brutal force, with a primal, terrible ferocity.

Dodging a blow, he hauled the demon against the wall, breaking his spine. A well-aimed strike with his powers finally hit home, paralyzed the other male, and Rhun tossed him to the floor. He jumped on top of him—and began a merciless butchery.

By the time he ripped the demon's heart from his chest, there wasn't a single unbroken bone in the male's body, not enough blood to squirt from the still beating heart, no tongue left in his mouth, the skin flayed off his hands.

Rhun stood above the battered shape of the demon, panting, drenched in blood—the demon's, his victims', as well as Rhun's. He stared at the carnage at his feet, squashed the heart in his hand, and dropped it on top of the other body parts.

His pulse hammered in his head, rushing waves of pain through his veins. Mind numb in the aftermath of a fight that had turned him into a raging mess of base instincts, he stood still for a moment. Darkness bucked within him. He'd unleashed his nature, had given it free reign, and it had almost consumed him.

Turning, Rhun looked for the one reason that had kept him sane.

Merle sat huddled in a corner, her legs pulled up tight to her front, her arms slung around her knees. She stared at him, unblinking, her face blank.

Rhun stumbled to her, dropped down in front of the woman he loved—who'd watched him tear apart another being with unspeakable violence.

"Merle..." His voice was barely more than a croak. He wanted to say he was sorry, that he hadn't meant for her to see him like this, hadn't wanted her to witness such slaughter at his hands. He wanted to touch her, reassure her, but he didn't dare brush her with a single finger, not when every inch of his skin dripped with blood and gore.

Trembling, he shook his head, knowing he'd broken something inside her he could never fix. He opened his mouth to speak—

Merle's hand shot out, grabbed his. Her fingers curled

around his blood-slick palm. Her eyes locked onto his. "Thank you," she whispered.

Rhun's breath caught in his throat. His heart stopped.

"Thank you," Merle said again, squeezing his hand, the hand that had torn out the demon's heart. "You made the bastard suffer." Her gaze held no fear, no revulsion, no shock. Only grim gratefulness, a deep, dark appreciation.

She'd seen him at his worst, and it hadn't made her hate him.

He was about to tell her how much her acceptance meant to him, but at that very moment, a blow of magic yanked him off her, hauling him across the room. He slammed into the opposite wall. Pain burst inside him in an explosion of nerves, and he slumped down on the bloody floor. Merle's anguished scream shook the air.

Groaning, Rhun looked up at the witch who'd struck him.

Isabel Murray's face was the last thing he saw before his mind drowned in darkness.

CHAPTER 22

"No!" Merle struggled to her feet, slipped in the blood on the floor. Her mind reeling, heart pounding, she stared at Isabel.

The Elder witch stood above Rhun's broken body, gazing down on him.

"Don't!" Merle yelled again. "He didn't hurt me!"

"I know." Said with such calm, it froze Merle where she stood. "I was hoping he might, though." Isabel's eyes darkened with a note of sadness. "Then I wouldn't have to do this."

As if cut like puppet strings, Merle's muscles and sinews didn't hold her up anymore, and she crumbled to the floor, crashing down on the bloodied concrete with a wet-sounding thud. Pain jolted through her hips, her shoulders, her head as they hit the ground hard. Up close, the metallic smell of all the blood in the room assaulted her nose, and she had to swallow down the bile rising in her throat.

Groaning in agony, she glanced up at Isabel, at the witch who'd once rocked her in comfort after Merle had squeezed her finger in a door as a child, who used to make her and the Murray children pancakes on the weekends after they'd had a slumber party. The witch who'd laughed and chatted with

Merle's grandmother while Merle and Maeve had sat under the table, stealing cookies from the plates until the two Elder witches had "punished" them with hugs and kisses and heartfelt words of affection.

The witch who now stood in a room drenched in pain and death, seemingly unaffected by the carnage she'd caused. Flicking a drop of blood off her pristine clothing, she met Merle's gaze.

Betrayal cut a gorge of raw pain through Merle's soul. Tears prickled in her eyes. "You," she whispered. "All this time. It was you."

Isabel heaved a sigh that seemed to shake the air. "Yes." Something akin to relief eased her features, as if she was glad she could speak about it freely. "I never meant for you to get involved, Merle. You should have stayed away, should have let it go. But you had to be so persistent, and just kept on digging." Isabel shook her head, her eyes shining with—pity? "You know I can't let you leave now. I've always loved you, Merle. Rowan did a great job of raising you by herself, and if the circumstances were different, I'd have gladly helped you grow into your powers now that she's gone. You would have made a formidable Elder, honey." A sheen of tears glistened on the witch's eyes. "Emily would have been so proud to see her daughter grow up to be you."

Merle's throat closed up, and her chest ached with a pain eclipsing the hurt where she'd crashed to the floor.

"However," Isabel went on, blinking away the tears and affection in her eyes, "you leave me no other choice now."

Magical vises tightened around Merle, squeezing her throat, her chest, her lungs, until pain pulsed in every cell of her body. The room swam before her eyes, darkness bleeding into her vision.

"Juneau won't question me if I tell her your demon went down the deep end and took you with him." Isabel's face was a blur of shadows.

Pain beyond the one wrecking her body jolted through Merle, ripping through her heart with cold, piercing fear—for Rhun. "Please don't kill him," she croaked past the strangulation in her throat.

"Oh, I won't," Isabel said. "I'll make good use of him—he can finish what his fellow demon didn't manage to accomplish. Turns out it's not the demon who takes the powers, but the witch who *gives* them. You didn't know that, did you? Neither did I. It's something I've learned over the past few days. Apparently it depends on the witch's mindset for it to work." A sigh. "Maeve has been...resistant, and sadly so. It would have all been easier on her if she'd just given in. Maybe she will be more inclined toward your demon. After all, he did successfully ensnare you to relinquish your powers, so chances are good Maeve will give in to him, too."

At that, Merle's dying senses snapped back to life, incited by burning fury. Blinking against the encroaching darkness, she focused all her remaining strength on the Elder witch. "How can you be so selfish?" she pressed out through gritted teeth.

Isabel sucked in air. "Selfish?"

The grip of death on Merle eased. The vises loosened by a fraction, giving her time to breathe, to recover enough to verbally charge forward. The least she could do was throw Isabel's hypocrisy in her face once more. "How can you do this? You, of all people—when you lost your own daughters to torture and murder? How can you betray and torture one of your own like this? And for what? Just to gain more power?"

The Elder witch's eyes widened. The air stood still.

Merle didn't back down. She'd verbally bitch-slap Isabel five ways 'til Sunday, and if it was the last thing she did. *Which it very likely would be.*

"Look at what you did!" Merle yelled. "Not enough that you tortured Maeve for your own gains. Look at this room—it's a fucking slaughterhouse, and you let it happen! Are you that far gone? Are you that power-hungry?"

The shocked expression on Isabel's face contorted into a grimace of outrage. "You think I'm doing this for myself?"

That struck Merle dumb, slowing her momentum.

Isabel's eyes darkened with indignation, laced with a deep hurt. "If I had done this years ago, right after Rowan died, my daughters would still be alive." Her jaw set in a tight line, she looked down at Merle with steely determination. "Now I'll make sure their deaths will be avenged—and that no other parent will ever have to mourn a child slain by demons' hands again."

Merle's heart skipped a beat. "What?"

There was an eerie glint in Isabel's eyes, a mixture of grief, regret—and a touch of madness. "I guess by now you figured out that Maeve contains incredibly strong magic. When Rowan confided in me after she locked it inside her, she told me she'd never felt anything like it. It eclipsed her own, and that was when Maeve was just a child. Now...her powers could be stronger even than Juneau's—and so much more destructive. You see, channeled in the right way, this kind of magic can anni-hilate whole species." A scary smile snuck onto Isabel's lips—scary because it was clearly on the wrong side of insanity. "Just imagine, Merle," she whispered with glee, "to live in a world without demons."

The breath rushed out of Merle. All feeling that was left in her body died away as she stared at the Elder witch in absolute horror. "You're building that world on dead bodies, Isabel."

Isabel's face softened, her lips trembled, and, for a moment, it was Lily's aunt who looked upon her, with eyes that held power, yes, but also love, such love and warmth. It was the woman who had held Maeve when she'd cried at Rowan's funeral. Had kissed Merle goodnight more times than she could count. Genuine regret edged her features, and she took a deep breath. Then, the moment was gone, and Isabel's expression iced over. "Nothing great has ever been achieved without making sacrifices."

Merle swallowed hard, feeling her time run out. "The other Elders won't tolerate this madness." Her heart raced away along with what remained of her life. "You won't be getting away with this."

"Once they see the benefit of the end result, they will thank me for it."

Her brain running in overdrive to find a way out of this, Merle glanced around the room. If only she had her powers, she'd have a fighting chance to take on Isabel. Her gaze fell on Rhun, still slumped down on the floor, motionless. It pierced her heart to see him like this, bloodied, bruised and broken. He hadn't stirred since Isabel had struck him down, he was still alive, Merle felt it in her very bones. Maybe, if he regained consciousness... She willed him to move with every ounce of her diminished mental strength.

Wake up, Rhun. Please wake up.

He stirred. Merle's heart stopped, then started a hysterical gallop. She turned her attention back to Isabel. The Elder witch hadn't noticed his movement. Relief flooded Merle.

Grasping for straws, she ventured forward. "This doesn't make sense, Isabel. How would you even get the powers from the demon once he's taken them from Maeve? He can't do anything with them and you can't either as long as the magic is locked inside him." Holding her breath, she tried to hide her anxiety. Would Isabel take the bait? Would she deem herself safe and close enough to victory to divulge the information?

"Oh, don't worry. The powers can be passed to another witch."

So close, so damn close. "How?"

Merle fought hard to keep her breathing calm, to avoid looking at Rhun, who'd shifted by the slightest fraction. Isabel stood between them, her attention on Merle. She still hadn't noticed Rhun had come to.

"Please tell me you won't have to take blood, pain, and pleasure from Rhun to get Maeve's powers." Merle looked at Isabel with an extra note of pleading in her eyes.

"Heavens, no." Isabel seemed genuinely disgusted by that idea. "Just the thought of laying a hand on a demon…" She shivered with obvious revulsion, then her eyes hardened. "It will be painful for him, though." Tilting her head, she regarded Merle for a moment, a slow smile spreading on her face.

"What—what will you do to him?" Merle didn't have to act one bit to put the tremor of fear in her voice.

"Oh," Isabel said with way too much delight, "he just needs to bleed himself dry with the intent to pass the magic to me, which I will make sure he does. And it will be my pleasure to persuade him to do so."

Behind Isabel, Rhun silently brought his wrist up to his mouth, his movements sluggish, exhausted. Using his fangs, he sliced his vein open until blood gushed forth. He repeated the action with his other wrist and then made sure the wounds stayed open. All without making a single sound.

Merle's breath caught in her throat. *"Rhun, no."*

There was no answer from him. Her heart broke into fine, fine splinters piercing her soul. She closed her eyes for a moment then looked back at Isabel. All she knew, right then, was that she had to stall, or else Rhun would drain himself for nothing.

"Isabel," she said, "you don't have to do this. Just…let Maeve go when it's over. Scrub her memory and let her go. She's been through so much…"

The blood kept flowing from Rhun's veins, mingling with the blood on the floor. His chest barely moved with his breaths anymore.

Isabel's expression was harsh, shuttered. And still a shadow of regret so deep passed over her face, revealing a heart inside her madness. "She *has* been through so much," she whispered, "that killing her would be a mercy, honey."

"No," Merle rasped, torn beyond the grasp of understanding.

"I'm sorry." Real pain trembled in Isabel's voice.

Merle knew the precise moment Rhun's heart stopped beating. It was the same moment her magic slammed back into her body, fused with her mind, her soul. Power rushed through her veins and beat against her skin with maddening euphoria. She gasped, flattened on her back by the force of it.

"No!" Isabel cried out, swiveled around and hit Rhun with a blow of power that sent him crashing into the wall once more.

And that was all Merle could take.

With a scream of pure fury, she lashed out at Isabel with the unadulterated force of her magic. It wasn't a spell. It was a visceral blast of her powers, a stroke that originated deep within her and sliced through the other witch's shields like a laser through metal. Isabel jerked, choked, and toppled over, her head hitting the concrete with a nauseating crack. It wasn't the impact that had killed her, though. Merle knew, with instinctive awareness, that the Elder's organs inside her had been fried, that her heart had exploded inside her chest.

Merle didn't care. The iron grasp keeping her down finally thrown off, she'd jumped up and run over to Rhun before Isabel had even hit the floor. Now she cradled Rhun's head in her lap, touched his wrists, muttered every damn healing spell she knew to close his many wounds.

To restart his heart.

"Don't you die on me, Rhun. Don't you fucking die on me!"

Tears clouded her vision, and she clutched him, willing him to live. Opening his mouth, she slit her wrist on his fangs, not even wincing at the pain. She pressed the wound against his lips, squeezed until her blood squirted out.

"Drink."

She prodded at his mind, brushed him with her powers, searching for a spark of life—however tiny—which she could nurture. He remained motionless, his mind a dark void, his aura gone. Still, Merle kept up her efforts, refusing to accept what would break her more than anything.

"Come back to me. Just come the fuck back to me!"

A glimmer of life deep inside his mind.

Merle drew in a sharp breath and mentally grasped for the tiny spark. She picked it up, cradled it like his head in her lap, wrapped it in her powers.

"Live."

Rhun's heart jolted into motion. He latched onto her wrist, and Merle gasped. Catching herself, she stroked his face as he sucked her blood in greedy pulls. Tingles of pleasure rolled through her veins, but the sensation soon subsided, her body growing numb from the amount of blood he was taking. The room spun. She slumped down next to him, her wrist in his grasp as he continued drinking. White spots in her vision, draining color from the world. Her own heart beat slower, slower.

"No." A deep voice in her head. *"Merle."* Power, stroking along her mental senses. *"My Merle."*

The spinning stopped. The little lights danced before her, faded. She blinked, sucked in air as her vision sharpened again, refocused—and filled with a face that, even coated in blood, was the most beautiful thing she'd ever seen.

"Rhun…" She gave him a shaky smile, relief a glowing warmth inside her. Raising a hand, she feathered her fingertips over his eyelids—closed to allow her touch—down to his mouth. "I was so scared you were dead."

A kiss on her fingers, a devastating smirk playing about his lips. "What's a little draining of blood?" His voice was as hoarse as if he'd been screaming for hours. "Takes more to kill me, little witch. After all, I'm used to bleeding for you."

"You're awful." Said around a desperate laugh, tears of joy spilling over. And she kissed him then, not caring about the blood on his lips. The only thing that mattered was the demon who'd somehow become the center of her world.

But—there *was* one other thing that mattered.

"Maeve," she rasped. "We have to find her."

He nodded, released her, got to his feet, and helped her stand as well. "She's around here. I can hear her heart beating." When Merle stared at him, he added, "Courtesy of my senses being in overdrive in this shithole."

"There's a door." Merle's voice trembled. She pointed to the corner of the room, where she'd spotted a door leading to the back of the warehouse while she'd been huddled against the wall during the demon fight.

Rhun was at the door within a second. A faint click as the lock became disabled. His hand on the knob, he paused, glancing at Merle over his shoulder.

"You should be the one to go in first," he said. "She needs to see your face."

Merle nodded, walked over on shaky legs, her body still weakened, and laid her hand on his. Together they opened the door.

What she saw when she stepped into the room would haunt her mind for the rest of her life.

Blocking out the assault of images and scents, Merle operated on automatic, her movements a blur. Rhun helped her release the shackles with mental commands, though he stayed back in the shadows. When Merle ripped the bloody sheets loose to wrap them around the nude, battered figure of what had once been her baby sister, she couldn't even sob. Couldn't break down.

Some pain was just too much.

In a face slashed beyond recognition, eyes fluttered open, homed in on Merle. Their color of fire and smoke was the only part of Maeve still familiar.

Split lips moved, formed words that wouldn't sound, but still, Merle heard them.

You came.

CHAPTER 23

The bedside lamp bathed Maeve's face in soft light, her features less haunted in sleep. Rhun had encountered his fair share of gruesome cruelty in his life, and still, what he'd seen in that room in the warehouse…it rivaled his darkest memories, chilled his soul.

Made him want to kill that fucker all over again.

Merle had taken care of Maeve after they'd returned to the old Victorian, had obviously cleaned her up after she'd carried her upstairs by herself, ignoring Rhun's offers of help. He understood, though. The only time Maeve had looked at him, her scent had spiked with gut-wrenching terror. He was, after all, a demon of the same species as the one who'd held her captive, and Maeve didn't know him, didn't know anything but to fear him. If he touched her, even with the intent to help, it would distress her beyond necessity.

Maeve hadn't spoken a word since they'd released her, or at least not that he'd heard. He'd stayed back as Merle had taken care of her, giving the sisters some much needed time alone. While Rhun had showered off the blood and gore sticking to his skin and had put on the spare clothes he'd taken from Bahram's apartment, Merle had put Maeve back in her old room, sitting down at her bedside after settling her in. For hours, she hadn't moved away, holding Maeve's hand, staring at her sister, and Rhun knew Merle hadn't once shifted from her position because he'd checked on her about once every hour.

The Elders' arrival had finally pulled her away.

Merle had called Lily on the way back from the warehouse, had explained what had gone down there and had asked her to hold the Elders at bay for a bit, give Maeve time to settle down. As usual, Lily had delivered, and it wasn't until an hour before dawn—after Merle had spent half the night watching over Maeve—that the witches came to call.

Now, after Basil had taken over Merle's spot at Maeve's side, after Merle had gone downstairs with Lily to face whatever was in store for her, Rhun stood in the upstairs hallway, looking into Maeve's room.

At a sister he'd been able to save.

Her face was marred with slashes, wounds some of which so severe not even the most powerful healing spells would be able to keep them from scarring. Rhun remembered the glimpse he'd gotten of the rest of her body, knew her face hadn't received the worst wounds of all. Not to mention the scars she'd carry in her soul and mind for quite possibly the rest of her life.

But underneath it all, she was alive, she'd survived, and as Rhun watched her breathe, he felt a knot ease deep in his chest, in the deep, dark corner that held the memory of another sister. One he hadn't been able to help. For the first time in his life, as he looked upon Maeve, he could let go of the guilt that had plagued him since he'd been a child.

I'm sorry, Siani.

With a sigh, he closed his eyes and let it go, let her rest, finally, in the peace she deserved.

When he opened his eyes again, he found Basil had lifted his head to scowl at him. The human male's resentment was palpable, his dislike of Rhun obviously only held in check by the fact he'd helped rescue Maeve. Yes, there was grudging gratitude in his features, but everything else in the look Basil shot him now said Rhun was and never would be welcome among Merle's friends and family.

And Rhun understood. It was a folly to ever think other witches, least of all the Elders, would accept a demon at Merle's side.

Merle had been determined to fight for him, had been convinced the Elders would allow him to be free in light of his contribution to Maeve's rescue. As voices raised in argument drifted up from below, Rhun knew she'd been wrong.

Backing away from Maeve's room under the watchful eyes of Basil, he made his way downstairs, following the sounds of the heated discussion. Merle's voice rose above the others, angry, pleading, telling them how he'd found Maeve, how he'd killed the other demon and helped put an end to the atrocities committed by Isabel.

"How can you insist on binding him again?" Merle's voice shook. "He's proven himself over and over!"

"He was bound in the Shadows for a reason," one of the Elders gave back. "His help in this matter is appreciated, but however good his recent deeds may be, they do not outweigh the innocent lives he took before he was leashed."

"He's only ever taken one innocent life!" Judging by her voice, Merle was close to tears now. "And it wasn't even cold-blooded murder, more like manslaughter—he was set up and manipulated. Doesn't that count as mitigating circumstances?"

If he hadn't been weighed down by misery, Rhun would have smirked at her use of law-speak.

"Do you have proof of that?" Juneau's voice.

A small silence.

"He told me what happened," Merle said with the stubborn strength Rhun had come to love.

"And you believe him." Not a question, more like an accusation.

"I know he's telling the truth." Ah, her adorable defiance was audible in every word.

"No," another Elder said, "you don't *know*. You believe him because you've become attached to him. And that is the problem—your feelings for him cloud your judgment."

"Which is why," another witch chimed in, "it is better you not have any say in this matter."

"We have already discussed this among ourselves before we came here," Juneau said. "Our decision stands—you will bind him again."

"The hell I will!"

"Watch your language, Merle." Juneau's voice was sharp as a whip, then gentled again. "If you cooperate and send him back to the Shadows, we will remit the punishment for your initial transgression of unbinding him without our consent."

"And if I refuse?"

A silence that stretched taut.

"You have shown a troublesome inclination for disobeying the laws we live by," Juneau said quietly. "If you continue to demonstrate disrespect for your Elders' orders, your punishments will become more severe."

Rhun could virtually hear Merle grind her teeth. "I'll take my chances," she said grimly.

"Don't be foolish," another Elder said. "He's just a demon."

"He's *my* fucking demon!"

"Easy, little witch," Rhun said in her mind. *"You don't want to cause an Elder-stampede, do you?"*

Merle swiveled around as he strolled into the living room, the corners of his lips twitching up at the sight of the shocked and alarmed expressions of the witches present.

"Ladies," he said, taking a bow.

Juneau's gaze hit him with the force of a swung baseball bat. "This is not a discussion you are invited to, demon."

"Ah." He came to stand next to Merle, his arm brushing against hers. "But I might have something to contribute."

"Rhun, what—" Merle began, but he covered her mouth with his hand, his gaze on Juneau.

"What will be the nature of Merle's punishment if she refuses to bind me?" He dropped all playfulness.

"That is none of your business," one of the other Elders said, a blonde with the aura of a healer.

"Tell me." His eyes were still intent on Juneau's, not backing down from the most powerful witch among the Elders.

After a long moment, Juneau answered calmly, "She will have to bear the burden of upholding the balance for all of the witch lines in our community for as long as she refuses to bind you."

Rhun barely kept himself from flinching. Such a punishment would render Merle in major pain for almost every day. Images of her bleeding in the car, screaming in agony, her flesh torn open to leech her magic, flashed through his mind, and his blood heated, burned in his veins.

"And if she does bind me," he managed to say past the raw pain inside him, "she'll go without punishment?"

"Yes," Juneau said.

His hand fell away from Merle's mouth.

Love, he thought, is feeling someone else's pain more than your own.

He turned to Merle, stroked a finger down her cheek, and stole a soft kiss.

"Bind me."

***

MERLE STARED AT RHUN, THUNDERSTRUCK, HER HEART SQUEEZED tight in her chest. "What?"

"I want you to bind me in the Shadows." His face was serious, as was his aura, vibrating with regret, grief—and grim determination.

"No." She shook her head, frantically, numb with denial.

"Merle." Juneau's voice filtered through the turmoil wrecking Merle's mind and heart. "Be reasonable and bind him."

"No!"

"*Do it, little witch,*" Rhun said in her head. "*I don't want them to hurt you because of me. And I sure as fuck won't stand around while you suffer for me. Bind me.*"

"*I can't.*" She shook her head again, her throat working hard to swallow what was a horrendous lump. "*I can't send you back. Don't ask me to do this.*"

"Bind him." The voice of another Elder, the head of the Michaels family line.

Merle couldn't see her, her vision narrowed on Rhun, her only focal point amid an unraveling world. His pale green-blue eyes studied her, took in her face as if drinking her in, like a desert plant would soak up the last drops of rain before the drought set in.

"*If you don't bind me now,*" Rhun said mentally, "*I will attack the Elders in front of you just to prove them right. I'll start with the hag with the bad wig over there.*" A pause. "*Seriously, with hair like that, she deserves to die.*"

How could he make a joke at such a time? And damn if that didn't break her heart even more with a rush of the impossible love she felt for him. "*Rhun, no, I can't…*"

A smile that shattered her. "*Don't force me to spill blood, little witch of mine.*"

"Merle," Juneau said, "don't stall any longer. Just bind him."

A chorus of voices rose around her, hailing down on her, demanding she do the impossible.

"*Do it.*" Rhun's mental tone softened, grew so quiet it was barely more than a whisper against her thoughts. "*You deserve better than a demon, Merle. Bind me.*"

She shook her head, her heart shriveled. Rhun cupped her face, kissed her softly, stepped away—and made as if to charge the Elders. With a silent sob, Merle broke.

> *"Into hunger, pain and darkness,*
> *hidden from the light,*
> *I bind thee in the Shadows,*
> *in never-ending night."*

Writhing, the Shadows came, tangling, snaking around Rhun's legs and upwards.

"Leashed and helpless, thou shalt pine..." Her voice cracked on a sob.

Rhun held her gaze, his aura steady, warm, trusting.

"...held ever after by the magic of my line."

His eyes stayed on her as the coiling, smoky blackness took him over, swallowed him soundlessly, and in the last seconds, he smiled at her.

Rhun's clothes fell to the floor, empty. The Shadows had taken him back.

Merle stood there, numb, feeling nothing. Around her, there were movements, sounds, scents and colors, people talking to her, touching her, and the world somehow demanded to keep moving. Merle moved along, said what was expected, what was necessary, but she was a wraith in a world that had lost meaning.

Acting on basic social survival mode, she finished the meeting with the Elders, walked them to the door, declined Lily's offers of staying over and comforting her, returned the twins' hugs without feeling, hanging on by a thread.

It was only after she'd politely forced Lily and Basil out of the house with promises of calling them if she needed support, only when the Victorian echoed with her lonely breaths, that Merle paused in front of Rhun's empty clothes—and broke down.

She collapsed onto the floor, sobs tearing out of her, tears spilling, the despair ripping her apart. Grabbing his T-shirt, she buried her face in it, breathing in his scent, while her body shook with her cries.

She rocked back and forth, her power bucking underneath her skin with the need to speak the words that would unbind Rhun again. Her heart broke with the knowledge she couldn't. Before they'd left, the Elders had cast a spell that would alert them if Merle tampered with the Shadows, and they would come after them both with a vengeance if she tried to bring him back.

And she knew, without a doubt, that Rhun wouldn't accept his freedom, that he would pressure her into binding him again as long the Elders threatened to hurt her for it.

"You damn stubborn demon," she whispered, her voice hoarse from crying, her heart an open wound that wouldn't stop bleeding. She kept crying, cursing, wailing at how fucking stubborn he was, how much she'd fallen for him, but above all, she cursed herself for not being strong enough. To fight for him, to hold on to him, to not give in under the pressure of Rhun and her Elders.

When after what seemed like an eternity of burning anguish, Merle finally wept in silence, only broken by her occasional sniffs, she heard it.

Soft footsteps on the hardwood floors, coming closer. Quietly, Maeve sat down beside her.

She hadn't once spoken to Merle since those silent words in the warehouse, hadn't reacted to anything Merle had said or done, as if she'd withdrawn deep inside herself, unresponsive to any stimuli. When Merle had bathed her, she'd stared into the distance, one step removed from this world. The food Merle had brought her had remained uneaten on the bedside table. Maeve hadn't touched or looked at Merle at all, not even giving a hint of recognition.

Now, she'd come to her.

Silently, Maeve put her scarred arms around her sister, stroked her back, her hair. She still didn't speak. She didn't have to.

Maeve held her while Merle cried until the ache in her lungs equaled the pain in her heart.

CHAPTER 24

The slant light of the afternoon sun streamed in through the kitchen window, glinted off the knife slicing the herbs. Merle watched Maeve wield the blade with calm precision. Her hands were steady, her movements sure, her eyes focused on her task. She was quiet in a way she hadn't been before. Her temper had always been calm, had never flared like Merle's, but now it seemed as if a part of Maeve had gone *silent*.

"Here" Merle handed her the next bundle of herbs to cut.

Maeve accepted them without a word, still not able—or ready—to speak. Merle had tried, at first, to get her to talk, just as she'd tried to convince Maeve to rest and recover. Stubborn though as her little sister was, she hadn't heeded Merle's advice. The day after Merle had bound Rhun in the Shadows again Maeve had started to quietly help out in the house while Merle had straightened out the chaos produced when the Elders had searched the Victorian in their hunt for Merle and Rhun. She'd found Maeve cleaning the bathrooms, doing the laundry, cooking lunch.

All without saying a single word.

Ignoring her protests, Maeve had smiled, eyes full of soft resistance. When Merle had found her leaning her head against the hallway wall during a pause in between dusting, had seen her stroking her fingers along the fading wallpaper as if caressing someone dear, she'd understood. Doing these tasks, helping out with the chores, it seemed to give Maeve a sense of belonging. Of being home.

Merle had stopped asking her to rest then. Instead, she'd given her a recipe to cook for dinner.

That night, Merle had woken to find Maeve had crept into her bed, snuggled up to her, holding her hand in sleep as she used to do when they'd been children. Merle had hugged her, her soul torn with the overwhelming happiness about having her back—and with the searing pain of knowing her baby sister had been broken on a fundamental level. The uncertainty of whether Maeve would ever fully recover from her ordeal burnt like corrosive acid in Merle's heart.

As she walked past Maeve now to mix the chopped herbs together in a bowl, she reached out to stroke her shoulders, one of many little gestures of comfort and reassurance—as much for Maeve as for herself. She still needed to touch her, feel her, to remind herself this was real, that Maeve was truly here.

She was about to add water to the bowl when the doorbell rang.

"I'll get it," Merle said, wiping her hands on a towel.

Dark foreboding whispered up her spine as she neared the front door, and her intuition proved right when she opened it to the one person—aside from all of the Elders—she'd least wanted to see again. Ever.

Arawn inclined his head in greeting, eyes of forest green intent on hers. Dressed in casual black attire that did nothing to lessen the lethal vibe of his power, he stood on her veranda like any other polite caller. The knowledge that he wasn't beat against Merle's skin with every fast thud of her heart.

"What do you want?" Of course, he'd come to collect his favor. Her question, then, was not aimed at the reason for his visit, but directly at the nature of the demand he'd make. With growing anxiety snapping at her nerves, she simply had no mind for playing nice.

Arawn tilted his head, a predator assessing its prey. "No word of thanks for my help in saving your sister?"

"We made a deal. Thanks are not necessary." She should probably be more courteous toward the Demon Lord, but the cocktail of emotions inside her—a mix of paralyzing fear and dangerous defiance—made her unabashedly blunt.

The ghost of a smile played about his lips. "Yes, we have a deal, do we not?" He leaned one shoulder against a porch post, his hands resting in the pockets of his pants. "I held up my end of the bargain. It is time for you to do the same." The verdant green of his eyes darkened as he raised his gaze, scanned the door and its immediate surroundings, seeing beyond the visible, before he looked back at Merle. "I believe it is polite to invite a guest inside."

Mentally checking the wards she'd put back up just this very morning, Merle held his intent stare. He couldn't enter unless she allowed him in. "You're not a guest." She straightened her spine, knowing better than to invite a being like Arawn into her house. "Tell me what it is you want from me in return for breaking the blocking spell."

His face hardened, though he didn't shift from his relaxed position against the porch post. "I see you do not care for courtesies, so I will be blunt as well. I want you to commit your sister to my custody."

All warmth left Merle's face, her heart beating a frantic tattoo against her ribs. Swaying, she grabbed the door to steady herself. "No."

"No?" Arawn's eyes narrowed, and even though his stance didn't change, his power pulsed as an almost visible force lurking just beneath his skin. "You swore a blood oath to grant me a favor," he said in a deceptively gentle tone. "Do you wish to break it?"

Merle shook her head, her fingers going numb from her

death grip on the door. "I... You said you wouldn't demand that. You agreed not to ask for fealty."

"I am not," Arawn calmly said, his bass voice rumbling in the afternoon quiet. "Our agreement specifically covered that neither you nor your sister would plead fealty. What I am asking for does not have to do with fealty. It goes beyond that." The air breathed magic all around him, such strange magic seeming at once contrary to and in tune with the fabric of the world. "I want you to transfer magical custodianship of her to me. Bind her life to me, and I will consider your debt paid."

Again, Merle shook her head, unable to react in any other way. Her mind was reeling. "I... I can't. How could you even ask this of me? Her life is not mine to give."

"Oh, but it is." The smile curving his lips was the one that had scared her lifeless before, when she and Rhun had appealed to him in his lair. "As the head of your line," he went on in a voice so very calm and friendly, they might as well have been discussing where to go for dinner, "you are ultimately in charge of the members of your family, a responsibility that includes liability for their magic and custodianship of their lives. In all matters magical, Maeve is your ward, and if you so wished you could magically force your sister's obedience by uttering a single word. You are fully authorized to bind her life to someone else, and transfer this power over her. Her pleading fealty is not necessary for that, which means my demand is in perfect compliance with the deal we made."

Merle stood there, staring at Arawn, as everything, everything slipped through her fingers. She'd lost the fight against her Elders, lost the man she loved, and now, after she'd just freed Maeve from the clutches of a monster, she was forced to cede her baby sister to a creature that made psychopathic demons tremble with fear. Something inside her snapped.

"Go to hell," Merle whispered, holding her power barely in check.

An easy shrug of one shoulder. "I am not sure they would

take me back." Arawn's gaze turned steely. "Now surrender your sister."

"No! Ask me for something else, anything else."

He glanced at the fine tendrils of smoke drifting up from underneath her fingers, where the wood of the door had begun to smolder. "Your magic is strong, fire witch, but it is not what I am interested in. Release Maeve into my custody."

"Fuck no!"

"Do not try my patience any longer. Give me your sister. And do not say something cliché like *over my dead body*, because that can easily be arranged. Breaking a blood oath will claim your life. Do you really want to go there?"

"No," a husky voice said from behind her.

Merle swiveled around on her heels, stared at Maeve. Her baby sister stood in the middle of the foyer, face pale, eyes wide, hands clenched to fists at her side. Trembling, breathing fast and shallow, her muscles under scarred skin flexed as if she'd like nothing better than to bolt and hide in the most faraway corner. And yet, she remained, looking past Merle at Arawn. At the powerful creature that was here to claim her, to end the short taste of freedom she'd just gotten.

"I will go with you," Maeve said, her voice but a rasp.

"No, you won't." Merle stared at her sister, her hand still clutching the door, her back to the male who threatened to take away the last piece of her soul. "Stay out of this, Maeve."

Eyes of amber and gray met her own, vivid in a face once so beautiful, now bearing the evidence of how close hell could come to earth. "You have done so much, more than I can ever give back. I can't let you risk your life too."

Maeve's voice still sounded so husky, so raw, as if it wasn't just temporarily rough from disuse or fear. Something inside Merle broke as she understood—Maeve's vocal cords had become irreparably damaged.

As could happen when one screamed for hours, days, on end.

She shook her head, her throat closed up tight. "Maeve, no. I..."

"You swore a blood oath," Maeve cut her off gently, her rough voice scraping over Merle's skin, a constant reminder of the torture she hadn't been able to protect her little sister from. "You have to keep it. If you don't, the Powers That Be will break you for it." Maeve made a small pause, and beyond the shadows of fear and pain in her eyes, there was love, such *love*. "I won't let that happen, Merle."

And with that, Maeve took a hesitant step toward the door, toward Arawn, who had been watching her with silent attention.

"Wait." Holding up a hand to halt Maeve, Merle swiveled around to Arawn. "You want her for her powers, don't you?"

Instead of an answer, he simply stared at Merle until her knees trembled.

She made herself speak. "You realize they're locked inside her? You can't access them. Look at her. She's been through hell, has been tortured over and over, and still, her powers haven't surfaced. They didn't break free under everything she's suffered, and even the demon was unable to take them from her. They won't ever emerge, so she'll be of no use to you."

Looking over her head at Maeve, Arawn quietly said, "That remains to be seen. Step aside and let her through."

All angry defiance left Merle in a rush of pure despair. "Please," she whispered, dropping the last of her pride in favor of pleading. "I just got her back. Please don't take her from me."

Tilting his head to the side, Arawn studied her with faint, detached interest, as one might examine a mutated lab animal. "I am curious. Why do you think begging me will help?"

Merle swallowed, holding back her tears, and spoke past the voice inside her telling her she fought a losing battle. "Because I'm hoping you maybe have a heart."

His lips tugged upwards while his eyes remained cold. "Pity

your demon is not here anymore. He would have told you better than to pin your hopes on that."

At the mention of Rhun, the reminder of how she'd lost him, Merle's chest constricted as if bound with a thousand tiny strands of barbed wire. The fact she was about to lose her sister too only added to the hurt spiraling out of control.

Those eyes the color of secrets hidden in the woods held her gaze. "No amount of begging will get me to change my mind, Merle."

Her name on his lips sounded wrong, as if he'd taken something private from her. She shivered, feeling bereft, vulnerable.

Pushing off the porch post, he pinned her with an adamant stare. "I *will* take her with me."

And she saw it then, that he meant it. Nothing she could do or say would ever sway his decision. She'd bartered away Maeve before she'd ever even saved her. The realization that she would have to let Maeve go sank into her blood, heart, and soul, and it was a violent, tearing pain.

Merle hauled in a breath, and with it, a last thread of resistance unfurled inside her. "Not yet," she told the lord of demons in front of her.

Arawn cocked a single eyebrow. It was enough to make power spark around him.

Merle wetted her suddenly dry lips. "She'll be yours, but leave her with me for now. You deal in favors, right? If you don't take her away for the time being, I will grant you another favor."

Arawn raised his other eyebrow as well.

"No," Maeve rasped behind her. "Don't do that, Merle. Not for me."

Merle shot a look at her sister. "This is not up for discussion." Turning back to Arawn, she said, "The favor will only put my magic at your disposal, nothing else."

Dark amusement in his eyes. "So you learn fast." He studied her for a long moment. "You will regularly make your magic available for my affairs," he said, steel underneath that voice of rough silk, "until I decide to take Maeve with me."

Merle bristled at the open-end contract, fighting hard not to snap at Arawn for his high-handedness. She gritted her teeth. "I will not kill for you."

He gave her a curious look, and just when she thought he couldn't possibly become more arrogant, he asked, "And just why would I need your help with that?"

"Maeve," Merle said without taking her eyes off Arawn, "get me a knife."

One side of his mouth tipped up in a wry smile. "Oh, I do not require a blood oath for this deal." The shadows in his eyes deepened. "You know I will come to collect my other favor when you refuse me your magic." And with a last glance at Maeve, he left, walking down the steps of the veranda to disappear in the thicket of trees near the driveway. The huge black bird of prey shooting out into the sky a few seconds later left tendrils of darkly curling magic in its wake.

Merle stood staring after it for a moment, pondering the price she'd have to pay for holding on to the last remnants of family she had left.

When Maeve took her hand, pulled her in a hug, she knew it was worth it.

"I'm sorry," Maeve whispered, a broken sound against Merle's shoulder.

"Don't." She hugged Maeve closer. "You'd have done the same."

❁

MERLE WAS BACK IN THE LIBRARY OF THE OLD VICTORIAN—FOR THE hundredth time this day. In between taking care of Maeve, she'd been here, in this room, leafing through the books looking for a way to unbind Rhun again without the Elders finding out.

With every passing minute, hour, day, another piece of

Merle died with the knowledge of him suffering in darkness. She had to find a way to get him back. His absence was a living, breathing source of pain, growing further with the passage of time. Merle missed him with every fiber of her being, had only fully realized how deeply he'd burrowed into her heart, how much she'd loved having him around when his loss had ripped a vicious, gaping hole into her soul.

She'd been right. Losing him hurt far more than being without her powers.

Shoving her hands through her hair, Merle groaned, her head thumping down on the desk she was sitting at. Memories of the past days floated up, rushed through her mind, and she ground her teeth together as she revisited all the times she'd felt helpless, powerless, controlled by the demands of those who held the reins. First the Elders, then Arawn. *Dammit*, she was sick and tired of being a mere pawn in a game others played!

Next to her, a book caught fire.

"Crap!" She jerked her head up, and with a wave of her hand and a muttered word, she extinguished the flames.

Grimacing at the damage, she gingerly set the book aside. She'd have to watch her temper, check her command over her powers, which had been failing due to the stress she'd been under.

Well, she thought sardonically, let's just add that to the growing list of things slipping from my control.

When the doorbell rang, Merle froze in the process of taking out another book to study. It likely wasn't Arawn again—he'd just left about an hour ago—and yet anxiety rippled through her as she got up and walked to the door.

Maybe it was just Lily or Basil—even though they would have called before showing up here. They'd come over in the last two days, to see Maeve, to check on Merle, giving her those looks that clearly said all they needed was one word from her and they'd permanently set up camp in the Victorian to keep her from falling apart.

She'd greatly appreciated it, same as the chocolate and ice cream Lily had brought over without asking. When Merle had started to thank her, Lily had threatened to beat her over the head with the pack of *Ben & Jerry's*. But when they'd left, Merle had made sure to hug Lily until every last cell in her best friend's body knew how much she meant to Merle. The quiver in Lily's aura and the tears in her eyes—quickly blinked away— were proof the message had gotten through.

As Merle now pulled open the door, she drew in a sharp breath and stood still for the longest moment, gaping at the woman who bore an eerie resemblance to the witch who'd broken Maeve. Swallowing, Merle could only stare at her. What could she say to a woman whose sister she'd killed?

"May I come in?" Hazel's voice broke through the awkward silence.

"Of course," Merle said, stepped aside and led her into the living room.

After offering her unexpected visitor refreshments, Merle sat there, self-conscious to a painful degree, the quiet of the house wrapping around her. With Maeve upstairs, taking a nap, it was only Merle and Hazel in the room, a strange meeting between two people whose lives had been touched by such darkness, it tainted the air.

Hazel cleared her throat, glanced at her hands. "I was wondering if I could see Maeve?"

Merle swallowed. "She's gone to lie down for a bit. Uh, I could wake her if you want."

"No, please, don't." Hazel shook her head. "Let her rest. She probably wouldn't want to see me anyway..." Her voice trailed away.

Once more, they sat in painful silence.

"I'm sorry," Hazel said, her magic a soft glow around her.

Startled, Merle looked at her, unsure how to reply.

"What Isabel did..." Closing her eyes, Hazel took a deep breath, laden with sorrow and grief. "You and Maeve, you girls

334

have always been like daughters to me, too. What happened to Maeve—it pains me, and I am ashamed that an evil like that has come from my own family. I am so very sorry."

The knot of awkwardness inside Merle's chest tightened impossibly further. "It wasn't your fault. You didn't do these things to Maeve…"

"I feel like I should have known. Isabel's my sister, I should have—" A poignant pause. "Was. She was my sister."

Merle's stomach lurched. Despite Isabel's evil, despite Merle's dark sense of satisfaction at the fact the Elder witch had paid with her life for torturing Maeve, Merle also felt Hazel's grief. No matter what Isabel had done, she'd been Hazel's sister, and if anyone understood the bond behind that, it was Merle.

Her fingers dug into the fabric of the armchair. Torn inside, unable to bring herself to apologize for taking Isabel's life, but ripped apart by visceral sympathy for Hazel's loss, Merle could only stare at her in strained silence.

"Do you love him?"

Hazel's sudden change of subject, her unexpected question, threw Merle off, though only for a second. Understanding immediately whom the older witch was referring to, she met her eyes, calmly said, "He's my heart."

Hazel regarded her for a long moment, then nodded. "And he obviously loves you, too—to go willingly into the Shadows, for you." Glancing down at her hands in her lap, she softly went on, "With so much death and pain around us, I think if we find love, we need to hold on to it." She paused, looked back at Merle with those warm brown eyes. "No matter what form it takes." Pulling out a book from her bag, she hesitated. "There is nothing I can do to right the wrong that Isabel caused. I just wish…" Hazel fell silent, swallowed, her eyes glistening as she glanced down. "If Maeve needs anything, don't hesitate to ask."

Merle nodded, waiting for Lily and Basil's mother to speak again, knowing she wasn't finished.

A heavy breath later, Hazel handed her the book. "I can't undo Maeve's pain. But I can do this for you."

Merle frowned at the small volume bound in black leather, inscribed with the title *On the Laws of Witches and Their Elders*. Glancing up at Hazel, she inhaled softly as realization sunk in. There had been a subtle difference in the other witch's aura, a change from when Merle had last seen her. "You're an Elder now."

Hazel nodded, rose to her feet. Merle followed suit.

"I have claimed my place as Isabel's successor." Smoothing down her skirt with calm hands, she met Merle's gaze. "It's time for a fresh breeze, don't you think?" She nodded at the book in Merle's hands. Giving her a small smile, she hesitated for a second, then closed the distance and enfolded Merle in a trembling hug. When Hazel withdrew again, she surreptitiously wiped at her eyes, said her goodbyes, and left.

Merle sank down on the armchair again, opening the book to where a mark was tucked inside. It was the section on privileges and duties of an Elder witch, and two of the paragraphs were highlighted. In between them, a small sticky note read, *You have my full support.*

As Merle read the two passages, she slowly started to smile, hope blooming inside her chest.

CHAPTER 25

Darkness. So thick, it penetrated his very being, each and every cell. It coiled around him, within him, *through* him. The worst part about the Shadows? They were sentient, and they were *hungry*.

The squirming black ate at his foundations, each bite a sharp sting spearing through him, gnawing at his soul until he wasn't Rhun anymore.

He was pain.

The starvation had hit him on the heels of the pain, depleting him of all his energy, leaving but a glimmer of life inside him. Enough to feel, while refusing him the mercy of death.

Burning anguish, gut-wrenching hunger, despair beyond hope, and still he held on to the image of sky-blue eyes and flaming hair, to the memory of a love that had broken and steeled him at the same time. Not even the most vicious darkness seeping into his mind could wrench this away from him.

Abruptly, the Shadows roiled as if agitated. If he'd had control over his physical form, he might have frowned at that. It felt like... Something pulled at him, called him forth, and the sentient black around him receded grudgingly. The Shadows sure as hell didn't want to release him, but they were *ordered* to.

He passed through the veil between the layers of the world, and as his form solidified under the night air's cool kiss, the Shadows let him go with waves of lingering pain. A breath— and he was free.

Rhun's eyes fluttered open, his vision predator sharp, homing in on the face of the witch leaning over him, the image of her branded into his heart. A single tear streaked down her cheek, her eyes a startling bright blue after the darkness he'd come from, her hair a spark of fire in the night. Color and life she was, his Merle.

Which was why he wouldn't allow her to be harmed in any way, least of all because of him. Fighting against the urge to hold on to this dream, he quietly said, "You know I'm going to force you to bind me again, little witch."

She shook her head, wiping at her damp cheek, and then held her wrist up to his mouth. "Drink." Her other hand stroked his jaw, his temple, feathered through his hair.

He didn't move. "*Merle.*"

Stubborn defiance in her eyes. "You're starving. Feed. We'll talk after."

When he still wouldn't bite her, she uttered a sound of frustration—which he couldn't help finding adorable—grabbed a knife from the bag lying next to her, and before he could stop her, she'd slit her wrist and pressed the bleeding wound against his lips.

A trickle of warm blood slipped into his mouth, touched his tongue. He was done for. Hunger and instincts took over, and against reason and his conscience, he latched on to her wrist, bit into her skin, and drank.

The aroma of her blood burst on his tongue like an explosion of exquisite pleasure. His body, his mind, regained strength with each deep and greedy pull on her vein. More of his senses came to life, and he breathed in her intoxicating scent, felt her aura, her power, infused with a new kind of strength. Something was different about her, a sense of completion in her magic, as if a missing piece had fallen into place.

Rhun broke away, licked the wound closed on her wrist and held it when she wanted to press it down to his mouth again to keep him drinking. "Enough." And damn if it didn't take a measure of superhuman self-control to say that. He'd pat himself on the back for it later, when he'd be starving in the Shadows again. "You shouldn't have unbound me." For all the roughness of his words, his touch was tender as he caressed her face, traced the freckles on her cheek with his fingers. Her skin was so, so soft, and he wanted to stroke her forever. But—"Send me back. I'm not going to let you get punished, Merle."

"I've found a way around that."

She rose to her feet, glanced behind her, and Rhun raised himself half-up on his elbows, looking around for the first time. He was lying on the lawn behind the MacKenna residence, the darkness of night illuminated dimly by a few candles on the back porch. Close by, behind Merle, stood Lily, Basil, and their mother, Hazel.

Further in the back, half-hidden in the shadows of the porch between the candles, lingered Maeve. One of her hands curled around a porch post, as one might hold on to someone dear, and her eyes were wary as she looked at Rhun.

In a fluid motion, he rose to his feet, accepted the clothes Merle handed him, pulled them on, and then turned to his witch. Before he could speak, or act on any of the numerous impulses of what he'd like to do with her, she took his hand and met his eyes, her face solemn.

"There is a way," she said, "to keep you here, with me. The Elders won't be able to punish me for it, and they can't force me to bind you again." A small intake of breath, a delicate quiver in her aura. "If you agree."

His eyes narrowed. "To what?"

She looked down on their linked hands, her fingers threaded

through his, and then she glanced to her side. Rhun followed the direction of her gaze, to the charred stump a few feet away, this relic of a tree that had witnessed the destruction of a family —as well as the bonding of hearts, generation after generation. Realization dawned on him, rushed through him in waves of exhilaration, and he looked back at Merle.

"Why, my little witch," he said, a smile flirting with his lips, "are you *proposing* to me?"

His acute hearing picked up how her heart skipped a beat then pounded at a double rate. Cheeks flushed a hot pink discernable even in the dark of night, she looked up at him, met his gaze.

"That depends," she said, her voice shaky, "on your answer." Her aura trembled with uncertainty, with *fear*.

He stared at her for a long moment, anger boiling inside him.

Then he lowered his shields.

⚬❧

THE FORCE OF RHUN'S MIND PULLED ON MERLE'S, AND SHE staggered, stumbled into his arms. Wrapping his power around her, he took her in, allowed her to see, feel, taste everything of him, nothing held back.

Gesturing for Basil and Lily to stand down when they made a move toward them, clearly worried about her, Merle held on to Rhun for support, gasped at the emotions crashing upon her.

At the depth of his love.

Beneath it, hot and raw, pulsed anger, formed into a snarled question. *"How could you ever doubt what my answer would be, witch volcano?"*

Smiling against his chest, where he held her pressed in a crushing hug, she couldn't help teasing him. *"So that's a yes?"*

His mind, body, and soul quaked with his growl, and she sent her smile straight into his mind.

"How can this work?" he asked, stroking her back, his other hand curving possessively, cherishingly over her hip.

"I've claimed my place among the Elders," Merle said, and in the small pause that followed, the surge of Rhun's pride and approval warmed her heart, *"and one of my prerogatives is unbinding any demon from the Shadows, if I have the backing of another Elder."*

"Isabel's sister." Understanding unfurled in his mind.

"Yes. She will also act as the one Elder necessary to marry another witch. As my husband—the husband of an Elder witch—you'll be protected from any hostilities by other witches, and they cannot force me to bind you again unless you are caught red-handed breaking our laws." She paused for a moment, gut knotted tight with unease. *"Rhun,"* she then said, her mental voice as serious as her heart, because she needed to be sure, needed him to understand, *"it's a binding commitment. I don't want to force you into this…"*

A rush of deep, lasting affection against her senses, not a single trace of hesitation, of doubt in his mind. *"I don't want to make anyone else's toes curl, little witch. Only yours. And I want to annoy you every day for the rest of my life."*

"That is a crappy way of saying I love you," she whispered even as her heart burst with joy, her mind drunk on the warmth of his emotions for her.

"All right," he said, his breath hot on her ear, his arms tightening around her, "how about this? When I was back in the Shadows, it was the thought of you that kept the pain at bay. It was the thought of you being safe and unhurt. And I'd go back into the Shadows any time, for as long as it takes, to keep you safe and unhurt, little witch of mine." A kiss on her hair, his aura enfolding her. "I love you."

She'd already seen the truth of it in his mind, had felt it rush over her in a caress of raw devotion, but to hear him put it in words, say it out loud, it undid her. Rising up on tiptoes, she wound her arms around his neck, pulled him down and kissed the living daylights out of him.

341

Well, at least she did so until he took over the kiss and threw her world off balance. Held upright only by Rhun's hands, she came back to her senses when Basil and Lily simultaneously cleared their throats.

"Right," Merle muttered and stepped back from her viciously talented demon, her lips tingling, her pulse shot up through the skies, her skin on fire. "Right. Um. Hazel?"

The Elder witch stepped forward with barely concealed amusement in her eyes, took Merle's left hand and then looked at Rhun, indicating him to give her his hand as well. He complied, his eyes never leaving Merle's. Hazel pulled out a scarf of soft silk and wrapped it around their joined hands.

"Speak your vows," Hazel said, her one hand resting on top of the scarf.

A slight drizzle of rain fell, feathering down on Merle and Rhun. His fingers closed around hers as he brushed her mind with his power, caressed her so most intimately.

"There you go, little witch. You've always wanted it to rain at your wedding, haven't you?"

Merle looked into eyes of palest green-blue, her soul going peacefully quiet in a way that breathed magic, yet had nothing to do with her powers. *"You remembered."* What she'd told her father, right here on the lawn, this little piece of her heart she'd pulled out, laid down in the open at a moment that had pained her so much. And just like that, Rhun had given it back to her, and, impossibly, soothed a part of this bittersweet ache.

"Of course," he said, his mental voice stroking her senses.

"I, Merle MacKenna, take thee, Rhun..." She suddenly faltered, frowning.

"Ap Owain," Rhun offered with a smirk that stole her heart again. *"My last name's ap Owain."*

She gave him a smile from the depth of her soul. "I take thee, Rhun ap Owain, to my wedded husband, 'til death us depart."

His thumb caressed the back of her hand. "I, Rhun ap

Owain, take thee, Merle MacKenna, to my wedded wife, 'til death us depart."

None of the weddings she'd witnessed could have ever prepared Merle for the sheer bliss of this moment, for the soaring joy that stole her breath. Hazel tied the ends of the scarf together, spoke the words that would seal the bond, but Merle didn't hear her anymore. Everything else faded away as her world centered on the demon who held her heart, her soul, who enveloped her mind in a blinding embrace of love.

Holding on to his hand, joined with hers in a scarf that would remain knotted for as long they both lived, she rose to meet his kiss—and groaned as Rhun snuck his other hand up to the back of her head, massaged her scalp and damn straight made her toes curl.

"Damn sneaky demon." A whisper against his lips.

But she could give as well as she took, and she grinned broadly when the circle pattern she scratched on his chest made Rhun's eyes cross and his thoughts dissolve into a puddle of goo inside his mind.

"Tricky little witch."

"Ahem." Lily's tap on her shoulder had Merle snapping back into the here and now.

Taking the knotted scarf in one hand, Merle turned to her best friend, who pulled her into a rib-threatening hug.

"Congratulations," Lily whispered in her ear. "I'm so happy for you, Merle."

"Thank you," she whispered back, squeezing Lily hard.

When she released Merle, Lily eyed Rhun for a moment, then extended her hand. "If you don't treat her right," she said as Rhun took it, "I will rip off your balls and feed them to the brownies in our backyard."

"Lil!" Merle gaped at her in shock.

Rhun's eyes, though, glinted with amusement. "Fair enough."

Before Merle could berate Lily any more, Basil stepped up to her, hugged her and kissed her hair. "I hope he'll make you happy, sweetie."

"He already does." Merle gave him a peck on his cheek as he released her, ignoring Rhun's low growl.

Basil's warm brown eyes, so much like his mother's, focused on Rhun then, turned cold. "Hurt her, and your balls won't be the only thing I'll rip off your body."

Rhun held his gaze, gave the other male a grim nod of understanding. His mind still open to Merle, she could see Rhun wasn't piqued by her friends' threats—if anything, his opinion of Basil and Lily had risen. Protectiveness, he understood all too well.

Basil took a breath, nodded, and then shook Rhun's hand. "Her favorite flowers are tulips. Remember that for when you screw up."

"Appreciated." He let go of Basil's hand, looked at Hazel and inclined his head in thanks.

The Elder witch nodded, then turned to Merle. "Cherish each other."

"We will."

Merle looked at Rhun, his dark hair wet from the rain, his gaze heated as it centered on her, and her heart was too small for what she felt for him. It would burst, she was sure, burst into a thousand tiny pieces, and each one would bear his name.

"Now that's just cheesy," he said, his mental voice affectionately teasing.

Merle gasped, realization sinking in with amazement—she'd opened her mind to him without thinking. Sneaky demon that he was, he'd read her thoughts and now grinned at her in the way that made her want to smack him over the head. When she narrowed her eyes at him, he simply laughed and pulled her in for a kiss she had no will to fight, not when she sensed the devastating depth of his love for her behind his teasing. She just melted, and, *damn*, it felt good.

"All right," Rhun said as he released her, glancing from Basil and Lily to Hazel, shooting a quick look at Maeve, "you might want to leave now." He made shooing gestures, sighed with annoyance when nobody moved. "I promised my witch I wouldn't embarrass her in front of her friends anymore, so you need to get going."

When Merle took a step back and looked at him quizzically, opened her mouth to ask him, he cut her off.

"You really don't want them to see this," he said for her ears only, dark heat in his eyes. He smirked when she tried to pick his intention from his mind and failed because he shielded it.

"Um, guys." Anticipation beat against her skin. Her eyes were riveted on Rhun, who had gone hunting quiet, studying her with predatory focus. "I'll see you tomorrow, okay?"

She didn't hear their goodbyes, was only half-aware of Maeve leaving with them, all her attention monopolized by the dark seduction of so much imposing *maleness* in front of her. The candlelight played over Rhun's face as he closed the distance between them, his power stroking over hers. The air between them flickered with sparks of magic.

Raising his wrist to his mouth, he bit down hard, opened his vein, and then held it up to her lips. "Drink." A rough command.

Her gaze steady on his eyes, she only hesitated for a second, then closed her mouth over the wound, licked. A jolt of power down her spine as his blood met her tongue. Rhun's aura shook. He curved his other hand around the back of her neck, squeezed.

"*Drink.*"

Merle sucked, and the warmth of his lifeblood flowed down her throat. She'd expected the taste to be bitter, as metallic as blood smelled, instead the flavor was...all Rhun. It was his essence, the darkness of his scent, the vibrancy of his power, and it meshed with hers, a clash of forces.

Without warning, Rhun angled her head to the side with his

other hand tangled in her hair, exposed her neck—and then he bit her.

Merle cried out, not from pain but from surprise at his sudden move. Pleasure exploded inside, and she saw, knew, felt it inside his mind, that he was deliberately careful not to take pain now as he sucked her blood, so as not to absorb her powers again.

"Keep drinking," he ordered her, his mental voice deep with the same desire tingeing his mind.

And she did, latching on to his wrist once more. The moment she pulled his blood from his vein at the same time as he drank from her, a rolling, consuming tsunami of pleasure razed her body and mind.

Her world unraveled.

Her nerves burst with too much sensation, Rhun in every part of her, down to the depths of her soul. Shaking, shaking, she couldn't stop jerking with the jolts of pleasure shooting through her, zinging back and forth between the pooling heat in her center and every last cell of her body. If he hadn't held her, she'd have collapsed onto the grass, her muscles turned to jelly by the damnedest best fucking orgasm she'd ever had, including when he'd taken blood, pain and pleasure from her.

When he stopped drinking—and thus halted those incredible, torturously intense surges of release inside her—and licked the puncture wounds closed, all she could do was peer up at him through eyes half-lidded with deep, devastating satisfaction.

"What the actual fuck was that?" Damn, she sounded like a woman well-used.

He effortlessly lifted her up, one arm around her back, the other underneath her knees. "That," he said in a voice that made her soul purr, "was what I've wanted to do with you ever since I marked you outside that demon bar."

She managed to raise one hand to stroke her fingers over his cheek, his lips, understanding blooming inside her as she noticed the new, amazing, wonderful bond of power pulsing between them.

"We're now mated by demon law," Rhun said and nipped her fingers, eyes gleaming with delight at her gasp. "Linked in the deepest way possible. Which also means your human life span will be extended to match mine. I won't ever have to lose you again." Such fierce tenderness glowed in his aura—no, not just his aura.

Merle felt it in this connection between them too, a bond that ran directly from his soul to hers, an intimacy that went even further than the merging of their minds when they'd dropped their shields.

This, it was a merging of hearts.

And Merle let him know, through the bond glowing invisible between her and him, how much it meant to her.

"Mine," she thought, pulling his head down for a kiss while he carried her home. "You're mine, Rhun."

His answer, it made her soul blaze with incandescent love.

"Always, little witch."

EPILOGUE

M erle shut the door behind her, put her purse on the dresser, shrugged out of her coat and hung it up on the rack—which had yet again been straightened while she'd been out. Bouncing with mischief, she deliberately rearranged the jackets, coats and scarves into a new mess, and then strolled over into the kitchen.

There she stopped dead in her tracks, blinking in disbelief at the sight.

"Are you *cooking*?" she asked, shell-shocked.

Rhun flinched as if caught, and stopped cutting the meat into small pieces. He surreptitiously shoved something with his foot around the corner of the kitchen island. "Well..."

"What are you hiding there?" She narrowed her eyes and stepped farther into the kitchen.

He pointed the knife at her, pursing his lips. "You know, I don't appreciate that assumption. Can't I just be cooking my mate a nice meal? But no, of course I have to be hiding—"

A loud meow made him freeze in mid-sentence.

Grinning, she sauntered closer. "Busted. Now drop the act and show me the cat."

Scowling, he put down the knife and bent to retrieve a black ball of fur from the floor.

She uttered a high-pitched squeal and rushed over. "It's a kitty!" Her sounds of delight turned into ones of compassion when she took a closer look at the tiny black cat. "Oh gods, he's got only one eye! Poor little fella…"

He scratched the kitten under his chin. "Yeah, he seems to have lost it in a fight. But it's healed already and he manages pretty well for being half-blind. He only ran into the door twice." He grimaced, probably remembering his own intimate contact with a door not too long ago. "I found him scrounging for scraps in the streets, and he looked so starved I thought I'd feed him…"

She held her finger out for the kitten to sniff. "Did you name him already?"

Rhun threw a sheepish look at her. "So… we'll keep him?"

That earned him a hearty swat on the shoulder. "What kind of question is that? Of course we'll keep him. So what's his name?"

"Sauron."

"Seriously?"

Holding up the kitten, he pointed at its one good eye. "The Eye? The Evil Eye? The Great Eye? Rimmed with fire, yellow like a cat's, slit pupils? Come on, the name's perfect."

She shook her head, a smile blooming in her heart. "Only you, Rhun, only you. Now let me hold him."

He took the kitten's paws and menacingly flailed them in her direction. "One does not simply *hold* the Dark Lord of Mordor. Lord of the Earth, King of Men, Base Master of Treachery… He will smite you, fool that you are, with his unfathomable power of—*purring*?" His face fell as the kitten rubbed against her outstretched hand and purred up a storm. "Traitor," he muttered under his breath.

Merle laughed and petted the adorable fur ball. "Come on. I'm a witch, he's a black cat—what did you expect?"

Smirking, Rhun handed her the kitten. His expression shadowed over. "How's Maeve?"

"Better." She rubbed Sauron's ears. "I saw her smile at something Basil said." The first time since her rescue, in fact, that her little sister had shown genuine amusement.

It was a day-by-day progress, and even though Maeve's voice still echoed the horror she'd been through, her behavior had become less that of an animal scared into a corner, and more that of a...person. There were moments when she'd retreat deep into herself, when her aura would freeze over as if a switch had been turned, and according to Lily, Maeve would wake screaming at night. Merle had been working with her, had tried to heal her emotional wounds with soothing, strengthening magic, and even though Maeve refused to speak of the details of her torture, the last two weeks had seen some improvement.

"I could still move out," Rhun now said, leaning against the kitchen island, his eyes solemn on hers. "This is her home. She should be here."

It had been difficult for Maeve to be around Rhun—rationally she knew he'd helped save her, that he didn't mean her harm even though he was a *bluotezzer* demon same as the one who'd broken her. Rationality, however, had a way of puffing into thin air in the face of lingering trauma, and after Maeve's second panic attack because Rhun had entered the room she'd been in, he'd decided to go crash at his friend Bahram's until he got his own place.

When Maeve had heard them talking about it, she'd offered to move out instead so Merle and Rhun could have the Victorian to themselves for the time being. Since she hadn't wanted to go back to her apartment—where she'd be alone, confronted with the memories of how the demon had abducted her from there—she'd asked Lily and Basil if she could stay with them for a while.

Hazel had immediately welcomed her into her home and

had designated one of the guest rooms for Maeve's permanent use.

Now, as Rhun looked at Merle with silent concern in his eyes, she shook her head, setting the kitten down on the floor. "No, really, don't worry. It was her choice, and I think it's actually good for her to be around Lily and Basil—those two can make anyone smile if they put their minds to it. Baz and Maeve have always been close, and he takes good care of her right now. And besides, she wouldn't let me kick you out of the house—she insists on you staying here. She can be just as stubborn as me sometimes." Her chest ached with affection. "You know what she said? She told me—and I quote here—to have some decent honeymoon quality time with you."

Rhun's eyebrows shot up. "*Maeve* said that?"

Grinning, she nodded.

He stroked his knuckles over her cheek, the bond between them pulsing with warmth, with love entwining their souls. "I'm glad she's coming back to herself." He stole a kiss that left her humming with contentment—as well as hunger for more.

"So," her darling demon then said, feeding the meat to Sauron on the floor, "now that we have a kitty, don't you think it's time we added some kids to the mix? How many do you want? Two? Three? Half a dozen? Of course, we have to get a new kitten for each one, so they won't argue over who gets to torture the furball. I have a list of names—"

"Whoa!" She held up her hands as he turned to her, slapped them against his chest. "Kids? We're talking kids now? And how come you already have a list of names for our unborn, un-ever-talked-about children?"

Rhun gave her a duh-kind-of look. "The names are for the kittens."

"I will not," Merle said, holding up finger into his face, "—*ever*—name a cat Gollum, just to make this clear right now."

He caught her finger in one hand, nibbled at the tip with his teeth. "Not even if we give him a collar studded with shiny, preciousssss stones?"

A giggle escaped her, her insides melting. "You are such a goofball." Cupping his face with her other hand, she quietly added, "You know we'll only have girls, right? The witch-gene and all…"

He sighed dramatically. "I'll live." One side of his mouth tipped up in a sly smile. "Unless they all turn out to be like you. Now *that* would kill me."

Her eyes narrowed, she drew her hand back to give him a good smack on his shoulder—and the very next second she found herself flat on her back on the kitchen island, Rhun's body hot and heavy as he pinned her down, his hips between her legs. His mouth covered hers in a demanding, hungry kiss, his tongue stroking, licking, tangling with hers with maddening intent until she wiggled her hips against him, strung tight with desire. Mounting passion zinged back and forth on the mating bond, mirroring, heightening, until their feelings seemed to merge as one and she couldn't tell anymore where her emotions ended and his began. The need to feel skin on skin was paramount, trumping all else.

"Now, Merle mine," he muttered against her kiss-swollen lips as she gasped for breath, her hands tangled in his hair, "let's go make some little witch volcanoes."

The thought of starting a family with her demon a sparkling wave of bliss inside, she could only wheeze in agreement as he hoisted her up on his shoulder and carried her upstairs.

ॐ

Thank you for reading *To Seduce a Witch's Heart!*
If you'd love more of my writing, sign up for my newsletter to receive my novella *To Caress a Demon's Soul* for free, and to be notified of new releases, and get more newsletter-exclusive goodies in the future.

My newsletter is low-volume and won't spam your inbox. I'll never share your information, not even with my demons. You can unsubscribe at any time.
Sign up here: www.nadinemutas.com/newsletter

If you enjoyed Rhun and Merle's story, consider leaving a review on your favorite store or on Goodreads. Reviews are great to help other readers find the books they'll love, and to support your favorite authors.
You're also welcome to contact me via email:
nadine@nadinemutas.com
I love to hear from readers!

Books in the *Love and Magic* series by Nadine Mutas:

Novels:

To Seduce a Witch's Heart (Love and Magic, #1)

To Win a Demon's Love (Love and Magic, #2)

To Stir a Fae's Passion (Love and Magic, #3)

To Enthrall the Demon Lord (Love and Magic, #4)

Novellas:

To Caress a Demon's Soul (Love and Magic, #1.5) **Sign up for my
newsletter to receive this novella as a free read!**

ABOUT THE AUTHOR

Polyglot Nadine Mutas has always loved tangling with words, whether in her native tongue German or in any of the other languages she's acquired over the years. The more challenging, the better, she thought, and thus she studied the languages of South Asia and Japan. She worked at a translation agency for a short while, putting to use her knowledge of English, French, Spanish, Japanese, and Hindi.

Before long, though, her lifelong passion for books and words eventually drove her to give voice to those story ideas floating around in her brain (which have kept her up at night and absent-minded at inopportune times). She now writes paranormal romances with wickedly sensual heroes and the fiery heroines who tame them. Her debut novel, *To Seduce a Witch's Heart* (first published as *Blood, Pain, and Pleasure*), won the Golden Quill Award 2016 for Paranormal Romance, the Published Maggie Award 2016 for Fantasy/Paranormal Romance, and was a finalist in the PRISM contest for Dark Paranormal and Best First Book, as well as nominated for the Passionate Plume award 2016 for Paranormal Romance Novels & Novellas. It also won several awards for excellence in unpublished romance.

She currently resides in California with her college sweetheart, beloved little demon spawn, and two black cats hellbent on cuddling her to death (Clarification: Both her husband and kid prefer her alive. The cats, she's not so sure about.)

Nadine Mutas is a proud member of the Romance Writers of

America (RWA) and the Silicon Valley Romance Writers of America (SVRWA), the Rose City Romance Writers (RCRW), as well as the Fantasy, Futuristic & Paranormal chapter of the RWA (FF&PRW).

Connect with Nadine:

www.nadinemutas.com
nadine@nadinemutas.com

Made in the USA
San Bernardino, CA
10 July 2018